4 14 DAYS NOT RENEWABLE

CONCORD
FREE PUBLIC LIBRARY

Concord, Massachusetts

Cabbage and Bones

Cabbage
and
Bones

AN ANTHOLOGY OF
IRISH AMERICAN WOMEN'S FICTION

Edited and with an Introduction
by Caledonia Kearns

FOREWORD BY MAUREEN HOWARD

Henry Holt and Company
New York

Henry Holt and Company, Inc.
Publishers since 1866
115 West 18th Street
New York, New York 10011

Henry Holt ® is a registered trademark
of Henry Holt and Company, Inc.

Copyright © 1997 by Caledonia Kearns
Owing to limitations of space, permissions acknowledgments appear on pages 357–58.
All rights reserved.
Published in Canada by Fitzhenry & Whiteside Ltd.,
195 Allstate Parkway, Markham, Ontario L3R 4T8.

Library of Congress Cataloging-in-Publication Data
Cabbage and bones : an anthology of Irish American women's fiction / edited and with an
introduction by Caledonia Kearns ; foreword by Maureen Howard. — 1st ed.
p.   cm.
ISBN 0-8050-5579-7 (hardcover : alk. paper)
1. American fiction—Irish-American authors. 2. United States—Social life and customs—
20th century—Fiction. 3. American fiction—Women authors. 4. American fiction—20th century.
5. Irish American women—Fiction. 6. Irish Americans—Fiction. I. Kearns, Caledonia.
PS647.I74C33 1997   97-13626
813'.50809287'0899162073—dc21

Henry Holt books are available for special promotions and premiums.
For details contact: Director, Special Markets.

First Edition 1997

Designed by Claire Naylon Vaccaro

Printed in the United States of America
All first editions are printed on acid-free paper. ∞

1   3   5   7   9   10   8   6   4   2

for the matriarchs:
my great-grandmother
Adelaide Burke Powers
my grandmothers
Marjorie Powers Farrell
Irene Sanders Kearns
Marie Curtin Reilly
and my great-aunt
Mary Patricia Farrell

and for
my mother
Marjorie Mary Farrell
"I carry your heart in mine"

IN MEMORIAM LESLIE BAKER

1945–1997

CONTENTS

Contents

Contents

FOREWORD

There is so much pleasure in reading this gathering of Irish American women's fiction that I feel I must caution the reader that there is also a good dollop of sorrow. Would that we could just revel in the humor, but then we would not be partaking of the whole loaf. No, these women of the Irish diaspora were all fated to be dutiful daughters, mothers, lovers, wives—and tellers of true and sometimes sorry stories. Dutiful. What a dreary notion, but I do not mean to say that what the reader will encounter here is all burden of family, parish, and the preordained woman's role. The duty that many of these writers take upon themselves is to discover what is wayward in their women's souls, where transgression in thought or deed may lead to a finer, at times more generous, understanding of a limiting world or to self-discovery.

Though the collection ranges from lace-curtain to shanty Irish, it is remarkable how repeatedly in *Cabbage and Bones* these women writers plumb the depths of their identities. The quest is often for imagination itself, the power to stray from the straight and narrow and connect to a liberating view, however wild or disreputable. In the work of Alice

Fulton, Tess Gallagher, and Mary Gordon, women yearn to cross boundaries that will project them beyond the prescription of dailiness. To cross over is, of course, a route to escape, yet another theme of the Irish American woman writer, and we may see this book to be a chronicle of many departures, the emotional and imaginative departures echoing the great emigration from Ireland. "Mary's Departure," by Kathleen Ford, is the most explicit retelling of the old story—a girl sent off to America when there is no work, no man, therefore no hope for her at home. This account, like many others of women sent forth alone, is familiar to us as a folk tale which, when urgently told, we listen to again and again for the confirmation, or is it the comfort, of a collective sorrow and the possibility of individual survival. The tone may be as breezy as Annie Callan's very current "How Ireland Lost the World Cup," but the loneliness of the voyage is always present, even when it is self-prescribed. The woman in Elizabeth Cullinan's moving "Life After Death" walks only the streets of her New York neighborhood, a somewhat glamorous locale, but she is as confined to her role as a village girl.

It has been said that the Irish had the advantage of language when we came to America; we still have, but that does not fully account for these writers' gifts. By tradition we are a talky lot, good mimics with good ears, and rather taken with speaking our piece whether we are bookish or not. For it is in the telling of our stories that we reveal how bound we are to the rituals of family life, yet how we strain against them. In Anna Quindlen's rendering of a mother's death, she is respectfully observant of each carefully spilled word, each final truth, though often the tradition of Gaelic irreverence describes pathos with an angry flow of humor. Written language is one way of counting ourselves present at the Irish American feast in which, as Caledonia Kearns points out, there remains our hunger for home. We do not translate from a foreign tongue but incorporate into the American vernacular our heritage of spoken and written words, from the scrappy arguments and quick wit of bedroom and kitchen to the instructive epistles and parables of the Catholic Mass and the narrative of Irish song. The cadences of Alice McDermott's sentences and the mounting rhythms of her amazing paragraphs propel the reader forward as in the ballad form.

Throughout *Cabbage and Bones*, there is a strong vein of the confessional. Who would know it better than our church-ridden women? Even the young writers, like Eileen FitzGerald or Erin McGraw, who only inherit the legend of that sacrament's once-dour performance, are given to telling their sins. But, of course, the fictional confession does not beg forgiveness. (I do not think St. Augustine, himself, begged forgiveness.) And isn't confession now pleasantly renamed the sacrament of reconciliation? In these stories it is the record itself that stands as written example, and more often than not these women write in the confessional mode with great good humor or with cleverness in an examination of memory, which we might once have called an examination of conscience. Both Mary McCarthy and Maura Stanton call back Catholic girlhood with exacting arguments against the shallows of their adolescence. With all the troubles of hearth and home, of the world paying no account, it is best to tell stories on oneself, to seek the absolution of laughter. So there is much enjoyment though little romance in this collection. These women writers are realistic, too smart to give in to the sentimental.

If there is a vision that draws together Irish American women writers, it is a culture of commerce as much as the duties and privileges of home and of proud, self-defining rebellion. The streets never were paved with gold and didn't we know it, nor was there any dream beyond a fair price for our service, or for truly told stories in which the domestic is upon occasion raised to the heroic. We seem a sturdy lot— sworn to both love and duty—though we can never cut free of our promise to others or to ourselves but can only write as best we can: green thoughts. We must thank Caledonia Kearns for her efforts in recovering the work of Mary Doyle Curran, with its emphasis on class and Irish exclusion, and the anecdotal passage from Ruth McKenney as well as discovering new voices such as Jennifer C Cornell's. What a redemptive myth of a woman's giving to husband and child, then returning to herself is Cornell's "Versus." I note that the subtitle of this collection bears no hyphen, for though the writers are more or less Irish, more or less American, they write, as all fair writers do, of an experience that is at once universal and particular.

I am an old party, the Irish kid with a mouth on her, from a mostly Irish parish where we combined the Puritan past with mockery of our cut-glass station. Like many women who are included in *Cabbage and Bones*, I have had to reach back to Ireland, to the strong pull of that legendary soil, rocky and generative. I am pleased to be any sort of gnarled root in Caledonia's garden.

MAUREEN HOWARD

ACKNOWLEDGMENTS

Some say the Irish have a tendency to go on, and I am no exception. Many thanks are due and must be acknowledged:

Special thanks to Margo Culley, who started this with me, to Gloria Naylor, who encouraged me to believe in my dreams, and to Victoria Sanders and Diane Dickensheid, who finished the job off—love and gratitude to you all.

I thank Theresa Burns, my editor, who helped shape the work with her vision, her assistant, Amy Rosenthal, for her commitment and efforts on my behalf, and Maureen Howard, who kindly contributed her valuable time and lovely words to the foreword. Hasia Diner graciously made sure my facts were straight and my contributors generously lent their work. In particular, Alice Fulton, Mary Gordon, Anna Quindlen, and Lisa Shea lent their support in the early stages. I deeply regret that I could not include everyone in the final draft and appreciate all the fine work I considered.

To Jen Stein, who gave me essential publishing tips—my thanks. Kudos to Amy Madanick and Casandra McIntyre, who gave me a computer which saw me through. Mikaela Beardsley gives me excellent professional advice along with her warm friendship. And Liza Feather-stone—listener and believer—girl, this would never have happened without you.

To my family: all the Farrells, the Kearns family, Bakers, Umstadt and James. To the Burke and Powers clans, Alice Denhard Riddle and her family, la familia Martinez, my father, Christopher, who gave me a name I could be proud to put on a book, and to my grandfather, John Aloysius Farrell, as always, much love.

I am blessed to have a large extended family who support and carry me. To the Cornells and the Williams-Tymoskis, the Dorchester crew: Bob, Cathy, and Jeremy Schwartz, the Luces, the Scharfenbergs, Sara McGlinchy, and Ann and Fran Grady. And to Ellen, Mary Elizabeth, and Kathleen Anne Grady—my soul sisters and fellow New York Irish–rooted Boston-bred lovies—how lucky I am.

And lastly, to Miguel Martinez—*mi corazon*—there are no words to say what's true.

Editor's Note

I am indebted beyond measure to three exemplary works of scholar-ship: Hasia Diner's *Erin's Daughters in America*, *The Irish Voice in America* by Charles Fanning, and *Irish-American Fiction: Essays in Criticism*, edited by Daniel J. Casey and Robert E. Rhodes.

INTRODUCTION

*Emigration is not just a chronicle of sorrow and
regret. It is also a story of contribution and adap-
tation.*—Mary Robinson, President of Ireland

*A woman writing thinks back through her moth-
ers.*—Virginia Woolf, A Room of One's Own

They immigrated in larger numbers than women of any other ethnic
group, the majority as single women. They accepted work women of
other ethnicities turned down and stigmatized; many became domestic
servants. They worked constantly before they married—if they married at all. Willing to marry later, they enjoyed their independent sta-
tus. Migrating in "chains," they used their wages, earned cleaning and
running other people's houses, to bring family in Ireland to America.
They left Ireland because there was nothing for them there. There was
no work. They had no food. They had no other choice.

Nineteen ninety-seven marks the 150th anniversary of the Great
Potato Famine in Ireland, which caused the first significant wave of
Irish immigration to the United States. While other waves of immigration preceded and have succeeded the famine, the reason for the
original exodus of so many from Ireland is clear: hunger.

The history of Irish American women in this country has been little recognized, with the exception of Hasia Diner's groundbreaking book *Erin's Daughters in America*. Without women's economic contributions to families in both Ireland and America, it is hard to imagine their survival and, ultimately, the success of the Irish. Once in the States, Irish American men had a harder time finding work than their female counterparts did, and when they did—on canals, digging tunnels, or building bridges—it was dangerous and often took them away from their families. Irish women, who almost always did not work outside the home after marriage, were frequently left alone as the heads of their households. In fact, abandonment of Irish American women by their spouses was epidemic when compared to other ethnic groups. As generation after generation settled in the States, many Irish American women worked their way toward greater economic stability by becoming schoolteachers and nurses.

There are few studies of Irish American fiction, and rarely is it discussed or considered a genre. When the question is considered, the focus tends to be on male writers such as F. Scott Fitzgerald, Eugene O'Neill, James Carroll, Pete Hamill, and William Kennedy, among others, and rarely on women's voices. A significant body of writing has never before been recognized until now: This is the very first collection of Irish American women's fiction. Certainly, neither historians nor literary critics have made a connection between the unique history of Irish American women's immigration to the United States and their literature; this is the motivation behind this anthology. Although there are a few stories included about immigration and the decision to immigrate, my point is not that the large scale of female Irish immigration created a disproportionate number of female Irish American writers, but that there is a legacy of hard work, independence, and perseverance that has carried on.

I first turned to the literature of Irish American women when I was in college. I wanted to prove what I knew instinctively: that there were many Irish American women writers and that there were more to discover. As I sat in the New York Public Library researching this book, I came upon many women whose writing had disappeared. I found Mary Deasy, a renowned short-story writer and novelist of the '40s and '50s, whose work has been largely forgotten. I discovered that Betty Keogh Smith, author of *A Tree Grows in Brooklyn*, was not Irish herself but had an Irish stepfather and that Flannery O'Connor was not emotionally tied to her Irish background. I laughed out loud over Ruth McKenney's truly wonderful *My Sister Eileen*, a collection of stories (almost all first published in *The New Yorker*) that later became a Broadway play and a movie. Weeks later, I was devastated by reading McKenney's *Love Story*, a sequel of sorts, where I learned Eileen died in a car accident on her way from California to New York for the Broadway premiere of *My Sister Eileen*, as did her husband, novelist Nathanael West.

The women in this anthology write because they must. They are the descendants of women whose voices were frequently lost as they struggled to work and provide for their families. (The auto-biographies of labor activists Elizabeth Gurley Flynn and Mary Harris "Mother" Jones came directly out of their work experience.) Yet there is an oral tradition among the Irish that prevailed and survived. The image of Irish women as storytellers, once buried, is now resurrected. In these stories, women are clearly defined as essential to the preservation of culture. In *The Parish and the Hill*, Mary Doyle Curran writes:

> *My mother would not leave because she could never abandon, defeated, a battle involving her race. She would remain, though ostracized by both sides; and before we left for the school of the Yankees and our lace-curtain cousins, my mother enjoined us to remember, in the battles which occurred every day, that we were O'Sullivans, descendants of the kings of Ireland, and we were not to come home crying.*

The mother in Alice Fulton's "Queen Wintergreen" directly acknowledges her place in Irish oral tradition when she states: "My tongue is the pen of a ready writer."

This collection is arranged chronologically to place the writing of these women in a historical context. "Noel Coward and Mrs. Griffin" by Ruth McKenney was written in 1938, nearly a century after the famine. Perhaps it took that long for Irish American women to gain the stability, the confidence in their voices, to begin to write. While there were Irish American women writing at the beginning of the century, my starting point here is the more realistic, more contemporary voice that began to appear in the 1930s. While this collection may not reflect the full breadth of Irish American women's writing—I have not included every Irish American woman writer of this century—my aim is to provide an overview of sorts. (Charles Fanning's important academic study *The Irish Voice in America* is the most comprehensive study of Irish American literature to date.) I have included Annie Callan and Helena Mulkerns, recent first-generation immigrants, as the Irish diaspora is fluid and constant.

Though all of these works are written by women of Irish American descent, not all of them have explicitly Irish American content. There are, however, some common themes. In the earlier stories, Mary McCarthy and Ruth McKenney provide levity, while Mary Doyle Curran and Mary Deasy reflect nostalgically on childhood and the origins of identity. Maureen Howard's work clearly departs from this, as her prose is bolder, more ironic than incantatory. Mothers are at the center of most of these works. They are the glue holding the family together, as in Anna Quindlen's *One True Thing*. In the excerpt from *Bridgeport Bus*, Maureen Howard's thirty-five-year-old virgin, Mary Agnes, is still controlled by her mother and is desperate to escape from her clutches. Kathleen Ford's "Mary's Departure" is a heartbreaking account of a mother who decides to send her daughter to America, as there is nothing left for her in Ireland. Tess Gallagher and Mary McGarry Morris both write movingly of their characters' connections to disappointing fathers, despite very different endings. "Daily Affirmations" by Erin McGraw tells the story of a woman who can't stop feeding herself to compensate for what her parents did not give her, highlighting how feelings of deprivation endure. Religion, and specifically Catholicism, is not always explicit in many of these stories, but it is commonly an underlying reference, from the convent schools in the work of Mary McCarthy and Maura Stanton to the Masses attended in Curran's *The Parish and the Hill*. Near the end of the collection, Helena Mulkerns imagines the famine and Jennifer C Cornell a silkie, while Annie Callan tells a more modern story, with characters caught between America and Ireland.

This book is needed not only to resurrect the work of writers like Deasy and McKenney, whose voices had been forgotten, but also to celebrate women writing. It distinguishes the voices of Irish American women and also affirms not only our place in the canon of American literature but perhaps, more important, our existence. While all of the writers included are gifted in their own rights, when combined their voices create a greater whole. Elizabeth Cullinan and Maureen Howard, both award-winning writers in the 1970s, now have a significant number of works that are not widely available. My greatest hope is that by placing them in the context of a tradition, their work and the work of all of the contributors will be better recognized.

In her introduction to *Black-Eyed Susans, Midnight Birds*, an anthology of African American women writers, Mary Helen Washington writes, "Editing this collection of short stories has been for me an autobiographical act," and I would have to say the same. I chose these works because I heard something in them that resonated. My family emigrated from Ireland around the time of the famine, and while the voices of my great-grandmothers may have been lost to me over generations as we assimilated into "white" America, there is something I got from my mother and she from hers that will not give up our feeling of connection to where we came from. And it is not just an idyllic image of an island bathed in what James Carroll calls "the green fog of sentiment, of nostalgia." It is a hunger: a hunger to remember.

The Ballad of Ballymote

TESS GALLAGHER

We stopped at her hut
on the road to Ballymote
but she did not look up
and her head was on her knee.

What is it, we asked.
As from the dreams of the dead
her voice came up.

My father, they shot him
as he looked up from his plate
and again as he stood and again
as he fell against the stove
and like a thrush his breath
bruised the room
and was gone.

A traveler would have asked directions
but saw she would not lift her face.
What is it, he asked.

My husband sits all day in a pub
and all night and I may as well
be a widow for the way he beats me
to prove he's alive.

What is it, asked the traveler's wife,
just come up to look.

My son's lost both eyes in a fight
to keep himself a man
and there he sits behind the door
where there is no door
and he sees by the stumps
of his hands.

And have you no daughters for comfort?

Two there are and gone to nuns
and a third to the North
with a fisherman.

What are you cooking?

Cabbage and bones, she said. Cabbage
and bones.

Cabbage and Bones

Noel Coward
and Mrs. Griffin

(1938)

RUTH MCKENNEY

My sister and I had a lot of trouble in our youth trying to get cultured. Every time we made a small attempt to explore science, religion, or the fine arts, public opinion was against us. In the end, Noel Coward blasted our reputations and in the opinion of our fond family, ruined our lives once and for all.

Of course, Noel Coward was only the climax. Before Noel Coward, Eileen and I got mixed up in a scandal about Michael Arlen, not to mention the time Father actually called in the pastor of the East Cleveland Evangelical Church to remonstrate with Eileen because she buried her doll on Good Friday and expected it, or said she expected it (no one ever knew the real truth of the matter), to resurrect itself on Easter.

That doll business caused a terrible uproar in the family. Of course, I admit it was a little thoughtless of Eileen to let the neighbors in on the big experiment. Inquiring minds, ought, I suppose, to operate only in the bosom of the family.

At least that was Father's position. He was certainly furious when Mrs. Griffin, a lady who was strongly pro bono publico, came rushing into the kitchen the night before Easter.

"Mr. McKenney," Mrs. Griffin bleated, sidestepping great pools of Easter egg dye, "do you KNOW that your little girl Eileen has been COMMITTING SACRILEGE?"

"Uhmmm?" Father murmured. He was engrossed in dying a hard-boiled egg half blue and half red, an operation which he had boasted he could do blindfolded, it was that easy. Eileen and I were watching his pitiful attempts with the contempt they merited. He had already spoiled four eggs.

"Bobbie came home tonight and wanted to borrow Sue's doll. He said he wanted to crucify it and hurry up and bury it so that it could Rise tomorrow." Mrs. Griffin's outraged squeal echoed in our quiet kitchen. Eileen looked up from her work, and an expression of gentle modesty, of unassuming pride, flickered in her large blue eyes.

"He did, huh?" Father remarked pleasantly, and added as an after-thought, "Tsk! Tsk!"

"Why, MR. MCKENNEY!" Mrs. Griffin's howl rang out at the same instant that Father's egg slipped from his spoon and fell into the kettle of red dye.

"God damn it to hell!" Father said. Eileen and I turned our heads so that he should not see our complacent smiles. It does not pay, we early learned, to gloat over the misfortunes, however merited, of one's parents.

"Why, Mr. McKenney," Mrs. Griffin repeated in a dying swan voice. You could see she was pretty shaken.

Father wheeled, the spoon, still dripping red dye, in his hand. "What do you want?" he screamed. Father had been trying to dye that egg two colors for more than an hour. He was a man who could never let a dare alone.

"Really! Mr. McKenney!"

"Well," said Father, gradually pulling himself together. He put down his spoon, very carefully, glanced murderously at his two daughters and led Mrs. Griffin into the living room.

"Bobbie Griffin," Eileen murmured, as the lad's mother disappeared around the door, "is a rat."

She was right. Ten minutes later, Bobbie, armed with a flashlight and goaded by his mother, pointed out the very spot where Eileen's doll, Joe, renamed for the big experiment, had been carefully buried in our backyard. Father dug Joe up with a hand trowel at a little after ten o'clock that night, in spite of Eileen's tearful complaints. "He'll Rise tomorrow and you won't have to trouble," Eileen kept moaning.

Mrs. Griffin and Father were of two minds about the whole situation. Mrs. Griffin said Eileen really didn't believe Joe would Rise, she was just trying to ruin the faith of Mrs. Griffin's angel-child Bobbie.

"Eileen!" Father intoned sternly, "if you were really trying to prove to Bobbie that Joe couldn't and wouldn't Rise, you are a bad little girl and need punishing, but if you were only a little confused about Easter I will have Dr. Ringing come to talk to you."

Eileen chose Dr. Ringing. She has been a realist from her tenderest years.

We lost interest in religion after the Easter fiasco and turned, rather suddenly, to Michael Arlen. Eileen and I have always believed that Michael Arlen was Father's fault, and we considered his behavior when the matter came, somewhat unfortunately, to public light, both unjust and extravagant. For Father, in the interests of teaching his twelve- and thirteen-year-old daughters the value of a penny, got us jobs minding infants while their parents were over playing bridge with the adult McKenneys.

It was a nice arrangement. Father was quite some bridge player and even at a tenth of a cent a point it was a dull evening when he couldn't collect a week's cigar money from his guests. In the meantime, his daughters, little business women that they were, were stripping the neighbors' shelves of all loose chocolate candy, peanuts, and other edibles and presumably listening for the night wails, if any, of scores of disagreeable little children, at $1.25 a night.

We were a little sullen about our work at first, since it was billed as a big character-building project and we had to put all our profits in the bank, but one night, while close on the scent of a box of chocolate candy we felt sure Mrs. Envry had hidden somewhere in her large house, we came across Michael Arlen. Mr. Arlen was hidden behind a volume of the collected works of Harold Bell Wright, on the Envry bookshelves. The Envrys lived across the street and had a mighty-lunged child named Little Cartwright. Big Cartwright was Mr. Envry. He wore glasses and sold insurance, although not to Father.

Eileen and I began to take a real interest in our work after we started reading *The Green Hat*. In fact, we couldn't wait to get back to the Envrys to see what happened next to poor, brave Iris March and her fascinating wonderful friends. Father got quite smug about us. He said we reminded him of himself when he was a little lad and sold newspapers at three o'clock on cold winter mornings.

"When was that, Father," Eileen asked once, "when you lived on that farm and milked the cows just as dawn came up over the snowy hills?" Eileen was always making Father mad.

Lenora MacAbee's mother, a somewhat hysterical lady who used to imagine her house was burning down twice every winter, broke the Michael Arlen scandal. She stuck her head in Lenora's little backyard playhouse just as I was assigning the parts in our big homemade drama, "The Green Hat."

"You," I was ordering Lenora, "are Iris' boy friend, and I am her husband, and Eileen gets to be Iris, but tomorrow I'm going to be."

"Eeeek!" Mrs. MacAbee said, calling our attention to her undesired presence.

It developed that Mrs. MacAbee was a woman of the world, at least on East Cleveland, Ohio, standards. She instantly recognized the name "Iris" which was more than Father did. When Mrs. MacAbee appeared dramatically in our living room, dragging Eileen and me behind her, she ran into something of an anti-climax. Father had to be told who

Iris March was, and who Michael Arlen was, and finally Mrs. MacAbee had to ask us to leave the room while she explained to the innocent Mr. McKenney just what was wrong with both Mr. Arlen and Iris. Father was never a great one for literary sensations.

Eileen and I and Mrs. Envry took the whole thing very hard. Mrs. Envry moved, taking along her Cartwrights, Big and Little, and Eileen kept saying stubbornly to any and all adults who would listen to her, "But WHY was Iris a bad lady?"

Father was never sure whether Eileen was just asking to be mean or whether she really didn't know. Mrs. Griffin said Eileen knew all right. Mrs. Griffin took rather a somber view of the general Michael Arlen situation. She said we were ruined for life and when Father somewhat uneasily demurred, Mrs. Griffin just said tartly, "You mark my words, they'll go from bad to worse."

Father didn't believe it at the time, but I guess he came around to Mrs. Griffin's point of view when we got embroiled in the Noel Coward incident a year or so later.

Surprising as it may seem, Noel Coward happened to us because our sextette of doting aunts on the Farrel side of the family thought we should sit at the feet of Shakespeare and quit going to those horrid movies all the time.

We were big girls, Aunt Molly said, already thirteen and fourteen years old, and it was about time we got some culture in our lives. She organized a sort of combine among the Farrel aunts. Every Saturday afternoon a different aunt bought us fifty-cent matinée tickets for the Ohio Theater, and every Saturday afternoon we got dressed in our best, hunted up our gloves and our handkerchiefs and trotted off, accompanied by a somewhat bored Farrel aunt to see Robert Mantell bang around the stage in "Macbeth," or Walter Hampden recite, "Love, I love beyond breath, beyond reason," etc.

It was our first season at the theatre and we had a wonderful time. We admired Mr. Mantell extravagantly and were very indignant when

Aunt Kate said, during the intermission, that she didn't know if she could sit through another act, he was better forty years before.

Then came the great Saturday when Aunt Molly had a cold and we went by ourselves to see Ethel Barrymore in "The Second Mrs. Tangueray." Miss Barrymore was, we thought, simply wonderful and the play was so wonderfully sad, especially where she killed herself, and we ate three chocolate bars in the intermission and altogether it was a wonderful Saturday afternoon.

The rest of the aunts immediately developed permanent Saturday afternoon colds and soon we got accustomed to trotting off to the matinées unchaperoned. Aunt Molly just went down to the box office at the Ohio Theater and ordered two fifty-cent matinée tickets for the rest of the season. The Ohio Theater had a new play every week, for in those days Cleveland got all the New York shows a season late. All that glorious winter Eileen and I throbbed to the drama with real people in it, which we much preferred even to Lon Chaney movies.

Every now and then we sat through some mighty mystifying plays on our Saturday excursions. We didn't mind obscurity, however; we rather liked it. We even thought Ibsen was fine because the costumes were so quaint and everybody seemed to be having such awfully sad times and all the characters had their lives ruined by something or other. The Saturday we saw "The Captive," a nasty old woman, a perfect stranger, walked right up to us in the lobby after Act II and said she didn't know what our parents, if any, were thinking of. This immediately revived our interest in what had seemed a very dull show.

Noel Coward didn't seem dull, however, even if "The Vortex" was one of the most mysterious dramas of the season, as far as we were concerned. Mr. Coward was very satisfying. He was constantly ripping around the stage talking about his ruined life and playing like mad on a big piano. He ran his fingers through his hair quite a lot, too, and appeared to be constantly, from the very beginning of Act I, on the verge of suicide.

Father was rather impatient with our idle prattle that night. We tried to tell him at dinner about Noel Coward and how sad the play had been but he said for Heaven's sake to stop talking all the time, we were driving him crazy, he had worries.

Poor Father, he developed a whole new set of worries when Mrs. Griffin came over to play bridge the next Tuesday night. She bustled into our house exuding virtue at every pore. Eileen and I retreated upstairs after sullenly shaking her dry wrinkled hand. We were engaged in pouring some of Father's eau de cologne over our hair brushes so that we would be beautiful like the tragic Irene Soames in Mr. Galsworthy's great epic, when we heard Mrs. Griffin's strident voice raised in excited conversation.

"And I said to Mr. Griffin, didn't I, Griffie, when I got home, I never knew such things were going on in the world."

We heard Father say, "Uhm" and then, "four hearts."

"Honestly, it was the first time I had been to the theatre since I was a girl and Mother took me to see little Eva, and if this is the kind of thing that's been going on in the theatre lately, I say, burn down the theatres."

"Double," Mr. Griffin said in his birdlike voice.

"Four spades, and really, I saw young girls in that audience. At least they ought to keep young girls away from that sort of filth."

"I'm sorry," Father replied pleasantly, as he put down his cards. "I haven't any spades. What was the play?"

"No spades! Well! Really, Mr. McKenney! Oh, the play was something called 'The Vortex' and there was a man called Howard or Coward I guess it was who wrote it and acted in it, too."

"Double trouble," Eileen said somberly, upstairs.

Downstairs we heard Father scrape his chair. He was getting to his feet. "Just what was the matter with the play, Mrs. Griffin?" His voice sounded pretty somber.

"The play?" Mrs. Griffin squeaked.

"I SAID WHAT WAS WRONG WITH THIS HOWARD OR COWARD OR WHATEVER YOU CALL HIM?"

"Why, Mr. McKenney!" Mrs. Griffin's bleat was tremolo. "I don't know what gets into you, shouting like that."

"Now listen, Mrs. Griffin." Father's voice was back down to sub-basement levels, although slightly shaky. "Just tell me as simply as you can why you do not consider this Howard or Coward or whoever he was fit for Eileen and Ruth to see."

"Eileen and Ruth!" Mrs. Griffin sounded pleased. "Mercy! Don't tell me they saw that awful business!"

"MRS. GRIFFIN," Father thundered, "PLEASE."

"Well, in the play, he was in love with his mother."

Father was gruff. "Go ahead."

"Well, that was it."

"WHAT WAS IT?" Father howled. Eileen and I were right with him there, all agog. But while we waited with baited breath to hear the worst, we were surprised to mark the sound of Father sinking into his chair and muttering, "My GOD."

"Isn't it terrible?" Mrs. Griffin twittered enthusiastically.

It *was* pretty terrible. Mrs. Griffin said she thought Father ought to send us to a convent or to a reform school, or somewhere. Eventually we were called downstairs and in the uproar Father shouted, "And you are never going to the theatre again until you are grown up and I can't stop you."

"Father!" Eileen wept, "PLEASE let us go just this next week."

"Please," I screeched through my tears.

"Well," Father muttered, weakening under the deluge of his daughters' watery grief, "what's coming next week you want to see so much?"

Eileen sniffled, blew her nose, and feeling that all was not yet lost, said hopefully, " 'What Price Glory.' "

Mrs. Griffin said that was the last straw. She said that *showed* you what Noel Coward could do.

C.Y.E.

(1944)

MARY MCCARTHY

Near the corner of Fourteenth Street and Fourth Avenue, there is a store called Cye Bernard. I passed it the other day on my way to the Union Square subway station. To my intense surprise, a heavy blush spread over my face and neck, and my insides contorted in that terrible grimace of shame that is generally associated with hangovers. I averted my eyes from the sign and hurried into the subway, my head bent so that no observer should discover my secret identity, which until that moment I had forgotten myself. Now I pass this sign every day, and it is always a question whether I shall look at it or not. Usually I do, but hastily, surreptitiously, with an ineffective air of casualness, lest anybody suspect that I am crucified there on that building, hanging exposed in black script lettering to advertise bargains in men's haberdashery.

The strangest part about it is that this unknown clothier on Fourteenth Street should not only incorporate in his name the mysterious, queerly spelled nickname I was given as a child in the convent, but that he should add to this the name of my patron saint, St. Bernard of Clairvaux, whom I chose for my special protector at a time when I was suffering from the nickname. It is nearly enough to convince me that life is a system of recurrent pairs, the poison and the antidote being eternally packaged together by some considerate heavenly druggist. St. Bernard, however, was, from my point of view, never so useful as the dog that bears his name, except in so far as he represented the contemplative, bookish element in the heavenly hierarchy, as opposed, say, to St. Martin of Tours, St. Francis Xavier or St. Aloysius of Gonzaga, who was of an ineffable purity and died young. The life of action was repellent to St. Bernard, though he engaged in it from time to time; on the other hand, he was not a true *exalté*—he was, in short, a sedentary man, and it was felt, in the convent, I think, that he was a rather odd choice for an eleven-year-old girl, the nuns themselves expressing some faint bewilderment and concern, as older people do when a child is presented with a great array of toys and selects from among them a homely and useful object.

It was marvelous, I said to myself that day on the subway, that I could have forgotten so easily. In the official version of my life the nickname does not appear. People have asked me, now and then, whether I have ever had a nickname and I have always replied, No, it is funny but I do not seem to be the type that gets one. I have even wondered about it a little myself, asking, Why is it that I have always been Mary, world without end, Amen, feeling a faint pinch of regret and privation, as though a cake had been cut and no favor, not even the old maid's thimble or the miser's penny, been found in my piece. How political indeed is the personality, I thought. What coalitions and cabals the party in power will not make to maintain its uncertain authority! Nothing is sacred. The past is manipulated to serve the interests of the present. For any bureaucracy, amnesia is convenient. The name of Trotsky drops out of the chapter on the revolution in the Soviet textbooks—what shamelessness, we say, while in the meantime our discarded selves languish in the Lubianka of the unconscious. But a moment comes at last, after the régime has fallen, after all interested parties are dead, when the archives are opened and the old ghosts walk, and history must be rewritten in the light of fresh discoveries.

It was happening to me then, as I sat frozen in my seat, staring at the picture of Miss Subways, February 1943, who loves New York and spends her spare time writing to her two officer-brothers in the Army and Navy. The heavy doors of the mind swung on their hinges. I was back in the convent, a pale new girl sitting in the front of the study hall next to a pretty, popular eighth-grader, whom I bored and who resented having me for a deskmate. I see myself perfectly: I am ambitious, I wish to make friends with the most exciting and powerful girls; at the same time, I am naïve, without stratagems, for I think that this project of mine will be readily accomplished, that I have only to be myself. The first rebuffs startle me. I look around and see that there is a social pyramid here and that I and my classmates are on the bottom. I study the disposition of stresses and strains and discover that two girls, Elinor Henehan and Mary Heinrichs, are important, and that their approval is essential to my happiness.

There were a great many exquisite and fashionable-looking girls in the convent, girls with Irish or German names, who used make-up in secret, had suitors, and always seemed to be on the verge of a romantic elopement. There were also some very pretty Protestant girls, whose personal charms were enhanced for us by the exoticism of their religion—the nuns telling us that we should always be especially considerate of them because they were Protestants, and, so to speak, our guests, with the result that we treated them reverently, like French dolls. These two groups made up the élite of the convent; the nuns adored them for their beauty, just as we younger girls did; and they enjoyed far more réclame than the few serious students who were thought to have the vocation.

Elinor Henehan and Mary Heinrichs fell into neither category. They were funny, lazy, dangling girls, fourteen or fifteen years old, with baritone voices, very black hair, and an insouciant attitude toward convent life. It was said that they came from east of the mountains. Elinor Henehan was tall and bony, with horn-rimmed glasses; Mary Heinrichs was shorter and plump. Their blue serge uniforms were always a mess, the collars and cuffs haphazardly sewn on and worn a day or so after they ought to have been sent to the laundry. They broke rules constantly, talking in study hall, giggling in chapel.

Yet out of these unpromising personal materials, they had created a unique position for themselves. They were the school clowns. And like all clowns they had made a shrewd bargain with life, exchanging dignity for power, and buying with servility to their betters immunity from the reprisals of their equals or inferiors. For the upper school they travestied themselves, exaggerating their own odd physical characteristics, their laziness, their eccentric manner of talking. With the lower school, it was another story: we were the performers, the school the audience, they the privileged commentators from the royal box. Now it was our foibles, our vanities, our mannerisms that were on display, and the spectacle was apparently so hilarious that it was a continual challenge to the two girls' self-control. They lived in a recurrent spasm of mirth. On the playground, at the dinner-table, laughter would dangerously overtake them; one would whisper to the other and then a wordless rocking would begin, till finally faint anguished screams were heard, and the nun in charge clapped her clapper for silence.

What was unnerving about this laughter—unnerving especially for the younger girls—was its general, almost abstract character. More often than not, we had no idea what it was that Elinor and Mary were laughing at. A public performance of any sort—a recital, a school play—instantly reduced them to jelly. Yet what was there about somebody's humble and pedestrian performance of *The Merry Peasant* that was so uniquely comic? Nobody could tell, least of all the performer. To be the butt of this kind of joke was a singularly painful experience, for you were never in a position to turn the tables, to join in the laughter at your own expense, because you could not possibly pretend to know what the joke was. Actually, as I see now, it was the intimacy of the two girls that set their standard: from the vantage point of their private world, anything outside seemed strange and ludicrous. It was our very existence they laughed at, as the peasant laughs at the stranger from another province. The occasions of mirth—a request for the salt, a trip to the dictionary in the study hall—were mere pretexts; our personalities *in themselves* were incredible to them. At the time, however, it was very confusing. Their laughter was a kind of crazy compass that was steering the school. Nobody knew, ever, where the whirling needle would stop, and many of us lived in a state of constant apprehension, lest it should point to *our* desk, lest we become, if only briefly, the personification of all that was absurd, the First Cause of this cosmic mirth.

Like all such inseparable friends, they delighted in nicknames, bestowing them in godlike fashion, as though by renaming their creatures they could perform a new act of creation, a secular baptism. And as at the baptismal font we had passed from being our parents' children to being God's children, so now we passed from God's estate to a societal trolls' world presided over by these two unpredictable deities. They did not give nicknames to everybody. You had to have some special quality to be singled out by Elinor and Mary, but what that quality was only Elinor and Mary could tell. I saw very soon (the beginnings of wisdom) that I had two chances of finding an honorable place in the convent system: one was to escape being nicknamed altogether, the other was to earn for myself an appellation that, while humorous, was still benevolent; rough, perhaps, but tender. On the whole, I would have preferred the first alternative, as being less chancy. Months passed, and no notice was taken of me; my anxiety diminished; it seemed as though I might get my wish.

They broke the news to me one night after study hall. We were filing out of the large room when Elinor stepped out of the line to speak to me. "We have got one for you," she said. "Yes?" I said calmly, for really (I now saw) I had known it all along, known that there was something about me that would inevitably appeal to these two strange girls. I stiffened up in readiness, feeling myself to be a sort of archery target: there was no doubt that they could hit me (I was an easy mark), but, pray God, it be one of the larger concentric circles, not, oh Blessed Virgin, the red, tender bull's-eye at the heart. I could not have imagined what was in store for me. "Cye," said Elinor and began to laugh, looking at me oddly because I did not laugh too. "Si?" I asked, puzzled. I was a new girl, it was true, but I did not come from the country. "C-Y-E," said Elinor, spelling. "But what does it mean?" I asked the two of them, for Mary had now caught up with her. They shook their dark heads and laughed. "Oh no," they said. "We can't tell you. But it's very, very good. Isn't it?" they asked each other. "It's one of our best."

I saw at once that it was useless to question them. They would never tell me, of course, and I would only make myself ridiculous, even more Cye-like, if I persisted. It occurred to me that if I showed no anxiety, they would soon forget about it, but my shrewdness was no match for theirs. The next day it was all over the school. It was called to me on the baseball field, when the young nun was at bat; it was whispered from head to head down the long refectory table at dinner. It rang through the corridors in the dormitory. "What does it mean?" I would hear a girl ask. Elinor or Mary would whisper in her ear, and the girl would cast me a quick glance, and then laugh. Plainly, they had hit me off to a T, and as I saw this my curiosity overcame my fear and my resentment. I no longer cared how derogatory the name might be; I would stand anything. I said to myself, if only I could know it. If only I had some special friend who could find out and then tell me. But I was new and a little queer, anyway, it seemed; I had no special friends, and now it was part of the joke that the whole school should know, and know that I wanted to know and not tell me. My isolation, which had been obscure, was now conspicuous, and, as it were, axiomatic. Nobody could ever become my friend, because to do so would involve telling me, and Elinor and Mary would never forgive that.

It was up to me to guess it, and I would lie in bed at night, guessing wildly, as though against time, like the miller's upstart daughter in Rumpelstiltskin. Outlandish phrases would present themselves: "Catch your elbow," "Cheat your end." Or, on the other hand, sensible ones that were humiliating: "Clean your ears." One night I got up and poured water into the china basin and washed my ears in the dark, but when I looked at the washcloth in the light the next morning, it was perfectly clean. And in any case, it seemed to me that the name must have some more profound meaning. My fault was nothing ordinary that you could do something about, like washing your ears. Plainly, it was something immanent and irremediable, a spiritual taint. And though I could not have told precisely what my wrongness consisted in, I felt its existence almost tangible during those nights, and knew that it had always been with me, even in the other school, where I had been popular, good at games, good at dramatics; I had always had it, a kind of miserable effluvium of the spirit that the ordinary sieves of report cards and weekly confessions had been powerless to catch.

Now I saw that I could never, as I had hoped, belong to the convent's inner circles, not to the tier of beauty, nor to the tier of manners and good deportment, which was signalized by wide moiré ribbons, awarded once a week, blue, green, or pink, depending on one's age, that were worn in a sort of bandolier style, crosswise from shoulder to hip. I could take my seat in the dowdy tier of scholarship, but my social acquaintance would be limited to a few frowzy little girls of my own age who were so insignificant, so contemptible, that they did not even know what my nickname stood for. Even they, I thought, were better off than I, for they knew their place, they accepted the fact that they were unimportant little girls. No older girl would bother to jeer at them, but in me there was something overweening, over-eager, over-intense, that had brought upon me the hateful name. Now my only desire was to be alone, and in the convent this was difficult, for the nuns believed that solitude was appropriate for anchorites, but for growing girls, unhealthy. I went to the library a great deal and read all of Cooper, and *Stoddard's Lectures*. I became passionately religious, made a retreat with a fiery missionary Jesuit, spent hours on my knees in adoration of the Blessed Sacrament, but even in the chapel, the name pursued me: glancing up at the cross, I would see the initials, I.N.R.I.; the name that had been given Christ in mockery now mocked me, for I was not a prig and I knew that my sufferings were ignoble and had nothing whatever in common with God's. And, always, there was no avoiding the communal life, the older girls passing as I crept along the corridor with a little knot of my classmates. "Hello, Cye."

Looking back, I see that if I had ever burst into tears publicly, begged for quarter, compunction would have been felt. Some goddess of the college department would have comforted me, spoken gently to Elinor and Mary, and the nickname would have been dropped. Perhaps it might even have been explained to me. But I did not cry, even alone in my room. I chose what was actually the more shameful part. I accepted the nickname, made a sort of joke of it, used it brazenly myself on the telephone, during vacations, calling up to ask a group of classmates to the movies: "This is Cye speaking." But all the time I was making plans, writing letters home, arranging my escape. I resolved that once I was out of the convent, I would never, never, never again let anybody see what I was like. That, I felt, had been my mistake.

The day I left the Mother Superior cried. "I think you will grow up to be a novelist," she said, "and that can be a fine thing, but I want you to remember all your life the training you have had here in the convent."

I was moved and thrilled by the moment, the prediction, the parting adjuration. "Yes," I said, weeping, but I intended to forget the convent within twenty-four hours. And in this I was quite successful.

The nickname followed me for a time, to the public high school I entered. One of the girls said to me, "I hear you are called Cye." "Yes," I replied easily. "How do you spell it?" she asked. "S-I," I said. "Oh," she said. "That's funny." "Yes," I said. "I don't know why they called me that." This version of the nickname lasted perhaps three weeks. At the end of that time, I dropped the group of girls who used it, and I never heard it again.

Now, however, the question has been reopened. What do the letters stand for? A happy solution occurred to me yesterday, on Fifteenth Street and Fourth Avenue. "Clever Young Egg," I said to myself out loud. The words had arranged themselves without my volition, and instantly I felt that sharp, cool sense of relief and triumph that one has on awakening from a nightmare. Could that have been it? Is it possible that that was all? Is it possible that Elinor and Mary really divined nothing, that they were paying me a sort of backhanded compliment, nothing certainly that anybody could object to? I began to laugh at myself, affectionately, as one does after a long worry, saying, "You fool, look how silly you've been." "Now I can go back," I thought happily, without reflection, just as though I were an absconding bank teller who had been living for years with his spiritual bags packed, waiting for the charges against him to be dropped that he might return to his native town. A vision of the study hall rose before me, with my favorite nun on the platform and the beautiful girls in their places. My heart rushed forward to embrace it.

But, alas, it is too late. Elinor Henehan is dead, my favorite nun has removed to another convent, the beautiful girls are married—I have seen them from time to time and no longer aspire to their friendship. And as for the pale, plain girl in the front of the study hall, her, too, I can no longer reach. I see her creeping down the corridor with a little knot of her classmates. "Hello, Cye," I say with a touch of disdain for her rawness, her guileless ambition. I should like to make her a pie-bed, or drop a snake down her back, but unfortunately the convent discipline forbids such open brutality. I hate her, for she is my natural victim, and it is I who have given her the name, the shameful, inscrutable name that she will never, sleepless in her bed at night, be able to puzzle out.

excerpt from

The Parish and the Hill

(1948)

MARY DOYLE CURRAN

Irish Parish and Money Hole Hill

I remember Irish Parish. It was Ward Four in the old days before the Irish began coming in. After the first great famine in Ireland, they came as rapidly as they could make up the passage money—Kerry men and women—and the one spot of green they named Kerry Park. They built their shanties around the park overlooking the river. Soon Ward Four was crammed with Kerryites, all coming for the money, and, above all, for the food that could be picked from the trees simply by lifting one hand. No one had told them about the work that waited for them. It was not until some of the first ones, consumed by a longing for the green land, went home to Ireland, sick with the consumption laid on them by their jobs, that the others learned it was the same work that the Irish were doing in the dark mills of Liverpool and Manchester. It was in the mills that they would earn their living, or laying the rails for the railway that was to stretch from one side of the new country to the other. There were those Kerry men who would not follow the rails, for laying the rails took them with every step away from the Atlantic Ocean and that much farther from the old country. It was those who settled down in Irish Parish, and the mill owners were made rich by their decision. Shrewd Yankees that they were, they harnessed the water power and created the great dam in full view of Kerry Park. The Irish had that always before them to remind them that the tales of travelers can sometimes be apocryphal.

These Irishmen soon found they had exchanged the English landlord for the Yankee mill owner; and they took off their hats, these shanty Irish, as reluctantly to this one as they had to the other. As time went on, the shanties disappeared, but the shanty Irishmen remained, housed now in the long row of red-brick tenements put up by the Yankee mill owners. The tenements were dark and small; children filled the five rooms to overflowing. There were five to a feather bed and three beds in one bedroom—the other bedroom, dedicated to the mother and father, held only one, though the youngest slept in a crib near the marriage bed, where the next occupant of the crib was being created. The marriage room also held the great chest stored with the linen brought from home. There was always the mingled musty smell of babies, tobacco, and bread in the house.

The front room was the one facing the street, and that was sacred to the dead, for it was here, in the early days, that the dead were waked. This room was filled with heavy furniture, bought at the local furniture store, and a few relics of the past: a colored picture of Ireland; perhaps a letter or two from home, placed prominently on the table; a pot containing some of the old sod that someone, in a last moment of desperation, had seized before he got onto the boat. Here, too, would be the most precious wedding presents carefully preserved, but the focal point of the room was the great family Bible sitting on a table in the center. In this all the names of the living and dead were carefully inscribed by the priest. Only for a death or a birth was the Bible ever opened. It was never read, for these Irishmen had no need to read the Bible stories—didn't they hear them often enough in church, and didn't they have, for entertainment, plenty of stories in their own heads, stories that had little to do with the Bible?

The dining room, with its great round table in the center, was not used much; often an extra cot was set up in there for the oldest of the children. Occasionally, when the old people wanted to escape the din of the children, they went in there to talk; but this was seldom, for an Irishman talks best when there is competition. The kitchen was the lived-in room. Here the family gathered to eat, talk, and play. Around the glowing wood stove the family, old friends, and even the cat, gathered on a dark winter night. The stove was the heart of the room, replacing the open hearth of the old country. The men were given the favored place, in front of the stove, where they could toast their wool-socked feet in the oven. The women gathered in another circle off to the side, sewing or knitting, hastily giving a full, round breast to a child whose crying interrupted a story. The child, spasmodically clutching and unclutching its hands, would fall asleep, its face still buried in the breast.

The teakettle stood always simmering, adding its steam to the damp smell of the room made by the diapers drying to one side of the stove. There was never a stove that did not have its teapot standing on the back of it to keep the strong tea warm but not boiling. The men and women both filled their bowls freely. On some occasions there was whiskey, or "poteen," as it was still called. The room was filled with the tobacco smoke that issued from the T.D.'s that both the men and the women smoked alternately. There was much talk of the cancer of the mouth that they thought was brought on by the rough stems of these clay pipes. It was a miracle that any of these women could hold a clay pipe, for most of them lost their teeth with the first child. Some of the older ones took snuff, carefully offering their paper packet to the one who sat next. The snuff was always accepted with a prayer for the dead—"The blessing of God be with the souls of your dead." Occasionally a thanksgiving was offered for a pipeful of tobacco, too. At seven-thirty the oldest children put the youngest to bed and came back to listen to the talk, until, overwhelmed by the heat of the room, they tumbled off the stools and were sent to bed. Determined to stay awake to hear the end of the story, they were soon asleep with ghosts and goblins haunting their dreams.

In telling the stories, there was always one man or woman who was favored, depending on the number of supernatural visions he or she had had. The one with the longest memory was best, for he could tell visions that were none of his own, but belonged to those dead ones whose names were forgotten. Whenever an Irishman told a story, it became his own.

" 'Twas after the birth of Johnny there," he would start. "I was watching him, for he had little strength from the mother who died giving him birth. I was sitting by the crib when I heard a step in the kitchen. It was after twelve, a bad time to be up, but I felt no fear, for I knew who would be in the kitchen rattling pans after twelve. I went out to her, and she said quietly, 'It is I, come back to look after him, for it's a great longing I have to keep him alive.' I said nothing, but nodded. 'I will stay only until morning to keep those off that are after his soul, though he but a child.' I nodded again, and remembered my old mother who had sprinkled holy water on the doorstep the night my father almost died. My grief! but I found the bottle quick and went and sat by the child. She gave him the breast and wrapped him in the warm cloth she had prepared with steam. Soon I heard a great rattling at the doors. 'Are they locked?' she asks. I nodded, for I dared say nothing for fear she would go—it is not good to speak to the dead."

An old woman in the corner sucked on her pipe ominously.

"Soon they were at the window. I could hear them crying and banging away. I tell you the hair stood straight on my head, for I could see her struggling to hold the child from them. It was a fearful struggle and her sitting all the time with no strength to speak. They near broke the glass with their hurling. I knew then there was no help against them. What are windows to the host?" he asked.

The whole room in a body shook its head, sighing.

"With that, I jumped up. If the dead could not keep them out, the living would. I took the holy water and poured it over the window. Everything was very quiet. When I turned around, she was gone and the child was in its crib breathing easy." He stopped to mop his face. "I never want another like it," he ended.

No one spoke for a long time. Then a woman began speaking. "It's about the O'Sullivans I would talk, and this is my story," she said. "In the old days of Ireland when the O'Sullivans were among its kings and there was wealth and glory for them—conversing daily with the Fianna and even, some say, with Crom Dubh himself, for there has always been some of the Devil about them—they had seven golden castles and seven silver, and there was some said it was fairy gold. There has ever been a story that they had more to do with the Sidhe than they would say. There was even one O'Sullivan who was gone for fifteen years, and there was no age upon her when she came back."

All the older people looked knowingly at one another.

"Well, it's that one gave birth to a child two months after her return, and it was no natural birth, for the swans were circling the house the whole day. It was a boy, and they say he heard the Sidhe, and since that time there is no one of the O'Sullivans who has not had to shut his door tight on a windy night for the fear of them. Some say they took to the hills of Kerry with the coming of the English and lost their wealth doing it. I have seen the black-browed ones come into the town of a Saturday and there is something else comes with them. Some say that the old ones that went to the hills buried their treasure and the young ones have been seeking it ever since. One of the girls looked for it in dreams and was told to seek it in a fairy forth. She did, and lifted the rock which it was supposed to be under and found nothing but a heap of dung. Some say the Sidhe removed the crock of gold to America and there will be O'Sullivans looking for it yet. They say the Banshee cries for the O'Sullivans as well as the O'Briens—they both being of the old Ireland. There is a John O'Sullivan come over this week hunting for gold. Well, he'll find no pot of gold here unless it be the one buried at the foot of Money Hole Hill and he's more than welcome to Yankee gold, for I'd want none of it."

Usually these evenings ended at eleven o'clock, for there was no Irishman wanting to be up after twelve. One could never tell what one would meet then. Too, they all had to get up early in the morning to get to the mill by six. When the windows were still dark with the night, the women would be up taking the hot soda bread out of the oven for breakfast and the men would be shaving themselves before the kitchen mirror. Excepting for the thump, thump, of the razor strap and an occasional fretful cry from the bedroom, this was one of the rare times that the house was silent.

Gradually the whole tenement came to life, though the streets outside were still quiet. Just as the first lightness appeared, the men would come out of the blocks with their lunchboxes in their hands and there would be greetings along the still dark street. Sometimes the women, too, would appear, with their shawls wrapped tightly around them to keep the cold away, on their way to church. The men would walk along with one another, but there was no talk—it was still too dark and too early for that. The women and men both hurried along so as not to be late for the daily Mass which began at five-fifteen and ended at five-forty, so that the men could get to the mill by six and the women back to the children.

The church would be very quiet and cold, and the people huddled there, waiting impatiently for the altar boy to light the candles so that the priest might appear and get on with the Mass. Though they wanted to start the day right, they didn't want it to take too long. The people would kneel, quietly saying their beads, their rattling the only sound in the church. They rose as a body when the priest appeared and began: *"Introibo ad altare Dei. Ad Deum qui laetificat juventutem meam."* The women received daily communion; the men received it only on Sundays—they needed the warm breakfast to get them through the twelve hours in the mill. After Mass, they all came out, ready for talk and banter now, for it was lighter and the day had started right. Some of the old women stopped to light a candle, but the younger ones hurried home to their children.

While the men worked their shift in the cotton and paper mills, the women worked theirs in the home. They baked their own bread, and indeed cooked everything their families ate. Flour was bought by the barrel and potatoes by the bushel. On Saturday and Wednesday mornings, the whole house was filled with the smell of fresh-made bread. On Monday, it was filled with the smell of damp laundry. There would be a great kettle of starch on the stove and soapsuds foaming over the edge of the set-tubs used on Saturday night for bathing children and on Monday morning for beating clothes into cleanliness. The back yards of the tenements were filled in winter with freshly washed clothes, hanging stiff as boards, iced by the wind. The women hanging them, their hands red and stiff with the cold, kept up a constant barrage of talk. "There'll be no drying today with the weather the way it is, and me with another tubful to replace these."

During the afternoon, the women would stop in on each other for a cup of tea, and they would talk over the latest news of the Parish—a birth, a death, a new one from the old country, or—and this they talked of most frequently—a new female complaint. The cures suggested interested them more than the complaint itself. They were all self-healers. Doctors seldom appeared in Irish Parish even for births. There was always a midwife, worn from childbirth herself, who would come to attend another's, her few instruments gathered in her apron when she came up the stairs. All the children were told it was the new child that made the apron bulge so.

Some of the older women were "knowledged" in herbs, and they knew a cure for everything under the sun. "There is nothing to a bad heart that dandelion will not sure." "Mullein is a fairy herb and it is dangerous to cut—do not pull it while the wind is changing or it's your head you'll be losing and not the ache in it. It's the one to bring children back when they are away." Children and childbirth formed the core of their conversation, and there was always a new story for them to talk and sometimes laugh over. "John Fitzgerald, who had so little sympathy for his wife and she in great pain," Bridgie Meehan would say; "you all know him, sour black man that he is. I put the pain on himself, and he all doubled up and roaring with it. He'll not be lacking in sympathy next time, I'm thinking, now that he's had a taste of it himself."

Great warnings were issued to the women that were carrying. "Don't be going to a house where there is one in labor or your own will come on you too soon. And be careful to keep out of the way of animals, especially cats—there is a woman I know whose last was born with a claw. She woke in the middle of the night and saw the cat staring at her; and she knew the one within her was doomed, for she could feel it scratching from then on. And if it's born with a caul, keep the child away from the fire, for it's in danger of death by burning."

Some of these shanty Irishmen were better off than others, but there was little social distinction in those days. All worked in the cotton and paper mills twelve hours a day, six days a week; all had large families and all were behind with the rent. In summer, they all sat out on their front stoops in their shirtsleeves, calling warnings to the children who played in the park and talking with one another. The old women smoked their T.D.'s, able with no discomfort to hold the hot bowls in their hands, hands calloused with whaling the bottoms of many children. The men talked and told stories—the mill and the work of the day were forgotten as their minds, freed from the present, recalled the past and explored the future.

There was no social ostracism if one of the children went down to John the Harp's to fetch home a pail of beer. Since God had provided these children, there should be use for them. On Saturday nights the men would gather in the back room at John the Harp's, drinking straight whiskey and talking. Some nights there would be music—one man would bring his accordion, another his fiddle. As the evening went on, the music grew faster and louder and there would be great singing and dancing. A man would take the center of the floor dancing and leaping to the music. The higher he could leap, the greater a dancer he was. Old Dineen, aged fifty-five, was the greatest "lepper" in Irish Parish. "Sure and it's up to the roof he can go, and it's wings on his feet he has surely." At twelve o'clock the men would come home gay and warm with the drinking and dancing. There was always a bottle of something for the old woman in one pocket.

Everyone belonged to Saint Jerome's Parish, for Saint Jerome's was the church these Irishmen had built out of their own pockets, even sending to Ireland for a Kerry man as their priest, "a fine strong man he was with a great flow of words from his tongue." They wanted none of these strange American priests who would be on bad terms with the Sidhe. A priest who had no charms against the powers of the "gentle folk" was of no consequence to them, no matter what titles he might have after his name. Above all, they wanted none of the skinflint sort, always dunning his parishoners for a new roof to the church when the old was as good as ever. They would give, but not on demand. And they could do without the theology if the man could sing a fine Mass. They wanted none of him who would give you a look if he saw a glass of whiskey in your hand either. There was no good to a man if he could not take a drink of whiskey at a gulp without gasping, priest or no priest.

Until Saint Jerome's Church was built, these Irishmen had no regular Mass on Sunday. Once every two months a priest traveling from one small New England town to another came through and said Mass for them. Along with a few others, he was sent out from the Boston Diocese to take care of every town in New England that contained Irish immigrants. When the church was finished, it was a fine building—red brick with five stained-glass windows and an altar that was the pride of the Parish. Inside, the church was a hodge-podge of color, every saint brightly painted. When my grandfather, John O'Sullivan, came to Irish Parish, the church had been added to, and a red-brick schoolhouse conducted by the nuns stood next to it.

John O'Sullivan was a Kerry man, born in the hills of Kerry. From the time he was born until he had set out to earn his living in a small Kerry town, he had heard nothing but pure Gaelic spoken, and he still spoke it himself as long as his wife lived. He was a strong, handsome man with the look of the blackbrowed O'Sullivans and there was many a girl who took more than one look at him. But John O'Sullivan had eyes for no one else from the time he first saw Johanna Sheehan walking down a country road in her bright red petticoat. She was the daughter of a fairly well-to-do farmer, well-to-do for those parts—didn't he own his own land and hadn't he more than one pig? John O'Sullivan was a hand on the farm next to the Sheehans', working for an old crochety man that had not the strength of a woman in either of his arms, and this from the great age upon him.

It was while he was sleeping in the loft that he heard the plotting going on down belowstairs between the old man and Mr. Sheehan. Though there was no strength left in the old man, he had eyes in his head.

"A girl like that would be a comfort to an old man in a cold bed, and a great one for the farm," the father said, "and she so straight and strong."

But the old man was crafty for all his great age; he knew the farms joining each other had more to do with the offer than wily Mr. Sheehan would say. "I'll take the pasture of yours in the hollow as the price for taking the woman off your hands."

"There's plenty who'd take her with nothing to go with her," the father indignantly replied. "There's not many women as fine and strong as she. I'll make no bargains with you, you old crow—not many fathers would be willing to give up a daughter to one with so many years on him. Come, settle your mind on her and she's yours with no bargains to it, free and clear."

"I know well," the old man said, "that it's the land you're after and I'm a part of that bargain, but I'll take her, for all that you're winning over me. I have but a few years, and the land may go to her as well as another. Be careful, though, that it's not begetting a son I am, one who'll be making muddle of your plans."

Mr. Sheehan only chuckled: "The Devil has your tail and you know it—no man, not even a Kerry man, begot a child after eighty." The wedding date was set as early as possible.

John O'Sullivan slept little that night, and in the morning he put himself in the way of Johanna Sheehan as she went singing down the road. He repeated to her the conversation he had heard, and she, being a girl of great spirit, resolved that she would never marry the old man. Johanna said never a word, listening to the ravings of John O'Sullivan gravely and quietly. One morning she did not appear on the road, but there was a letter for John O'Sullivan left in the rocks where they used to sit. The letter said simply: "I have gone to America. I have saved all that I earned from my eggs and taken the bit Aunt Bridgie left me. If you want me, you will find me in a place where there are Kerry men. Signed Thomas Heffernan, Schoolmaster, written for Johanna Sheehan, in secrecy."

That was all John O'Sullivan knew when he left Ireland for America. He collected his wages at the end of the season; for he was not one to renege on an old man, no matter how much bitterness he felt in his heart toward him. He worked till after the harvest and then left. He had enough for passage and enough for some shoes. He sailed to America with other immigrants in the cold of the winter. When the boat docked at Boston, he was told then that it was there he would find most of the Irish immigrants. He took a job on the docks, and in the evening, tired and weary, he hunted for Johanna Sheehan, but no one had heard of her. Most of the Irish girls were working as house servants, but he could find no Johanna Sheehan registered at any of the agencies. In a saloon one night, he heard two men talking of Irish Parish and how it had become a settlement for Kerry people. He asked them where it was, and the next day he left for Irish Parish. He found Johanna there waiting for him to come. They were married, and Johnny O'Sullivan went to work in one of the paper mills.

Johanna Sheehan gave John O'Sullivan seventeen children. She was a good wife and mother, and, though she told no stories herself, she never tired of her husband's. She died of excessive childbearing, as most of the women of the Parish did, at the age of fifty. After her death my grandfather came to live with my mother, who was his favorite child.

All of the O'Sullivans went to church and sang in the choir, and the O'Sullivan girls were known far and away for their sweet, clear voices. The whole family was a singing one, and on the Feast of Corpus Christi they led the procession around the park. John O'Sullivan and his family occupied one of the tenements in the "Row," and, as he became better known, he was one of the men whom all Irish Parish turned to for advice. Even the priest would come to him if there was a Parish problem he could not cope with. And the priest, too, acknowledged that John O'Sullivan was the finest story-teller in the Parish. On summer evenings people would gather on the steps of the O'Sullivans' to listen to him, and there were plenty went home quaking with the fear he put into them.

For forty years the O'Sullivans lived in Irish Parish, and there were changes that took place, not within the old but within the young. No one thought of the Hill in the old days, nor much about education either. The seventeen children, with the exception of Agnes (God rest her soul, marked for death by the words of the blasphemous comparing her to an angel) had, as a matter of course, been sent to Sister School. The Order of Notre Dame, stern and severe in habit, taught them. They learned nothing much except to read, write, and spell. My mother's handwriting was medieval, each letter carefully and conscientiously drawn.

I was born in Irish Parish, but was lifted out of it, and with my family was one of the group to move to Money Hole Hill. The influx up there came gradually, and our move from Johnny O'Sullivan's block made us aliens for many years. The slow migration really began in my grandfather's day. It began with the marriage of Sidney Whitney to Bridie Flannagan. Irish Parish acquaintance with the Hill had only been a geographical one till then; but the Hill came to the Parish when it wanted a wife for its foremost son; for beauty and health, and a fine aristocracy, an aristocracy of the spirit, resided there.

Bridie was a paper cutter in the Whitney Mill. In six months, she was a lady in the Money Hole Hill sense of the term. My grandfather could see no difference and told her so—"a few more feathers in your hat," he would say. But he was secretly pleased that she came to hear his stories, as she always had. But who wouldn't come to hear my grandfather tell stories! "He would have scared the Devil himself and kept him from his evil work," my grandmother used to say.

Bridie was one of the first wedges, but there was another. Nelly Finn moved up to Money Hole Hill, but her invitation was not so legitimate. Nelly was a great source of amusement to the ladies of Irish Parish whose husbands couldn't afford her. In their secret hearts, they were rather tickled to know that the men on Money Hole Hill were frail, even if their wives did wear so much whalebone. The ladies of Irish Parish were fond of Nelly Finn; the ladies on the Hill scorned her. They had their reasons. Many were the nudges and sly winks when, after Mass on Sunday mornings, she drove through Kerry Park, her parasol tilted rakishly, and as many birds in her hat as there were in a bush. My grandfather was fond of Nelly, too; he would wait for her to pass his corner on Sunday morning and inquire, "How's business, Nelly?" Nelly became a myth for Irish Parish. Long after her death, my mother would say, when I was pestering her, "Don't bother me now. I'm as busy as Nelly Finn."

We moved to the Hill because of my father, who was a foreigner and had little understanding of Irish Parish for all his having been born in Ireland. My grandfather blamed it on County Cork—"It's English he is, not Irish at all," he would grumble. Others moved because the old ties were disappearing, and the Irish had little but the church and the mill in common any more. When we moved, Irish Parish was still at one with itself. Ours was looked on as the first great apostasy; for my grandfather, now old and childish, was still considered one of the archangels of Irish Parish. Everyone protested his departure, and none more than himself; for in Irish Parish, at least, he could still be shanty Irish with impunity.

And so we left Irish Parish for less green fields; and we became outcasts from our own race, and aliens among the race of Yankees into whose hallowed circle we moved. There were, it is true, a few Irish on Money Hole Hill; and they were the worst of all, imitators of imitators, neither Yankee nor Irish, but of that species known as the lace-curtain Irish. They put the curtains up in their parlors, and decked out their souls in the same cheap lace. It was into this circle that a lace-curtain father moved a set of the most shanty Irish people that have ever been. My grandfather refused to go back to Irish Parish because he would not leave my mother, whom he considered the root and flower of our whole family. My mother would not leave because she could never abandon, defeated, a battle involving her race. She would remain, though ostracized by both sides; and before we left for the school of the Yankees and our lace-curtain cousins, my mother enjoined us to remember, in the battles which occurred every day, that we were O'Sullivans, descendants of the kings of Ireland, and we were not to come home crying. We never did; and to the end of my days, I shall remember my mother standing in the door, her black eyes flashing out a fire that still serves to warm the worlds of the Money Hole Hills that I have lived in since.

excerpt from

Hour of Spring

(1948)

MARY DEASY

In the spring, Bride thought, there would be the child; but born not deep in a continent's center as she had been born, as her father had been born: sent forth instead, like those who had gone before them, to draw into his wailing lungs the sharp salt air of the land that meets the sea. It did not matter that this was not the same ocean that curved long tongues of spray over the rocks in the west of County Kerry; the sea that hurls itself against the land and slips away speaks in the same voice to those who stand on the shore, whether it be Kerry or the other side of the world, across a sea's and a continent's width. He would know the big boom of the surf when the green water rushed along the beach, and the stiff beat of the wings of the gulls, wheeling in the wind under a high morning sky.

Or it might be that it would not mean the same to him, half his blood being the solid New England line that lay behind his father; it might be that he would grow up no true Joyce at all, as her great-granduncle Matt would have put it, unsmiling, the words coming out hard and disapproving in his rapid Irish speech.

But there was no one left to care for that now: not Old Matt now, nor her father, nor her grandfather Joyce; not even Aunt Maggie lost in the dim print of press notices always more obscure, nor Granny Joyce triumphantly immortal in her circle of nonagenarian Cratty kin. They were all dead or careless, scattered and lost in America's huge earth, even their children unidentifiable in their starched prosperity, heedless alike of clan and of past.

She remembered her great-granduncle Matt as a tall old man who wore a loose-fitting dark suit and a derby hat, and who came to visit them twice a year on holiday afternoons, when he talked to them about the old days when he had lived on Burke Street. There were long silences in the conversation while he sat staring stubbornly at the heavy blacked shoe swinging from his carefully crossed knee, silences which he would finally break with a bit of news, uttered suddenly in his uncompromising voice, about some member of the Joyce connection. Sometimes he went farther back and began to talk about Ireland, and of his experiences with the little people there. He told them once that his grandmother had the glamour, and could see the fairies and traffic with them. She was a beautiful gray woman, he said; and told how she would put an empty chair by the peats on a stormy night for some poor ghost to come in and rest.

He believed all that, Bride thought; he believed it as implicitly as he believed in the Lord God sitting in His golden chair, and the angels and the blessed saints standing round. People who never knew the old Irish might think it incredible that a man could live for more than half a century in a modern American city and still believe in the existence of fairies, particularly a man as hardheadedly matter-of-fact as her great-granduncle Matt. There wasn't an ounce of whimsy in him that she had ever discovered. It must all have been perfectly literal with him, and I suppose, she thought, no one will ever know what kind of bizarre world it was in his head, with banshees and changelings all mixed up with Ty Cobb's lifetime batting average and what William Jennings Bryan said during the 1908 presidential campaign.

She wished now that she had known him better. She had been only ten years old when he had gotten his death in a spring rain of 1927, coming from the opening baseball game of the season, and her grandfather Joyce had died hardly more than a year later, so that she had never really learned to know him either. All that she knew was about two old men; but there was so much more than that to know.

There was that day in 1870, for example, when a pair of County Kerry Irishmen, Timothy and Matthew Joyce by name—nephew and uncle, although, as it frequently happens in the generations of large families, there was not so much as ten years' difference in their ages— arrived in the sprawling Midwestern town on the spring flood of the broad yellow river. The town must already have been a full two hundred thousand when they walked up the steep cobblestoned streets from the wharf for the first time, carrying their bulging green bag between them and looking about suspiciously and curiously as they went, their hats drawn down half-belligerently, half-shyly, over their foreheads. There were factories, schools, shops, warehouses, theaters, telegraph offices, railroad stations, hotels—all the appurtenances of a thriving American postbellum city.

Nobody could have blamed them if they were bewildered: two young greenhorns who had grown up in the same row of yellow-roofed cottages staggering crookedly uphill, under a washed blue-gray sky, in which their fathers and their grandfathers had grown up before them. What was there behind them but the rock and the furze, the swift Irish speech, the wet wild land? Oh, if I could go back, she thought, I would walk through the years, carrying my son in my arms to see the thick-walled Kerry cottages with their honey-colored thatch, the whin and the bog, and the sea that rolls endlessly out of the west. I would stand on the high hills and show him his past that will run in his veins to his own hunger and bewilderment and rich joy, the past that will give the form to his limbs and the color to his mind, bending his life to its pattern even before his birth. I would show him the troubled land, and the faces of his fathers. I would show him . . .

Ireland? Staffy Brady said. No, there's not much of it sticks in my memory. The sea, maybe, and the little fields of stooks with the western light on them of an evening, and the night smells that came up out of the bogs. I was only a lad when they brought me over.

He sucked for a moment on the stem of his unlit pipe, his small, shrewd-eyed face, with its tremblingly shorn gray stubble about the lean jaws, pleased but a little sardonic as he spoke.

You didn't know, maybe, he said, that I'd been in the ring when I was a young man? I knew them all: Corbett, Ryan, John L. Sullivan, Jack Dempsey—not the Dempsey you'll be thinking of, but the Nonpareil. They were all Irish, every one of them. There's a saying somewhere that the Irish are never at peace but when they're fighting. God forgive us, and it's a saying that doesn't stop for its meaning with the men.

It was on a Sunday in 1941, the summer before she had left for California, that she had sat talking to Staffy Brady in the room behind his little candy-and-tobacco shop on Burke Street. It was a hot August afternoon; the air was thick with the smell of dust and tobacco, and there was a baby crying upstairs, and a tinny phonograph playing a fast tune on a scratched record over and over again.

By God, you're a fine slip of a girl, Bride Joyce, Staffy said. You take after your father to the very eyes in your head. They're the Carroll eyes, light gray, with all them black lashes.

The Carroll eyes, she said. Then it was my grandmother Joyce's family he got his looks from?

Oh yes, he said. You've never seen your grandmother Joyce's father, old Denny Carroll, or you'd know what I mean. He was the tall whip of a man even after he'd begun to stoop down with age; and the peculiar gray eyes he had, just like your own.

He swayed back and forth a few times, meditatively, in his creaky rocker, sucking on his unlit pipe. The baby stopped crying for a moment or two, and in the breathless heat the phonograph went grinding quickly on, unopposed and insistent.

Your grandmother Joyce, Staffy said, had the name of being the holiest woman in this parish, but it was not from her da that she got that at all. The old people had a saying, there was never a time Denny Carroll went into the church that he could stay out of it without losing his soul. Wasn't it many a Sunday morning, they used to tell it, he was down by the rocks in the old country, watching the sea with his pipe in his mouth, the time his missus would be running about looking for him with his Sunday breeches in her hands? They were always the latest couple in the church; when the Carrolls were inside, the Mass could begin.

Your great-grandmother was a wild one, the same as Denny, Staffy said, and the disputes they had in their time—sure the whole village would come to stand outside and listen, and they keeping it up the grander for knowing the audience they had! She was more than a match for Denny, and no mistake. I remember him telling about a day when they were courting together in the old country, and he had taken her to the races that they would hold in them days down on the hard sand of one of the beaches, maybe a dozen miles from the place where they lived. Didn't it happen that they were going back that night in the cart he was driving, and the axle broke the time they were halfway home, and could never be mended till the morning? There was only one bed in the world for them to sleep in, at the lone houseen where they stopped, but the woman said they could make it serve with a pillow between them, the way they would both be as single as if they was lying in separate counties.

The next day the axle was fixed, and they went riding off home together. It was a fine windy day, and your great-grandmother had pushed her shawl back loose around her shoulders; well then, as they were passing along the road, it blew off entirely and over a wall. Denny stopped the horse, and was for climbing over the wall and fetching it back for her, but wasn't she down herself before he could ever set foot on the ground?

God help you, Dennis Carroll, she said, if you couldn't get over the pillow, you can never get over that wall!

And she climbed it herself before he could open his mouth, and came back fetching her own shawl with her. Staffy smiled, nodding slightly, the pipe clenched in his teeth. She was an O'Neill, he said, and the O'Neills was always ready ones with their tongues.

They sat there in silence for a few moments, the music hurrying their thoughts to its nagging rhythm.

Tell me about Ireland, Bride said to him.

He shook his head. Devil a more. It's all mixed up with the stories the old folks would be telling, the way I don't know in the world what I saw and what I didn't. I can remember the sea and that's all of it.

But Burke Street? he said. That's another story. I can tell you all you'll want to know about Burke Street. *Mo léir*, it's not what it was in the old days.

My mother, God rest her soul, never knew the day for years on end in those times when she didn't have a couple of greenhorns in the house. They'd come straggling in with their bags and their bundles, looking half-starved after their long trip from the old country, and the lice on them that every one of them could not help but be getting on them filthy boats. My mother would feed them, and clean them, and give them a bed to sleep in, and it was in our house they would be staying till they had a job, and could set up someplace for themselves.

Matt and Timothy Joyce, he said, lived in our house when they first came over. Timothy's mother and mine were own sisters to each other, the way it was a natural thing for him and Matt to come to this town, where they had relatives already settled before them. I was maybe ten years old at that time, and that would have made them near thirty and twenty. You knew your grandfather only when he was an old man, and so you may not believe that he was thought to be a handsome young buck when he came over. He was a great, powerfully built chap in those days, a wrestler's build, I'd say: thick back, and solid legs, and shoulder muscles like knots of iron. And he had them blue eyes, and a sandy mustache, and taffy-brown hair growing low on his forehead. There was more than one girl on Burke Street would have been willing to lay down for him in those days. Not that he was ever much for the women. He was as awkward with them even then as his uncle Matt.

The Carrolls lived upstairs of us then, Staffy said, rocking back and forth slowly in the thick moted heat of the room. There were two girls, Ellen and Brigid—your grandaunt Brigid, the one you were named for, he said, pointing the end of his pipe at Bride. Both fair-looking girls, nothing to what their mother had been, maybe; they had the long Carroll upper lip that spoiled their looks a bit, to my mind. I think Timothy had known them over in Ireland. Maybe there they would have thought they were a good bit above him: oh, he could read and write and figure, but they had taught in a school themselves; they'd read about things then he hadn't even known were in the world. They did say Denny Carroll had a bit of the Latin and the Greek itself, that he'd learned from his own grandfather; and it's many a time I heard him say myself there were great lands and windy fields in Munster that his fathers before him had owned till the days of the con-fiscations, and they with the long blood running in them that went back to King Miledh and the heathen times.

But in this country things turned out a bit different for them. There was Denny hitting the bottle steady since his wife had died on the boat coming over—they had to bury her at sea, and when he was bad with the drink he used to say he saw her standing up in front of him, with the water running from her clothes and the seaweed tangled in her hair—and there was Timothy with a fine job with the railroad, a steady young fellow looking for a wife. Yes, he was steady, even in those days. He would have his drop or two now and then, and there was that black Joyce temper would break out once in a while or so; but you could see he had all the makings of a steady man.

Nobody ever knew which one of the Carroll girls he was courting, Staffy said. Brigid was a bit older than him, maybe a year or two, but she was the handsomer of the sisters, and seemed to favor him more than Ellen did. The whole thing was hanging fire, dragging on from month to month, till the old women of the parish had their tongues fair hanging out of their heads for a drop of real gossip to wet them with, when Johnny Fogarty came over from Ireland, and after two weeks had the banns up in church for Brigid and himself. That was Christy Fogarty's father; it's likely you never laid eyes on him. He must have been in his grave long before you were ever born. He was the grand plain fellow, Johnny Fogarty, and the fine tenor voice he had, would make you think you were listening to one of the holy saints themselves. He'd sing a *come-all-ye* like nobody else in the world could sing it.

Timothy and Ellen waited maybe a month after Johnny and Brigid were married, Staffy said, and then their banns were read out in the church, and they were married as if neither of them had ever had a thought of doing anything else. Oh, there were some ill-tempered enough to say Ellen was taking her sister's leavings, and that Timothy was making second best do when first best was gone; but there was never anyone could put it on them that they weren't true to each other once the marriage words were spoken. And if Timothy never seemed to know or care what was going on in Ellen's mind, or whether she was happy or sad or what, as long as his life with her went on according to the way he had it in his head was the proper way for it to go—why, you know yourself there was something in the man that was always solitary, unkindly, poor at sharing what was in the hearts and minds of even the few that were closest to him in life. Timothy was—Staffy squinted his eyes for a moment, seeking a word—Timothy was what you might have called a *believer*. Oh, I don't mean only that he was a good Catholic, though that was part of it, of course; I mean he believed that people ought to act and did act according to certain rules in life. It made for a kind of blindness in him. He was like a man following a road on an old map that's been out of date for a hundred years; he couldn't see that there were other newer roads now that people were using, or that a few people were even cutting across fields to build newer ones still. No, he walked along his road like it was the only one in the universe and, like everybody that took a step off it, one side or the other, was on his way to the devil, as fast as might be.

I must have been at his wedding, Staffy said, but devil a bit about it I remember. The Irish have never made so much of a wedding as, say now, the Italians do: the two people will stand up together in the church as stiff as if they was maybe going to try to spell each other down in a spelling bee, and there will be a bit of a celebration after. But an Irish wedding is a tame thing to an Irish funeral.

A finger of sunlight reached through a long slit in the cracked green blind that flapped listlessly at the open window, and rested an emphatic tip on the littered table, which still held the dishes from which Staffy had eaten that morning. Bride sat in a straight-backed wooden chair just out of the light, and listened while he came slowly forward through the past.

Johnny Fogarty, if I remember it right, he said, was on his keeping in the western islands before he came over to this country in the fall of '71. He was a wild Fenian to the end of his days, and knew all of the big ones from O'Donovan Rossa to Tom Clarke. Maybe Timothy had a bit of a part in that kind of business too, though I never heard him speak of it in later days; for the whole of Ireland was like a boiling pot the time he was coming from a boy to a man. You may have noticed there are three things an Irishman always puts his soul in: his religion, his sports, and his politics. If you ever find an Irishman who is wishy-washy on any one of those, you can make up your mind to it he is not the true article at all.

Those two, Johnny Fogarty and Timothy, he said, were maybe a bit in the way of being in a race with each other, those early years, which one of them would get ahead fastest in the world. There was Johnny after buying his own house on Burke Street, and Timothy as fast behind him as he could sign the papers on the mortgage. The two sisters, they were the ones were behind it, of course; for all Ellen had turned into the holy woman of the parish since she'd married, she was like all the rest of the females that I ever heard of in the world: she did not want to be behind any other woman of her own flesh and blood. It was the great sorrow to her that it was Brigid who had the first boy of the two of them, and herself having nothing but girls that while. She went to the church and made novenas to Saint Anne, and Saint Elizabeth, and every other woman-saint in the calendar that had ever brought a child into the world, and the whole time there was Brigid having one boy after the other, three of them in a row, and all of them born living and healthy. It got so she couldn't bear the sight of Brigid, and there were times they had high words together on the head of it. They had dull hard lives surely, the women in those days, and a bit of a quarrel was the thing that was like the spice in the pudding to them.

That was till the great misfortune that came on Brigid, the time she lost two of her three boys in the river. The two oldest it was, that was drowned through the ice in '82. Didn't the one fall through, and the other after him, trying to pull him out? And there was Brigid left with only the one boy from all that brood, and she never the same from that day out.

She and Ellen were nearer each other after that. It might have been that your own father, Young Matt, that was born the same year to Timothy and Ellen, was growing into the image of the oldest boy Brigid had lost in the river, and she had a softness for him that kept her from quarreling with his mother, the way she could see him every day. When Maggie, that was the next of Ellen's children, was born, it was Brigid that left her own house and husband alone to do for her sister, and the same three years later when Hughie, the last of them all, came into the world. You'll maybe have noticed it is the way with some women—and it is mostly those that have had some great misfortune in their own family—that they will go around looking for worries to take up from other people, while their own house shifts along the best way it can. That was the way it was with Brigid after her boys were lost: there was not a house in the parish did not have to thank her for some kindness or other from her own two hands; but Johnny and Christy, the boy that was left, they had mostly to get along by themselves, and many's the time they made a supper of bread and tea while Brigid was off cooking a fine meal in some other house.

Staffy half-closed his eyes for a moment, and through the slit of the lids Bride saw the pupils fixing into their focus on the past.

I remember that day that Hughie was born, he said after a time, like it was all painted out for me on them colored pictures we used to look at through the stereoscope. That was sometime past the middle of the eighties, when Timothy was going on toward forty years old and I was ten or eleven years younger, the way it was. I came out of our house on Burke Street just as Timothy came out of his house that was directly opposite, and we walked up the street to the church together. He was holding Young Matt by the hand.

It was about a quarter past seven on a morning in May, and we could see the sun just starting to break through the early morning river mist that was all around us in the street, and the sky getting higher and rosier as we walked along. We passed Johnny Fogarty's house and Johnny came running out, sticking his arms in the sleeves of his coat, with his derby on the back of his head and his shoes half-blacked, like a man that had come from his bed in a hurry.

How is herself this morning? he called out to us.

No farther on than she was last night, Timothy said. It's a bad time, Johnny, a very bad time.

To see him walking along the street, with his eyes staring straight ahead in a stubborn gloomy look over his sandy mustache, you might have thought it was the worry over Ellen that was pulling his face the long way it was, but never believe that! Timothy was one that dearly loved a comfortable life, and the low way he was in when we first saw him that morning had little to do with Ellen's trouble, I'm much afraid, and more than a bit to do with the upset in his habits that it was making. There was Ellen in labor now for more than eighteen hours, and what he was scowling over was drinking cold tea and having strange women dish up his meals to him.

Strange women! I remember Johnny said. Is it Brigid you're calling a strange woman then? And he laughed. He was a man to hear laugh, Johnny Fogarty was.

Well, we went on to the church so; it was First Communion Sunday, and you could hardly find yourself a place inside the doors for the crowd. Timothy's oldest girl, Kate, was one of the First Communicants: a fine handsome girl of fourteen she was then, blue-eyed like her father, with the same taffy-colored hair he had, thick and curly and growing low on her forehead. You could see the gloom sliding off Timothy's back like butter off a hot knife when he saw her come in with the others in her white dress and veil, carrying the prayer book that he had bought her for her First Communion, and looking the handsomest and the holiest of the lot. A fine lovely girl like Kate, Young Matt beside him with that black curly head the women were always making over, another son maybe that very minute being born at home—you couldn't blame him for arching up a bit like a prize bull, and looking around the church the way everybody would know this was Timothy Joyce, that had such a fine family and a fine job and a fine Catholic home. Those were the good old days for Timothy and no mistake. Oh, he had plans then—or Ellen had, and she'd kept after him about them till he was almost thinking by that time they were his own—about the children: there were to be no words about Kate's getting a job in one of the big new department stores in town, the way some of the girls in the parish had done; she was to go to the Sisters' academy on Fremont Street next year, and Young Matt, when he grew up, would go to St. Francis College and be a lawyer or a doctor, if so it was that he didn't have the vocation to be a priest.

At any rate, Staffy went on, there was Timothy, casting his eyes ahead to the future, as it might be, and having no more thought of Ellen at home than of the devil himself, when all of a sudden there was a twitch of his sleeve, and he looked around to see Old Matt standing next to him in the aisle.

You had better come now, I heard Matt say, in a stage whisper that had half the people in the pew ahead of us looking around. Herself is worse, and they have sent for the priest.

Timothy looked at him without a change of expression that I could see. Then he looked at the altar; it was past the Communion, so he had heard enough of the Mass for his Sunday duty. After a bit he picked up his derby and got up, saying something to me, in a whisper like Matt's, about Johnny and me bringing Young Matt home when the Mass was over.

I'll walk along with you, I said, getting up myself.

We went out of the church together, the three of us, creaking down the aisle in our heavy shoes.

How bad is it then, that they have called the priest? Timothy said, when we were outside the door.

I don't know that, Matt said. She is very bad indeed, the women say.

You'll have seen your great-granduncle Matt and heard him speak yourself, the way I don't have to tell you the Irish bang that came at the end of his sentences, like he had a personal grudge against every soul he was talking to. They do say there is a hard streak in every Kerryman, and sure there was one a foot wide in Matt Joyce; he was never the man for any softness, or laughing, or even smiling whatever. A queer solitary world it was he lived in, in the middle of that brood of Timothy's; many's the time I've seen him sitting in his rocker with his pipe in the evening, spelling out the newspaper to himself with a look on his face like he mistrusted the very words he was reading, and all the while the rest of them talking away sixteen to a dozen, and laughing, or fighting, or whatever it was. He used to go off by himself of a Sunday afternoon and watch the boys playing football in the vacant lot there used to be down on the corner of River Street. Him in his derby and his Sunday blacks, you know, or, if it was a warm day, with his coat over his arm, and sleeve garters, and a shirt with a small purple figure, and a black bow tie. They did say he had been grand at the sports himself the time he was a young fellow over in Ireland.

The three of us walked on after that for a bit without speaking. I remember the way the street looked, so queer and still; there wasn't another soul in sight. The sun had gone higher in the sky, and you could smell the fresh dampness of the walks.

Is it Father O'Malley that is at the house now? Timothy asked, after a short while had passed.

And who else would it be? Matt said. Father Devanney had the seven-thirty, as you very well know.

I saw the stubborn look settling on Timothy's face.

She will not like that then, he said, shaking his head. It was always to Father Devanney that she went. Your soul to the devil, Matt said to him, would you like her to die without the priest?

You could see it in Timothy's face, Staffy said, that that was the first time it had so much as come into his head that she might die. But he kept walking on—even when he was a young man he had that way of walking you'll remember, deliberatelike, that powerful figure of his resting for a moment on the flat of each foot before going on to the next—and after a bit, as if he had figured it out, he came out with his answer.

She will never die, he said to Matt. A fine strong woman like herself—she will never die over a baby, and that her fifth.

It is a boy, Matt said. I meant to have told you before. It is a fine boy with hair on its head like a year-old child.

Timothy only said—A boy, is it?—and walked on as deliberate as before, but I saw the arch of his chest as he breathed in the air; from the soles of his feet, up through his broad limbs and trunk to the top of his head, he looked strong and powerful and serene. Oh, a prize bull, all right! It made me feel queer and a little respectful for a minute, as if he might be one of them heathen gods that used to go about—what's the word that was in the book?—*fructifying* mortal females. He was sound as a good apple in those days, your grandfather was.

Well, we walked on down the street toward Timothy's house, and when we came up to it we noticed that the front door was ajar, like somebody had come in at it and the people inside were too flurried to close it after him. We went in, first Timothy, then Matt, and last myself; I remember the feeling of hush that came over us, and the way our shoes creaked on the floor in the narrow hallway. It was that quiet, we could hear the clock ticking from behind the closed door of the parlor on our right. We stood there looking at each other for a minute, and then all at once we heard the sound of a woman's sobbing from the floor above. By God, there was the same wail of death in it that you would have heard in the old days in the *keen*, and I knew then in my soul that Ellen was gone.

You'll never have heard a keening in your life: the piercing howl that used to go out of the women's throats in the old times, and they crouching at the foot of the bed where the fresh corpse of one of their blood was lying. It was a long wail, like sorrow itself rushing out of the body, and then it would fall slow and choke off in a kind of sob. I remember a keening in the old country when I was a bit of a lad; in the evening it was, and two or three gossoons like myself ran off after supper and looked through the open door at the women inside. It was one of them wet gray evenings, with the darkness coming, and the great rush of the sea behind us. It seemed to me like the sound I heard was the howling of the whole universe over its sorrows.

I saw Matt cross himself quickly when he heard that woman's sob from above.

She is dead then—God rest her soul! he said.

I looked over at Timothy. He was standing the same way as before; the expression on his face had not changed at all, except to set itself a little more stubbornly in place.

She is never dead, he said, after a minute. His voice sounded flat and almost angry. A fine strong woman like herself—she is never dead.

He walked over toward the stairs and started up. But at the halfway he stopped. Somebody was coming down the stairs; standing below in the hall, I could see a man's legs in good black broadcloth trousers coming into sight. It was Father O'Malley, the new assistant in the parish. He was a tall pale curly-headed young priest, with one of them sunken-eyed, high-nosed faces that always look a bit arrogant whether they are or not.

You must resign yourself, Mr. Joyce, I heard him say. It was the will of God to take her.

Timothy stared at him. She is never dead, he said again. He went on up a few more steps. A fine strong woman—

She was one of God's saints, Father O'Malley put in, quicklike. You must think of her as having gained her eternal reward.

He was a young priest then, just out of the seminary, and for all the soothing way he spoke, like he was used to things like this happening to him every day in his life, he looked like he wished himself fair out of it. He came out of a neighborhood a bit less rough-and-ready than St. Michael's was in those days, and he had a hard time of it getting himself used to this comedown in the world. Musha, he didn't stay long; I don't doubt Father Devanney put a bug in the Bishop's ear, and before the year was out he was packing off to another parish.

Timothy stood there listening to what he was saying, but it was plain to be seen that he didn't understand one word in ten. He looked a bit dazed, like he hardly knew he was standing on the stairs of his own house on Burke Street, and his face had flushed up red to the roots of his hair. After a few moments he began going on up the stairs to the second floor, walking right past the priest as if he didn't see him, and not so much as turning his head when Matt and I came running after him to try couldn't we stop him from going up for a minute or two, till he'd had time to get the straight of it in his head about what had happened. I had the queer sort of feeling that it was not sorrow but black anger that was eating inside him, like it might be he thought somebody had played a mucky trick on him one way or another.

We followed him up, and watched him walk into the room where Ellen was. Brigid was sitting at the foot of the bed, crying; she didn't look up at the sound of his footsteps, but Mrs. Heeny, the midwife, straightened up from doing something over the bed and stared around at him.

Oh, the poor man! she said. She bent over again and drew back the sheet that was covering the dead woman's face. It's too late you are, Timothy Joyce; have they been telling you that? she said. The angel, the treasure, she's gone to heaven. Her life went out of her like the tide, and as much good it did us to try to hold it back.

Timothy went over closer to the bed, and I saw him looking down at the face on the pillow. I remember the way the warm thick braid of the corpse, not yet begun to gray, dragged over one shoulder, and the look of the mouth that had something rigid and unnatural about it, like if someone had pressed it shut a bit off the true line after death. Mrs. Heeny said something more to Timothy, but I doubt much if he ever heard her. There was the look on his face, as he stood by the bed, that

I could not tell if he was in anger, or in fear, or in grief, or in all three at once; it was like someone had struck him a blow and he could not find the striker to lay his hands on him. And all the while the face on the pillow, with its queerly shut mouth, lay there sleeping and careless, like all that meant nothing to it now.

Matt came tiptoeing past me into the room, and went over and put his hand on Timothy's arm.

Now come away, Tim, he said to him. There is John Fogarty downstairs, and Father O'Malley waiting for another word with you.

Timothy looked around at him; after a bit he said in a thick kind of voice, Eh, Matt, I was too late, a bit too late.

Oh yes, he may have had some kind of idea in the back of his head that if he'd been there he might have put a stop some way to her going; it must have seemed to him just then like something she had the choice of, whether to die or not, and that, if he'd been with her at the moment when she had to decide, he could have made her see what her duty was to him and that brood of children she'd brought into the world. Maybe it was a queer reaction for a man to be having to his wife's death, but a man in his troubles is not apt to be reasonable any more than a man that is in the drink. The world seems a wild new place to both of them, and both of them see things by strange lights.

Matt had hold of his arm that while, and he turned him around and started him over toward the door.

Sure it was God's will, and she had a fine holy death, he said. There is no good at all in taking on now.

They started down the stairs together, and I followed after them. Downstairs in the hall Kate was standing with Johnny Fogarty and Father O'Malley; she wasn't crying, but there was a queer scared staring look on her face. She looked at Timothy and Matt like she was seeing them for the first time in her life; you can imagine what was going on inside her head. She grew up in that minute, Kate did, from a girl that went to school, and minded her book, and honored her father and mother according to the catechism, to a woman with two grown men and a brood of kids to boss and do for, just like any other woman on the street. It made her a bit hard, maybe, coming on her the way it did; a woman will mellow down to a life like that when she goes into it the ordinary way, with first a man to look after, and then the children coming along one by one; but it's different happening the way it did to Kate. She got a bit hard—oh, the sharp ways of a settled woman, you know, when she wasn't more than a slip of a girl herself—and you couldn't rightly blame her for it. It was a great thing to fall on any woman, and she no more than a child at the time.

Johnny Fogarty, I remember, came over to the stairs to meet Timothy as he came down.

I've sent the boy over to Peg Killian's with the other children, he said to him. You will not be wanting them underfoot at this time. He looked embarrassed and solemn, and kept turning his derby round and round in his two hands; he was never one of your Irishmen that feel easy and merry in the smell of death. The new baby is in the kitchen with Mary Lynch, he said. Will you be going in now to look at it?

I will not, Timothy said.

He seemed to pull himself together a bit again at that; I suppose there was a dim kind of feeling working in him somewhere that Ellen's dying had given him importance for that time, and I thought maybe he was going to draw himself out of the queer way he'd been acting ever since he'd been upstairs in that room. He pushed open the door of the parlor then and went inside, and we all followed him, Matt and Johnny and the Father and me.

You won't be old enough to remember what an Irish parlor was like in those days: the horsehair furniture, and the long lace curtains, and the colored holy pictures on the walls. Oh, and shut up behind closed doors and drawn blinds the most of the time, of course, the way they smelled of stale air and wax when you went into them. The Joyces' parlor had a dark red patterned carpet on the floor, and on a stiff round table between the windows there was a book with a purple velvet marker falling out of the middle of it, and one of them glass bells with wax flowers under it.

Will you be taking a chair, Father? Matt said to the priest.

Timothy had already sat down himself; I remember the way his eyes, with the stubborn look like a hard glaze on them, went over the three of us, Matt, Johnny, and me, who had perched ourselves on the slippery black sofa, and then moved over to Father O'Malley, who took the other chair, sitting a bit on the edge, as if he would have liked well enough to be out of the room and the house. For a while there wasn't a sound but the ticking of the clock on the mantel and the heavy breathing of all of us—queer, how the bare idea of having something to be quiet about makes a man labor at his breath like his lungs was a pair of bellows in full action.

It was Father O'Malley that started first to speak. Oh yes, he'd made up his little speech and out it tumbled: Death comes to each of us; we must—aw—you must console yourself with the thought that she had the sacraments of the Church to comfort her in her last moments—and Timothy sat there listening to him, only the glaze on his eyes growing harder and harder, and the color reddening up higher in his face. Father O'Malley, poor man, he'd no way of knowing then how the Joyce temper went, but something in Timothy's look must finally have struck him a bit odd, for the words began wavering out of his mouth, and then stopped altogether. When Timothy didn't move, he took courage again and went on.

Your wife, Mr. Joyce—was how he began.

I watched Timothy get up. His face by that time was a purple-red, and you could see the rich color of his lips under his sandy mustache.

My wife, he said. His voice sounded thick; by God, I knew then we were in for it. My wife, he said again, very deliberate and plain. The devil fly away with her for a black-hearted bitch.

Father O'Malley stammered out something—Mr. Joyce, Mr.

Joyce!—like he'd had the shock of the world; now, if it had been Father Devanney was there, he'd have handled it as cool as any bishop, but this fine young man—yerrah, he didn't know if he was on his head or his feet or his tail at all.

There was them wax flowers under the glass bell on the table; I mind the time Ellen bought the thing, and she lording it over Brigid, that had no such bit of stylishness in her parlor. Timothy picked it up and sailed it across the room, straight for the fireplace, and the next minute there was the glass flying around our ears. The Father got a bit of it in his cheek; I can still see him standing there, staring wildlike at the blood on his handkerchief, and the rest of us hurrying around trying to soothe down Timothy, and Mary Lynch coming in from the kitchen to see what was the matter, and she with the tongue in her head would skin a man alive with no trouble at all. Staffy chuckled, sucking on his unlit pipe. The wild Irish we were then, and no mistake. But it was a shame it was, we to be acting such a shindy, and Ellen lying cold in her bed upstairs.

excerpt from

Bridgeport Bus

(1965)

MAUREEN HOWARD

First I will write:

When I go home I walk through all the dim two-family-house streets where the colors are brown and gray with what they call cream trim. On the route I take—eight-thirty in the morning, five at night—there are four houses which are repainted in pastels, pink and pale green, with aluminum around the doors and windows: their front stoops are faced with quarter-inch fake stone. When my nerves are raw from the meaningless day at work I see nothing more than four ugly houses, their vulgar shapes, their sameness defined by the light colors and bright metal. On better days I think these houses have beauty, reflect some hope shared by the Italians who own them: I suppose their blank painted faces would look fine in the Mediterranean sun or in a summer town on the Long Island shore.

I turn and walk up the hill where I live. Here the dark houses are equally bad, though presumed to be better, with an extra bedroom in each flat and the upstairs flat bulged out over the downstairs porch. When I look up the hill there are dirty window-eyes and huge indolent growths on each idiot brow—a row of monster heads to greet me. I turn back and see the city stretched out dead at my feet; I think about New York or San Francisco or Paris—the scene in which young Gide (it's the first entry in his journal) looks down on beautiful mist-gray Paris across the imaginary writing desk of an artist. I started reading that book, but something happened—my brother's children, my mother's gall bladder; something happened so I never finished.

The actor says: "You see all that down there . . ." (panorama of city at night) "all that," he says to Rita Hayworth, "will be yours." When I look down I see my city on the banks of the exhausted Naugatuck. There is a line of rust along the shore that smells of rubber—the gardens, if I may be allowed, of factories; and then the hills with all the streets of brown houses coming up toward me and toward my street of superior brown houses.

When I go home my mother and I play a cannibal game; we eat each other over the years, tender morsel by morsel until there is nothing left but dry bone and wig. She is winning—needless to say she has had so much more experience. She meets me in the front room, hiding behind the evening paper, a fat self-indulgent body, her starved mind hungry for me. I am on guard when I first come from work—what means for devouring me has she devised during the day? I stand under the dark-stained arch, an anxious thrill rising in me, and just wait, watching but not seeing the elephant chairs and my bloated old mother behind her paper. The room, stuffed with darkness day or night, any season, is a monochrome of immobility: heavy chairs, lame tables, parchment shades and curtains of ecru lace—all colorless as time, all under a layer of antediluvian silt.

Arrangement in gray and black—portrait of my mother profiled, soft and bulky in her sagging chair: a big Irishwoman "fulla life" with eyes ready to cry. For contrast, her white hair crimped in a prim Protestant roll seen against the walls (a deeper tone) papered in potato skins. A coat of yellow varnish, the years of our aboriginal love, over the entire picture. I have not long to wait, contemplating the classic scene of home, for she never misses a cue.

"Ag?" she says, not looking at me, and I don't answer. I entertain myself with the notion that one day it will be someone else come in the front door, a rapist or a mad killer, and she'll be caught there reading the obituaries or looking up her TV programs for the night.

"Ag, I bought snowsuits today for the children—downtown."

"In April? That's fine."

"On sale, Ag. Sometimes I don't think you use your head. There's been sales advertised downtown all week. I bought them big for next year." She smiles, puffy and red in the face, self-satisfied, imitating the well-to-do Irish.

"I don't read that paper. How much?"

"Well, that's it—only twenty dollars."

"Sixty dollars?"

"Yes, for *three* children. I guess I can multiply as well as you, Mary Agnes." Then she's had enough and pushes herself out of the chair, waddling off to get supper.

"Sixty dollars," I say after her, "and what's wrong with the ones you bought last year, not on sale. Can't they pass the clothes on? Can't Catherine wear Patrick's snowsuit? I didn't know a goddamn girl's coat buttoned from right to left when I was their age."

"I don't like to hear you talk that way, Mary Agnes." And then she says, hurt to wrench my heart—and it works every time; my heart *is* wrenched during her big scenes—the spectacle of her raw face, tears swelling, her blood pressure up: "Your father, rest his soul, was poor. It's a sad thing, Ag, when you've no more feeling left for your brother and his family way up there in Buffalo. It doesn't matter about me, but it's sad."

We never get more violent than that. I am cursed with gentility and can hardly do better than an occasional name-of-the-Lord-in-vain, but after each argument I like to look at myself in my own room or in the blue glass mirror in the dining room. There I can see what part of me she has picked at—her favorite soft flesh around the eyes, or my shamefully concave chest. I am gaunt—you might guess it, five foot eleven, one hundred and eighteen pounds.

But why do I start with such heightened drama when there are the usual tidbits: my mail opened, my bureau drawers "arranged." Clorox put in the wash with a new dress. Or: "Ag?" (Once again it is only me, not the sex maniac I dream of, and she goes on at me behind the paper.) "Christine Doyle called about the Sodality Tea and she said wouldn't you pour. Isn't that nice?"

"And you said yes?"

"Yes, isn't that nice." Then she is wise enough to hurry right on and read me something out of the paper: "Well poor Tom Heffernan died, that's a blessing. They say his body was full of it."

You will think now that I am stupid and incompetent, but you'd be surprised how I gnaw at my mother just by reading for hours, or not speaking, or muttering "Christ" in the direction of the television set as I pass through the front room. And, my choicest bone of contention, I take night courses instead of making myself one bit attractive to the gelded, balding boys that my mother finds in limitless supply.

"Tess Mueller is coming over with that nice son who works in the bank," she announces from behind her paper. I get a quick flash of Fred Mueller, a harmless pudding-beast caged at the People's Trust, counting out my money and saying, "Cold enough for you?" or "Long time no see."

"That's a shame," I tell my mother, "because tonight I'm going to the library in New Haven."

"The library, the *library*!"—shrieks of coronary outrage.

"The University library, Mother. Hundreds of men."

But she is gasping now and slaps her beloved *Evening American* against the brown velour chair. "That's what I'm to tell Tess when she brings that nice boy—that you've gone to the *library*?"

"Oh, you'd be surprised—hundreds of men . . ." But then never use even the simplest sarcasm on children, because they don't get it, and I wonder if I should illustrate my point for mother: maybe a story of a nun, a Sister of Mercy working on Cardinal Newman in the stacks; she meets up with an emeritus professor, a medievalist who has just been writing a piece on the clerical orgies at Cluny.

Scene: Sterling Memorial Library in the 9860.2n's.

Time: Four o'clock in the week of Septuagesima. It is a moment of transition. The lights have not yet been turned on. . . .

Mother smooths out the newspaper, folds it, tucks it under her arm with finality: she is finished, through with me.

"Ag, you are thirty-five years old." This is her master stroke.

What I should have written to begin with is that I am Mary Agnes Keely, a thirty-five-year-old virgin. Narrative should begin with essentials, not the oblique device—picture of a city, a house—that flirts with the truth in a maidenly way. I am called Ag, named Mary after guess who and Agnes after the child martyr who defended her virginity before it had even a literary value—I have never had much sympathy with her. At the age of thirteen can you honestly say there's a choice—I mean between a lion and a dirty, nasty man. I cannot believe in a world which honors that prissy little girl and dishonors me as one of a million social misfits—lets me be fed daily to my ravenous old mother.

"Ag," she will say, her mouth watering, "you are thirty-five years old."

As I write this I am at peace for the first time in years, sitting at my desk (an old dressing table) where I can look at myself often. I admire the freshness that has come to my cheeks this evening and what appears to be a new firmness to my throat. I have laid out a thick pad of yellow theme paper, and with a smooth, satisfying ball-point pen have begun to write. I can hear my mother at the telephone out in the kitchen. She is aggrieved, whining to the long-distance operator and asking again, the fifth time in the hour, if the girl will dial her son in Buffalo. My brother and his family don't seem to be home. That's the straw, she tells my Aunt Mae in a lengthy call, that broke the camel's back in her already broken heart. She has told her sad story to Aunt Mae and to her younger sister, Lil, and from what I can overhear, Aunt Lil will be over after supper, done up in her ranch mink stole, to reason with me and try to straighten things out—though nothing is tangled as far as I'm concerned: things are straighter than they have ever been, and I intend to set the whole scene down on this pleasant yellow pad.

It is spring now, but nine weeks ago tonight it was winter, the beginning of February. I came in from the wet gloom of the brown streets to the shriveled gloom of our house. There was mother with the *Evening American*, but she didn't ask who was standing under the arch; so at once I knew there was to be an announcement on a grand scale.

"Is it still raining, Ag?" she asked, sweetness itself.

"Yes," I said.

Then she put down the paper so I could see that she had been to the Edna-Lou Beauty Shop. Her hair had a fresh purple rinse and was kinked in to the head. She was wearing her best stylish-stout wine crepe with a surplice top and her new Enna Jettick shoes.

"Well, wouldn't you just know," my mother said with put-on petulance, "wouldn't you just know it would rain tonight." She waited, preening her fat bosom, but I wouldn't ask, so she heaved out of the chair. "Dinner is almost on the table. We have to eat early tonight, Ag, because of the novena."

"The novena!" I gasped. Her backside looked broader than ever as she hustled out to the kitchen. Ever since I was a girl, for over twenty years that would be, I have had to drag my mother to that novena in the winter, tugging her up the church steps like an impossible rolled mattress and stuffing her into a pew. Then the Rosary, the Aspirations, the Benediction, the Prayer for Peace . . . The whole thing started just before the war and was addressed to Our Lady of Fatima, who as I recall appeared to some prepubescent Portuguese and said the world was coming to an end—as though that were news.

So off to the novena, and afterwards from St. Augustine's to Friedman's Dairy with the Scanlon sisters, Aunt Mae, and a toothy schoolteacher named Louise Conroy—there to reap the reward: heavenly hot-fudge sundaes toped with whipped cream, and a symposium on every hysterectomy in town. Unfortunately, when the novena was four-ninths or five-ninths over it coincided with Lent, so my mother and her friends would stand in the back of the church and debate about going to Friedman's. But they always went, denying themselves nuts and whipped cream to commemorate the forty days and forty nights in the desert. Nine weeks ago tonight the novena began.

"I've put your dinner out," my mother called, and I walked slowly out to the kitchen, switching en route from the Spenser-Milton seminar, which was given on Friday evenings, to Modern French Poetry. She had already settled herself behind a dish of glutinous brown stew.

"I have my course tonight, Mother."

"You have what?" Poor Mother, she saw I was serious.

I sat down opposite her, just as loose and easy. "My French course. It comes on Thursdays."

"God knows"—she started the harangue right away—"you were brought up a good Catholic girl, that you should choose a lot of dirty French books over your religion. And thank the good Lord" (with a tremolo) "your father is not here to see you an ingrate to your mother ... a woman the age of you, Mary Agnes, thirty-five years old ... ," and on and on with a sad scum forming on her stew. She looked hateful with the veins jumping in her face, yet I almost cried, out of a perverse love for her ravings. I was consumed, ready to say yes I would go with her and try to stop the end of the world, until she said: "I will pray for you, Mary Agnes," with her lips all pursed up as though she were sucking the marrow out of my bones. That was new, and for eight weeks I have heard it—how she is praying for me, for a woman who would let her old mother climb the slippery hills and go up the church steps alone at night.

It must have been her praying for me that started me on the pastel houses. I had to have something to come back with after all. Three or four times a week when I came in from work, I talked about the Italian houses, the houses painted pink and pale green. I mentioned how gay they looked on a rainy day or remarked what a lovely aluminum curlicued "C" the Capizzolis had put on their front door, or how I admired the Riccios' empty urn, a cemetery urn painted red, standing in front of their peachy-pink house. And all the while I had no knowledge, I'll swear to it, that I was provoking her more than usual. Sure I was nibbling, and there were the expected retorts about foreigners: "They weren't stupid. They knew how to improve their property." But when I told her I liked the Italian houses it was only partially true; I had come to love them. I left the house early to hurry down my street and around the corner to the first one, the Marcuccis', who had left corrugated metal awnings up all winter long, waiting for sun, and then on to the Riccios' splendid red urn that promised to have flowers, and to the Capizzolis' with all the twisted aluminum and the pressed stone that knew no geological limitations. A few gray blocks on, near my office, was the last house—I don't know the people—a three-family aqua wonder with glass bricks set around the old frame windows to modernize, and the front yard cemented up except for a small patch of dirt the shape of an irrigation pan. There some hardy ivy grew all winter—green. It was an oasis I rushed to, and one day I walked into the cement yard and picked an ivy leaf. The urn, the awnings, the ivy remembered another season, though I suppose it was the future that I really admired in them, because I had none.

One night I told my mother, "That's how I get to work and back, from one bright house to the next. I think lots of people go on that way, from one bowling night to the next or even from meal to meal."

I thought she hadn't heard—she hardly ever did when I took it upon myself to explain things—but later by the blue light of the television set she remarked, "You used to be a good, plain girl, Ag. I can't see what's changed you."

I bought a red silk dress at this time and let my hair grow. At the office they all said how snappy Miss Ag was looking—there I command respect for seventeen years as a cheerful drudge. I am secretary to the president of the Standard Zipper Company. Everyone knows the type: a pinch-faced lady who supports an old mother, can locate every paper clip and advise her boss not to merge with Reddi-Zip, Inc. It makes the salesmen laugh to say I know all the ups and downs. Pathetic—I think of a million flies all over America, zip, zip, zip down the trolley—miners, truck drivers, farmers, junior executives, Hollywood stars—never an embarrassing moment, due to the efficiency and diligence of Miss Mary Agnes Keely. I think of harassed women catching their flesh (you must never hurry it, *I* know that), and tossing babies kept warm for the night, and the suitcases and tents and silver bags—everything closing and opening like breath going in and out, while I am sealed—as though our 72-inch model were stitched into me from the toes up, and the zipper stuck forever on a broken track under my hawk-Irish nose. It's pathetic, but funny.

I mentioned the dress, the novena naturally, and I shall want to write about my course. After my father died, my brother went to college anyway, but my mother sent me to work to pay off the mortgage on our wen-browed, dark house so we'd always have a roof over our empty heads. I started filing at Standard Zipper and taking courses at night, and I discovered that being a homely gawk I was smart. Well, I was smarter than anyone at the teachers' college and as smart as the Saturday morning crowd at Columbia. I have a world now, the size of a circle of light thrown by a desk lamp, that is mine, safe from my mother and the zipper company and my brother's children. It is the one space in which I am free of self-pity, and I hold it as sacred as some impossible belief in guardian angels, though when I am outside my circle of light I see that it is dim and small. Someone is always saying how fine it is and what a mark of maturity to be able to think, to read; but I am sure for most people it's cowardice. I mean, we should want to stand in an amphitheater with spotlights on us, like F.D.R. in a black cape, and say something significant:

"At last, my friends, we know the world can come to an end."

Well, the small circle of light thrown by the reading lamp has been shining with special brightness since the beginning of February because of my course in the modern French poets—they speak to me. That happens now and again, though I fancy myself a sophisticated reader with all kinds of critical impedimenta: I read something so direct, so pertinent to exactly where I am—the way I feel, my precise frame of mind. That is the rapport I had—I still have—with Nerval, with Baudelaire, with Rimbaud. Not only what they say in brilliant, disparate images but with their diseased, eccentric lives. I feel pain where I have never been touched, dissipation in my early-to-bed soul. There now: have I written an illumination?

(My mother has got through to my brother in Buffalo. She has only to hear his voice to cry, so what must it be tonight—an endless keening, ancient, racially remembered. I wonder if she will ask me to talk to him, way up there in Buffalo. "Hello," I will say, "how are you? How are the kids? Yes," I will assure him, "everything is *fine* here. The weather is fine. I am going away." She is wailing. She will not give me the satisfaction of defending myself to Francis on the phone, but no matter where I may go I will get the bill—I always pay. If I were to steal out of my room and hidden in the murky nite-lite of the hallway spy on the succulent sight—my mother leaning heavily on the refrigerator, dabbing at her wet eyes and nose with a disintegrated Kleenex, weeping and weeping to the child she loves, my brother—then I could not go. I would offer myself to her, the last sweet bite, a soupçon airy and delicious to restore her, humanity fudge. Warriors did that—not as long ago as we like to think—ate the heart of the enemy. I will stay in my room.)

Now let me tell what has happened:

I have told about the red dress, the novena, the pastel houses, and the French poets. Tonight I came home, a Thursday, and turned up the hill to my house. The scene was wrong: the weather had been fine all day from the window of the zipper factory, and the sun still glowed, low and late on my dirty brown street, but now I saw a flash of electric blue—intense Immigrant Blue. And I ran up the hill to my house, because it was *my* house with that blue all over the front and halfway down the side, and I ran up the steps ignoring the luminous sign of warning, my feet sticking to the gluey wet paint. Inside, there she was with the newspaper held up higher than usual, waiting—

"Ag, is that you?"

"You know it's me," I shouted. "You know that." I tore the *Evening American* from her face. The smile she had prepared to greet me with was plastered on her speechless mouth.

"You have gone out of your mind," I said evenly, *"out of your mind!"*

"Now, Mary Agnes, the painters came today . . ."

"The house is blue."

". . . the painters came today, Mary Agnes, and I had it in mind for a while with the house so run down, and I wanted to do something for you, something to please you, Ag."

"The house is blue."

"Well, that's it." Her voice rose an octave—her face was flushed. "For weeks now you've been talking up those houses the Italians own, every day it seems you're at me about the colors and the decoration." Now she got up and began to gather the torn newspaper, stooping as best she could with the blood rushing to her head and those veins jumping faster than I've ever seen. "You've been plaguing me with those colored houses, but there is no pleasing you, Mary Agnes."

"In the first place we are not Italians," I said.

"Well you don't have to tell me," she screamed, "you're the big mixer, aren't you, with all your talk about those wops . . . It wasn't me wanted the house blue."

"We are not Italians." Then in a whisper: "We are withered brown people. Can't you see that? Can't you see one rotten thing?"

"No, I don't like the way you speak to your mother—out of dirty French books I've seen in your room. I bless the day your father died, not to see you like this, a heretic and a spiteful woman."

I grabbed her fat arm when she turned from me and held her. "Now tell me," I said, "how much does it cost to paint a house?"

But she only started to cry, so I had to answer. "It's my bank account, isn't it?—spread all over the front of this house."

"You'd go off and leave your mother to die, Mary Agnes." Then I saw the working of her voracious mind. Her words grated through the sobs, "You've no more feeling than stone; you'd go way off to the other side with the money and let me walk up to church in the winter, and go off on your summer vacation and leave me alone—all alone when I chose that color for you."

Then *I* began to cry, and it wasn't the Economy Flight I mourned. I had dreamed, indeed put my deposit down on seven magic lands in twenty days—too far away, unreal. I don't for a moment think it would have come off. Now I threw myself into an elephant chair. "For me. For *me*. That's the color for your Holy Mary. Must the whole street know, the whole city, that I am a virgin and thirty-five?" I pounded the bulky chair, thinking it was my mother's body. She must have felt I was wild—staring up at her with my ravaged face. Suddenly I was smiling and sure.

"All this," I said pleasantly, looking around the front room, "has no importance." My mother thought I meant our house. "I am going to play Bridgeport Bus, once and for all I am going to play Bridgeport Bus and go away." (It's a wonderful game, Bridgeport Bus: you line up the dining-room chairs in two rows and you collect fares and joggle along through the Naugatuck valley talking to all the passengers and then get off at Bridgeport.) Mother went out weeping into the kitchen, but I stayed there hugging the large bosom back of the chair.

Aunt Lil has come and gone. She stuck her head into my room and seeing that I was calm, writing on a yellow pad (school work no doubt), she went to comfort my mother, saying it was only one of our arguments like any other. Then I could hear Mother, loud and choking to Aunt Lil, that tonight was to end her novena and the girls would think it queer, waiting for her in the vestibule of the church. She is too ill from the exertion and all the shouting. O, M. Rimbaud, say it: "This can only be the end of the world, kept going." It is obvious that I will not finish my course . . . no matter.

I intend to travel light: only the red silk dress, some books, my cosmetics—though my face has a surprising fullness and the skin on my neck seems tight, like the skin on an out-of-season hothouse fruit. I am like that, maturing too late—will I be more valuable, that is one of the questions to be asked, still unplucked? My girlish head luxuriates in absurd decisions: I will take the Bridgeport Bus and joggle to the rail- road station and choose between Boston and New York. I will wear my rhinestone earrings or leave them behind. I will call a taxi to take me to the bus depot, or I will walk so I can see for the last time my obscure, night-dark city with its hills rising—unlit funeral pyres, gray and brown, rising from the beach of industrial rubble . . . and the river used up, ashamed like a deserted woman.

"So long!" I will say, "you have loved me like a mother; I take nothing from you but bare necessities: one suitcase, the beginning of this story. So long, sweet Mother, good night, good night."

The wise boy Rimbaud writes: "The hour of flight will be the hour of death for me." Let me establish that I *know* this as concretely as I comprehend a world of zippers. So having cleared myself of some naïveté, I have only to put on my coat and go—through the living room where my mother is soothed at last by her television, watching lives much more professional than ours.

"Let's not say good-bye, only *Adieu, bon appetit.* . . ."

Life After Death

(1976)

ELIZABETH CULLINAN

Yesterday evening I passed one of President Kennedy's sisters in the street again. They must live in New York—and in this neighborhood—the sister I saw and one of the others. They're good-looking women with a subdued, possibly unconscious air of importance that catches your attention. Then you recognize them. I react to them in the flesh the way I've reacted over the years to their pictures in the papers. I feel called on to account for what they do with their time, as if it were my business as well as theirs. I find myself captioning these moments when our paths cross. *Sister of the late President looks in shop window. Sister of slain leader buys magazine. Kennedy kin hails taxi on Madison Avenue.* And yesterday: *Kennedy sister and friend wait for light to change at Sixty-eighth and Lexington.* That was the new picture I added to the spread that opens out in my mind under the headline "LIFE AFTER DEATH."

It was beautifully cold and clear yesterday, and sunny and windless, so you could enjoy the cold without having to fight it, but I was dressed for the worst, thanks to my mother. At three o'clock she called to tell me it was bitter out, and though her idea of bitter and mine aren't the same, when I went outside I wore boots and put on a heavy sweater under my coat. I used to be overwhelmed by my mother's love; now it fills me with admiration. I've learned what it means to keep on loving in the face of resistance, though the resistance my two sisters and I offered wasn't to the love itself but to its superabundance, too much for our reasonable natures to cope with. My mother should have had simple, good-hearted daughters, girls who'd tell her everything, seated at the kitchen table, walking arm in arm with her in and out of department stores. But Grace and Rosemary and I aren't like that, not simple at all, and what goodness of heart we possess is qualified by the disposition we inherited from our father. We have a sense of irony that my mother with the purity of instinct and the passion of innocence sees as a threat to our happiness and thus to hers. Not one of us is someone she has complete confidence in.

Grace, the oldest of us, is married and has six children and lives in another city. Grace is a vivid person—vivid-looking with her black hair and high color, vivid in her strong opinions, her definite tastes. And Grace is a perfectionist who day after day must face the facts— that her son, Jimmy, never opens a book unless he has to and not always then; that her daughter Carolyn has plenty of boyfriends but no close girlfriends; that just when she gets a new refrigerator the washing machine will break down, then the dryer, then the house will need to be painted. My mother tells Grace that what can't be cured must be endured, but any such attitude would be a betrayal of Grace's ideals.

My middle sister, Rosemary, is about to marry a man of another religion. Rosemary is forty and has lived in Brussels and Stuttgart and Rome and had a wonderful time everywhere. No one thought she'd ever settle down, and my mother is torn between relief at the coming marriage and a new anxiety—just as she's torn, when Rosemary cooks Christmas dinner, between pleasure and irritation. Rosemary rubs the turkey with butter, she whips the potatoes with heavy cream; before Rosemary is through, every pot in the kitchen will have been used. This is virtue carried to extremes and no virtue at all in the eyes of my mother, whose knowledge of life springs from the same homely frame of reference as my sister's but has led to a different sort of conclusion: Rubbed with margarine the turkey will brown perfectly well; to bring the unbeliever into the fold, you needn't go so far as to marry him.

Every so often I have a certain kind of dream about Mother—a dream that's like a work of art in the way it reveals character and throws light on situations. In one of these dreams she's just died— within minutes. We're in the house where I grew up, which was my grandmother's house. There are things to be done, and Grace and Rosemary and I are doing them, but the scene is one of lethargy, of a reluctance to get moving that belongs to adolescence, though in the dream, as in reality, my sisters and I are grown women. Suddenly I realize that Mother, though still dead, has got up and taken charge. There's immense weariness but no reproach in this act. It's simply that she's been through it all before, has helped bury her own mother and father and three of her brothers. She knows what has to be done but she's kept this grim knowledge from Grace and Rosemary and me. She's always tried to spare the three of us, with the result that we lack her sheer competence, her strength, her powers of endurance, her devotedness. In another dream Mother is being held captive in a house the rest of us have escaped from and can't get back into. We stand in the street, helpless, while inside she's being beaten for no reason. The anguish I feel, the tears that wake me are not so much for the pain she's suffering as for the fact that this should be happening to her of all people, someone so ill-equipped to make sense of it. Harshness of various kinds and degrees has been a continuing presence and yet a continuing mystery to her, the enemy she's fought blindly all her life. "I don't think that gray coat of yours is warm enough," she said to me yesterday.

"Sure it is," I said.

"It isn't roomy enough." As she spoke, she'd have been throwing her shoulders back in some great imaginary blanket of a coat she was picturing on me.

"It fits so close, the wind can't get in," I explained. "That's its great virtue."

"Let me give you a new coat," she said.

When I was four years old I had nephrosis, a kidney disease that was almost unheard of and nearly always fatal then. It singled me out. I became a drama, then a miracle, then my mother's special cause in life. From this it of course follows that I should be living the life she'd have liked for herself—a life of comfort—but desire has always struck me as closer to the truth of things than comfort could ever be. "I don't really want a new coat," I told her yesterday. "I like my gray one."

"Dress warmly when you go out," she said. "It's bitter cold."

As I was hanging up there was an explosion—down the street from me, half a block on either side of Lexington Avenue is being reconstructed. The School for the Deaf and the local Social Services Office were torn down, and now in place of those old, ugly buildings, battered into likenesses of the trouble they'd tried to mend, there are two huge pits where men drill and break rocks and drain water, yelling to each other like industrious children in some innovative playground. And all day long there are these explosions. There was another; then the phone rang again. It was Francis, for the second time that day. "Constance," he said. "What a halfwit I am."

I said, "You are?"

He gave the flat, quick, automatic laugh I hate, knowing it to be false. When Francis truly finds something funny, he silently shakes his head. "Yes, I am," he said. "I'm a halfwit. Here I made an appointment with you for tomorrow afternoon and I just turned the page of my calendar and found I've got some sort of affair to go to."

"What sort of affair?" I asked. It could have been anything from a school play to a war. Francis produces documentaries for television. He's also married and has four sons, two of them grown. He's a popular man, a man everyone loves, and when I think of why, I think of his face, his expression, which is of someone whose prevailing mood is both buoyant and sorrowful. He has bright brown eyes. His mouth is practically a straight line, bold and pessimistic. He has a long nose and a high forehead and these give his face severity, but his thick, curly, untidy gray-blond hair softens the effect.

"I'm down for some sort of cocktail party," he said. "This stupid, busy life of mine," he added.

This life of his, in which I figure only marginally, is an epic of obligation and entertainment. Work, eat, drink, and be merry is one way of putting it. It could also be put, as Francis might, this way: Talent, beauty, charm, taste, money, art, love—these are the real good in life, and each of these goods borrows from the others. Beauty is the talent of the body. Charm and taste must sooner or later come down to money. Art is an aspect of love, and love is a variable. And all this being, to Francis's way of thinking, so—our gifts being contingents— we can do nothing better than pool them. Use me, use each other, he all but demands. I say, no—we're none of us unique, but neither are we interchangeable. "Well, if you've got something else to do, Francis," I said to him yesterday, "I guess you'd better do it."

He said, "Why don't I come by the day after tomorrow instead?"

I said, "I'm not sure."

"Not sure you're free or not sure you want to?"

"Both." I wasn't exactly angry or hurt. I have no designs on Francis Hughes, no claim on him. It would be laughable if I thought I did.

"Ah," he said, "Inconstance."

I said, "No, indefinite."

He said, "Well, I'm going to put Thursday down on my calendar and I'll call you in the morning and see how you feel about it."

"All right," I said, but on Thursday morning I won't be here—if people aren't interchangeable, how much less so are people and events.

"Tell me you love me," said Francis.

I said, "I do."

He said, "I'll talk to you Thursday."

"Goodbye, Francis," I said, and I hung up and put on my boots and my heavy sweater and my gray coat and went out.

The college I went to is a few blocks from this brownstone where I have an apartment. It's a nice school, and I was happy there and I can feel that happiness still, as though these well-kept streets, these beautiful houses are an account that was held open for me here. But New York has closed out certain other accounts of mine, such as the one over in the West Fifties. Down one of those streets is the building where I used to work and where I first knew Francis. His office was across the hall from mine. His life was an open book, a big, busy novel in several different styles—part French romance, part character study, part stylish avant-garde, part nineteenth-century storytelling, all plot and manners, part Russian blockbuster, crammed with characters. His phone rang constantly. He had streams of visitors. People sent him presents—plants, books, cheeses, bottles of wine, boxes of English crackers. I was twenty-two or three at the time, but I saw quite clearly that the man didn't need more love, that he needed to spend some of what he'd accumulated, and being twenty-two or three I saw no reason why I shouldn't be the one to make that point. Or rather, what should have put me off struck me as reason for going ahead—for the truth is I'm not Francis's type. The girls who came to see him were more or less voluptuous, more or less blonde, girls who looked as if they were ready to run any risk, whereas I'm thin, and my hair is brown, and the risks I run with Francis are calculated, based on the fact that the love of someone like me can matter to someone like him only by virtue of its being in doubt. And having, as I say, no designs, I find myself able to be as hard on him as if he meant very little to me when, in fact, he means the world. I try now to avoid the West Fifties. Whenever I'm in that part of the city, the present seems lifeless, drained of all intensity in relation to that lost time when my days were full of Francis, when for hours on end he was close by.

I also try to avoid Thirty-fourth Street, where my father's brother-in-law used to own a restaurant, over toward Third Avenue. Flynn's was the name of it, and when I was twelve my father left the insurance business to become manager of Flynn's. He's an intelligent man, a man who again and again redeems himself with a word, the right word he's hit on effortlessly. His new raincoat, he told me the other day, "creaks." I asked if there was much snow left after a recent storm, and he said only a "batch" here and there. Sometimes he hits on the wrong word and only partly accidentally. "Pompadour," he was always calling French Premier Pompidou. He also has a perfect ear and a loathing for the current cliché. He likes to speak, with cheery sarcasm, of his "life-style." He also likes to throw out the vapid "Have a good day!" "No way" is an expression that simply drives him crazy.

The other night I dreamed a work of art about my father. He was in prison, about to be executed for some crime having to do with money. Rosemary and my mother and I had tried everything, but we failed to save him. At the end we were allowed—or obliged—to sit with him in his cell, sharing his terror and his misery and his amazing pluck. For it turned out that he'd arranged to have his last meal not at night but in the morning—so he'd have it to look forward to, he said. I woke up in despair. My father's spirit is something I love, as I love his sense of language, but common sense is more to the point in fathers, and mine has hardly any. As for business sense—after eight months at Flynn's, it was found that he'd been tampering with the books; six thousand dollars was unaccounted for. No charges were pressed, but my father went back to the insurance business, and from then on we didn't meet his family at Christmas and Easter, they didn't come to any more graduations or to Grace's wedding, Rosemary no longer got a birthday check from Aunt Kay Flynn, her godmother. You could say those people disappeared from our lives except that they didn't, at least not from mine. Once, when I was shopping with some friends in a department store, I spotted my Aunt Dorothy, another of my father's sisters. She was looking at skirts with my cousins Joan and Patricia, who are Grace's age—I must have been about sixteen at the time. A couple of summers later I had a job at an advertising agency where my cousin Bobby Norris turned out to be a copywriter. He was a tall, skinny, good-natured fellow, and he used to come and talk to me, and once or twice he took me out to lunch. He never showed any hard feelings toward our family, and neither did he seem to suspect how ashamed of us I was. Around this time I began running into my cousin Paul Halloran, who was my own age. At school dances and at the Biltmore, where everybody used to meet, he'd turn up with his friends and I with mine. Then one Christmas I got a part-time job as a salesgirl at Altman's. A boy I knew worked in the stockroom, and sometimes we went for coffee after work, and once he asked me to have a drink. We were walking down Thirty-fourth Street when he told me where we were going—a bar that he passed every day and that he wanted me to inspect with him. Too late to back out, I realized he was taking me to Flynn's. As soon as I walked in, I saw my father's brother-in-law sitting at a table, talking to one of the waiters. He didn't recognize me, but I couldn't believe he wouldn't. I'm the image of my mother and I was convinced this would have to dawn on him, and that he'd come over and demand to know if I was who he thought I was, and so I drank my whiskey sour sitting sideways in the booth, one hand shielding my face, like a fugitive from justice. Or like the character in a movie who, when shot, will keep on going, finish the business at hand, and then keel over, dead.

It's three blocks north and three blocks east from the house where I live to the building where I went to college. Sometimes, of an afternoon, I work there now, in the Admissions Office, and yesterday I had to pick up a check that was due me. The Admissions Office is in a brownstone. The school has expanded. Times have changed. On the way in I met Sister Catherine, who once taught me a little biology. "Is it going to snow?" she asked.

I said, "It doesn't look like snow to me."

In the old days these nuns wore habits with diamond-shaped headpieces that made them resemble figures on playing cards, always looking askance. Yesterday Sister Catherine had on a pants suit and an imitation-fur jacket with a matching hat on her short, curly gray hair, and it was I who gave the sidelong glance, abashed in the face of this flowering of self where self had for so long been denied.

"It's cold enough for snow," Sister Catherine said.

I said, "It certainly is," and fled inside.

The house was adapted rather than converted into offices, which is to say the job was only half done. Outside Admissions there's a pullman kitchen—stove, sink, cabinets, refrigerator, dishes draining on a rack. Food plays an important part in the life of this office, probably because the clerical staff is made up of students who, at any given moment, may get the urge for a carton of yogurt, or a cup of soup, or an apple, or a can of diet soda. I went and stood in the doorway of the room where they sit: Delia, Yeshi, Eileen, Maggie. They knew someone was there, but no one looked up. They always wait to make a move until they must, and then they wait to see who'll take the initiative. One reason they like it when I'm in the office is that I can be counted on to reach for the phone on the first ring, to ask at once if I can help the visitor. But the routine of Admissions is complicated; every applicant seems to be a special case, and I work there on such an irregular basis that I can also be counted on not to be able to answer the simplest questions, and this makes the students laugh, which is another reason they like having me around. That someone like me, someone who's past their own inherently subordinate phase of life, should come in and stuff promotional material into envelopes, take down telephone requests for information, type up lists and labels— and do none of this particularly well—cheers them. I stepped into the office and said, "Hello, everybody." They stopped everything. I said, "Guess what I want."

"You want your check," said Yeshi, who comes from Ethiopia— the cradle of mankind. Lately I've been studying history. A friend of mine who's an Egyptologist lent me the text of a survey course, and now there are these facts lodged in my mind among the heaps of miscellaneous information accumulating there. "Where is Constance's check?" asked Yeshi. She speaks with a quaver of a French accent. Her hands are tiny, her deft brown fingers as thin as pencils. She has enormous eyes. "Who made out Constance's time sheet?" she asked.

Maggie said, "I did." She wheeled her chair over to the file cabinet where the checks are kept. "It should be here. I'm sure I saw it this morning with the others." Maggie is Haitian. Her hair is cut close and to the shape of her head. She has a quick temper, a need to be listened to, and a need, every bit as great, to receive inspiration. "Uh-oh," she said.

"Not there?" I asked.

"It's got to be. I made out that time sheet myself," said Maggie. "I remember it was on Thursday—I'm not in on Wednesdays, and Friday would have been too late."

I said, "Well, I don't suppose anyone ran off with it. It was only for a few dollars."

"Money is money around here." This came from Delia, a pre-med student and the brightest of the girls. Her wavy light-brown hair hangs below her waist. She has prominent features—large hazel eyes, an almost exaggeratedly curved mouth, and a nose that manages to be both thin and full; but there's a black-haired, black-eyed sister, the beauty of the family, and so Delia must make fun of her own looks. She's Puerto Rican and must also make fun of that. She speaks in sagas of self-deprecation that now and again register, with perfect pitch, some truth of her existence. "There's no poor like the student poor," she said yesterday.

"That's a fact, Delia," I said. "But I don't plan on contributing my wages to the relief of the Student Poor."

Maggie began pounding the file cabinet. "I made out that time sheet *myself*. I brought it in *myself* and had Mrs. Keene sign it; then I took it right over to the business office and handed it to feebleminded Freddy. He gave me a hard time because it wasn't with the others. I hate that guy." She pounded the cabinet again.

Yeshi said, "Maybe Mrs. Keene has it."

"Is she in her office?" I could see for myself by stepping back; Olivia was at her desk.

"Come on in," she called.

I said to the students, "I'll be back," and I went to talk to my friend.

"You're just in time for tea and strumpets," she said.

Olivia was in school with me here, but her name then was McGrath. She's been married and divorced and has two sons, and I say to myself, almost seriously, that the troubled course of her life must be the right course since it's given her the name Keene, which describes her perfectly. She's clever, capable, resilient, dresses well, wears good jewelry, leads a busy life. Except for the divorce, Olivia is an example of what my mother would like me to be, though her own mother continually finds fault. "I wonder what it's like to be proud of your children," Mrs. McGrath will say.

Olivia reached for the teapot on her desk and said, "Have a cup."

"No thanks," I said. "I only came by to pick up my check, but it doesn't seem to be outside."

She opened her desk drawer, fished around, and came up with a brown envelope. "Someone must have put it here for safest keeping." She handed me the envelope and said, "Come on, sit down for a minute. Hear the latest outrage."

I sat down in the blue canvas chair beside the desk. I love offices and in particular that office, where the person I am has very little fault to find with the person I was. I begin to wonder, when I'm there, whether the movement of all things isn't toward reconciliation, not division. I'm half convinced that time is on our side, that nothing is ever lost, that we need only have a little more faith, we need only believe a little more and the endings will be happy. Grace's children will be a credit to her. Rosemary will find herself living in a style in keeping with her generous nature. My mother will come to trust the three of us. Olivia's mother will learn to appreciate Olivia. Francis will see how truly I love him. I'll be able to walk down Thirty-fourth Street and not give it a thought. "All right," I said to Olivia, "let's hear the latest outrage."

"Yesterday was High School Day."

"How many came?" I asked.

"A record hundred and seventy, of whom one had her gloves stolen, five got stuck in the elevator, and twelve sat in on a psychology class where the visiting lecturer was a transsexual."

"Oh God," I said.

"Tomorrow I get twelve letters from twelve mothers and dads."

"Maybe they won't tell their parents." I never told mine about seeing Aunt Dorothy shopping for skirts, or about the time I went to Flynn's for a drink, or how my first boyfriend, Gene Kirk, tried to get me to go to bed with him. To this day, I tell people nothing. No one knows about Francis.

Olivia said, "Nowadays kids tell all. Last week Barney came home and announced that his teacher doesn't wear a bra."

I looked at the two little boys in the picture on Olivia's desk. "How old is Barney?" I asked.

"Ten."

He has blond hair that covers his ears, and light-brown eyes with a faraway look. He calls the office and says, "Can I speak to Mrs. Keene? It's me." His brother, Bartholomew, is a couple of years older. Like Olivia, Bart has small, neat features and an astute expression. He sometimes does the grocery shopping after school. He'll call the office and discuss steaks and lamb chops with his mother, and I remember how when I was a little older than he I used to have to cook supper most evenings. The job fell to me because Grace wasn't at home—she'd won a board-and-tuition scholarship to college—and Rosemary was studying piano, which kept her late most evenings, practicing or at her lessons. And after my father's trouble at Flynn's my mother had to go back to teaching music herself. She's a good—a born—musician, but the circumstances that made her take it up again also made her resent it. I resented it, too, because of what it did to my life. After school, I'd hang around till the last minute at the coffee shop where everyone went; then I'd rush home and peel the potatoes, shove the leftover roast in the oven or make the ground beef into hamburgers, heat the gravy, set the table—all grudgingly. But Bartholomew Keene takes pride in his shopping and so does Olivia. In our time, people have made trouble manageable. I sat forward and said, "I'd better get going."

"Think of it," said Olivia. "A transsexual."

I said, "Put it out of your mind."

In the main office, the students were in a semi-demoralized state. Their feelings are in constant flux; anything can set them up or down, and though they work hard, they work in spurts. My turning up was an excuse to come to a halt. I showed them my pay envelope.

Maggie pounded the desk and said, "I *knew* it had to be around here somewhere."

"And I believed in you, Maggie," I said.

" 'I be-lieve for ev-ry drop of rain that falls,' " sang Delia, " 'a flow-er grows.' " They love to sing—when they're tired, when they're fresh, when they're bored or happy or upset.

" 'I be-lieve in mu-sic!' " Maggie snapped her fingers, switching to the rock beat that comes naturally to them. Eileen got up and went into her dance—she's a thin, pretty blonde with a sweet disposition and the soul of a stripper.

" 'I be-lieve in mu-sic!' " they all yelled—all except Yeshi, who only smiled. Yeshi is as quiet as the others are noisy but she loves their noise. Noise gives me eyestrain. I began backing off.

"When are you coming in again?" asked Delia.

I said, "Next week, I think."

Yeshi laughed. Her full name is Yeshimebet. Her sisters are named Astair, Neghist, Azeb, Selamawit, and Etsegenet. Ethiopia lies between Somalia and the Sudan on the Red Sea, whose parting for Moses may have been the effect of winds on its shallow waters.

After I left the office yesterday, I went to evening Mass. I often do. I love that calm at the end of the day. I love the routine, the prayers, the ranks of monks in their white habits, who sit in choir stalls on the altar—I go to a Dominican church, all gray stone and vaulting and blue stained glass. Since it's a city parish, my companions at Mass are diverse—businessmen and students and women in beautiful fur coats side by side with nuns and pious old people, the backbone of congregations. I identify myself among them as someone who must be hard to place—sometimes properly dressed, sometimes in jeans, not so much devout as serious, good-looking but in some undefined way. It's a true picture of me but not, of course, the whole truth. There's no such thing as the whole truth with respect to the living, which is why history appeals to me. I like the finality. Whatever new finds the archeologists may make for scholars to dispute, the facts stand. Battles have been won or lost, civilizations born or laid waste, and the labor and sacrifice entailed are over, can perhaps even be viewed as necessary or at least inevitable. The reasons I love the Mass are somewhat the same. During those twenty or so minutes, I feel my own past to be not quite coherent but capable of eventually proving to be that. And if my life, like every other, contains elements of the outrageous, that ceremony of death and transfiguration is a means of reckoning with the outrageousness, as work and study are means of reckoning with time.

Yesterday Father Henshaw said the five-o'clock Mass. He doesn't linger over the prayers—out of consideration, you can tell, for these people who've come to church at the end of a day's work—but he's a conscientious priest and he places his voice firmly on each syllable of each word as he addresses God on behalf of us all, begging for pardon, mercy, pity, understanding, protection, love. By the time Mass was over yesterday, the sun had set, and as I stepped onto the sidewalk I had the feeling I was leaving one of the side chapels for the body of the church. The buildings were like huge, lighted altars. The sky was streaked with color—a magnificent fresco, too distant for the figures to be identified. The rush hour had started. The street was crowded with people—flesh-and-blood images, living tableaux representing virtue and temptation: greed on one face, faith on another, on another charity, or sloth, fortitude, or purity. And there, straight out of Ecclesiastes, I thought—vanity of vanities, all is vanity. Then I realized I was looking at President Kennedy's sister. She was with a dark-haired man in a navy-blue overcoat. I had the impression at first that he was one of the Irish cousins, but I changed my mind as she smiled at him. It was a full and formal smile, too full and formal for a cousin and for that drab stretch of Lexington Avenue. It was a smile better given at official receptions to heads of state, and I got a sense, as I walked behind the couple, of how events leave people stranded, how from a certain point in our lives on—a different point for each life—we seem only to be passing time. I thought of the Kennedys in Washington, the Kennedys in London, the Kennedys in Boston and Hyannis Port. Which were the important days? The days in the White House? The days at the Court of St. James's? Or had everything that mattered taken place long before, on the beaches of Cape Cod where we saw them sailing and swimming and playing games with one another?

We reached the corner of Sixty-eighth and had to wait for the light to change. It's a busy corner, with a subway station, a newsstand, a hot-dog stand, and a flower stand operated by a man and his wife. The flower sellers are relative newcomers to the corner. I began noticing them last summer, when they were there all day, but when winter came they took to setting up shop in late afternoon. For the cold they dress alike in parkas, and boots, and trousers, and gloves with the fingers cut out. They have the dark features of the Mediterranean countries and they speak to each other in a foreign language. They have a little boy who's almost always with them. I'd guess he's about five, though he's big for five, but at the same time he also seems young for whatever age he may be, possibly because he appears to be so contented on that street corner. A more sophisticated child might sulk or whine or get into trouble, but not that little boy. Sometimes he has a toy with him— a truck or an airplane or a jump rope. He also has a tricycle that he rides when the weather is good. If it's very cold he may shelter in the warmth of the garage a few doors down from the corner, or he'll sit in his parents' old car, surrounded by flowers that will replenish the stock as it runs out. In hot weather, he sometimes stretches out on the side- walk, but that's the closest I've ever seen him come to being at loose ends. He's a resourceful little boy, and he's independent like his par- ents, who work hard and for the most part silently. I've never seen them talking with the owner of the hot-dog stand or the newsdealer. Business is business on that corner, and not much of it comes from me.

I never buy hot dogs, flowers only once in a blue moon, and newspapers not as a rule but on impulse. Yesterday, I put my hand in my pocket and found a dollar bill there and I decided to get a paper. I picked up a *Post* and put my money in the dealer's hand. As he felt through his pockets full of coins, the flower sellers' little boy suddenly appeared, dashed over to his parents' cart, seized a daisy, and put his nose to the yellow center. The newsdealer gave me three quarters back. The traffic lights changed. President Kennedy's sister started across the street. The flower seller's wife grabbed the daisy from her son, and he ran off. I put the quarters in my pocket and moved on.

Yesterday's headlines told of trouble in the Middle East—Israel of the two kingdoms, Israel and Judah; Iran that was Alexander's Persia; Egypt of the Pharaohs and the Ptolemies. I love those ancient peoples. I know them. They form a frieze, a band of images carved in thought across my mind—emperors, princesses, slaves, scribes, farmers, soldiers, musicians, priests. I see them hunting, harvesting, dancing, embracing, fighting, eating, praying. The attitudes are all familiar. The figures are noble and beautiful and still.

One of Them
Gets Married

(1985)

JEAN MCGARRY

April was eighteen and a half and away at school, St. Bernard's College in Wrentham, all girls, when Margery married an Italian and would have given her father a heart attack, on top of everything else, if things hadn't changed since the old days, but they had. Mrs. Dooley died of cancer in 1969. They had her up at the institution for a year, thought she had gone mental, then someone discovered the tumor and gave her five months to live but she died in one. Sad funeral, her father told April when she came home Thanksgiving; a lovely woman, he said, and all those kids. The kids were married except for Terrence, who had gone into the seminary early, come out, gone in again when he was seventeen, and was now buying and selling property, as her father put it; condemned buildings, was what her mother said. Married, little Alice Dooley already had three of her own. Her father said this at least six times. Alice and her husband moved out-of-state, he told her another time; she was pregnant with the fourth and they were hoping for a boy, three girls and a boy, but her real interest in life (April knew by this kind of talk that her father was drinking again) was to get as fat as she could and now she was already big as a house.

April had never heard him so cynical. He had white hair now; he had made himself go white, Margery said, because he was anxious to be dead and get it over with. Their mother—she was not white, but had her hair done at the Palace Beauty Salon; autumn auburn was the color she used until it got brassy and they mixed it with medium light brown—told Margery she shouldn't talk like that. Oh nobody around here should do anything but you, Margery said in that tone no one liked. What did she say? their mother asked April. Don't tell me; two of the world's biggest hypocrites you are. Well here (handing the dishtowel to April), if you're so smart, you can take over my job and see if you can keep this stinking family going. She was going to leave the room in a temper but Margery left instead: I've had it, she said, I'm getting out of here.

"Tell me (to April), you're smart, what's gotten into her?" Before April could say anything—and she had her ideas; she had been taking psychology for a year now just so she could tackle problems like this and was only too willing—her mother said, "Oh I know, it's getting married. If she's upset now, just think how she'll be after, if she thinks this is bad." April sat down, but her mother had gotten up already and was at the foot of the stairs yelling to Margery to bring down the magazines and show her sister here the patterns she had picked for her china and silver.

"I don't feel like it."

"Well, just throw them down. I'll show her if you won't."

"I'll show her. I don't want you showing her."

They looked at the pictures and Margery told stories about the big Italian dinners she had gone to at the Tagliatellas, with all the relatives and a hundred and one courses, one right on top of the other. You'll get money from them, her mother said; they like to give money for weddings, but I'll tell them your patterns anyway, they can afford a couple of place settings at least.

"Ma!"

"What do you mean 'Ma?' You'll be glad to have it. They don't bring home much from Unemployment you know (Joey Tag, as Margery called him, worked for the state), get it while you can."

They were starting up again. April said she had studying to do.

"Don't clutter. I just broke my back cleaning."

Other things had changed. They didn't say the Mass in Latin, the nuns wore dresses and you could see their hair. The old ones looked older in street clothes, April thought, but the poor things are cooler in summer—that's what everybody said. The pastor had died; April was away at school for the funeral, but her father said he had brass from the state house and the chancellery: the bishop, the auxiliary bishop, and a bishop nobody knew from out-of-state. They put on the dog, April's father said, but then, this is a big parish to open up all of a sudden, a real plum for whoever gets it. Your friend's uncle there, you know, Fr. O'Reilly, that cousin of the Dooleys, they say he's high on the list. I'd like to see a man like that get it, do the parish good.

They had bingo at the church Saturday nights after cutting out Saturday confessions. But the real blow came, her father told April, when the acting pastor announced in the church bulletin that he was forced to hire a lay person to teach at Holy Savior. There just weren't enough vocations to go around; people aren't making the sacrifice, April's father said. It's a scandal when a parish this size can't produce the vocations to staff the parochial school. Thank God my kids aren't there anymore.

April wondered if he were criticizing her for not making the sacrifice, but he had hardly noticed when she went up to St. Bernard's in the fall instead of off to the Mother House to be a postulant, after she had announced her vocation the year she started high, and every year after. Her mother noticed. "See, I told you you'd outgrow it." But even *she* didn't rub it in. April couldn't imagine ever wanting to be a nun. One of the first things the lay theology teacher had given her when she explained she was doing a year of college before maybe joining a semi-cloistered order in Providence was a book about the crimes the pope had committed in World War II. She brought home another book by a minister about God's death and by then, starting to have different thoughts and wondering whether to bother going to Mass or not; it didn't seem to matter. There was only the one discussion at home about this change, when her mother asked her if she thought she was smarter than God. It struck April as funny, but she didn't laugh out loud.

"The church doesn't have the support it used to," her father was saying. They were sitting together on the porch. "My mother and father built that church with their collection money; they wouldn't be able to build a shack with the pittance they get Sundays. You're lucky if some of them show up for Palm Sunday and Christmas, doing you a big favor to be there, too."

He was talking about the Italians. The parish had always had Italians, but now they were moving into the neighborhood and taking over. Two Irish families had moved out just this year down the street, he said (April couldn't think whom he meant until she remembered the two old ladies in the Gallagher house, and the old guy, Mr. Burke, dead now, who rented a room over Adams Drugstore and had to be put in the institution), and Italians moved in. Young children too, he said, so they'll be around for a while. You can hear the mothers shrieking, he said, up and down the street all hours of the night. You can always hear mothers, April wanted to say, Italian or not. She was too flip these days, they were always saying, especially for a college girl.

Other things had changed. The mayor had left his wife for a hairdresser, and the name dragged in the mud, April's father said. He wasn't reelected to the fifth term. Who'd they elect? A Guinea, he said, Carbone, first time in the city's history. Not only was it an Italian, but Republican party. "Oh, they're thrilled up there on the Hill, first place urban renewal goes, you watch; they're tickled pink."

Margery's Guinea (her father called him that only to April) had at least gone to junior college and was trying to make something of himself, which was more than he could say for most of them. Joey Tag had made himself into an insurance man before his uncle got him in at Unemployment. He had worked for Metropolitan Life down the avenue across from the drugstore, and Margery and her mother used to go down and peek in the window. "He looks busy in there," her mother said, "you can at least say that for him."

April was not surprised to hear that Margery and her mother were doing things together. Margery had changed, or maybe the mother had changed, but they were thick now, that's how her father put it, and went everywhere together.

Her mother had gotten Margery a job at the butterfly valve company she worked for. Margery was a clerk typist across the hall in accounts receivable. They loved to talk about the "personalities" at work. The mother was always coming home with a tale about how the younger guys were trying their best to get in with her so she'd put in a good word with Margery. Her mother loved the attention, April could see that.

"And such a stick in the mud she is. I tell her to have her fun now *before* she's married and cooped up. But she won't give them the right time of day, so stuck she is on that Joey. I can tell you're really in love, Margery." April didn't know whether she was kidding or not.

The wedding was a week from Saturday. They were going to be married by Fr. Doyle, April's friend from high school, used to run the CYO and take them to skating parties till he decided all of a sudden to go down to the missions in Peru. There was nothing left for him to do in Providence, was what he told April and she never forgot the weird look on his face when he said it (probably losing his marbles, her mother said at the time). Fr. Doyle hoped they—the kids in the CYO, April figured, although it was just herself there during one of the vocation sessions they had twice a week—would help him make the sacrifice.

He went away in February after they announced it over the pulpit at all the Masses. April's mother said she felt sad, because he was a holy man and not like the other phonies with a new Buick every year. He came back the next summer. April's father heard he'd had a nervous collapse and the bishop shipped him to Narragansett to recuperate. At first, they weren't going to let him back in at Holy Savior, even though he wanted to come back. Eventually, he did get back. "He was good with the kids," April's mother piped up from the kitchen. That's what they say, her father said, but you and I know it had a lot to do with that cousin of his that's a bishop of Hartford or something. Anyway, he got back in (April's father), and you were embarrassed running into him on the street, you didn't know what to say. "He looked like Hell," the mother said, "skin and bones, lost all his hair." Next thing you know, April's father went on, they're rushing him to Rhode Island Hospital dying of cancer, although I heard from someone they had him drying out up there. If you were still in good with him (to April), you could get the real story.

But it was Margery who was friends with Fr. Doyle now. She got to know him (April's mother) in that ecumenical group she was involved with when she was dating the funny guy from Cumberland, remember him? But I could have told her she'd never marry that guy—plus, he had diabetes to boot. Once a week, she and that Charlie Muncie, I think his name was, went up to the rectory with one other couple and two single girls who left the convent and wanted a little exposure to life, that's what Margery said, but they picked a funny place to get it.

Margery kept going to the sessions even after Charlie was gone, and no more danger of a mixed marriage. The group dwindled to just the two girls; the nuns had departed too. "We talk," April heard Margery telling her mother; "sometimes we go out for coffee." Is he okay? the mother wanted to know. "You wouldn't recognize him, he's so different-acting. Always criticizing you-know-who." April thought for a minute this might be herself, but it had to mean the new pastor nobody liked.

Does he ever say to say hi to me? (April from the dining room).

I wasn't talking to you so just butt out.

I'd just like to know, Margery.

No.

He must say *something*.

April had run into Fr. Doyle once on the avenue. He spoke, but she could tell he didn't know who it was. Maybe it's because I've lost so much weight, she told her mother. Oh, I think he recognized you, April, her mother said; he just didn't want to admit it. You know how they are when they've been on sick leave, they don't like people judging them.

"I'm not judging him." (An old friend of April's who knew Fr. Doyle in the old days and was the only girl from St. Mary's Academy to go up to Brown University, non-Catholic, said she wasn't surprised he didn't recognize her; he was probably in bad faith. April explained that meant a bad conscience. She always goes too far, was what her mother said to this.)

Margery got married at the ten o'clock Mass, riding down with her girlfriend Harriet and April in a limousine from the Callaghan Funeral Home. "This is how he does business," her father told April about Buddy Callaghan, the funeral director. "I told him he already had this family, he didn't have to worry, but he always extends the courtesy. All he asks is to get invited to the wedding so people can see him there."

Nothing seemed funny about the limousine, Margery told April when she asked, it was just a limousine. "Don't *you* get started," her mother said from the bathroom. That was Thursday, two days before the wedding when things were at their worst.

"The bride wore an off-white sateen gown with Venice lace and empire waist," they read on Sunday, sitting at the kitchen table eating from a foil-covered platter of cold roast beef and ham. The picture had come out too dark and on the second to the last page with weddings from out of town. Margery was next to a Polish girl—Irene Dombrowski to Harold Zinciewicz—which didn't help matters. She was still a pretty girl, her father kept saying over and over. No one paid any attention; April saw her mother rolling her eyes. "I'm sick of weddings; I don't want to go to another wedding for the next ten years," she said. April could tell she was pleased.

She had never had so much fun in her life, April had heard her mother say at the wedding. She had been up dancing the whole night. She had danced with the neighbors, with April's Uncle Bernie, with the bridegroom's father. She had danced more than Margery had. She was up and down all afternoon too, having to talk to people and introduce them to the bridegroom's family. They kept coming over—his mother and father—and telling the bride to bring their son over to the table, somebody wanted to talk to him. "Already," Margery said to April, "they're making me out to be his servant." "Are you talking to me?" April said. Margery got up, took the bridegroom by the arm and led him over to the table of relatives.

Margery had not spoken to April before the wedding. She was grouchy all the time and could not even take the trouble (her mother) to be civil to the people who were forking over the money so she could have the goddamned wedding in the first place. April could see she wasn't having the kind of fun you read about in the bride magazines.

She acted as it if were an ordeal, even getting the presents. The only thing she got excited about was when his mother sent over two antique gold candlesticks which had been the grandmother's in the old country. Margery said she never expected anything that good. Her mother was making a joke to April about how hideous they were and Margery would have to drag them out every time she had the in-laws, as she called them, over to dinner. Margery said they could both go to hell. April thought the two of them would have another blow-out, but her mother acted as if she hadn't heard it. Later April heard her mother telling their father's Aunt Helen, "as high hat (April's grandmother) as they come," that Margery had gotten a set of solid gold candlesticks from his people. Aunt Helen said they'd be expecting something in return for that. April's mother overlooked that comment. "The girl's thrilled," she said, "you'd think it was a million dollars."

"I should say so," said Aunt Helen, all red in the face from the hot roast beef and two glasses of cold duck. Each table had a carafe of wine—that was part of the package deal they had from the caterers. After that, it was paying for your own. "That's the best your father and I can do for you, Margery," her mother said, "so don't knock it. She'll be wanting a wedding too sooner or later and your father's got to give one what he gives the other; fair's fair."

Margery and Joey rented a tenement over in the Fruit Hill neighborhood. Margery and her mother spent the month before the wedding fixing it up. They scrubbed the bathroom tile with toothbrushes, laid in shelfpaper, and washed and waxed all the floors. It was backbreaking work, April's mother wrote in a letter to her, describing all the jobs they had done in detail, "and that Margery's no ball of fire either. She let me do most of it."

When April came home for the weekend, her father took her right over to the tenement. ("You take her," the mother said, "I'm sick of the place.") He told April what they were paying, that it was an ideal location—so handy to the bus lines—and how nice the girl had fixed it up. He was the most excited about it. April had never seen him so excited. He ran up the flight of stairs and pulled April in the door. She saw the whole place: the linen closet, the back hall, the kitchen cabinets with the everyday glasses they had gotten at the January sale at Sears, the broom closet. The new dinette set and the bedroom set were there but otherwise the place was empty, except for the braided rug (*my* aunt, he said) in the living room. "You'd like something like this, wouldn't you?" April said she would. "You'll have your turn, just wait and see. You're both beautiful girls. Don't belittle yourself," he said, when he saw the smile. "You'll do as good as her easy, plus you've got the education. Don't be in a hurry," he said. "Be smart. You can get married any time."

The way he said this, so friendly and enthusiastic, made April feel enthusiastic. They were both enthusiastic and looked through all the rooms again, but in the car there was nothing to say all the way home.

"What did you say to him (April's mother) that got him into such a stinking mood?"

He was on and off like that right up till the day of the wedding: full of it (April's mother) one minute; sitting in the dark smoking a cigarette, the next. When he got like that, everybody tiptoed around and made sure not to slam the cupboard doors and best just to stay out of his way. April was starting abnormal psych at school and paid close attention to the symptoms of all the mental diseases, but she couldn't find one that fit him and his ways. Margery and her mother didn't think there was anything wrong with him. "He (the mother) brings it on himself, *we* know that much." But April didn't think the things he was doing were normal. He was still up during the night throwing up, but they were used to that. It was more the things he did during the day. Sometimes at dinner he just stared at the wall and sighed. He looked unhappy—that was one way to describe it, April thought—but there was more. "You have to remember to handle him with kid gloves," April's mother kept saying, "and that's something *you* can't seem to learn how to do."

Sometimes April thought she was better off at school, but she wasn't happy there either. Margery told her she was lucky to be away and should thank her lucky stars, rotten roommate or not. When April told her mother how the girls in her end of the hall were against her, her mother said she should learn not to let people walk all over her. "You were always like that, you know, a doormat."

Seeing Margery's tenement and thinking about what it would be like to live there—Joey Tag, easy-going and cute—even though it was small and everything old-fashioned, funny colors, gave April the idea that even for her, things might get better by and by, as her grandmother said. She could always get married and move out of the dorm junior year. She told Margery how lucky she was. Margery shrugged, but April knew she'd been dying to get married.

"You can get married too, anybody can. It doesn't take talent—*they* did."

Who?

"Them. Them, stupid," pointing downstairs, "who do you think I meant, Jackie Kennedy? Don't kid yourself, April, nobody's got it that great. You're so naïve. Who's that happy you know? If you'd get your nose out of a book once in a while, you'd see the world and see how it stinks."

April didn't think she'd ever heard Margery talk like this before. Even though it was negative, it was something Margery was telling her personally and she was grateful. When Margery saw this—and she never (her mother) missed a trick—she told April to get out, she was going to take a nap.

The Lover of Horses

(1986)

TESS GALLAGHER

They say my great-grandfather was a gypsy, but the most popular explanation for his behavior was that he was a drunk. How else could the women have kept up the scourge of his memory all these years, had they not had the usual malady of our family to blame? Probably he was both, a gypsy and a drunk.

Still, I have reason to believe the gypsy in him had more to do with the turn his life took than his drinking. I used to argue with my mother about this, even though most of the information I have about my great-grandfather came from my mother, who got it from her mother. A drunk, I kept telling her, would have had no initiative. He would simply have gone down with his failures and had nothing to show for it. But my great-grandfather had eleven children, surely a sign of industry, and he was a lover of horses. He had so many horses he was what people called "horse poor."

I did not learn, until I traveled to where my family originated at Collenamore in the west of Ireland, that my great-grandfather had most likely been a "whisperer," a breed of men among the gypsies who were said to possess the power of talking sense into horses. These men had no fear of even the most malicious and dangerous horses. In fact, they would often take the wild animal into a closed stall in order to perform their skills.

Whether a certain intimacy was needed or whether the whisperers simply wanted to protect their secret conversations with horses is not known. One thing was certain—that such men gained power over horses by whispering. What they whispered no one knew. But the effectiveness of their methods was renowned, and anyone for counties around who had an unruly horse could send for a whisperer and be sure that the horse would take to heart whatever was said and reform his behavior from that day forth.

By all accounts, my great-grandfather was like a huge stallion himself, and when he went into a field where a herd of horses was grazing, the horses would suddenly lift their heads and call to him. Then his bearded mouth would move, and though he was making sounds that could have been words, which no horse would have had reason to understand, the horses would want to hear; and one by one they would move toward him across the open space of the field. He could turn his back and walk down the road, and they would follow him. He was probably drunk my mother said, because he was swaying and mumbling all the while. Sometimes he would stop dead-still in the road and the horses would press up against him and raise and lower their heads as he moved his lips. But because these things were only seen from a distance, and because they have eroded in the telling, it is now impossible to know whether my great-grandfather said anything of importance to the horses. Or even if it was his whispering that had brought about their good behavior. Nor was it clear, when he left them in some barnyard as suddenly as he'd come to them, whether they had arrived at some new understanding of the difficult and complex relationship between men and horses.

Only the aberrations of my great-grandfather's relationship with horses have survived—as when he would bathe in the river with his favorite horse or when, as my grandmother told my mother, he insisted on conceiving his ninth child in the stall of a bay mare named Redwing. Not until I was grown and going through the family Bible did I discover that my grandmother had been this ninth child, and so must have known something about the matter.

These oddities in behavior lead me to believe that when my great-grandfather, at the age of fifty-two, abandoned his wife and family to join a circus that was passing through the area, it was not simply drunken bravado, nor even the understandable wish to escape family obligations. I believe the gypsy in him finally got the upper hand, and it led to such a remarkable happening that no one in the family has so far been willing to admit it: not the obvious transgression—that he had run away to join the circus—but that he was in all likelihood a man who had been stolen by a horse.

This is not an easy view to sustain in the society we live in. But I have not come to it frivolously, and have some basis for my belief. For although I have heard the story of my great-grandfather's defection time and again since childhood, the one image which prevails in all versions is that of a dappled gray stallion that had been trained to dance a variation of the mazurka. So impressive was this animal that he mesmerized crowds with his sliding step-and-hop to the side through the complicated figures of the dance, which he performed, not in the way of Lippizaners—with other horses and their riders—but riderless and with the men of the circus company as his partners.

It is known that my great-grandfather became one of these dancers. After that he was reputed, in my mother's words, to have gone "completely to ruin." The fact that he walked from the house with only the clothes on his back, leaving behind his own beloved horses (twenty-nine of them to be exact), further supports my idea that a powerful force must have held sway over him, something more profound than the miseries of drink or the harsh imaginings of his abandoned wife.

Not even the fact that seven years later he returned and knocked on his wife's door, asking to be taken back, could exonerate him from what he had done, even though his wife did take him in and looked after him until he died some years later. But the detail that no one takes note of in the account is that when my great-grandfather returned, he was carrying a saddle blanket and the black plumes from the headgear of one of the circus horses. This passes by even my mother as simply a sign of the ridiculousness of my great-grandfather's plight—for after all, he was homeless and heading for old age as a "good for nothing drunk" and a "fool for horses."

No one has bothered to conjecture what these curious emblems—saddle blanket and plumes—must have meant to my great-grandfather. But he hung them over the foot of his bed—"like a fool," my mother said. And sometimes when he got very drunk he would take up the blanket and, wrapping it like a shawl over his shoulders, he would grasp the plumes. Then he would dance the mazurka. He did not dance in the living room but took himself out into the field, where the horses stood at attention and watched as if suddenly experiencing the smell of the sea or a change of wind in the valley. "Drunks don't care what they do," my mother would say as she finished her story about my great-grandfather. "Talking to a drunk is like talking to a stump."

Ever since my great-grandfather's outbreaks of gypsy-necessity, members of my family have been stolen by things—by mad ambitions, by musical instruments, by otherwise harmless pursuits from mushroom hunting to childbearing or, as was my father's case, by the more easily recognized and popular obsession with card playing. To some extent, I still think it was failure of imagination in this respect that brought about his diminished prospects in the life of our family.

But even my mother had been powerless against the attraction of a man so convincingly driven. When she met him at a birthday dance held at the country house of one of her young friends, she asked him what he did for a living. My father pointed to a deck of cards in his shirt pocket and said, "I play cards." But love is such as it is, and although my mother was otherwise a deadly practical woman, it seemed she could fall in love with no man but my father.

So it is possible that the propensity to be stolen is somewhat contagious when ordinary people come into contact with people such as my father. Though my mother loved him at the time of the marriage, she soon began to behave as if she had been stolen from a more fruitful and upright life which she was always imagining might have been hers.

My father's card playing was accompanied, to no one's surprise, by bouts of drinking. The only thing that may have saved our family from a life of poverty was the fact that my father seldom gambled with money. Such were his charm and powers of persuasion that he was able to convince other players to accept his notes on everything from the fish he intended to catch next season to the sale of his daughter's hair.

I know about this last wager because I remember the day he came to me with a pair of scissors and said it was time to cut my hair. Two snips and it was done. I cannot forget the way he wept onto the backs of his hands and held the braids together like a broken noose from which a life had suddenly slipped. I was thirteen at the time and my hair had never been cut. It was his pride and joy that I had such hair. But for me it was only a burdensome difference between me and my classmates, so I was glad to be rid of it. What anyone else could have wanted with my long shiny braids is still a mystery to me.

When my father was seventy-three he fell ill and the doctors gave him only a few weeks to live. My father was convinced that his illness had come on him because he'd hit a particularly bad losing streak at cards. He had lost heavily the previous month, and items of value, mostly belonging to my mother, had disappeared from the house. He developed the strange idea that if he could win at cards he could cheat the prediction of the doctors and live at least into his eighties.

By this time I had moved away from home and made a life for myself in an attempt to follow the reasonable dictates of my mother, who had counseled her children severely against all manner of rash ambition and foolhardiness. Her entreaties were leveled especially in my direction since I had shown a suspect enthusiasm for a certain pony at around the age of five. And it is true I felt I had lost a dear friend when my mother saw to it that the neighbors who owned this pony moved it to pasture elsewhere.

But there were other signs that I might wander off into unpredictable pursuits. The most telling of these was that I refused to speak aloud to anyone until the age of eleven. I whispered everything, as if my mind were a repository of secrets which could only be divulged in this intimate manner. If anyone asked me a question, I was always polite about answering, but I had to do it by putting my mouth near the head of my inquisitor and using only my breath and lips to make my reply.

My teachers put my whispering down to shyness and made special accommodations for me. When it came time for recitations I would accompany the teacher into the cloakroom and there whisper to her the memorized verses or the speech I was to have prepared. God knows, I might have continued on like this into the present if my mother hadn't plotted with some neighborhood boys to put burrs into my long hair. She knew by other signs that I had a terrible temper, and she was counting on that to deliver me into the world where people shouted and railed at one another and talked in an audible fashion about things both common and sacred.

When the boys shut me into a shed, according to plan, there was nothing for me to do but to cry out for help and to curse them in a torrent of words I had only heard used by adults. When my mother heard this she rejoiced, thinking that at last she had broken the treacherous hold of the past over me, of my great-grandfather's gypsy blood and the fear that against all her efforts I might be stolen away, as she had been, and as my father had, by some as yet unforeseen predilection. Had I not already experienced the consequences of such a life in our household, I doubt she would have been successful, but the advantages of an ordinary existence among people of a less volatile nature had begun to appeal to me.

It was strange, then, that after all the care my mother had taken for me in this regard, when my father's illness came on him, my mother brought her appeal to me. "Can you do something?" she wrote, in her cramped, left-handed scrawl. "He's been drinking and playing cards for three days and nights. I am at my wit's end. Come home at once."

Somehow I knew this was a message addressed to the very part of me that most baffled and frightened my mother—the part that belonged exclusively to my father and his family's inexplicable manias.

When I arrived home my father was not there.

"He's at the tavern. In the back room," my mother said. "He hasn't eaten for days. And if he's slept, he hasn't done it here."

I made up a strong broth, and as I poured the steaming liquid into a Thermos I heard myself utter syllables and other vestiges of language which I could not reproduce if I wanted to. "What do you mean by that?" my mother demanded, as if a demon had leapt out of me. "What did you say?" I didn't—I couldn't—answer her. But suddenly I felt that an unsuspected network of sympathies and distant connections had begun to reveal itself to me in my father's behalf.

There is a saying that when lovers have need of moonlight, it is there. So it seemed, as I made my way through the deserted town toward the tavern and card room, that all nature had been given notice of my father's predicament, and that the response I was waiting for would not be far off.

But when I arrived at the tavern and had talked my way past the barman and into the card room itself, I saw that my father had an enormous pile of blue chips at his elbow. Several players had fallen out to watch, heavy-lidded and smoking their cigarettes like weary gangsters.

Others were slumped on folding chairs near the coffee urn with its empty "Pay Here" styrofoam cup.

My father's cap was pushed to the back of his head so that his forehead shone in the dim light, and he grinned over his cigarette at me with the serious preoccupation of a child who has no intention of obeying anyone. And why should he, I thought as I sat down just behind him and loosened the stopper on the Thermos. The five or six players still at the table casually appraised my presence to see if it had tipped the scales of their luck in an even more unfavorable direction. Then they tossed their cards aside, drew fresh cards, or folded.

In the center of the table were more blue chips, and poking out from my father's coat pocket I recognized the promissory slips he must have redeemed, for he leaned to me and in a low voice, without taking his eyes from his cards, said "I'm having a hell of a good time. The time of my life."

He was winning. His face seemed ravaged by the effort, but he was clearly playing on a level that had carried the game far beyond the realm of mere card playing and everyone seemed to know it. The dealer cocked an eyebrow as I poured broth into the plastic Thermos cup and handed it to my father, who slurped from it noisily, then set it down.

"Tell the old kettle she's got to put up with me a few more years," he said, and lit up a fresh cigarette. His eyes as he looked at me, however, seemed over-brilliant, as if doubt, despite all his efforts, had gained a permanent seat at his table. I squeezed his shoulder and kissed him hurriedly on his forehead. The men kept their eyes down, and as I paused at the door, there was a shifting of chairs and a clearing of throats. Just outside the room I nearly collided with the barman, who was carrying in a fresh round of beer. His heavy jowls waggled as he recovered himself and looked hard at me over the icy bottles. Then he disappeared into the card room with his provisions.

I took the long way home, finding pleasure in the fact that at this hour all the stoplights had switched onto a flashing-yellow caution cycle. Even the teenagers who usually cruised the town had gone home or to more secluded spots. *Doubt,* I kept thinking as I drove with my father's face before me, that's the real thief. And I knew my mother had brought me home because of it, because she knew that once again a member of our family was about to be stolen.

Two more days and nights I ministered to my father at the card room. I would never stay long because I had the fear myself that I might spoil his luck. But many unspoken tendernesses passed between us in those brief appearances as he accepted the nourishment I offered, or when he looked up and handed me his beer bottle to take a swig from—a ritual we'd shared since my childhood.

My father continued to win—to the amazement of the local barflies who poked their faces in and out of the card room and gave the dwindling three or four stalwarts who remained at the table a commiserating shake of their heads. There had never been a winning streak like it in the history of the tavern, and indeed, we heard later that the man who owned the card room and tavern had to sell out and open a fruit stand on the edge of town as a result of my father's extraordinary good luck.

Twice during this period my mother urged the doctor to order my father home. She was sure my father would, at some fateful moment, risk the entire winnings in some mad rush toward oblivion. But his doctor spoke of a new "gaming therapy" for the terminally ill, based on my father's surge of energies in the pursuit of his gambling. Little did he know that my father was, by that stage, oblivious to even his winning, he had gone so far into exhaustion.

Luckily for my father, the hour came when, for lack of players, the game folded. Two old friends drove him home and helped him down from the pickup. They paused in the driveway, one on either side of him, letting him steady himself. When the card playing had ended there had been nothing for my father to do but to get drunk.

My mother and I watched from the window as the men steered my father toward the hydrangea bush at the side of the house, where he relieved himself with perfect precision on one mammoth blossom. Then they hoisted him up the stairs and into the entryway. My mother and I took over from there.

"Give 'em hell, boys," my father shouted after the men, concluding some conversation he was having with himself.

"You betcha," the driver called back, laughing. Then he climbed with his companion into the cab of his truck and roared away.

Tied around my father's waist was a cloth sack full of bills and coins which flapped and jingled against his knees as we bore his weight between us up the next flight of stairs and into the living room. There we deposited him on the couch, where he took up residence, refusing to sleep in his bed—for fear, my mother claimed, that death would know where to find him. But I preferred to think he enjoyed the rhythms of the household; from where he lay at the center of the house, he could overhear all conversations that took place and add his opinions when he felt like it.

My mother was so stricken by the signs of his further decline that she did everything he asked, instead of arguing with him or simply refusing. Instead of taking his winnings straight to the bank so as not to miss a day's interest, she washed an old goldfish bowl and dumped all the money into it, most of it in twenty-dollar bills. Then she placed it on the coffee table near his head so he could run his hand through it at will, or let his visitors do the same.

"Money feels good on your elbow," he would say to them. "I played them under the table for that. Yes sir, take a feel of that!" Then he would lean back on his pillows and tell my mother to bring his guests a shot of whiskey. "Make sure she fills my glass up," he'd say to me so that my mother was certain to overhear. And my mother, who'd never allowed a bottle of whiskey to be brought into her house before now, would look at me as if the two of us were more than any woman should have to bear.

"If you'd only brought him home from that card room," she said again and again. "Maybe it wouldn't have come to this."

This included the fact that my father had radically altered his diet. He lived only on greens. If it was green he would eat it. By my mother's reckoning, the reason for his change of diet was that if he stopped eating what he usually ate, death would think it wasn't him and go look for somebody else.

Another request my father made was asking my mother to sweep the doorway after anyone came in or went out.

"To make sure death wasn't on their heels; to make sure death didn't slip in as they left." This was my mother's reasoning. But my father didn't give any reasons. Nor did he tell us finally why he wanted all the furniture moved out of the room except for the couch where he lay. And the money, they could take that away too.

But soon his strength began to ebb, and more and more family and friends crowded into the vacant room to pass the time with him, to laugh about stories remembered from his childhood or from his nights as a young man at the country dances when he and his older brother would work all day in the cotton fields, hop a freight train to town and dance all night. Then they would have to walk home, getting there just at daybreak in time to go straight to work again in the cotton fields.

"We were like bulls then," my father would say in a burst of the old vigor, then close his eyes suddenly as if he hadn't said anything at all.

As long as he spoke to us, the inevitability of his condition seemed easier to bear. But when, at the last, he simply opened his mouth for food or stared silently toward the far wall, no one knew what to do with themselves.

My own part in that uncertain time came to me accidentally. I found myself in the yard sitting on a stone bench under a little cedar tree my father loved because he liked to sit there and stare at the ocean. The tree whispered, he said. He said it had a way of knowing what your troubles were. Suddenly a craving came over me. I wanted a cigarette, even though I don't smoke, hate smoking, in fact. I was sitting where my father had sat, and to smoke seemed a part of some rightness that had begun to work its way within me. I went into the house and bummed a pack of cigarettes from my brother. For the rest of the morning I sat under the cedar tree and smoked. My thoughts drifted with its shiftings and murmurings, and it struck me what a wonderful thing nature is because it knows the value of silence, the innuendos of silence and what they could mean for a word-bound creature such as I was.

I passed the rest of the day in a trance of silences, moving from place to place, revisiting the sites I knew my father loved—the "dragon tree," a hemlock which stood at the far end of the orchard, so named for how the wind tossed its triangular head; the rose arbor where he and my mother had courted; the little marina where I sat in his fishing boat and dutifully smoked the hated cigarettes, flinging them one by one into the brackish water.

I was waiting to know what to do for him, he who would soon be a piece of useless matter of no more consequence than the cigarette butts that floated and washed against the side of his boat. I could feel some action accumulating in me through the steadiness of water raising and lowering the boat, through the sad petal-fall of roses in the arbor and the tossing of the dragon tree.

That night when I walked from the house I was full of purpose. I headed toward the little cedar tree. Without stopping to question the necessity of what I was doing, I began to break off the boughs I could reach and to pile them on the ground.

"What are you doing?" my brother's children wanted to know, crowding around me as if I might be inventing some new game for them.

"What does it look like?" I said.

"Pulling limbs off the tree," the oldest said. Then they dashed away in a pack under the orchard trees, giggling and shrieking.

As I pulled the boughs from the trunk I felt a painful permission, as when two silences, tired of holding back, give over to each other some shared regret. I made my bed on the boughs and resolved to spend the night there in the yard, under the stars, with the hiss of the ocean in my ear, and the maimed cedar tree standing over me like a gift torn out of its wrappings.

My brothers, their wives and my sister had now begun their nightly vigil near my father, taking turns at staying awake. The windows were open for the breeze and I heard my mother trying to answer the question of why I was sleeping outside on the ground—"like a damned fool" I knew they wanted to add.

"She doesn't want to be here when death comes for him," my mother said, with an air of clairvoyance she had developed from a lifetime with my father. "They're too much alike," she said.

The ritual of night games played by the children went on and on long past their bedtimes. Inside the house, the kerosene lantern, saved from my father's childhood home, had been lit—another of his strange requests during the time before his silence. He liked the shadows it made and the sweet smell of the kerosene. I watched the darkness as the shapes of my brothers and sister passed near it, gigantic and misshapen where they bent or raised themselves or crossed the room.

Out on the water the wind had come up. In the orchard the children were spinning around in a circle, faster and faster until they were giddy and reeling with speed and darkness. Then they would stop, rest a moment, taking quick ecstatic breaths before plunging again into the opposite direction, swirling round and round in the circle until the excitement could rise no higher, their laughter and cries brimming over, then scattering as they flung one another by the arms or chased each other toward the house as if their lives depended on it.

I lay awake for a long while after their footsteps had died away and the car doors had slammed over the good-byes of the children being taken home to bed and the last of the others had been bedded down in the house while the adults went on waiting.

It was important to be out there alone and close to the ground. The pungent smell of the cedar boughs was around me, rising up in the crisp night air toward the tree, whose turnings and swayings had altered, as they had to, in order to accompany the changes about to overtake my father and me. I thought of my great-grandfather bathing with his horse in the river, and of my father who had just passed through the longest period in his life without the clean feel of cards falling through his hands as he shuffled or dealt them. He was too weak now even to hold a cigarette; there was a burn mark on the hard-wood floor where his last cigarette had fallen. His winnings were safely in the bank and the luck that was to have saved him had gone back to that place luck goes to when it is finished with us.

So this is what it comes to, I thought, and listened to the wind as it mixed gradually with the memory of children's voices which still seemed to rise and fall in the orchard. There was a soft crooning of syllables that was satisfying to my ears, but ultimately useless and absurd. Then it came to me that I was the author of those unwieldy sounds, and that my lips had begun to work of themselves.

In a raw pulsing of language I could not account for, I lay awake through the long night and spoke to my father as one might speak to an ocean or the wind, letting him know by that threadbare accompaniment that the vastness he was about to enter had its rhythms in me also. And that he was not forsaken. And that I was letting him go. That so far I had denied the disreputable world of dancers and drunkards, gamblers and lovers of horses to which I most surely belonged. But from that night forward I vowed to be filled with the first unsavory desire that would have me. To plunge myself into the heart of my life and be ruthlessly lost forever.

Nijinsky

(1988)

MAURA STANTON

I pushed open the red door of my new high school. I still thought of
it as my new school, although I had been enrolled since September and
now it was almost the end of November. The low, modern hall was
brightly lit. I was late. The doors were already shut on the sound-
proofed classrooms, and I could hear the hum of the fluorescent tubes
hidden behind the translucent glass squares of the ceiling. I stopped at
my locker and slowly changed into my heavy uniform saddle oxfords.
I had nothing to fear. I had merely to go to the office, explain that my
bus had broken down, and take an approved tardy slip to my first hour
teacher. My new school was so different from the old school I had
transferred from after three years that sometimes I felt light and thin,
as if I were a person in a dream. I half expected the hands of the other
girls to slide right through my body, especially when I stepped into the
bright, noisy cafeteria with its small tables for four and its huge,
abstract mural, or watched one of the softly veiled sisters, her head
thrown back, laughing with a group of girls in the lounge.

My old school had been celebrating its Centennial when my family moved to Minnesota. Its high, sooty walls, its dim hallways and

enormous flights of stairs had made me dread waking up on school mornings. The sisters were bitter and grim-faced; they were always collecting money for charity. There were even placards on the candy bar machine down in the sour-smelling basement cafeteria, where we ate our bag lunches in silence at long green tables.

I liked to think that I had changed since starting my senior year at the new school. But I was still nervous. I remembered the pinched-lipped Latin teacher, who used to humiliate me at the blackboard, with great vividness. Even though I had so far, in this new school, been able to recite my Spanish dialogues by heart, my throat clenched painfully when I rose to speak. But the black, kindly eyebrows of Sister Rosa reassured me.

I felt cheerful as I entered the main office. Waxy plants in straw baskets hung from the ceiling. Some oddly shaped leather chairs were grouped around a chrome coffee table. The secretary, typing at her blond wood desk, nodded routinely when I muttered my excuse, and handed me a slip of paper to fill in. She was young, and her nails were polished a frosty rose. She buzzed the principal's office, and in a minute Sister Olga swished out in her black and white habit, her rosary clicking against the metal door frame.

Sister Olga had a freckled, moon-shaped face. She smiled, and glanced at my excuse when I handed it to her. Then she bent over the desk and signed it with a felt-tipped pen.

"You're a senior, aren't you?" she asked.

"Yes, Sister."

"The seniors are meeting in the Little Theater this morning—and every Friday at this hour from now on."

"Yes, Sister."

She handed me the tardy slip. "One of our older sisters, from the Mother House in Wisconsin, is visiting us for a few months. She'll be giving lectures on music."

"Yes, Sister." I folded the paper in my hand. "Thank you, Sister."

I felt dismayed as I walked back down the hall to the Little Theater. It was one thing to appear late in my small religion class, which met first hour, and was taught by a friendly, overweight sister who liked to interrupt her theology with personal stories about her girlhood in Kansas City. But it was quite another thing to open the door of the Little Theater, where the whole senior class was assembled, and face a stranger. Still, the sisters who taught at this school were pleasant and modern in their views. I expected that I could slip unnoticed into a back row seat. A few months ago, in my old school, I could not have done it. I would have hidden in the lavatory. But I felt I had changed. I was much less timid now, and could even talk animatedly to the other girls in my classes—I was not always pretending to read in homeroom.

The back of the Little Theater was dim when I opened the door. The aisle slanted steeply down past bolted rows of red and yellow and blue chairs. I heard the rustle of the other girls craning around to see who I was. I kept my eyes lowered, but managed to spot an empty seat down on the left. I moved toward it, trying to appear casual.

"Young lady? Young lady, stop right where you are!"

The voice calling up to me was so sharp and querulous that a great wave of heat washed across my face. I was stunned. I could hear the girls around me holding in their breath.

"What do you think you are doing?"

I looked in the direction of the voice. The stage lights fell in a circle, illuminating a tall sister who stood at the podium, just below the rim of the stage itself. She wore the huge, old-fashioned headdress which all the other sisters of this order had abandoned.

"I asked you a question, young lady!"

I felt betrayed. I held out my slip of paper and struggled for words. "I have a tardy slip, please, Sister."

"You have what?"

"A tardy slip," I repeated.

"And do you think that excuses you? I was talking, and you interrupted me. You opened that door. I was talking about one of the most beautiful pieces of music in the world, and you came in late!" Her voice rose. She raised her right hand and shook her index finger wildly in the air.

"Sister, I'm sorry." The skin around my lips began to tingle. I had always expected this kind of attack in my old school, but I suddenly realized how much I had lowered my guard in the last few months. I felt faint with humiliation, but at the same time I knew that the salty lump in my throat was caused as much by anger as by tears.

"Sit down!"

"Yes, Sister."

"And if you ever interrupt me again—if any of you girls ever interrupt me again when I'm talking about art and beauty—I will deal with you personally, after school."

I sat down as quickly as possible. The girl beside me, who had long, straight hair that she must have ironed carefully every morning, raised her pale eyebrows discreetly and shook her head in the direction of the podium. I felt immediately comforted. I reached up to wipe the sweat off my forehead, but the same girl leaned toward me warningly.

"Don't touch your face," she hissed.

"What?"

She was unable to answer, for the sister at the podium was staring in our direction. I dropped my hands to my lap.

"Now I want you girls to listen to this music with pure souls," the tall sister said, her voice lower and calmer. At first I thought her white face was fuzzy, but looking at her more closely, I realized that her skin was only heavily wrinkled—her face, in the frame of her pleated wimple, looked like a drawing by Picasso. She extended her arms on either side of her body. "I don't want you to have any erotic thoughts when you listen to this music. It's beautiful music. Nijinsky was sorry afterwards for the evil way he danced. He was a pure man, a good man, but sometimes he was tormented. He always asked for forgiveness. We were close friends. Perhaps I'll tell you more about him sometime. But now I want you to listen to this beautiful music by Debussy."

She turned to a record player with fold-out speakers on the edge of the stage behind her, and touched the switch very quickly, as if she were afraid of it. A record dropped to the turntable and in a minute the haunting notes filled the Little Theater. The sister kept her back to us, and watched the record spin around as attentively as if it were a whole orchestra of musicians.

I took advantage of the music: "Are we going to be tested on this?"

The girl next to me shrugged. She shifted in her chair so that her mouth was close to my ear. "Her name's Sister Ursula. She says if you touch your face, you'll touch anything."

"What do you mean, touch your face?"

"Sex." The girl stifled a giggle. "She means sex."

Next Friday, we seniors were reminded over the P.A. system that we were to assemble in the Little Theater for another music lecture. It had begun to snow outside, and I was reluctant to leave my desk by the window. I could have sat there watching the flakes all day.

Sister Ursula was waiting for us at the podium, her arms folded. She watched us file silently to our seats. The room was chilly and damp, as if the registers, which were beginning to blow dry heat from the ceiling, had only just now been turned on. I rubbed my cold hands together, then tried to stick them up the sleeves of my brown uniform jacket. I thought I could see the shadow of the snow on the skylight above my head.

For a long time Sister Ursula only stared at us—she seemed to be looking us over row by row and face by face. I heard embarrassed coughs and nervous stirrings all around me. I kept my eyes focused at a point above Sister Ursula's headdress, hoping she did not remember me from last week. I had deliberately changed the part in my hair this morning.

My friend, Andrea, who sat beside me, scrunched down in her chair. Behind her hand she whispered: "I wish she'd get started."

"Me, too."

"She's spooky, isn't she?"

I nodded. Sister Ursula reminded me of the sisters who had terrified me in my old school—the Latin teacher, of course, and Sister Mary St. David, who measured our skirt lengths and rummaged through our purses, and the principal, Sister Vincent de Paul, who had once pinched my arm for breaking line to get a drink of water. I felt annoyed that I should be confronted with a specter from my gloomy, depressing past just as I was feeling comfortable in this brighter and more modern world.

"What man," Sister Ursula asked in a loud voice, "is the greatest dancer in the world?"

We looked uneasily at each other. Finally a thin girl with blond, greasy bangs raised her hand.

Sister Ursula nodded at her. "Stand when you answer."

The girl stood up. "Nijinsky was the greatest dancer, Sister."

"What do you mean—was?" Sister Ursula gripped the podium with both hands. She began to rock it back and forth.

The girl swallowed. "I mean—I think he's dead."

"Dead!" Sister Ursula shouted. "Of course he's not dead. Where did you get such an idea?"

"I don't know," the girl whispered, her neck and face coloring brightly. "I thought I read it somewhere."

"Sit down. Don't you ever answer a question with misinformation."

The girl sat down. I realized that the muscles in my stomach were clenched as tightly as if I myself had been Sister Ursula's victim.

"Now Nijinsky, of course, loved Stravinsky's music. One day he tried to explain how the 'Firebird' reminded him of God—we were walking together in Paris. I remember it was raining, and his hair was soaked." Sister Ursula shook her head. "But he was so happy—he didn't notice. He looked like an angel. Later we went to Mass together."

Sister Ursula went on to talk about bassoons and oboes and descending chords, gesturing with her claw-like hands. I knew nothing about music. I had never heard of Nijinsky or Stravinsky or the other people that Sister Ursula kept talking about. I looked up at the skylight, hoping that the snow was still falling. I had no boots with me, but if it continued to fall all day it would nevertheless be a pleasure to feel the cold lumps in the arch of my shoe as I walked through the drifts. I began to hum Christmas carols in my head. I think I almost fell asleep, for I was startled by the first notes of the strange music which Sister Ursula suddenly began to play. But she switched the record off abruptly after a minute. She came a few steps up the center aisle and stood looming over the red-haired girl who sat at the end of my row, resting her chin on her hands.

"What are you doing?" she hissed.

The girl gasped. "Sister?"

"What are you doing with your hands?"

"Nothing, Sister."

"Nothing? What do you mean, nothing? Take your hands away from your face, do you hear?"

"Sister, I wasn't doing—I was just leaning—" the girl's voice shook. She pressed both her freckled hands against her chest.

"You don't understand yet, do you?" Sister Ursula softened her voice. She let out a sigh. She looked around at the rest of us. "Never touch your faces, girls. Never. It's a terrible habit. If you touch your face, if you play with your bangs, rub your nose, if you even rest your chin on your fist no matter how innocently—someone watching you knows what it means."

We stared at her blankly and uneasily. Andrea was pinching the hem of her plaid skirt convulsively between her thumb and index finger, and the girl on the other side of me had splayed her fingers rigidly across both knees.

The snow fell slowly but steadily for the rest of the day. Hour to hour and class to class I watched it stick and finally thicken on the brown grass. Then it began to cover the sidewalks, and during Art, my last class, I could hear the clank of the janitor's shovel around the corner of the building. I kept looking up from the piece of wood I was sanding to check on the flakes: they kept coming down in eddying but satisfactory gusts. The Art teacher, a young sister with strong hands and a bad complexion, kept breaking out into bits of song as she went from table to table checking on our work. In my old school we had done nothing in Art except drawing exercises and still lifes, but in this class we were always working with power tools, pouring cement into molds, folding paper, breaking colored glass with hammers and twisting copper wire into shapes.

"You can go ahead with your first coat of stain," Sister Melissa said, bending over my shoulders.

But by the time I got my newspapers spread, my brush cleaned, and waited my turn for the can, the bell had rung.

"Shall I wait until Monday?" I asked.

"It shouldn't take you more than ten minutes," Sister Melissa laughed. "Artists don't work by the hour, you know."

I spread the reddish stain rather hastily across my piece of wood. The other girls in the class were rolling up their newspapers and gathering their books. My strokes were uneven and a hair from the brush stuck to the wood. I picked it off with my finger and left an ugly streak. I brushed over the wood again, trying to keep my strokes smooth. But I was impatient to get out in the snow.

At last I finished staining the edges and propped my piece of wood against the wall to dry. I was all alone in the Art room. Even Sister Melissa had disappeared. I pressed the lid back onto the can of stain, but as I gathered up my newspapers I knocked over the plastic cup holding the camel's hair brushes, scattering them across the floor. I got down on my hands and knees.

"What are you doing!" a familiar voice shouted at me. "Get up at once!"

I looked back over my shoulder. Sister Ursula stood in the middle of the Art room, her hands on her hips. She seemed very tall from my position on the floor. Her brown eyes shone under her heavily drooping lids. Her skin had the texture of a boiled potato.

"I'm picking up these brushes, Sister," I said, trying to keep my voice steady.

"Get up! You look like a dog down on all fours like that—what a shameful way to use your body."

I got slowly to my feet.

"Clumsy," she said, watching me. "Why are you so clumsy? And what terrible posture."

I stood facing Sister Ursula, my face burning. The windows behind her were steamed up now, and I couldn't tell whether it was snowing or not.

"Touch your toes!"

"What, Sister?"

I stared at her headdress, with its elaborate pleats. Up close the linen seemed yellow—or it may have been the light. All day the story about Nijinsky's madness and death had been passed from senior to senior, for the girl Sister Ursula had humiliated had looked him up in the encyclopedia.

"Why are you standing there? Touch your toes," she repeated. "And don't crook your knees."

I leaned over and let my arms dangle. I felt frightened and light-headed. The muscles behind my knees strained sharply.

"Go on!"

I straightened up. "I can't, Sister. I'm too stiff."

"Stiff! You're a child."

"I can't do it, Sister."

She must have caught the note of hysteria in my voice, for she cocked her head and moved back a step. Suddenly she leaned over and with heavy, panting breaths began to touch the floor with the palms of her hands. She did it over and over. I stood watching her in horror. Her veil flew up over her headdress so that I saw its stiff underpinning. Each time she rose up, her face was redder and more congested than before. Finally she stopped and leaned against the blue cinder block wall, gasping for air.

"Are you all right, Sister?"

"Of course," she sputtered. She rearranged the front panel of her habit. "Just remember——" she began.

"Yes, Sister?"

"Just remember——" She took one final, deep breath, then seemed to recover, although her face was still a deep pink. "Just remember that when you dance, when you walk, when you move even a finger—you are praising God."

"Yes, Sister."

"When Nijinsky danced, he danced for God." She lowered her voice almost to a whisper. "He used to come to my room and dance. That was before I took my vows, you understand?"

I nodded. My whole face felt numb. I wanted to run past her but my books and folders were on the radiator across the room, and I needed them to do my homework that weekend.

"Right before my boat sailed," Sister Ursula went on, "he came to see me at the hotel. He begged me not to leave. I had to throw myself on the ground in front of my crucifix—I couldn't bear to look at him. He wanted to dance for me one more time but I was afraid to watch—

I had dedicated myself to God, you see, just as he had dedicated himself—" She broke off with a sigh. Then her eyes seemed to focus on me more sharply. "Why are you so fidgety?"

"I have to catch a bus," I said quickly.

She looked at me sternly. "Then go. And keep your hair clean—you should be ashamed to let it get so oily."

I gathered up my books, my eyes stinging with unshed tears. Sister Ursula's last remark—since I had washed my hair only yesterday—caused me to mutter and blink my eyes in anger all the way home on the bus. I hardly noticed the snow. I kept going over the scene in my head—refusing, in many bitter phrases, to touch my toes. I told her over and over that Nijinsky was dead.

On Saturday I went tobogganing with Andrea. The sky was a deep and perfect blue; the snow seemed whiter than any snow I remembered. The sharp, cold air filling my lungs as we sped down the hill in the park was exhilarating; but each time, as Andrea steered us away from Minnehaha Creek, and we slid to a halt under the spruce trees where the ground was bumpy, I felt depressed. I could not keep the thought of Sister Ursula out of my mind, no matter how I tried. I was especially perplexed by the contrast between my dark uneasiness and the cheerfulness of everything around me—the glowing faces, the red and blue knit scarves, the laughter, and the flying mist of snow which rose up from under the speeding toboggans.

My fingers moved stiffly inside my mittens by the time we began to pull the toboggan home. We took the short cut around Lake Nokomis, kicking up smooth, untrodden snow. My toes felt swollen in my boots even though I was wearing two pairs of socks. Nothing remained of the sun but a cold pink glow in the west.

"Why are they letting her do this to us?" I asked Andrea.

"Are you talking about that crazy nun again?" Her voice was muffled in her scarf. "If you're afraid she'll recognize you next Friday, cut class."

"And what about the Friday after? Anyway," I said, looking out at the gray lake which was beginning to thicken and freeze around the edges. "It's not just me. It's all of us. Do we have to sit there and be humiliated? Do we have to put up with all her weird ideas—next she'll tell us that Lincoln is still alive!"

"Ignore her, then." Andrea pointed to a shed which two men in red earmuffs were hammering together on the shore of the lake opposite the bridge. "Look! They're putting up the warming house—we'll be able to skate pretty soon."

"That's right where the woman drowned last summer, isn't it?"

"You have a morbid mind," Andrea said, jerking the rope on the toboggan so that it bumped across the sidewalk which circled the lake.

A wind was blowing across the snow. Andrea's words depressed me even more. I had been part of the crowd which watched the divers dredge the lake. I had seen the woman—who had committed suicide—brought up, and although she was wrapped immediately in plastic, I had glimpsed her heel, shriveled and gray as my own when I stayed too long in the bathtub.

I decided to speak to the principal about Sister Ursula Monday morning. I knew it was partly cowardice—I wanted to cover myself in the event that Sister Ursula singled me out again—but it was also partly benevolence, I told myself. The other seniors had never experienced these erratic and unpredictable outbursts from a teacher. There was no reason they should have to put up with the ugly and terrifying behavior that had finally given me—in Andrea's words—"a morbid mind." It also occurred to me that the other sisters on the staff had no way of knowing what was going on in the Little Theater on Friday mornings.

I was given an appointment to see Sister Olga during my afternoon study hour. I was tormented by the delay, for I knew from experience that my power to act diminished with reflection. I imagined the cold stare that would replace Sister Olga's friendly glance when I dared to criticize another sister. She would hate me for the rest of the year.

I could hardly swallow my bologna sandwich in the cafeteria. I sat by myself at a table by the window. The temperature had risen, and the dead grass was beginning to show in patches through the melting snow, which was by now heavily trodden and gray. I tried to invent another reason for wanting to see Sister Olga, but only half-heartedly. I knew I was doomed to go through with my idea. I had been deformed by the sisters at my old school—there was no other way of viewing it. I knew I hadn't been born with this morbid and gloomy vision. But years of submission to ridiculous whims had turned me into an unsmiling outcast—I looked at the groups of relaxed and normal girls at the tables around me with envy and despair.

At two o'clock I presented myself to the secretary. My face was already flaming with embarrassment, and my mouth felt dry. I was told to go into Sister Olga's office. She sat in a swivel chair behind her large, uncluttered desk. A metal crucifix with a burnished silver Christ hung behind her on the yellow cinder block wall. The wall behind the canvas Captain's chair, where Sister Olga gestured for me to sit, was covered with a huge pastel painting of indeterminate shapes—clouds or flower petals or waves.

"You're new this year, aren't you?" Sister Olga said. She nodded at me encouragingly. "What can I do for you?"

I swallowed. "I want to talk about—" My voice cracked. My lips felt so numb I could hardly move them.

Sister Olga stopped smiling. She leaned forward across her desk. Her eyes were intensely blue. "Don't be nervous," she said. "Anything you say to me will be held in the strictest confidence."

"Yes, Sister," I said.

"Are you having trouble with one of your classes, is that it?"

"No, Sister—not exactly, Sister. It's about Sister Ursula," I blurted out.

"Ah!" She blinked. She leaned back in her chair, folding her arms. "Go on. I think I know what you're going to say."

"She says if we touch our faces, it means we're evil—we're thinking about sex. She frightens people—she yells at us for no reason." I felt my voice warming, for the expression on Sister Olga's face was one of concern, not anger. "She thinks that Nijinsky—he was a famous ballet dancer—is still alive. But he died in 1950. She says she used to know him."

Sister Olga sighed. "Let me explain to you about Sister Ursula. I'd rather you didn't repeat this to any of the other girls, but since you've come to see me, I think it's only fair that I explain." She looked at me shrewdly. "You think Sister Ursula's crazy, don't you—because she thinks Nijinsky is alive?"

"I don't know, Sister," I murmured.

She shook her head. Her heavy nylon veil rustled against her round collar. "A very small part of our order has always been cloistered, you see. But we've agreed—in consultation with the Bishop—that the cloister is not a valid response to the modern world. Anyway, no one entering our order has made that choice for years. Mother Superior has decided that we should bring our few cloistered sisters back into the world. We plan to put their secular abilities to use—Sister Ursula, we knew, had been composing hymns for years—so we brought her here to lecture to you girls on music." Sister Olga picked up a pencil from her desk and began to roll it absently between her fingers. "You *are* learning about music, aren't you?"

"Oh, yes, Sister," I said quickly.

"Sister Ursula has not seen a newspaper or magazine since she took her vows—she's not uninformed about history, of course—the wars, the presidents, the new Pope, that sort of thing—but she only knows what she's been told. And since no one ever guessed that she was interested in Nijinsky—" Sister Olga coughed discreetly. "We've just told her. She seemed to take it calmly. We showed her the article in the encyclopedia."

I leaned back in my chair, beginning to feel relaxed. "Was she a dancer? Did she used to live in Paris?"

Sister Olga shrugged. "We know nothing about her except what she herself tells us. There weren't any files kept on girls who entered the convent before the First World War. We don't even know her exact age—she seems to have forgotten. Now as for the other part of your complaint—" Sister Olga laughed. "When I was a girl we were warned about patent leather shoes."

"My mother told me about that," I said.

"Sister Ursula has very old-fashioned notions about decency." Sister Olga stood up, her rosary clicking. "But you get the Church's modern view in your Family and Marriage class, don't you."

I nodded vigorously.

"Just relax and be a little understanding. Sister Ursula doesn't have advanced views about the behavior of young women—but you shouldn't let her upset you." Sister Olga moved across to the door, and stood holding the knob.

I rose to go. "Thank you, Sister. I feel much better."

"Good. I'm glad to get those cobwebs out of your head. I'd rather you didn't gossip about poor Sister Ursula, however—we're trying to make her adjustment to the modern world as easy as possible."

"I won't say a word to anyone," I promised.

Sister Olga opened the door for me. I heard the clatter of the typewriter as I passed the secretary's desk, but I was suddenly so lightheaded and buoyant that I could hardly see ahead of me. The bell rang for the change of classes. I was caught up in the stream of brown-uniformed girls moving down the main hallway.

The Little Theater was empty on Friday when we filed in for our music lecture. Andrea found a seat beside me. She blew her nose into a pink tissue, then rolled the tissue into a ball. "Are you scared?" she asked.

"Not any more."

"Good." She stuffed her tissue into her torn jacket pocket. "She's just a crazy old nun."

"I don't think she's crazy," I said carefully. "She's just old. I feel sorry for her."

The side door near the stage opened, and Sister Ursula entered. We all quieted and coughed and cleared our throats. The movie screen had been rolled down, and Sister Ursula's headdress made a fantastic shadow against the white as she passed in front of it.

She stopped at the podium. She stretched out her arms and gripped it tightly. Her face once again seemed fuzzy to me—I decided that the eerie paleness of her skin was due to her many years in the cloister.

"She doesn't have any eyebrows," Andrea whispered.

"They're white. You just can't see them," I whispered back.

"Girls," Sister Ursula said sharply, "I have an apology to make to one of you." She turned her head slowly from side to side. "Where is the girl who told me that Nijinsky was dead?"

We looked around at each other. Finally someone said, "She's not here today, Sister."

Sister Ursula bowed her head. Her chin seemed to fold into the stiff cloth of her wimple. When she looked up again, she was squinting. The skin beneath her eyes appeared swollen.

"Then let me," she said, her voice cracking, "apologize to the rest of you instead. That girl was right. Nijinsky is dead. Nijinsky is dead," she repeated. "It's written down, so it must be true." She paused and looked blankly around as if she did not know where she was. "And he was mad—all those years he was mad."

I saw the curly head of the girl in the row ahead of me nodding in agreement.

"Let me tell you something," Sister Ursula went on, her voice stronger than before but still hollow and directed more at herself than at us. "I never had a vocation."

Again she paused. She seemed to be shivering and I leaned forward nervously. I was afraid she might have a stroke. Sister Olga had said that she took the news of Nijinsky's death calmly, but she did not look calm now. Beside me, Andrea reached down for her Spanish book. Out of the corner of my eye I saw her surreptitiously open it on her lap.

"I didn't go into the convent because I wanted to serve God. I went into the convent because I thought I was going mad myself. You see, I was never happy, girls. Never! Never in my whole life—I was born with an iron band around my heart, I think. There are weights in the tips of my fingers."

Sister Ursula extended her arm in front of her, trying to spread out her fingers which curled inward toward her palm. I could not take my eyes away from her face. It no longer seemed fuzzy to me. I could see every line in her skin and below it the pulsations of her muscles.

She brought her arm slowly back to her side. "And what about the wings on my shoulders?" she asked. "Can you see them?"

I heard someone snickering behind me, but most of the girls whose faces I could see had their eyes rigidly downcast.

"Can any one of you see my black wings?" she asked again. "Of course not. That's why I went into the convent—to hide them under my habit. At night, when I'm sleeping, the wings close over my body. I have the most evil dreams about Nijinsky. I've tried to live a holy life, but it's no use—when I'm writing my hymns, the evil wings brush the paper—I write horrible things."

I found I was gripping the metal armrests until my fingers ached. I glanced desperately at Andrea, but she was hunched over her book, mouthing Spanish words to herself. No one in the whole room seemed to be looking directly at Sister Ursula. Every girl I saw when I turned my head was slumped down in her seat as far as possible, horrified or embarrassed. I was the only one up on the edge of my chair. I tried to shut my eyes, but they opened of their own accord. I fought hard against the idea that was growing in the back of my mind: I had more in common with Sister Ursula than with anyone else in my new school.

Sister Ursula groaned loudly. "What have I done? I've frightened all of you, haven't I? But I only meant to apologize, I only meant to make you understand—oh, I'm wretched, wretched!"

She buried her face in her hands.

Queen Wintergreen

(1992)

ALICE FULTON

Margaret Merns was on her knees in the front yard, picking dandelions for wine, when she spotted a snowy mystery on the ground. Jarvis Fitzgerald's sight was surer than her own. Yet she had to call his attention to the crumpled whiteness. Jarvis picked it up and settled spectacles on his face. Although the temperature was over eighty at seven A.M., he wore his best heavy coat with no tatters at the cuffs and a vest smooth as a new sail. There must be some high fussing on him to send him into his holiday clothes, she thought. I suppose he thinks we're keeping company. But it must be a brother and sister state of affairs at our age. He curled the wire spectacles like tiny ram's horns around his ears and read the white circular aloud: "Americans who believe in the demands of Ireland that they be allowed to govern themselves will hold a meeting the night of July 1, 1919, at St. Comin's Hall."

Peg Merns didn't listen. He is here again, as he is every morning, she thought. He is here, reading to me with the vast gaze in his granite blue eyes. Since the girls in her hamlet weren't sent to school, she'd never learned to read. Was it just three years since her husband Michael had read to her the accounts of the Irish and the Strangers?

Although she was tired of the Troubles, she would have liked to read on her own about the girls of the city fighting shoulder to shoulder with the boys.

Jarvis braced his feet apart like a horse in rough country as he concluded, ". . . so cognizant of their rights, and so determined to remain what God made them—a distinct and independent nation." He folded the flier and put down the sack he'd been holding for her. "Except for the shoes on your feet, you could be a pilgrim circling the stone beds of St. Patrick's Purgatory," he said. "Get yourself up from the dirt, and we'll have a word."

Her straightening was hampered by the arthritis, the shingles and the bee buzz in her head. These days she had no pluck in her limbs to walk without a hard blackthorn stick. The heat weighed like a basket of wet seaweed on her back. Peg Merns had never lived far from water. First the sea, so full of itself; now the state waterway calm and contained as a pint of bitter behind their house. Addled, she'd lately mistaken this canal for Irish water.

"Dandelion wine, is it?" Jarvis said, steadying her elbow.

"I'll hold in big esteem the man that gets a great country to take the pledge."

She knew the tale of the king who had another head darned with blond wool inside his skull. All her life she'd felt there was another, arguing head sewn within her own. And lately she'd begun to see glowing stitches on the outside of things. There was a wreath of rubbery shimmer around each yellow flower, and Port Schuyler, New York, had taken on the cloud colors of Ireland. America, once so brashly bright, was getting dim as a chapel.

They sat on the stoop. Peg separated the roots from the greens in her apron, and Jarvis began to fill his pipe. "On my soul, if it's not good to yourself you are," she said. He hesitated. "The appearance of desire is on your face. Go on, put fire to your pipe." But he planked it down on the step. At this hour the kitchen was full of her son's family launching themselves on another day of dust. It hadn't rained in over a month. With so many bodies inside, the house would be close and hot. And her son's wife, Dolly, had nerves. Still, Peg felt sorry for Jarvis, who had no people. She could well imagine his rented room with its cracked shaving mug and yellowed brush, the pictures of Thomas Ashe and the heroes of 1916 on the walls.

"I'd say come in, but the children would be in a hundred pieces around us," she told him.

"How are you this Saturday morning, Peg Merns?" he said, and he wasn't one for pleasantries. She had sized him up as a direct man with no mischief in him. Straight as the hands on a clock.

"Ailing I am, and wasting. It's a grief to be old."

"And a sorrow." He glanced at her. "But you've still got a fine physique. Will you be at the freedom meeting tonight?" He gestured with the circular.

"Oh, it's the Cause you've come for, is it?" There's little taste of Gaelic in his language, she thought. If I said some, he wouldn't know but it was Latin I spoke.

Jarvis hooked a thumb in each lapel. "I have more than the one Cause today. But every Irishman wants her to remain a distinct and independent nation. This notice is signed by the men and the Fathers. I know you'll take an interest in their manly and dignified stand."

She secretly believed that Ireland was a bad-luck country, where people were sent to dine on rocks and hope. As a girl she'd looked at the messy stone fences full of voids and thought they should turn the place into a tombstone quarry. She'd stood on the point to watch the ships coming home in a lather, the ghost of a mountain in every wave.

"I wish them well, indeed I do. But a woman isn't welcome when the talk is of the Troubles. A woman has no vote nor did she ever."

She watched a rivulet of sweat run down his neck, which was long and clean as a gander's. He laced his fingers together over his vest. "Now, Peg, if women got the vote the Blessed Mother would blush."

"It's only a man who'd think that Mary Mother of Sorrows would care at all about such a thing after losing the idol of her heart." There was a spark on his small finger. A diamond pinkie ring. Holiday clothes! Isn't that the spit for the venison and the deer not yet killed, thought the head inside her own.

"If Irish freedom don't interest you, there's another wonder in town you'll want to see. The flying boat is coming. It gave an exhibition and raced with a train, and tonight it stops in the water." He fiddled with his watch chain. "Will you come along with me to see it?"

A flying boat! exclaimed the royal voice inside. What would such a thing resemble at the departing of day for night? Would it have the two sails set and a nice following wind? Would it have wings? " 'Come along,' he says to a woman with the gait of a three-legged horse, the third leg being a cane," she said.

"Then let me be the fourth," Jarvis said. There was a small gap in his smile so you could tell it was not store-bought. She was reminded of the spaces her son Tom, a train conductor, punched in tickets. Jarvis took the flat cap off his head and revolved it in his hands. She'd wondered whether he had hair underneath, but there it was, calm as carded wool. "Peg, we understand each other. You're a bold woman, and I like that. As for myself, I don't spit or wipe my mouth on my sleeve. It would be an honor and a pleasure—"

"Not to come before you in your speech, but can I fetch you a cup of cold milk? I'm sure that's what you're after asking."

Jarvis paused. His collar had dug a ring into his neck, and he touched the red brand. "Like I said, you're a woman full of sport, and I get a fit on my heart when I think of you." He tapped his toe on each word. "It would be an honor and a pleasure if you'd consider this an offer of matrimony. I've been meaning this while back to ask you."

Thank the Lord for faces to cover what you felt, though it caper behind the smile or frown, she thought. A vain bit of her warmed to think of Jarvis's words. It was a triumph to be proposed to at the age of sixty-five by a man not given to drinking or fisticuffs, neither God-beset nor from a family of soupers—those who'd turned in their religion for broth during the famine years—a man, what's more, without the ring-worm or the twitch, neither a brute nor a murderer. A fine physique, he'd said. He must be touched in the head to want me, she thought and thought, I'll not have him anyway. Don't be a gloat, she told her tri-umphant self and felt shamed in advance at the scandal. The scorn of the world her wedding would bring upon her family! And she wasn't about to give up her pleasures. She had a clay pipe to smoke on the sly and no wish to serve a husband like a Christ on earth. A wife must sit to the side of the fire and let her husband warm his vamps in front. She could still hear her children cry "Oh, Ma, Daddy is coming and Katey has taken his newspaper!" In the pinch times, she'd said she'd already eaten so Michael could have his plenty. He had passed away a year ago.

"I'm not the one to hold a man to a rash word. To think of a wed-ding at our age! Wouldn't that be the grand occasion—with none to hand me over but my own son and the neighbors lined up to laugh on either side. No, I had the one good man, and one is all I'll have. I'll lay it down flat. Even if I were an airy girl again I'd not be the one for you who wants a female mild as turnip water. Have sense," she told him.

He knocked the fresh tobacco from his pipe. "You misjudge me, Peg. A man alone is a great pity, but a wife is company. I'll pray you change your mind."

In a pig's rump I will, said the voice in her skull's vault. "Then pray to Saint Jude who loves a lost cause," she said aloud. A long straying on you, said the voice, as Jarvis Fitzgerald, a fine, well-standing figure of a man got smaller in her sight.

She stood toiling with her hair before the little mirror in her room, sick to her soul of the body: the constant caring for it and its constant complaints. The shingles illness stung like a bodice of briars. Soon she'd get soft in the head, and they'd have to lead her on a leash to the state home. A fine physique. Well, what did he know. In the long ago she'd stood tall as a guarding goat. She'd had hair the yellow of Indian meal. Now it is as the psalm says, she thought, "My moisture is turned into the drought of summer." She'd pulled down the shades to make a cool night season. Her room was a welter of feathery doilies, china figurines, and patterned fabrics. She had three clocks, counting her lavaliere watch, and each told a different hour. There was a small fireplace of marble, its hearth blocked by a piece of green tin. Scapulars hung from the lamp, and you had to walk a slim path around the iron bed to get somewhere. On the dresser she kept an altar to the Virgin, a jar of pennies for the Missions, and a heap of bone jewelry. She stood toiling with her hair, remembering the long-ago when the sea bashed the cliffs by the cottage where they'd lived.

She was born in 1854, six years after the famine. She'd heard tales of that time—the people living on barnacles and nettles, the coffin ships sent out with sacred medals and holy water fastened to their prows. Her father swore he'd never trust Ireland to feed them again. She'd gone into service under an English gentlewoman when she was fourteen. Behind the diamond windows of the rich she'd learned there was nothing worse than being under the hand of other people. And she'd learned about the secret yearnings of men. She attributed the worse vices to the English. As a domestic she'd learned that the jerky walk and glandular madness of certain old men stemmed from their wild ways as boys. Some of them believed that if they sinned with a virgin they'd be cured. Her employer's second cousin had come into her room one night, and she'd poured the washbowl's water over his head. The next morning she gave her notice. By that time she was sixteen, and her father had saved enough money for the trip to America. They piled their belongings behind them in the wagon, and Peg turned to fix the West country in her head. She saw a woman walking with a load of brushwood on her back like a pair of raveling wings. In the distance, the ashen water and a figure sitting on the sea wall with her head in her hands.

In her day, girls were raised to be pure and not transgress. Then, my sorrow! she thought, some learned all the mortifications of the saints at their husband's hands. Not that Jarvis would expect wifely duties of that kind. He was as godly as De Valera. She knew he'd not tamper with her. Like herself, he'd believe the act was for procreation—or sin. Still she didn't want his flannel breeches on her bedside chair, his skin next to her sleeping skin, a crescent of hair oil on her pillows, a bedful of tobacco sweat. Her own smell of camphor and wintergreen was a place to live. Not once had Michael told her to belt up or had a rod onto her. He was a gent. On their wedding night he had dropped to his knees and prayed before entering the high iron frame and coarse sheets. That first time she was reminded of a visit from the dentist: the screech along the nerves and the duty to open against your deepest instinct. She had no good words but the Irish for the body and what happened in the marriage bed. Gaelic was more direct, less soiled than English. A month before a niece gave birth, the young woman had asked Peg where the baby would come out, and Peg hadn't the words to make her much the wiser.

And the things she knew how to tell in English wouldn't have comforted the girl. Many a strong tough woman I've seen laid low in the anguish, bellowing to Mary, and some never came to themselves again, she thought. Wasn't God far from the words of their roaring! In some houses, the men sat round the fire nice and chatty wondering why didn't the woman stir herself and pass the babe in a mad rush, getting the release from her task. Or a husband would run in and cry, Oh, God be with us stop, his blood shaking from the sound. Her Michael had always gone to his brother's house when her time came, which suited Peg nicely. She'd put a tea towel between her teeth, so her courage might be firm as Queen Maeve's of long ago. It wasn't the pain down in the bowels but the fiery needle of no heed sewing through your spine that put the amazement on you. Each time was different except for her thinking this time I'm at the end of my soul! This time I'll be cliff grass when it's over! Now some women were more nicely formed. But for her the family way meant the toothache, the leg cramps, the vomiting, the dropsy and the jaundice. One infant was born yellow, and Peg's hands swelled fat as cream crocks, so she could hardly haul water from the well to wash the baby's clothes. She'd had three girls and three boys. Once the doctor had used instruments to pull from her a dead child, black and blue, her skin peeling off in places. Only the baby's fingers had their natural color. They said that once you touched a dead person you wouldn't have any loneliness in you. But stroking that sweet and goodly girl had put the solitude of the world in her. And then Joseph had died at two—of empyema, the doctor said.

Well, she had always feared God and done her duty. Now she had four grandchildren, each more afraid of her than the other, all of them too shy to give sharp ear to her marvels. And that is a shame, she thought, for it is as the psalm says, "My tongue is the pen of a ready writer." A woman didn't tell hero stories, after all, only ghost stories. Hers were so potent the children ran when they saw her coming, though she gave them Mary Janes and more at Christmas.

"I hear you had a visitor this morning," her son Tom said from the doorway. He was in his suspenders and rolled-up shirt-sleeves. Peg stopped sorting her baubles into groups on the bed and began knitting to put the appearance of work upon her. "A gentleman caller."

"You wouldn't mean Jarvis Fitzgerald." Tom's Dolly must have been listening from the kitchen. Peg could imagine her picking with her ears by the window, her hair in rags around her Temperance Lady face, to hear what Jarvis had to say. Dolly has the spite in her nose for me; she'd give me the ropes side of the house if she had her way, thought the head inside Peg's head.

"Is that who it was?" Tom sat himself down on the spread. He was her pet son, a boy of fun and tricks. It was years since she had seen him clearly. She remembered him dressed finely on his days off, his hat at an angle. And there were spokes of blue and gray in his glance, which she had memorized. His eyes had rays in them like a dartboard's. Even as a child he wouldn't flinch when things hit him. No matter how hot the day, Tom Merns would assure you the breeze would soon be in from the river, people said. People said he'd stake his last dollar against the sun's setting. And she couldn't deny his liking for a wager. But those people hadn't heard his fine wide laugh. She thought he looked always as if he should have an accordion strapped to his chest, so ready for happiness he was. It wasn't true either that he was bone-lazy. He worked as a train conductor five days a week, but she'd seen his Dolly place a quarter of a pound of butter out for tea, squandering his pay. And didn't she, his mother, eat out of his pocket, pushing him to the poorhouse with every bite?

"What did you and Mr. Fitzgerald discuss, might I ask?" Tom said. He toyed with a coral necklace, staring idly into nothing. Then he removed a small pad of paper from his pocket.

"Home rule." Her eyes fell on a garnet ring given her by Michael.

"Ah. And I heard he touched on matters of the heart. I heard he asked you to be his lady wife." Tom scribbled on the pad. Toting up his bill with the turf accountant, she thought.

"At his great age he'll be wanting a lady nurse. You'd have to buy a pair of wheelbarrows to roll us to the altar. That would be a sweet sight for the parish, indeed. But I'll not shame your father's memory with such talk."

He smiled. "What's wrong with old Fitz? The man has no vices that I know of. And he's here every morning, so don't say you don't like his company."

"Would you have your own mother marry a stranger? You get the award."

"He couldn't be more of a stranger than Dad was when you married. You'd only known him a day, remember?"

"God rest him." She kissed the crucifix she wore on a chain, thinking we were a made match. When I die, will the dust praise him? "And what are you composing as we speak?" she asked.

"Young Michael has a touch of the croup. I'm just reminding myself to buy mustard for a plaster. But to return to our subject, Mr. Fitzgerald is a decent, God-fearing citizen. Well-spoken, too." Tom grinned, and put the pad away. Jarvis was famous for his earnest sermons on political matters.

"His talk is like a peat fire. Lovely at first, but it chokes you after a while. Your father and I were as close as the Shannon and the Suck."

"Jarvis is a widower himself, isn't he?"

"So he's not of a queer nature," she conceded. "Oh, he's a good enough creature. But I'd sooner walk naked through the streets than take a husband at my age." Here she'd been thinking how ashamed they'd be to have her marry, yet it seemed the very thing Tom wanted. And why wouldn't he? Didn't he have the full of the house of croupy children, and she and Dolly in each other's haircombs all day?

"Wasn't he married to Mary Hurlehey?" Tom asked. His hands flew over the tobacco he was rolling. He didn't once look down.

"Now there was a ramblin' rose. He might as well have put a roof of stone on a house of thatch." If she left, they'd have room for the children, and she wouldn't be pushing in on them. But she'd be on the shift for shelter, living like a tink in the weather unless she married. And if she stayed, she'd have to hide in her room or have on her conscience the spoiling of a home.

"I just wanted to point out that a man has his pride." He picked up the garnet ring and studied it. "If you offend him he'll be without a wife forever before he'll have you. You're a stubborn woman, but don't be too hasty in saying no to a fair offer."

"Your father said, 'Peg, I might as well argue with the wind that strokes the water as with yourself.' A rare man he was!"

Tom sighed and rose to leave. Then he hesitated. "What's that noise? Hear it? In the chimney?"

"The chirping and scratching? I heard it but was afraid to say aught in case it was the imagination of the ears."

"It sounds as if some animal's caught there. I don't see how it got in with the flue sealed."

"The flue sealed, is it! This morning after Jarvis left I was down to the canal with a sack like a picaroon. Didn't I trap a seagull and put it up the chimney because yourself said it needed cleaning and so we couldn't use it. Last winter I wished for a good blaze." There hadn't been a fire in the hearth since she and Michael were young.

Tom's broad face furrowed in a scowl. "Oh, Ma, you didn't! Jesus, Mary and Joseph! Have you taken leave of your senses? How did you ever sneak the bird past Dolly?" He continued, greatly stirred, saying he would buy her a stove if she felt chilly. And how could she remember winter on a ninety-degree day? At last he left to get the long-handled broom. She would put her hair in a snood, take her shawl and go to Edward McWilliams's wake. Then Tom's family could have the house to themselves for a while. How wearisome it must be to live with an old woman who brought livestock in the building. She was shaking with humiliation. Hadn't she raised Tom from a tiny mite only to find the back of his hand given her now? He had said Jarvis was proud. She knew the Fitzgeralds had been the most spoken-of family in Western Ireland. Even during the famine they'd had a budgetful of yellow gold and sauce with their potatoes. "Well, he's cold poor now," she said aloud. Though he thought he'd be a mouthful in this country, he'd never advanced beyond foreman at the mill. As for those who whispered of a fortune hidden in his house, let them try to live on whispers. His lady wife! As if she'd be rich and wear white stockings. She'd planned on having safe moorings here for the rest of her life.

But when a person thinks it's nice 'tis how it's a mocking trick, she thought, overcome with self-pity.

Tom hurried in with his stern face on. "A seagull! You'd sell your shawl rather than do anything the normal way." He opened the flue and pushed the straw end of the broom up the chimney. The beating stopped, and his face cleared. "I think it's gone. Are you going to see the hydroairplane? I hear it's docked in the canal."

"I am not." She selected an earring from the trinkets on the spread and held it out to him. "Would you be giving this to your Dolly from myself? It's lost its mate, but it'll make a lovely brooch."

Edward McWilliams was stretched in the front parlor with eleven lit candles at his head and feet. The twelfth candle went unlit to stand for Judas. A lamp glowed red in the corner of the room, and the air hung thick as a blanket of flowers. People stood around chatting or sat in rows before the casket, waiting for the lovely young priest to say a prayer. None of the women could do enough for the young Father. They at least would stay until he spoke. Jarvis was there, looking ill at ease since the afternoon mourners were mostly female. Peg waited until he stood alone, then went over.

"Did you know Edward McWilliams well?" he asked.

"Not at all," she admitted.

"Then why are you here to pay respects?"

"They say death makes your praying more sincere," she said with a flick of her shawl. Putting her hand to her mouth she added, "I heard it was the cancer killed him. But whisper! I have a recipe for that." She had to get someone to write down her cancer cure before she cleared off.

"I heard his last words were 'Show me the mercy you'd show a beast and shoot me,'" Jarvis whispered back.

"He was a great dramatist then, was he?"

"The despair runs in that family," he told her. "They're from the

West Country, you know. His father died after leaping in a holy well, may they be safe where it's told."

"They say a holy death is a happy death," she noted piously.

"But to die without penance, or anointing rites, without the Host!" Jarvis sighed. "And didn't he change his mind after the leap and come up with the moss in his hair. And Jim Boyle, staggering home on a toot, shot him for the anti-Christ."

"It is short until we join him on high," she said sweetly.

"There's nothing but a while in this life for anyone," Jarvis agreed. After a bit he added, "I've heard that heaven's a yard and a half above the height of a man."

"Wouldn't that be the way of it," she said. "To be just out of reach." The subqueen in her mind wondered why people feared death if death meant entering forever to bright welcomes from your darling dear ones. But she held her tongue.

"I was after coming to inquire for you tonight. I don't suppose you've considered the story I opened this morning?"

So he'd still want her, though she poured a hundred discouragements on his head! "I have," she said.

"Well, let it to me, woman. Has your answer changed?"

"It has." She wouldn't dig her heels in any longer.

Jarvis brightened. "Then the matter is right. God never failed the patient heart."

"Patient, is it? It's been all of the eight hours since you honored me with your attentions, my good gentleman."

"You're right, Peg," he said. "It's well late for us to be patient." She would have to do for him for the rest of his life. The thought made her want to flee the fuzzy, red-lit room. Talking with Jarvis was like trying to sit still on a prickly horsehair couch, she thought.

She went home and told them right before supper. Then, entering the little room off the kitchen where they ate, she saw that Tom's Dolly had set out enough cutlery for courses. And a fruitcake left from

Christmas, jeweled with candied fruit like a dark crown, sat on the sideboard. They had to eat in shifts or suffer bruised elbows at the table. Usually she took a tray of tea to her room, but tonight Tom insisted she join them. The babies would eat in the parlor. But when Tom's Dolly placed a chop before her she found she had no edge on her teeth. "I thought you were partial to lamb," Dolly chided.

"I'll have a tomato with a whiff of sugar on it. I have the liking of the world for that," she said.

"Why didn't you invite Jarvis over to see his new home?" Tom asked.

"When a woman marries she goes to her husband," Peg said. She thought of Jarvis's rented room, the hunks of sun falling through its windows and herself perishing with the heat. What wouldn't she give for a hole of her own! A steady hut on a stump of land out of the water, an old boat turned upside down as hens would live in.

"Nonsense!" said Tom. "You have to stay here with your family, with all of your things."

"You really must live with us, Mother," Dolly added. "This was your house before we moved in."

Why is it my nose would bleed if I met her without warning in the dark, Peg thought. You can't hate a woman because she has no complexion on her. Isn't it that when I sit with her for thirty minutes I feel I've been dead and buried that full half hour? How it must distress Tom, the two women raking each other! But what if she'd been wrong, and her son had no grudge against her living here? There was still no going against the promise she'd made Jarvis. And she'd never bring a husband into their crowded lot, another someone to bump into on the backstairs.

Later, as her room grew dark, Tom came up with a bottle he'd stashed before Prohibition became law. "What if herself finds out you've been drinking?" Peg asked. "She'll Carry Nation you for a week."

"A man has a right to celebrate his mother's wedding."

They had a glass and laid into talk with each other. Peg said a psalm that went, "The king's daughter is all glorious within: her clothing is of wrought gold," having learned it by heart from her mother. And Tom told her of the great events he'd read in the evening's paper. Does it not seem Tom would like me to stay, she thought.

"It's much I admire those people whose lives would make books you'd need two hands to lift," she told him. It would be grand to do one bold, soul-gambling deed before she died. But a wedding! The ancient bride and groom hobnobbing with the gossiping guests . . . that was never it. Who would dance on the table to "The Hard Summer"? Then to live with Jarvis Fitzgerald's worryings until the end day of her life. And wouldn't he seem the wisp in place of the brush whenever she thought of Michael? "It's close in here. I'm thinking I need a breath of air. I won't be long," she said.

It was a dusky nine o'clock by then, and the evening was made dimmer by her fading eyes. She walked along the towpath near the canal until she saw a new shape near the opposite shore. Was this the flying thing? She moved closer to the water to get a better look. It was moored next to a grove of gas lamps and hallowed by their churchly yellow glow. The canal was tall and dark as a priest's gown; the Northern locks must be open wide, she thought. It was a perfect night: calm and desolate. Since there was no one to see, she sat down on the bank, dangling her feet over the darkness like a girl. She let one foot, then the other, dip into the water, brogues and all. It was the first cool she'd felt in weeks. She set down her cane, and slid forward a bit so that the waves reached up her shins, wetting the dense black lisle of her stockings. She'd never understood why a person was urged to pray for the souls of the faithful departed. The subqueen inside said to pray for the unfaithful: tinker, hawker, gypsy, Protestant and Jew. Oh my God, I am heartfully sorry, she said, easing herself into the state waterway, which at first felt coldly foreign, then as her skirts turned to fetters, warmer, more familiar.

excerpt from

At Weddings and Wakes

(1992)

ALICE MCDERMOTT

Once or twice each winter they would climb into the family car and retrace in full daylight the route that usually brought them home. It would be Thanksgiving and Christmas when it happened twice in one winter. Christmas only those years that their father, calling them their own little family, insisted they eat their turkey alone. (Giving his children in those years the oddest of holidays, what with the television on all day despite his attempts to interest them in checkers or pick-up sticks, games they played only in their rented cabins in the summer, and with all their neighborhood friends gone to grandmothers in Brooklyn or Queens or Jersey; with the strangeness of changing into Sunday clothes at three o'clock in the afternoon to eat a quiet dinner in the dining room with their tight-lipped mother and their weary father, who seemed ready by then to admit that the strife and mournfulness of Momma's table lent some texture to the day, after all. That the strife and mournfulness had become, after all, the personal, the familial mark his family made on the general celebration.)

From the three passenger windows the children would watch the winter trees fall away and the buildings slowly rise against the lowering colorless sky. Now, as they entered the labyrinth of city streets and elevated subway tracks, they saw the stores and the buildings and the people in full daylight, so that they began to feel, watching carefully, that they had peeled back the swarming darkness and had glimpsed, at last, the pale underside of what they could now see was this tattered place. Newspapers and broken paper cartons wheeled across the curbs and the holiday silence, the stores with their heavy steel shutters, the empty parking lots, the few stunned people in the street with their coats flapping around them, all added to the sense that what the daylight revealed was puny and empty, a refutation of what had been the night's illusion. A subway rattled overhead but its sound was weaker than it had been in the darkness, more short-lived, perhaps because they imagined it to be empty. At a stoplight they noticed a small church, squeezed into a row of stores and named by a handful of cramped words that stretched across its entire face on a white handwritten sign. Its single stained-glass window was broken in one corner and repaired with cardboard. Its door was closed and barred. As were the doors of all the shops and the windows and doors of every apartment house. In one of these they saw the branches of a Christmas tree pressed into a pale curtain behind a pane of glass as if the rooms beyond had lacked the space to accommodate it. Under the shadow of the El, in what seemed a concentration of the pale beige light that filled the deserted city, a man pawed at a trash can, lifting and sorting. Two more men in worn gray coats stood at another corner, their hands deep in their pockets. They talked together, shifting their feet, moving their shoulders, laughing, arguing, who could tell? But unaware, certainly, of the miracle that had taken place sometime past midnight, of the way the day had been transformed. A woman in a short coat with cold bare stockinged legs ran along the sidewalk in black high heels. A swag of greenery had come down from a storefront and lay unclaimed at the edge of a curb, a single strand of red plastic ribbon rising and falling above it.

Earlier, on the highway, they had glanced into the cars on either side of them and seen families like themselves, girls and women in fur collars and hats, boys and men in dark Sunday coats, some with bright presents piled in their back windows, but now they felt that they alone had gotten the good news of the miraculous birth and they sensed vaguely that their new clothes and the shopping bags of wrapped gifts put them at some risk here in this empty, colorless, tattered place—at some risk of being proven mistaken: it had not happened. The angels had not sung last night in the black winter sky and Santa (although only the younger girl still truly believed in him) had not filled their stockings. The morning they had just lived, from the cold living room at dawn with its surprise (despite all their confident expectations, always a surprise) of presents and toys, of all hope realized, to the sweet breakfast in the tiny kitchen and the joyous, overcrowded Mass, had not happened, could not have happened, given the bleak light of this cold, deserted, dirty place.

"There's the prison," their brother said on those Christmas mornings they took this particular route to Momma's street, and the three children felt the cold that must have whistled through the bars. Felt, looking at the long, square tiles of pale turquoise that ran up the building's side, like the tiles in a subway station, in dirty public bathrooms, that this was the punishment, then: to be banned forever to a public place, to know nothing else but its barrenness and chill.

Following this, following the empty street and the prison, the rattle of the empty trains and the bone-colored light of the city, Momma's place, on this day, was a warm redemption; a confirmation, a restoration, of all that the day had begun with and had, in their spirits at least, been in danger of losing.

Aunt May opened the door on which Aunt Agnes had hung a small gold wreath and there, moored to the barren world below by the length of brown stairs and the narrow, skylit landing, was the living room transformed. Before the boarded fireplace, where the coffee table had last stood, a white tree strung with small soft pink lights and shining pink beads, hung with pink Christmas balls of a dozen different sizes that caught the shine of the lights and the glint of the small metallic beads and their faces in round distortion as they stood closer to take it all in. The rest of the room was dim and the apartment smelled sweet and warm from days of baking. The children's presents were piled in three neat groups at the foot of the tree; their parents' gifts and the presents for each of their aunts were on the large green armchair, behind which Aunt Agnes had placed her Victrola—taken from her room for just this one day. The sounds of Christmas in these rooms moored above the city's silence were the Vienna Boys' Choir and the rat-tat-tat of Momma's pressure cooker and, while she lived, Aunt May's soft and breathy voice admiring their Christmas clothes, their packages, the pink lights in their eyes.

It might have been a different place entirely in these first few minutes, a place they had never visited before. The dining-room table was pulled to its full extent and covered with a pure-white cloth and set with the white-and-green Belleek and the rainbow-lit Waterford that were used only on Christmas and Easter. The heavy silverware was the same that they used at every dinner, but its polish was so high that it, too, seemed transformed. Momma was in the kitchen. There was powder on her cool soft cheek when they kissed her and the surprise of pale lipstick, the ruffle of white lace at her throat. It was she, on this day, who poured their Cokes, one inch in each glass, although Aunt May smiled wildly at them from the kitchen doorway as they took their first sip. On the server in the dining room there were cut-glass bowls full of green olives and celery stalks and tiny sweet gherkins, and Aunt May let the children choose from these before she carried them into the living room, where Aunt Agnes in black silk pajamas or a green velvet dress or, once, a quilted satin skirt that touched the floor was reaching to turn on another light, where—oh yes, it might have been another place entirely, another world moored some four stories above that barren, loveless one—their parents sat side by side on the wide horsehair couch, holding hands.

"Turn around," Aunt Agnes would say to the girls in their holiday dresses and then always declare before she had given them what they considered sufficient praise, "Oh, but he is always impeccable," as she accepted their brother's kiss. There was holly along the mantel behind the white tree, holly in a tall white vase on the cocktail cart. Sitting on the dark carpet they would study the piles of presents they knew they could not touch, trying to determine which pile was whose and what it might contain, while their father and Aunt Agnes discussed the stock market or the company or something the President had said, and Aunt May, on a dining-room chair beside their mother, fretted over them (Are you all right on the floor? Is there a draft? Are you children hungry?) and then, in another year, leaned to whisper something to her sister just as the downstairs buzzer rang and without a word she stood, touched her hair, and went out to meet him.

He was larger in his dark suit and overcoat, and his big, gloveless hands were reddened by the cold. He had taken the subway from Queens. As they'd heard him crossing the outside landing their mother and father and aunt had stood and hurriedly told the three children to get up and brush out their clothes and so what first greeted him when he entered the room were their three solemn faces and it seemed to be them he meant when he said, first off, "Ah, this is Christmas itself."

He, too, carried a shopping bag of gifts and he placed it beside the couch as he shook hands with their mother and their father, saying, How do you do, and received such a tender, Merry Christmas, Fred, from Aunt Agnes that the children as well as their parents glanced at her quickly and in so doing recognized the claim she had made on this day. Most mornings of the year she might leave the apartment at seven and head for her office in Manhattan, or on weekends at noon for her concerts and matinees there, without a thought for the life of the place once she was gone from it. But this day was hers, as were the white tree and the holly and the stiff, glimmering bows of old rose that had been placed on top of every picture frame.

"Momma's in the kitchen," she said softly, directing them because the lovely, transformed day was hers, and Aunt May said, "Oh, yes, let me take you in" (as if, it seemed to the children, the apartment on this new day had expanded, the kitchen grown some distance from where they stood). "I'll just put down your hat and coat."

She hurried into Momma's bedroom with his coat on her arm, and in that second's pause after she'd gone, he looked at the children and smiled and winked.

All of them were still standing. "I imagine the trains were pretty empty this morning," their mother said, and the mailman rubbed his hands and shook his head. "Well, no," he said. "You'd be surprised."

"But isn't it brisk today?" Aunt Agnes offered, moving to the cocktail cart between the rooms, her long, elegant hands made whiter still by the thick black silk of her sleeves. "You should have something to warm you up." She paused, her arms held gracefully. "Bob," she said, "will you do the honors?"

Their father moved quickly toward her, both men seemed like children under her cool and gentle gaze. "Certainly," he said. "Ladies, what will it be?" Just as Aunt May returned from the bedroom and—would the day never cease to amaze and delight them?—easily took the mailman's arm. He began to walk forward with her and then paused and bent down to his bag of gifts, taking a long, thin box from the top. Handkerchiefs, even the children knew it, for Momma.

"Manhattans, please," Aunt Agnes said, answering for them all.

At dinner the mailman's face was flushed again and he praised every morsel of the meal, remarking again and again how many years had passed since he'd had creamed onions such as these, sage dressing, mashed potatoes so light and giblet gravy as rich as this; since he'd had buttermilk biscuits—"Not since the last batch my own mother made, God rest her soul"—as if, the children thought, he'd been in prison or exile. As if he'd been keeping track, year after year, of what he'd been deprived of.

Their father liked him. They could tell by his own red cheek and his bright eyes as he carved the turkey, by the way he joked with the three of them, winking at the girls as he transferred the meat to their plates, and joked even with their aunts and Momma ("Mrs. Towne") as he piled their own plates high. The two men had discovered before dinner that they'd seen many of the same cities during the war and so there was that to give them their pleasure in each other, and, another discovery, a mutual youthful infatuation with basketball and crystal radios. There was the sense too, the children understood, that their father at last had someone from the outside to see him among these difficult women, someone who might see, as he sometimes asked his children to, what he was up against here. He spoke over the women's heads as he stood again to carve second helpings and his buoyancy seemed to include his anticipation of all future commiseration with this man, as well as his awareness of his own expertise, his experience. It would not be long before he would have the pleasure of telling him: I know these gals. Believe me.

"And how about you, Fred?" he asked from across the table that held all the women in his life. "What can I get for you?" And it might have been this buoyancy, this unaccustomed camaraderie in their father's voice that made the children notice, suddenly, and for the first time, how striking was the family resemblance between their mother and her sisters and even Momma. There was an unaccustomed stillness about them with Fred here, and because of this, too, the children looked up from their own plates to see that the women had the same coloring under the bright light of the small chandelier, the same high white foreheads and arched brows and, beneath their eyes, the same pale, washed delicate skin, so that their father's confidence suddenly struck them as mistaken, even foolish. Of course he didn't know them, who could know them, marked as they were, each identically, by all they had lived.

"Oh, a little of this and a little of that," Fred told him, passing the thin dish. He couldn't count how many years it had been since he'd had a Christmas dinner such as this.

Aunt Agnes put her knife on the edge of her plate and crossed her fork into her right hand. She placed her left hand on her lap and leaned forward ever so slightly. "And how long ago was it?" she asked. "That you lost your mother."

"It will be six years on April the second," he said, taking the plate again and nodding a thank you. He shifted a little in his seat, placed his elbow on the tablecloth and then slipped it off as he spoke. "She died on Good Friday."

"That's a blessed day to die," their mother said, but the mailman, accepting more turnips, shook his head. "I'd hoped she'd last to Easter." He looked around the table. This might have been something he'd never before revealed. "Past the mourning," he said, and apparently fearing they would think he meant morning, added, "The mournful part. Of Holy Week. The sad part. I'd thought it would be nice if she'd just once more lived through that."

She had been sick, it seemed, for a good while, perhaps ever since he'd returned from the war, but had only begun to fail noticeably in her last few years. She was an Irish girl, come here alone at nineteen, much like yourself, Mrs. Towne, and married to a big Swede who died when he, their only child, was nine. No one in this room (except, of course, for the little ones here, who should be grateful for their ignorance) needed to be told what a hard time it was for a widow with children to make a good living, but then the room itself and all the lovely women in it were testimony enough to the strength of character those young Irish girls had. She worked for a wonderful Jewish family on Central Park West and sent him to the Paulist Fathers. After school he'd go up the back elevator and sit in their kitchen with his homework until seven o'clock or so when he and his mother would make the trip together back to Queens. At seven the next morning they'd be back again. When he returned from overseas she was still with the same family, but he saw right away that the three years alone had taken their toll. It might have been the cancer just beginning—"I've heard its onset can sometimes take years"—it might have been the loneliness. A GI buddy (he nodded to their father as if he'd just named a mutual friend) told him to apply at the post office and when he got the job he said, "Okay, Mom, now I work for you." The Jewish family gave her one hundred dollars and took her to lunch at some fancy restaurant. You couldn't have asked for nicer people.

"And you're still in Queens?" Aunt Agnes said. She might have only heard rumor of the place.

"Still," he said and then added, "But not in the same apartment." He shook his head. "No," and then said no again, as if still resisting the notion. "I wouldn't stay in the same place once Mom was gone. It didn't make sense. I mean the building was fine and all, close to the subway, but I took another apartment two flights down. A smaller place." He held his empty fork in his hand and looked down at the plate of food and for an instant the children felt they recognized him from their own time on the subways. They had seen him there: a florid man riding alone, his eyes closed and his body absorbing every shock of the banging cars, every shift and lurching curve with such gentle, practiced resignation that for a moment they thought it was the subway he was referring to when he looked up again and smiled and, shrugging, told them, "I'm just not one to hang on."

"There's a young family in our place now," he added. "Cubans. Nice people. They still sometimes get our mail. We make a big joke about it, me being with the postal service and all."

"That would be Mr. Castro," Aunt May said softly. She was sitting beside him, their shoulders well apart, but her words seemed effectively to place her hand in his. They had had quiet conversations, she had learned the names of the people in his life. A blush rose under the gold rims of her glasses and the mailman, perhaps blushing too, turned to them all to say, "Yeah, Castro, wouldn't you know it? They invite me up there every Christmas, but"—he raised his hand and shook his head, some part of that old argument that made him say no, no—"I couldn't go in there again. Much as I've sometimes thought I'd like to. I was a boy there," and because it seemed he could not go on, Aunt May explained, "Fred's mother was very ill at the end. Very ill."

"Oh, sure," their father added, supporting his new ally. "That's cancer for you. It's a terrible disease."

But from her end of the table Momma said, "My husband died right outside this apartment door." She raised her finger and pointed toward the living room. "My sister, the mother of these girls, died in that far room." Her head trembled slightly as she spoke but when she nodded it was a firm, single nod and it seemed to show them all at once where their sympathy should lie. For even as he traveled back and forth, his schoolbooks in his lap and his mother's warm thigh beside his own, the earth was falling away beneath her feet.

"I didn't know," the mailman said. It was all she had left him to say. "Right here it was?" He shook his head and glanced at May. "That's part of a story I haven't heard," he said and in the moment's pause that followed it seemed someone might actually begin to tell it. But he added, "God bless you, Mrs. Towne, you've had your trouble," and Aunt Agnes lifted a cut-glass bowl of cranberries. "The children haven't had any of these," she said.

The rule was that only wrapping paper came off at Momma's apartment. They could peek inside the boxes or look to their hearts' content at the pictures on the lids but they could take nothing out for fear of lost parts, doll shoes or tiny dice, that Momma or any one of their aunts might step on or stumble over in the darkness that would follow their departure. The children understood the wisdom of this and though they objected to it annually they found, too, that it prolonged the pleasure of their anticipation. After dinner, while the women cleared the table and their father smoked a cigarette in the green armchair the children would study the pile of presents they had opened at the cocktail hour, peering through cellophane at the baby doll they could not yet hold or tracing with a finger (his mouth puffing out for soft, devastating explosions) the picture of a model battleship whose many and complex pieces he could not study until the next morning. It was like getting the gifts but not quite fully getting them, like having their longing for these toys remain temporarily undiminished by their receipt. As they stretched out on the floor around the white tree they were vaguely aware of the fact that Christmas was once again nearly past but for the time being there were their plans for these opened and yet untouched gifts to keep them from the full acknowledgment of the approaching end of the day.

In the chair above them their father slowly turned the pages of one of the dull magazines, smoking and lifting small pieces of tobacco from his tongue. On the Christmas Fred was there, both men smoked and talked softly about people they had known and the city as it had been when they were young, categorizing both the people and the place by parish names, Saint Vincent's and Saint Peter's, Holy Sacrament, Saint Joachim and Ann.

In the kitchen and the dining room cabinets slammed and pots rattled together, voices rose although they remained, especially on that Christmas that Fred was there, encased in a hard, crusty whisper. At some point Agnes or May or Veronica or their mother would stride silently through the living room and shut a door. At some point the children would catch the breathy sound of tears.

It was the same every year as whatever it was that had transformed the day now faced the long night and the prospect of tomorrow and the day after. As their father turned the pages of the dull magazines and the children rehearsed strategies for as yet unopened board games, the women seemed to pull the old grievances from kitchen drawers and rattling china cabinets, testing them, it seemed, against the day's peace and proving in this final hour that it had been a temporary and paltry and unreliable peace.

Aunt Agnes said she was not looking for gratitude. She had learned long ago never to look for gratitude. Veronica cried throatily, "Well, what about me?" And May once said fiercely, "All this is the past," seeming to indicate with the cutting, physical motion of her voice the five women in the dining room and their father with his cigarette and even the small children themselves stretched on their stomachs beneath the tree.

On the Christmas Fred was there Momma said from her chair, "If your own father doesn't deserve a mention I don't know what I can ask."

Watching their own wide faces in the distorted pink glass of the Christmas balls the children heard her say, "Forgotten, I suppose," and out of the well of silence that followed this pronouncement came the sniff of tears, the hushed pleas for peace and reconciliation. Still Christmas, someone said. Oh, Momma—they recognized their mother's voice. Aunt May was explaining something, softly, plead-ingly, but the silence that followed her voice spilled out into the living room and silenced the men as well. Even the children saw it was as their father had once described: Old Momma Towne giving her step-daughters a taste of the silence of the grave.

Christmas was passing and even before the merry fog of it had cleared they caught the stony shapes of Golgotha. The mournful part.

And then, in the day's last, limp miracle, the downstairs buzzer rang.

It would happen any time after dinner: while their father smoked and the women cleared the table, when they'd returned again to the dining room for pumpkin pie and coffee, peppermint ice cream and Christmas cookies, sometimes after even the dessert dishes had been cleared, but because he always arrived late in the day, after each of the day's long-anticipated events had passed and Christmas, the last Christmas Day for one long year, was finally used up, the children met him and his box of Fanny Farmer candy with more enthusiasm than they might have shown if the discovery of a chocolate-covered cherry was not the day's last joy.

Uncle John was tall and broad with dark hair and dark eyes and white, white skin that seemed to shine as if it was pulled too tautly under the persistent stubble of his beard. He said, "How are you, sis?" to each of the four sisters, and "Hiya, Momma, dear," to the old woman, and then added each year, "I'd kiss you, but I'd hate for you to get this cold."

He would present the box of candy to Momma in her chair and then Aunt Agnes would stand, disregarding whatever argument he had interrupted in much the same way she might snub an old friend, and ask, "What can I get for you, John?"

Every Christmas he would say, "Just a little ginger ale, sis, please," although even the children understood—by the hushed pause between her question and his answer, by the general sense of relief that would accompany Aunt Agnes to the cocktail cart—that a more difficult, more troublesome reply was always possible, and remained a possibility for next year as well, even as he accepted his tumbler and raised it to say Merry Christmas.

His sisters and his mother watched him drink, their anger and their tears and even, on the Christmas Fred was there, that stony silence of the grave suspended now on what seemed the delicate promise of his sobriety. He was a handsome man but handsome in such a broad, exaggerated way that the children found him comical. His eyes were dark and his thick eyebrows bristled and his black hair waved across the top of his head. He had broad cheeks and thin red lips and a strong square jaw and it was part of everything they knew that girls had swooned over him when he was young; girls his own age and younger and girls as old as each of his four sisters.

He had a wife and a family in Staten Island but as far as the children knew he always appeared here alone and for just this single hour of the year.

If they were still at the table a place would be cleared for him, a cup of tea offered and accepted, a piece of pumpkin pie. On the Christmas Fred was there Aunt May merely said, "Johnny, this is Mr. Castle," and the two men shook hands, their uncle showing no more surprise or interest than he might have shown had the mailman been as familiar as everyone else in the room; or had everyone else in the room been as much a stranger.

Their father, even on that Christmas, retreated in their uncle's presence, sat back and stared out and said little more than what candy his daughter might choose if it was a cherry she was after from the box Momma had opened and passed around so proudly, passed around as if, he would say later, the reprobate had brought her pure gold.

But then he was her own baby boy. The son who had been curled in her stomach even as she crouched in the hallway just outside the apartment door and held in her arms her dead husband's bloody head. Her own son whose birth had held the three oldest girls in speechless terror that she, too, would die and then rewarded them not only with the return of the only living adult who gave them any value but a living baby doll as well, whose hair they curled and carriage they pushed, whose clothes they bought and washed and ironed right up until the time he made their girlfriends swoon and made Momma, sitting long into the night in the window seat of the bedroom she and Lucy shared, call out to the girls to go downstairs to help their brother up out of the street.

He was her own baby boy, her joy, more charming and more beautiful than she had ever dared imagine and it seemed it was her unchecked pride in him, her delirious mother love, her failure to acknowledge each time she touched his dark thick hair that if her sister had not died in giving birth to Veronica she never would have had him for her own, that invited disaster. By seventeen he was an incorrigible drunk. She threw him out for good when he was twenty-one.

And how is Arlene, Aunt Agnes would ask him at the Christmas table, her effort to return the very tail of this day to what it had been, to retain some elegant control, reminding the children themselves of the way they might gather up the chocolate crumbs on a cake plate and press them together with the prongs of their fork, trying to get some last flavor from what in its substance was long gone.

And did his children enjoy their Christmas?

He would eat his small piece of pie and drink his tea with a pinky raised. He had the arrested charm of a man who had discovered fairly young that given his looks a little personality went a long way. "Oh, she's fine," he said. "Oh yeah, sure, they had a great time."

Suspended above their heads was the argument or the tears he had interrupted. Suspended, too, was the memory of those late nights and early mornings when they had thrown their coats over their nightgowns and gone downstairs to peel him from the sidewalk or from the floor of the vestibule and work his dead weight step by step up four floors and across the moonlit or dawn-lit landing and onto the couch in the living room. Momma would be there in her robe, her long graying braid over her shoulder, and if he was conscious enough she would tell him, her steady voice growing louder and shriller with each word, that she was hardening her heart against him: hardening her heart against the time when she would refuse to spend the night waiting at the window, when she would simply lock the door and turn out the light and go to bed, because she had seen enough tragedy in these rooms, her darling sister cold dead and her husband gone before she'd reached him. She was hardening her heart so that she would never have to see him with that same gray pallor on his lovely face when they brought him home with his neck broken or his liver gone or his flesh frozen stiff in some alleyway. He was her own baby boy, her comfort in sorrow, her gift from the dead, and yet she would harden her heart against him to spare herself that. To spare herself the loss of her dearest joy.

All four girls would be weeping by the time she finished (and on more nights than one the downstairs neighbor pounding at the floor) and as he turned his handsome face into the pillow she would angrily send them back to bed and then, since she hadn't slept at all and couldn't afford to try at this hour, she would dress herself for work.

Watching from the bed they shared, Lucy, their mother, would see the fury in Momma's movements as she walked between the bureau and the dressing table or sat before her many broad reflections to pin up her hair, muttering to herself all the while, slamming brushes and drawers, and in the failing darkness she would see how the anger seemed to straighten Momma's spine and set firm her face, how it propelled her out of the room, into the living day. Lying alone on the high bed in the now quickly dispersing darkness, Lucy would see that, given the muddle of life, loss following as it did every gain, and death and disappointment so inevitable, anger was the only appropriate emotion; that for any human being with any sense, any memory or foresight, every breath taken should be tinged with outrage.

He said, sitting back, that work was as always although he wasn't traveling much, no farther than Jersey City this year. And his daughter had had her appendix out back in September, missed some school. Oh yeah, she was fine now, nothing to it. His black eyes were hooded by his salt-and-pepper brows and his mouth, like Momma's, was narrow, his lips thin.

Their mother asked if there were many people on the ferry tonight and he answered, "Not a soul," although you'd be surprised, he said, how busy the trains were. And on the Christmas he was there, Aunt May added that Fred had said just the same thing earlier in the day. The two men looked at each other then, recognizing that what they had in common was not the women at the table nor this warm room, but the cold dark public world they had emerged from and would, one within a half an hour of the other, rise to return to.

"Is that so?" Uncle John asked with a handsome man's license to feign halfhearted interest. He placed his teacup in its saucer and glanced at his watch. "Speaking of which," he said. He had not looked directly at the children since his arrival, would not, they realized, give them his full attention if they were set ablaze, but it was the children he addressed now, as if, spying them, he spied a back door through which he could safely make his escape. "I've got a reservation on the next ferry."

Momma, with papal dignity, did not move from her chair as he stood and, this time, bent to touch his lips to her cheek. He called her Momma dear again and only the older girl noticed how, when he touched her hand, her fingers curled up suddenly to meet his. And yet did not hold. He turned to his sisters, touching his cheek to theirs as well. He patted the children's heads and shook hands with the men and waved briefly from the dark street below when the children ran into Momma's bedroom to see which way he would go.

When they returned to the living room again, Aunt May and her mailman were still standing by the front door and their parents and Aunt Agnes had begun to bind up their presents with bakery string. Momma was still in her chair, a large white handkerchief in her hand now and her hand in her lap, her black eyes furious. The mailman was saying what a glorious Christmas it had been and wasn't it a shame that all good things must come to an end. When Aunt May brought him his coat and had thrown a sweater over her shoulders so she could walk him down he reached into his pocket and drew out three quarters for the children, although he had already given the girls silver bracelets and the boy a tortoiseshell penknife. He could not remember, he said, when he had last spent Christmas in the company of such fine children and so saying would have made a brilliant exit if he had not hesitated for a moment and leaned past May to call another good night to Mrs. Towne. Agnes froze in front of him and May took his arm and shook her head and their mother made the softest hushing sound, and suddenly confused the man looked up to see their father's shrug and frown: Now you see what I'm up against. He floundered for a puzzled minute and then, with May's help, it seemed, recovered and said again a less buoyant good night. The children listened for the sound of their footsteps on the stairs and saw in their minds' eye the silent two of them descending slowly, their faces lit from below by the single downstairs light. Their father had just lifted the last shopping bag of presents by the time she returned, and what with the children's wool hats and mufflers and buttoned coats there were only a few minutes for them to admire the gold ring with its single clear stone that Aunt May took from her finger and held out in her palm.

Outside, beneath the heavy wheels of their car, subways ran, brightly lit trains crowded with people, Fred the mailman among them, regretting the decision he had made six years ago in haste and sorrow, with no idea of what a miracle the future could be, to send his mother's wedding band to the foreign missions where it would help to form a chalice for some poor young priest. And somewhere on the water whose scent reached them just as the lights and the buildings had fallen away, Uncle John stood alone on the prow of the ferry, his collar upturned and the wind whipping his pants legs, off already on his year-long journey to Stat and nigh land (as the younger girl thought of it), where he had a wife and a family they had not met—not, their father was now saying into the darkness as he drove, because of all the torment John had put Momma through in his wild days, oh no. That was not what had so thoroughly hardened her heart. What had done it, what had made her mad as hell, he said, was that the bastard had stopped. "She feels the same way about God," he said as their mother chuckled and clucked her tongue and whispered again, "Imagine May married."

Suddenly the younger girl raised her head from her mother's breast and felt the coolness on her flushed cheek. She saw the dark back of her father's hair and then the silhouette of her brother's leather cap. She looked across her mother's coat to her sister as she leaned against the far window and then turned her head around and realized that from the window on her side she could see only small distant lights, single lights that could only mark desolate, uninhabited places. She sat up a little farther, moving with enough urgency to get her mother to shift and turn to her even before she said, "Was Aunt Veronica there?"

Her sister looked at her from over her shoulder. "Where?" their mother asked.

"Today," the girl said and she saw that her brother in the front seat had turned too, sharing her revelation. "She wasn't there."

Their father laughed and said, "She just noticed."

Their mother placed her black kid glove on the girl's cheek and then brought her back under her arm. "She was there," she said softly, "but she wasn't feeling well. She had a little virus. She was in her room."

The girls caught each other's eyes shining in the darkness. They hadn't even noticed. And it was clear from their brother's silence, from the way he dipped his profile and turned away from them and did not say, I can't believe you just realized that, that he had not noticed either. Had not noticed that the joyous day had proceeded entirely without Veronica and that, perhaps because of the joy itself, she had not been thought of, she had not been missed, not even by the younger girl, who had given her her loyalty.

But then, they would tell each other later, much later, as teenagers or adults, when had there ever been a Christmas or an Easter, a gathering of any sort, when one of them had not disappeared, retreated to a bedroom or crossed the outside hallway or torn off down the street (hadn't Aunt May once spent an entire evening on the fire escape?), just to prove what? That life would indeed go on without them, that they would have no part of the joy. Just to prove, perhaps, no matter that the children on that Christmas had well proved them to be wrong, that like the dead their presence would be all the more inescapable when they were gone.

Mary's Departure

(1993)

KATHLEEN FORD

*Dolly Bogs, Ballyconneely Bay,
County Galway, Ireland 1903.*

The slick gray stones poked out of the cliff like the polished claws of an animal. Below, the green Atlantic swirled and sent sprays of water into the air. The water could not reach Mary Flarity, who sat in her rocky alcove pondering her double pair of socks and her dead brother's boots. She would have examined the nits on a chicken if it would have postponed her return to the cottage where her mother waited.

Mary had discovered the stone crevice twelve years earlier, when she was seven. She'd come upon it after wandering away from a game of hide-and-seek she'd been playing with her brother. She still remembered how Sean had called to her from the rocks even higher up the hill. She had not answered, and when he'd left to search for her, she'd crept out of the shelter, looking again and again to make certain she was alone. She'd not told anyone about her place.

At ten, Mary kept a writing tablet on the stone ledge inside her alcove. Sitting under the slate roof, protected on three sides from the wind, she'd written about the water that swirled below and about the fishermen who'd defied it for centuries. Sometimes, by sliding forward, she could see activity on the shore. But often the men were too far away and there was no color to catch her eye. After keeping the diary for six months, Mary's book disappeared. Birds, Mary thought, or wind. She knew some creature or force had carried her words into the ocean; it did not occur to her that anyone had found her hideaway.

Mary leaned against the far wall and stretched her legs in front of her, dismissing her feet from further inspection. She held her head in her hands and, quite suddenly, began sobbing against the sound of the surf. She felt the warm tears trickling through her fingers and her throat ached. Mary focused on the pulse in her throat which was keeping time with the pulse behind her eyes. When her throat expanded, Mary imagined it was bleeding; when it contracted, she thought she might choke.

Mary's cries became louder and louder until even the crash of surf on rock was diminished. Finally, after sustaining the full volume of her cries for five minutes, Mary stopped. As she regulated her breathing, she realized there was no real pain in her heart or chest—there was no feeling of desolation either. "I didn't want him anyway," Mary said to the air. The wind pushed the words back in her face.

Dermott McMahon was not Mary's idea of a perfect bridegroom. Mary had never formulated any such notion, not that it would have mattered if she had. There was only Dermott—and now that he'd decided "to abide with me mother," he was no longer a possibility. The other bachelors in Dolly Bogs were over fifty years old or had about as much business getting married as Father Cregan. Among the bunch of them, there wasn't a barrelful of dirt they could call their own.

Mary smoothed her skirt, folding her hands on top of it. Her fingers were as red as the fuchsia which grew on the cliffs. Thick dirt-colored scabs had formed in the cuts beside her fingernails. A large burn, once as purple as Lenten cloths but now the color of freckles, sat like a coin between her thumb and first finger. Her hand had been burned two years ago when she'd reached into the fire to remove a potato. Nora, Mary's mother, had grabbed her daughter's hand and spit on it. And it was while comforting Mary that Nora first mentioned Dermott McMahon.

"There, there," Nora said, leading Mary to her bed beside the hearth. "I know it hurts." Nora seemed to be transfixed by her daughter's hands, looking first to one and then the other. Finally, she spoke again. "You're just a girl, but already your hands are getting old."

Mary looked into her mother's gray eyes. The eyelashes were pale and thin; Mary wondered if her own would look the same in forty years.

"You know Andrew McMahon has died," Nora said, taking a breath before continuing. "That will leave Dermott alone with his mother. It makes me think he'll be looking for a wife in the next year or two, Lord willing."

Nora rarely spoke of the McMahons, who lived on a large parcel of land on the other side of Clifton Stream. The McMahons were a reclusive lot. They left their grazing sheep only for Sunday Mass, and then it was usually through a blur that the other residents of Dolly Bogs saw them. Dermott had a way of whipping the donkey so it sped up just as he was passing a group of his neighbors.

"And what is that to me, Mother?" Mary had asked.

"Look at your own hands, girl, to answer that question. It would be a fine thing to have land to pass down to your sons—fine, too, not to struggle every day of your life. Just keep your eye out for Dermott, that's all I'll say. Keep your eye out. I believe Dermott is a great one for noticing the girls."

After Nora's instructions Mary kept her eyes on the back of

Dermott's head each Sunday morning. Her eyes followed him as he stood, sat, and knelt—followed as he allowed sinful thoughts to distract him from his weekly duty. Because Dermott was a head taller than his mother, it was easy to follow where he was looking. Dermott's eyes were always scanning the family groups in front of him. As Nora had said, Dermott's eyes did roam. First they'd light on Kathleen McBride in the second pew, then they'd go to Bridget Hogan in the fifth. By the time Father Cregan got to the *Lavabo*, Dermott's eyes were on Patsy O'Rourke in the seventh pew.

From her seat in the tenth row—two in front of the dark vestibule—Mary watched as Dermott's hair became grayer and grayer. She watched Will McMahon, Dermott's uncle, become too crippled to kneel. In two years time, Will's neck had become so stiff, his back so bent, that he could no longer look up; his only view was the top of his muddy shoes on the church floor.

Only Agnes McMahon, Dermott's mother, seemed to be thriving. Instead of shrinking, she grew taller. The week before Will died, the top of Mrs. McMahon's bony skull (which in church was always covered with a wool kerchief) had reached to her son's shoulder. But it wasn't just height she'd gained. Since Mary had been observing the McMahons, the old woman had become broader and stouter until she resembled one of her own hearty gray donkeys.

Plumpness was rare in women with grown children. "A sign of good health," Nora said, not too happily. The other old women of Dolly Bogs had become as wispy as candles; they were outweighed by twelve-year-old children.

After Will McMahon's funeral, Nora spoke to Mary again. "Andrew and Will McMahon—may they rest in peace—were not poor men. They were able to hold their land through thick and thin. And while they had their share of rocks and boulders, they always made a good living with their sheep. I've heard they have over a hundred head and I've no reason to doubt it."

Mary pictured the dumb animals always running and standing, running and standing. The McMahon sheep had always seemed dirtier than anyone else's. Twigs and clumps of mud dangled from their wool so their undersides always looked as if they were filled with teats.

"Mary, are you listening?" Nora asked.

Mary nodded, turning back to her mother.

"All the McMahon property went to Dermott when his father died. Now with the uncle gone to his eternal reward, Dermott will be feeling more alone. He'll be thinking about getting help to manage it. There's only Dermott and his mother. He'll surely be settling on a wife."

"I see," Mary said.

"You could be a woman with property. A landowner's wife."

The next Sunday Mary found a linen blouse on her bed. Lace as delicate as a spider's web decorated the collar and sleeves. Mary had never seen anything so beautiful.

"A young lady should have something fine," Nora said.

Mary had no idea where her mother had found such a luxury, let alone how she'd obtained it. Since Sean and Dada had died, the two women had sold eggs and repaired fishing nets, but the income from that was just enough to keep them alive. Still, it seemed to Mary that Mam had a secret well where she could go for money. Half a dozen times, Mary had seen money appear overnight in the tin which Mam kept over the hearth.

Mary did not ask how the blouse had arrived on her bed. She touched it lightly with her fingertips, then bent to smell its dry stiffness. When her mother wasn't watching, she ran her tongue over the fabric to feel the imprint of the weave. Although she had washed the night before, she removed the large metal tub from its peg. Without being asked, Nora heated the water and when Mary sat in the tub, her mother braided her daughter's hair. Instead of the usual braid which hung down Mary's back and was tight enough to make her eyes water, this braid left soft mounds of hair beside her face. Nora pinned it up to expose Mary's neck.

Nora brushed Mary's skirt, then removed mud from Mary's hand-me-down boots. When the two women set out for Holy Apostles Church, hardly a word had passed between them.

Mary could feel the wind at her neck. She pretended the sweater, which rested on her shoulders, was a shawl. Though she would want its warmth in the cold church, this day she would do without it. She would drop the sweater to the floor or let it fall onto the wooden pew behind her. She squeezed her arms across her thin chest, causing her shoulders to hunch and her blouse to stand out from her body. Mary peered down at her small breasts and breathed in the odor of soap. For an instant, she had a desire to take off the blouse and to kiss her own skin. She could kiss her shoulders and her arms; she could run her hands down the sides of her body, down her thighs and legs. It would be wonderful to twirl her feet, to massage her calves, to hook her thumbs on her prominent hip bones and strut through the fragrant field beside her.

Mary ended her reverie when she heard the clop of the McMahon donkey. "Stand aside," Nora whispered, "but don't hurry yourself." The women stepped into the muddy rut on the left as Dermott and Agnes McMahon passed. Walking the final quarter-mile to the church, Nora fell behind Mary, though she continued to instruct her. "Stand straight, Mary, the back of a woman is a lovely thing. I'll guarantee that today you won't see anyone you like better than yourself."

Dermott was standing beside his donkey as they approached. His mother had gone into the church. Nora too went directly into the church, but Mary nodded toward the donkey cart and then paused for a second. Dermott followed Mary into the church. In the damp vestibule, sensing Dermott was behind her, Mary lifted a tiny lock of unruly hair from the back of her neck. With a finger she managed to poke it back into the heavy braid. A second later, she removed her sweater. Next, she lingered at the holy water font. "His eyes are on my neck," Mary thought, as she reached down to brush a thistle off her skirt. Slowly, she walked to where her mother sat in the tenth pew. A second later Dermott entered the church to take his place beside Agnes.

As Father Cregan prayed for the dead, Mary thought of Dermott. His face was lined and the last two fingers on both hands were twisted with arthritis, but at thirty-eight he was still a young man. Nora said he'd get even better with age. "When the gray turns to white he'll be a fine figure of a man," Nora had said.

"Thy holy apostles and martyrs," Father Cregan prayed, "with John, Stephen, Matthias, Barnabas, Ignatius, Alexander, Marcellinus, Peter, Felicitas, Perpetua, Agatha, Lucy, Agnes, Cecilia, Anastasia, and all Thy saints; into whose company we implore Thee to admit us, not weighing our merits, but freely granting us pardon. Through Christ our Lord."

Mary knew Dermott would approach her after church let out, but she was not prepared for the directness of his question. "Would you walk with me this afternoon?" he'd asked. Mary had blushed deeply before agreeing.

In the months that followed, Dermott McMahon became as much a part of Mary's weekly routine as Wednesday's baking. He arrived at the house each Sunday at two. Nora greeted him, and together they stood silently on the path looking out to the sky. They exchanged a few words about the weather before Nora called to Mary, who then stepped through the threshold.

"You're off then," Nora would say, and Mary and Dermott would nod before beginning their walk.

Sometimes they'd turn east to the inland road where they could hear the stones crunch under their feet. If people were out in the road they'd have a chat. Occasionally, they'd walk as far as the wider road which ran into a still wider road that went to Galway. Usually, though, they'd go west to the ocean. They'd walk through small rocky pastures and patches of gorse; they'd walk onto rocky ledges and hills, always keeping their eyes on the changing sky which moved from gray to purple or from blue to black within minutes.

"A sky like nowhere else," Dermott would say when Mary looked to the heavens. "That's true," Mary would answer, but she'd wonder how Dermott could know such a thing. The McMahons, like the Flaritys, had never gone anywhere.

After they'd been walking out for a couple of months, Dermott began talking to Mary about his farm. He'd tell her how he was rethatching the barn or mending a wall. Often there were stories about his sheep—about cloven hooves caught in rocky vises, about lambs found dead after being born in the night. "They can't take the chill and I've got to find them before they die," Dermott said once, explaining that he didn't always know when the ewes would lamb. "I've got to check them through the night when their time has come."

Mary would listen intently, surprised by Dermott's feeling for his animals. On the day he told her a young ewe had died while lambing his voice actually shook. "A Suffolk she was. They don't usually have twins the first time so I only expected a single. Well, the second lamb was a breech and wouldn't come. I reached in to twist, but it just wouldn't come. They both died."

"The first lamb?" Mary asked.

"Too weak. I couldn't find another to take him."

Mary had twice seen shepherds pull slippery lambs from their mother's bodies but she couldn't imagine Dermott doing this. Her face turned red when she thought of it; quickly, she looked to the Atlantic, which was crashing noisily forty yards beneath where they sat.

Mary remembered the birth of Eileen O'Malley's first baby four years ago. Old Tabbie, the midwife, was down in Limerick with a grandniece when Eileen's time came. Mike O'Malley had come for Nora and Mary had gone too. While Nora and two other women looked between Eileen's legs, Mary had been told to get into bed with Eileen.

"Dampen her forehead," they'd said, but Mary hadn't been able to pry Eileen's hands from her own. "Don't leave me," Eileen screamed, holding tightly to Mary's fingers. By the time Mary had been able to substitute an iron crucifix for her hand, Eileen was screaming in her ear.

"I've got hold of you," Mary said over and over, pressing Eileen's shoulders. Mary had positioned herself behind Eileen with one leg on either side of her so it might have seemed that Mary herself was giving birth, only instead of a baby it was a grown woman being born—a grown woman screaming to the ceiling for all the saints to come and help her. When the baby, a boy, finally arrived, Mary was so stiff she could barely move from the bed. Eileen, who kept crying big gusty cries, had been cleaned and given the child.

Dermott's cough brought Mary back to the oceanside, but instead of the ocean all she could see was Dermott bent over the female animal. He was looking inside the ewe's body, to the silvery red blood and the long mucus strings that appeared before the lamb showed itself. Mary shuddered. "Thank God you have other animals," she said, just to have *something* to say.

"I have over a hundred and twenty sheep, but few as fine as that Suffolk."

Mary knew her mother would be very interested in having the number of McMahon sheep. Guessing and village gossip were no match for the words of the shepherd himself. Dermott took Mary's hand in his own. "I've told my mother you'd come for tea today," he said.

"I thank you very kindly," Mary said, wondering if Mrs. McMahon would be waiting by the door, ready to pounce on her when she entered.

Later, Mary thought she might have managed better if Agnes McMahon *had* pounced. Then, at least, Mary would have known to lie still in the way of a helpless animal in the grip of a vicious predator. As it was, Mary had to learn on her own not to enter into any argument with Agnes. She had to learn not to look directly into the old woman's face, because such glances were considered brazen. She had to understand that, in Agnes's words, "Those looks were the sign of brassy girls and hussies without shame."

But at the moment when Dermott first extended the invitation, Mary allowed the picture of Mrs. McMahon to fade. Instead, she thought of how happy Nora would be to learn that Dermott had finally invited her to tea. She thought how exciting it would be to announce her wedding engagement to the village and, someday soon, to hear Father Cregan read the banns of marriage on three consecutive Sundays.

Now, sitting in her rocky alcove, Mary was able to review the many teas she'd had with the McMahons. The review didn't take much effort because each Sunday afternoon was like the one before. Only today's visit, which Mary knew would be her last, had been different.

Each Sunday at five Dermott would lead Mary into his house. Agnes, sitting in a red velvet armchair beside the fire, would look up from her missal as if she were the most surprised woman in all of Ireland. "Why it's you, dear heart. And I see you've got Mary with you."

Mary hugged her knees against the black ocean wind. She did not doubt that Dermott's mother had been working against her, and that she would work against any girl who wanted to move into the McMahon house. Over the months Mary had watched the old woman protect her prerogatives. Never once, in all the Sundays Mary had been taking tea at the house, had Agnes let Mary pour from the china teapot—nor had she allowed Mary to pass the plates where her misshapen scones sat like rocks on a beach. "Dermott, we can't allow our company to serve us," Mrs. McMahon said whenever Mary was bold enough to look up and make this offer. "Sure, it's something you do in your own house, Mary, but here you are the guest."

"True enough," Mary thought, "and if you have your way a guest is all I'll ever be."

Instead of relaxing as time went on, Mary grew more and more anxious during the visits. On the day Mary tried to bring the conversation around to how much work there must be on such a fine large farm, Mrs. McMahon nearly spit in her cup with laughter. "Work?" she asked. "Who better could manage this place than me and my boy? We can hire on a man or two when it's shearing time, but we don't need to have them eating off our plates all the other times. No, dearie, I can assure you, extra help is not wanted."

Mary looked down to the plate on which the scones rested while the words "not wanted" rang in her ears.

Later, in front of her own fire, Mary had recounted the events to Nora. "She calls him 'boy' and 'dear heart,' " Mary said. Nora only nodded.

"Sure, and he'll always be her dear boy, make no mistake. It's Dermott you must bring round. He can't be dead to your charms."

"He isn't," Mary said. But she did not tell her mother how Dermott removed her hair from its braid so he could hold it to his face. She said nothing about how Dermott braided it himself, sitting at Mary's back so Mary couldn't see his face, but could only feel her long hairs catching on his callused hands—could only hear his breathing.

"This takes concentration," Dermott said once, when Mary asked what he was thinking. "I can't talk while I'm sifting through gold, now

can I?" Mary had kept her chin on her knee. She had not asked him to
speak again until this very day.

Today they'd been caught in a downpour just as they began their
walk. "Let's run to my house," Dermott said. Mary pulled her sweater
over her head and ran behind him, not looking to the green-black
clouds or to Dermott's back, which was bent into the wind. She'd
kept her eyes on the muddy road and tried to place her feet where
Dermott's had been seconds before. In this way, Mary had no gauge to
measure how far they'd gone nor how much farther they had to go.
When they'd tumbled onto the McMahon porch, all mucky and dripping, Mary had been so happy for the dryness she'd said what came
into her head without thinking.

"Wouldn't it be fine, Dermott, if this were my house too and we
could put our feet by the fire and pass the day without thinking of my getting back to my own house?" she'd asked. The moment the words were
spoken Mary knew she'd made a terrible error. Dermott's face became as
hard as the granite church. Mary, beginning to understand the full extent
of her blunder, might have apologized right away, but just then Dermott
put his head down and began unlacing his boots. A moment later, when
he unlaced Mary's boots, her apology died on her lips. Instead, she com-
pounded her mistake. "I mean, Dermott," she said, "it would be good to
marry now and have some wee ones before we're old."

Dermott couldn't get into the parlor fast enough. "Early because of
the weather," Mary heard him say to his mother.

"When the rain lessens, Mary," Mrs. McMahon said, "you should
be on your way."

Dermott had placed both pairs of boots side by side on the bricks
in front of the hearth. Seeing them that way—Dermott's large black
boots and her own smaller brown ones which had once belonged to

Sean—made Mary as sad as she'd ever been. "It's hardly worth drying them out," she said to no one. When Mary looked up, she'd seen Dermott and his mother in silent communion. Both had thin closed smiles on their faces.

A second later, Mrs. McMahon put what might well have been a curse on Mary and her family. "Mary," she said, "I hear that Patricia Kelly from over in Leenane is going to America. She'll be working for a fine family in New York."

Mary looked at the balding head of her enemy. She was beaten and she knew it. Tears as big as Christmas currants spilled down Mary's cheeks. "Good on her," Mary managed to say before letting loud sobs burst forth. Her shoulders shook with the full force of her body. Saliva ran from her mouth onto her blouse, but Mary couldn't stop. The crying, unlike the tears she'd shed when Sean died, felt good. She wanted to keep them going as long and as loud as she could.

"I have no idea," Dermott said to his mother when Mary was quiet long enough to hear.

"I'm sure," Mrs. McMahon replied.

When the storm, like Mary's crying, died from exhaustion, Mary put on her boots.

"I'll be abiding with me mother," Dermott said, unnecessarily, at Mary's gate. Mary let him go back to his mother before she ran to her hideaway.

Mary tied her damp sweater around her shoulders. Although the dark was coming fast, she was still able to pick her way along the stones. At the top of the hill she turned to look back to the water. It might have been a big hole rather than the sea. If it hadn't been for the spray that blew in her face and for the loud crashing noises that deafened her ears, Mary would have thought she was at the end of the world.

Nora sat close to the fire. A picture of the Sacred Heart was propped on the ledge above the fire, and beside it was a statue of the Blessed Mother. Nora still wore the dark blue serge dress she'd worn to church that morning, but in place of her black oxfords, she wore a pair of green socks which had once belonged to Mary's father, Francis.

"Mother, it's over and done," Mary said. She let the words fly out, knowing that if she reflected on them they might remain unspoken until another week had passed. Then, of course, she'd have to explain Dermott's absence.

Mary put her arms on Nora's shoulders to prevent her mother from getting up. Next, Mary pulled the step stool from under the bed and, perching herself on the tiny wooden seat, looked up to her mother's gray eyes. Mary told Nora everything.

Eventually, after shaking her head back and forth, Nora said, "He'll never marry with his mother alive. She'll not let another woman in the house."

"Mam, you didn't tell me," Mary said. "Did you know I could never have him?"

"Of course not, my dear, I thought Dermott was a different sort. I didn't know the old woman's influence."

"Do you think she will keep for years?" Mary asked. She didn't know any other way of asking.

"Agnes McMahon is a Tooney. The Tooneys all live into their nineties. Ed Tooney lived to be one hundred and his brother Thomas lived to be one hundred and two."

Mary laughed. She could see Agnes McMahon with a head as bald as one of her newly shorn sheep. She'd be pouring her weak tea from its pink flowered pot, serving her rocklike scones to Dermott, who would be too old to braid anyone's hair. Too old to even see it.

The next Sunday, at the time when Dermott ordinarily would have come to the house, Nora led Mary to the end of the lane. "Stand in front of the stone shrine," Nora said. "And look to the road. Tell me if you see anyone coming."

Mary turned away from the shrine which Nora had built with her own hands after Sean had drowned. She did not turn back even though she heard her mother digging. When she was told to look, she saw Nora lifting a flat slate stone. Under the stone was a small hole. From it Nora drew out a metal chest. "Everything is here," Nora said. "Come sit by me while I show you."

"What's this, Mother?"

"That's a ring your father's mother never wanted me to get, but once she died your father took it from her before his sisters could get it. It's a real ruby. And this is your baptismal certificate and Sean's too. Here's my wedding paper and the plenary indulgence Father Cregan got from Rome after your father died. Here, Mary, look at this. This is the money your father left me—more than anyone thought, more than enough for me to live on, even if I never sell another egg or darn another net. There's enough here for you to buy a ticket to America."

"No, Mother," Mary said.

"Yes, you must go. There's nothing here for you."

Mary was unable to speak, but she knew she would fight her mother on this no matter what. She would not go to America and leave her life. She had no other life. "Mother," Mary managed to say, "I can't leave you."

"There's nothing for you here and the sooner you realize that, the better. Listen, Mary, there may never be a time as good as this. Patricia Kelly will take you with her. She has family connections there. She can help you find work in a fine house."

"Don't make me go," Mary said. The words came out with the force of a great wind. They left her hanging on her mother's shoulders. They left her bleeding internally where no one could see.

Nora counted her bills, saying the numbers aloud so that Mary felt she, too, was counting. "You'll need money for the boat and some money to pay Dennis to take you to the Kellys in Leenane. We must write Patricia tonight."

"I can't leave. I don't want to." The ache in her chest had turned to pain.

Nora put the money in her sock. "We shall pray on the matter," she said. The tiny box, like a coffin, was put back into the earth. The slab of stone was returned to its place; Mary remained frozen beside the shrine while Nora walked off to the cottage. Nora's walk was decisive—the walk of a determined woman. Mary feared that the prayers would be answered quickly.

Before first light Mary went to her hideaway. "Remember!" she told her brain, but her mind wasn't working normally. Thoughts were not coming in words and sentences but in sharp quick flashes like the drops of saltwater which blew into her face. "Calm yourself," she said aloud, then sat to watch the sun appear. First, it was a yellow thread on the horizon; next, a pale pink ship. Finally, the sky became the bright rose of a new day. "Good-bye!" Mary called before running back to the cottage and throwing herself onto her mother's bed. She pushed her cold face against Nora's warm neck and breathed in the smell of Nora's harsh soap. "Mam," she said, hugging her mother's frail body to her own wiry one.

"With boots on, too," Nora said, looking down to the quilt. "Come, we'll have a fine breakfast before Father Cregan comes to give you his blessing."

The valise which had once belonged to Nora's sister stood by the door like a dog waiting to be let out. Mary's hat and gloves were on its back. Mary turned her chair so she would not see them while she ate. When they were finished eating they did not put their plates in the enamel pan by the fire as they usually did, but pushed them aside as if they expected a servant to clear the table.

Nora took Mary's hands in her own. "I know you will be a good girl. You will remember to say your morning and evening prayers and write to me every week."

"Mam," Mary said, bending to kiss her mother's hands.

"There's no reason to think we won't see each other again in five or six years. You'll be coming back for visits. Maybe even sending for me so I can visit you in America."

"It is so," Mary said. She knew her mother would never leave the shrine down the lane or the graves in the parish churchyard. But she could save her wages for a visit home. If Patricia's letter was true, there was money all over America. Patricia had written that the people in America had two houses, one for winter and one for summer.

Father Cregan came on the back of his donkey just as Mary and Nora walked to the gate to look for him. It was a cool morning; the sky was violet and the air was misting. The tip of Mary's nose dripped; the tops of her ears stung. Mary looked across the fields and rock walls to the purple clouds above the water.

"Good morning, Father," the women said in unison when the priest got off his donkey. But just as they were about to return to the house, Dennis could be seen coming down the lane in his cart. Mary gave a panicked look to her mother. A second later the priest spoke: "Come here, Mary. I can give you the blessing now."

Mary knelt on the rocky path and bent her head. The priest was quick with his words and even quicker with the sign of the cross which he made over Mary's head. A second later Father Cregan had squeezed Mary's shoulders and helped her to her feet.

"I expect you want a private word with your mother now," he said. Before Mary knew what was happening, the priest had put her suitcase in the cart and was leaning against the wide wooden wheel having a chat with Dennis.

Nora put her arm around Mary's back so when Mary looked down to her new cloak her mother's hand was clutching the wool. Veins like earthworms stood up from the rough skin. "Mary," Nora said, "you're to go off like a brave woman."

Mary took her mother's face in her hands then pulled it toward her. She kissed her mother's lips. "We'll see each other again before seven years have passed," she said.

"I know it," Nora replied.

They walked toward the waiting cart with their heads down. A minute later, Mary was bouncing beside Dennis. She was turned so she could see her mother and Father Cregan standing beside the short posts on either side of the gate. They might have been decorations for all their stillness. Neither raised a hand to wave until Dennis prepared to turn onto the ocean road. Then, as if it had been rehearsed, Nora and the priest waved frantically. For an instant, Mary thought they were calling her back. Perhaps she had forgotten something, or there'd been a sudden change in plan. But while Dennis slowed so Mary could stand beside him, her hand on his shoulder for balance, the waving continued in the exact same way. Mary waved, too. Then the cart lurched, and Dennis clucked for the donkey to pick up the pace.

"I won't see her face again in this world," Nora said when the cart was out of sight. The boulder which held the wooden plank over the well was no match for Nora's heart. Her heart felt so heavy in her chest she would have sat on the lane like a beggar if the priest hadn't been there.

"Sure, there's lots of money in America. You and Mary will be visiting each other before long," the priest said.

Nora made herself smile, but she was glad when Father Cregan decided not to join her for a cup of tea. She wanted only to sit quietly by the door and look off to the ocean.

My Father's Boat

(1993)

MARY MCGARRY MORRIS

Time has stopped. My eyes open this glistening spring morning to my watch's blank face. The battery is dead but a new one will have to wait because I'm determined to spend the day preparing the garden for tomorrow's planting. This is our first sunshine after a week of rain.

I dress quickly, but then waste the next half hour searching for my green rubber boots. They stand just inside the attic door, cobwebbed and reeking of the moth crystals tossed in here every few months against foraging squadrons of squirrels and bats and mice. As I lace the boots with a wary eye, my naked wrist reminds me of another watch, one my stepfather gave me years ago on my sixteenth birthday.

I clomp through the dusty clutter to a paint-chipped blue bureau that holds my first jewelry box, an elegant deep purple flecked with gold bursts. Here, beneath a tangle of class rings, circle pins, and pop-off bead necklaces, is the dark green velvet case and, inside, a delicate gold watch. I wind it up, amazed when it starts to tick, its gears still willing to turn after a quarter century's dormancy. Under the skylight, the watch glimmers with the diamond chips that mark the six and the twelve, and all the old guilt washes over me.

My mother was angry that my stepfather had bought me such an expensive present. It cost him one hundred dollars—fifteen down and the rest spread over a two-year installment plan. One month after my birthday, the watch and case disappeared from my room. When I finally worked up the courage to tell my mother, she declared me careless and my stepfather foolish. I shrugged it off, feeling strangely relieved of one more of my stepfather's intrusions, this watch that could be allowed no space in the flimsy outpost of loyalty and pride I so dutifully manned for the father who had forgotten my birthday. It was not my stepfather I resented, but his munificence that made my own father's neglect all the more real and bewildering.

My stepfather was certain the watch had been stolen. He reminded my mother of the missing bottle of anisette.

"Tommy wouldn't do that," my mother said. "Not his own daughter's watch. No," she protested in a weakening voice, "Alice must have lost it."

"The case, too?" he demanded, his hands in the air. "Tell me how she did that!"

"Now I remember!" I spoke up, anxious to bear this sin of my father's, as my mother had done for years. "I put the watch in the case and then I took it to school to show everyone! I remember because in fourth period Mrs. Lawson said, 'Alice Fermoyle, what are you passing up the aisle?'"

My mother nodded eagerly.

"And then the lunch bell rang and I went to my locker and put it on the shelf and the door wouldn't close tight so I had to fiddle around with the lock and kick it shut at the same time, and it must not have caught. Remember, I told you what a lousy locker that was?"

"Yes, you said that," she nodded. "Yes, I remember you told me that at the beginning of the year, and I told you . . ." Her eyes darted to the front door where my stepfather was zipping his frayed Legion jacket.

He was gone all afternoon. First he checked with the three jewelers in town. No one had seen the watch. Then he drove over to Wexford. There, in a secondhand store, a clerk remembered having bought a watch in a velvet case the previous week. He checked his records. Yes, he had paid twenty-five dollars to a Mr. Fermoyle who wanted fifty for it. The clerk confided that Mr. Fermoyle had seemed "a little under the weather." The clerk also remembered that Fermoyle had said his daughter hadn't liked the watch, so he was going to get her a better one.

When my stepfather offered to buy back the watch, the clerk explained that he had already sold it for forty dollars to a dealer in Hammond. My stepfather drove to Hammond. The dealer there was sorry, but he had sold the watch just the day before to a place up in Lewisville. My stepfather drove the half hour to Lewisville, where the jeweler agreed to let him have the watch for seventy dollars, "a real steal." My stepfather had only ten dollars with him. He signed a note promising to pay the difference over the next six months.

I can still remember the commotion of his car squealing into the driveway, his breathless voice up the stairs, calling, "Alice! Alice!" He knocked on my door, then raced into the room. "Look! I got it back!" he said, slipping the watch over my hand. "I told your mother it wasn't your fault. You just thought you were being careful, but the best way to take care of something, Honey, is to use it." He patted my cheek and winked. "Believe me."

"Thanks," I said. Just thanks. And before he was halfway down the stairs I was regaling my brothers with a Chaplinesque performance of our father's catlike stealth as he looted our home. We rolled off the beds, writhing with muffled laughter at the notion of Dominick buying the watch back every time Dad would take it and hock it. With that sleight of mind that makes the darkest universe navigable, we turned the theft to a gallant deed, and the quest, the recovery, to folly. I seldom wore the watch except when my stepfather would ask where it was. After a while, he must have stopped asking.

On my way out of the attic, I step over the shoe box containing Aunt Almadene's letters and my father's pictures. I should put the pictures into an album, instead of leaving them up here to crack and curl up in the attic's extremes of heat and cold. The only reason I haven't is out of consideration for my stepfather, who is about the only one who looks through the albums anymore. Loyalty. Guilt. One fed on the other. They still do, all these years later.

There are a few pictures of my aunt sitting on the beach or in their tiny living room, cluttered with furniture I remember from Almadene's gracious house. But most of these photographs are of my father and his boat. As I flip through them, it strikes me as odd that this boat, a boat I have never seen, this dinghy powered by a salvaged motor, seems more familiar, more real to me than this fragile-looking man. It is because I know what boats do. There are rules for boats and all the parts have names. And of all the myriad kinds of boats there are, a boat is still a boat, a thing that floats.

My father is sixty-nine. In some of these pictures, he wears a yachting cap, white with gold braid beneath a crest whose insignia I am certain stands for nothing. I have not seen my father for a few years now. Except in these pictures. When my son was graduating from high school he sent an invitation to my father, who wrote back saying he'd love to come if he only had the money. I wired him the plane fare. He never came, but a few months later he sent a picture of his new boat.

In this most recent photo, my father wears a double-breasted blazer with glinting brass buttons. With one foot braced against a piling, he leans over the dock, pointing proudly down at his boat that is all but submerged in the shadows of larger boats. It makes me smile to see how he has hitched up his pant leg so as not to bag the sharp crease of his white pants. My father always called them slacks, even if they were rancid, even if they'd been slept in for weeks.

He has a deep tan and a skinny black mustache. His self-conscious grin makes me suspect that the pictures are taken by tourists he approaches with his camera and the sad tale of his only daughter's abandonment.

He lives with his widowed, older sister, Almadene, in a Florida retirement complex. Almadene writes every few months. She misses the snow and the mountains and our cool summer nights. But it is worth it, she says, having my father so happy. It is in these letters that the pictures are always enclosed.

> *Your dad goes out in the boat every day. The fishing hasn't been too good because, he says, the big boats scare them all away. So he buys our fish down at the dock before he comes home.*

My father adds a few lines telling me that the winter was great—or the summer not nearly so hot as Almadene complains. And he hopes that we'll come down real soon. Or at least send the children.

Almadene always adds the final postscript. This one reads,

> *Your dad would love to hear from all of you. He checks the mailbox every day. Of course you are all so busy now bringing up your families, I know—and I tell him that. But a letter would help—or a phone call. Sundays and holidays, especially. Those are his blue days, he says. He thinks you have all washed your hands of him.*

When we were children, my mother divorced him "because of the drinking." He doesn't drink anymore. In fact, last year one of Almadene's postscripts varied a little.

> *Your dad and I went to McDonald's tonight to celebrate his tenth anniversary away from the drinking. Maybe you and the boys could send him a congratulations card.*

The "boys," men now, laughed and said they didn't think Hallmark had come up with an anniversary card yet for alcoholic reform.

We have always managed to laugh. We laughed when our father fashioned a key during occupational therapy and made his way in the night from the state hospital's alcoholic ward. We laughed after he was picked up three consecutive weekends for public drunkenness and then, on the third weekend, landed in jail because Almadene's long-suffering husband, Uncle Durant McBride, was up for reelection as mayor and his opponent had charged him with shielding his relatives behind the power of his office. We laughed so hard that tears filmed our eyes that third Monday on our way to school past the jail on whose barred windows our father beat, crying out when he saw us, "Help! Help! I'm a prisoner in here!" We laughed when we heard how he had locked Almadene's housekeeper in the bathroom for an entire day so that he could drink "in dignity and peace" at the dining room table. We laughed the night he burst through our front door, with the slurred announcement that he was through with the drinking and was ready to be a husband and father again. And after the cruiser left with him weeping in the back seat, we laughed again, but into our pillows because our mother cried in the kitchen.

Early in my teens, my mother married burly, gentle Dominick. They had a child, a son, late in my mother's childbearing years. That August birth brought Dominick's mother from Brooklyn, where she sat for countless summers on her front stoop, revered and unaccosted.

Maria was uncomfortable speaking English, suspicious of her busy new daughter-in-law, and bewildered by the sudden inclusion of three raucous redheads in her realm of dark-eyed, respectful grandchildren. We pinched and elbowed one another, straining to keep straight faces as Dominick proudly introduced her to us as Grandmother. Her baleful glance made it clear that we were not Dominick's children, but Clara's. She was not our grandmother, but Jimmy's, the baby who looked like us but whose last name was hers.

"Scavolna," she said, pronouncing it in a way Dominick never had, with a dark, rolling ferocity that spoke of popes and sauces and Mafia chieftains. We could call her Mrs. Scavolna.

In our tiny house, she slept with Jimmy and me in the crowded bedroom overlooking the little flagstone patio that Dominick had laid the previous spring. She didn't like our blaring radios. We were determined not to like her.

Two weeks after the birth, my mother returned to her job as an office manager in a downtown clothing store. Dominick worked not only days on construction, but nights as well, guarding an empty factory. My brothers and I had summer jobs, so during the day when Jimmy slept, Maria was alone with little to do. Because her sight was too poor for television, she spent most sunny afternoons sitting on what she called "Dominick's porch," not a porch at all, but three steps topped by a wider board. The house was "Dominick's house," her son's, the only one of three to own his own home. It was the first house we had ever lived in. Before Dominick, there had been many apartments.

Dominick was disappointed that Maria would not use his patio, but she explained, in her mysterious Italian and fluent hands, that there was nothing to see out there in the back but bushes and trees. It was cars passing by and children playing on the sidewalks and busy pedes-

trians to which she was accustomed, not birdsong and neighbors'
lawnmowers and Dominick's skimpy forsythia and spindly silver
maples.

So the top step became her stoop where she perched precariously in
an aluminum lawn chair, wearing any one of three black dresses, her
long white hair skeined rigidly at the nape of her neck. The empty
street she watched had no sidewalks and ended in a culvert of plowed
rubble, the scarred hiatus of a development of five-room Capes, all
undormered, and all under five thousand dollars.

Day after day she sat out there with her black rosary beads slipping
between her fingers. She stared over the heat-shimmered asphalt.
Once, she told Dominick, a car stalled and the driver asked to use the
phone. She let him in. Dominick scolded her, telling her in Italian how
dangerous that could have been. Another time, a saleswoman gave her
three packets of hand lotion, which she ordered Dominick to shut up
about because they were to be her present for Clara when she left in
September. Her next visitor was my father.

It was late afternoon. He had been drinking all the night before and
had run out of money. A taxi bore him into Maria's expectant gaze. He
stood by the cabbie's window, searching his pockets for the fare. He
took off his shoes and made a show of shaking them out. Apologizing
to the driver, he directed him to 4 Cranmoore Street where one
Almadene McBride would gladly reimburse him.

He staggered up Dominick's flagstone walk toward Maria. He had
to see Clara. The old woman told him that Clara wasn't home from
work yet. His kids, then; where were his kids? At work, she told him.
He shook his head, then demanded to know who the hell she was.

"Mrs. Scavolna," she said. "Dominick's mother."

"Dominick?" He peered up at her. "You mean the wop? The wop
that stole away my kids and my wife and my whole goddamn life?"
Teetering, he caught the iron railing. "You think tha's a nice thing for
your son to do? Do you?" he demanded.

Her jaw clamped shut, Maria stared fiercely past him.

"But you know, Mrs. Slar-whas-your-name, you know what really, really hurts?" He closed his eyes and sighed. "He got Clara, my wife, kicked out of the Church. He did."

Tears ran down his cheeks, and the beads tightened on her knuckles.

"She's living in sin, ma'am. And that baby, that baby of theirs is a bastard in the eyes of God, ma'am. Tha's the truth."

"Go!" the old woman groaned, pointing toward the street. "You go or I call Dominick now!"

He held up his hands. "No-no-no. I don't want any trouble. I just wanna get Clara back to God where she belongs, Mrs. Ya-know-who-ya're, I forget."

"Go!" she insisted, rising from the chair.

"I'll go. I'll go," he muttered. "But their sins won't go away. They're gonna burn in hell, ma'am. Your own son. Gonna just burn in eternity. Never gonna see God, ma'am. Isn't that sad? I've lost my wunnerful wife and my wunnerful kids and you've lost your wunner-ful son!" he moaned.

The old woman sank into the chair, her head bowed with shame.

"Tha's why I drink, ma'am." He struck his breast. "The pain! In here! I pray for them. I do!" His chin hit his chest as he began to sob.

She buried her face in her hands.

"Do you have fifty cents, ma'am?" he cried. " 'Cause I tell you what I'm gonna do," he said, wiping his nose on his arm. "I'm gonna go to church and light a candle and I'm gonna pray."

From the folds of her black dress, the old woman drew out fifty cents. She could not look at this man Dominick had ruined. Her own son, an altar boy.

"Do you have a buck, ma'am, and I'll light two candles. One for your boy and one for that poor innocent baby."

She gave him a dollar.

"Could you call me a cab, ma'am?"

After my father left, Maria went upstairs and packed. She threw the lotion samples into the trash. That night, Dominick and my mother had their first real fight. Dominick accused her of always looking the other way, always making excuses, always being too nice to "that bum" who deserved nothing better than to be beaten to a pulp for his disrespect to that saintly old woman.

"I want him out of my life, do you understand?" Dominick demanded of my mother, who continued to cut meat and pass on mashed potatoes and pork gravy as if none of this could really be happening. "This is my home! This is my family!" he insisted, pounding the table. In giddy horror, we kicked one another under the rattling flatware. Overhead, the baby screamed and Maria's rocking chair creaked back and forth, back and forth, the gnawing dolorous rhythm more than Dominick could bear. "I'm gonna get him," he vowed. "I'm gonna get him and I'm gonna make him fight me like a man."

"Phew!" my older brother whispered. "For a minute there, I thought he meant Dad!"

A mouthful of milky laughter burst from my younger brother, splattering the supper plates. With machine-gun precision, my mother slapped my older brother, who cuffed my younger brother, who bellowed and turned to me, a volatile vessel of guilt, shame, and indignation, my father's daughter, who jumped to her feet, denouncing as brutal and ignorant anyone who would strike an intoxicated man, a sick man, all the while pointing, damning Dominick Scavolna, sweet, gentle Dominick, who not only rose but seemed to swell from the table like a monster unchained, a beast that, with a sickening roar, drove its fist through the newly papered wall. Dominick fled from our stunned silence to the sanctuary of his night job.

The bright spring morning shines through all the windows. Before I go outside, I put the letters and the photographs back into the shoe box. Monday, when I take my watch to the jewelers, I will buy one of those narrow-slotted albums for my father's pictures.

I have been digging in the garden for almost an hour. My squatting legs ache as I pluck more rocks from the warm, wet soil. The wheelbarrow bottom is already covered with muddy stones and long hairy roots as well as shards of pottery and glass and yellowed bones, and now a delicate blue teacup handle. I trace my thumb along the dirt-pocked glaze. This is not mine. I have never seen this before. I am startled now as I am every spring by this debris, this winter harvest of secrets the earth keeps, stubbornly yielding but a few at a time. One year it was the unbroken lens from eyeglasses, though no one in our family wore them. Other years it has been marbles, bits of cloth, chunks of coal, a rust-bloated horseshoe, a Tootsie truck.

It is noon now, and the sun presses like dead weight on my bent back. Every muscle throbs. On the way into the house, I check the mailbox. Bills, magazines, and a letter from Aunt Almadene. She says:

> *Your dad is in the hospital. He had been sick with emphysema and bleeding ulcers all winter and now the doctor tells him he has angina very bad. He is very depressed. He says he is dying and will die alone. He is so very lonely . . .*

Immediately, I call Almadene to see which hospital he is in. To my surprise, it is my father who answers the phone. When he hears my voice he cries and, for a few seconds, cannot speak.

"Dad . . . oh, Dad," I whisper, closing my eyes to the ruffled curtains, the ceramic coffee pot, the paintings on the walls of this life I have built away from him. All the old resentment—that he has never once been in my home, that he does not really know my children, that it is Dominick they love and call Grandpa—all that is washed away. This is a pathetic old man, alone and dying. And I am his child. Blood is the bond. The truest bond. I will fly him here. I will nurse him forever. We will rework our lives. It is not too late. "Dad, what are you doing home? Almadene's letter says you're . . . very sick."

"Pet," he chokes, gasping for breath enough to speak.

It makes me cringe. I will take away his pain. I have been a negligent daughter.

"Pet, can you come?" he wheezes. "Can you see me just once before I die? Is that too much to ask? Just one time? Tell your brothers to come. For your old man, Pet?" He sobs and his voice breaks, the flap of his lungs so weak in my ears that I cannot bring myself to remind him of the times we tried to come and he did not want us. "I'm afraid, baby. I'm so scared, I'm afraid to close my eyes at night. I need you kids . . ."

"Dad, why aren't you in the hospital?" I gently probe. "You shouldn't be home. Almadene's too old. She can't take care of you."

There is movement. A hinge squeaks as he closes a door, not wanting his sister to hear. He whispers hoarsely, "It's my boat. Remember that storm we had in March? It did a job on my boat, so I patched it up. Then I had more trouble . . ."

He goes on, describing the split in the bow, the battered motor for which he thinks he can get more secondhand parts from a fellow at the marina, the same fellow who had him rescued two weeks ago . . .

"What? What do you mean, rescued?"

"It was terrible, Pet. I went out early in the morning and was going along just fine when the lousy motor conked out and I kept waving at the big boats heading in and they kept waving back. Anyway, a storm was coming, chasing them all in, and I knew I couldn't sit out there much longer in those swells, so I swam to an island and sat out the storm until about ten that night when the young fellow from the marina sent out the Coast Guard."

"You swam?" Is it my imagination, or is his voice stronger now, his breathing unlabored.

He laughs. "The old man's still got it, Pet. I fact, I was just getting ready to swim out to the boat when they came."

"Dad!"

"I figured if it started I could find my way back by the stars." He laughs again. "I always wanted to do that."

"You should be in the hospital," I interrupt weakly.

"No. I should be a rich man, Pet, on one of those fancy yachts with—"

"Dad, listen. Almadene's in her eighties. She can't take care of you! I want you to—"

"Pet!" he whispers urgently. "Yesterday I called a carpenter and he's coming this afternoon. That's why I left the hospital—to make sure he does a good job, and I have to see about spare parts off—"

"Dad, forget the boat. You're in no shape for that now. Besides, I want you to come up here. With us. Both of you."

"I don't have that kind of money, Pet."

"But you won't even need the boat, Dad!" I laugh. All he will finally need is us.

There is silence.

"Will you come?" I persist.

Another silence, another of the long, familiar corridors I have raced down only to find him cringing at its end, his widened eyes darting past me, desperate for a place to hide, each of us feeling as trapped as the other.

"Pet?" The wheezing again. "Do me a favor. Will you tell the boys to come down here?" His voice cracks. "Will you tell them that? Tell them I need them?"

"Yes," my weak reply. He knows they will not come this time unless he asks.

"Don't let go now, Pet. I'm all alone. I'm still your father, you know," he says with an uneasy laugh.

"Of course you are."

"Will you write and tell me when you can all come?"

"I'll write."

"Promise?"

"Yes," I promise, in the wordless struggle of the gagged and bound. How does he do this? How does he keep me on this trail that is always a circle?

"Pet!" he says quickly. "I just thought. You know that money you just said? For the tickets? I bet for half that I could get a brand-new motor."

His voice is still with me as I hang up the phone, my hands trembling with this rage, this powerlessness of the little girl who would rather have had it be all her fault than admit he simply did not care enough.

Don't let go, he said. Don't let go. I wish I knew how. My brothers let go years ago, as did my mother. He keeps me a child, a little girl, like the watch buried all these years in an attic drawer. He uses me in disuse.

"Damn it, damn it! Damn you!" I explode, driving my fist into the shoe box cover. "I'll write! I'll write, you bastard!"

I return to the garden and dig with a fury I have never felt before, digging deeper, deeper down through the black humusy topsoil and the packed clay and the dismal yellow-streaked silt, all the while composing my letter.

> *Dear Dad,*
>
> *I refuse to feel guilty. You were a lousy father. I was a good daughter, doggedly pursuing you those first eighteen years of my life, refusing to be forgotten, refusing to be relinquished.*

With every stone the shovel strikes, my foot stings and pain shoots up my arm. Of course, of course. Again and again. It is through forging that tensile strength endures. I know what I am doing. And I do it well because this is the way I have been taught to prepare a garden, my mother's way, trenching the perimeter and mounding each bed.

Dear Father, Dear Dad, Dear Daddy,
Your little girl is grown and gone because she had to. This woman writes her letter, this woman you have never known; this woman, a mother now, as all your women had to be for you, forever child, my child since both our births, whom no one could make into a father.

I am working compost, lime, and dry manure into the soil when it occurs to me that this garden, which began as two meager rows of tomatoes and two of radishes, is now as large as a family burial plot. Perhaps soon after the house was built, a child died and was laid to rest out here with his Tootsie truck, his marbles, and his baby spoon. And then some years later, his mother was buried beside him with her china and with her glasses on. I close my eyes. My father is dying. My father dies. He dies alone.

My dearest child,
My little boy of the legion of lost boys, who never needed compasses and only dreamed on stars, even in death your course is now, your passage blithe, brief with the wind.

Inside the house, the phone is ringing and ringing and ringing. Great mounds of soil are piled around me, their paler caps baking in the sun, ready to be hoed down into rows. I keep at it, sifting out more and more debris, dizzy now with the suspicion that old plates and teacups might actually grow in here, ripening, a perpetual harvest of human rubble.

Dear Dad,

Now I know what it was you gave: something of a quality whose name I never knew. This, your legacy: that because of your weakness, we plumbed inward for nourishment; because of your pain, we took joy from the world; because of your sins, we honored virtue; because you were selfish, we gave; because you broke promises, we clung to ours; because you stayed a child, we passed early into adulthood, outdistanced you at almost the same speed with which you fled from us. How juxtaposed our journeys, our roots seeking sun and blossoms, yours needing shade and silt, never daring to push upward past rock and drought and trampling feet.

I love you and I'll miss you, the way you were, the way you are, wanting your boat and your yachting cap more than anything else in this world.

The little girl you kept in me will miss the boy at the wheel of Uncle Durant's mayoral car, the wicked, wicked father-child who thumbed his nose at the world and raced us into a cornfield where we hid from the cruiser's siren, then, when it had passed, sped out with stalks and cobs snagged in the wipers and bumpers as we drove past the elegant home of Clyde Norton, Mother's lawyer, with you blasting the horn while we hung out the windows, all of us screaming—as if the divorce had been no one's fault but Norton's. And in the wonder of that reckless moment, you had us believing that if it weren't for that old man's legal villainy, we might all be together again, forever with corn silk in our hair, flying along railroad tracks you swore were safer and quicker than any roads, on our way to Melvin's Home-Maid Ice Cream stand, where you handed back the cones for us to

lick, then turned out your pockets in a great show of
mortification at having forgotten your wallet at home.
"Sorry, kids, you have to give the lady back her ice
cream," you said, and when she refused, you thanked
her. "My name is Durant McBride," you called, hurry-
ing us into the car. "I'm going to go get my wallet now
and I'll be right back. Rest assured your honorable
mayor won't leave such a debt unpaid."

By midafternoon, the rows have been mounded, the narrow ones
for tomatoes, pole beans, and peppers, and in the back, the flatter,
wider rows for squash, pumpkins, and cucumbers.

I load my tools onto the wheelbarrow and then walk stiffly around
the garden, pleased with my work, pleased to be done. In the farthest
trench, a yellow protrusion catches my eye. Kneeling down, I extract a
spongy, rotting pencil. I rake my fingers deeper and find glinting brittle pieces of a roof shingle. There is more, a rusty crippled nail, a
clump of petrified dog stools, and now a seashell fluted with dirt—a
seashell, though we are so many miles inland. I hold it to my ear, listening for wind and waves. What I hear is the tick tick tick of my stepfather's watch.

My Father's Alcoholism

(1994)

EILEEN MYLES

All through my childhood I was a devotee of the dark-haired man. There was Tyrone Power, there were endless boys in comic books: Super Boy, Reggie, Walter in Little Lulu. Obscure brunet boys who I based my fantasy life on. They were beautiful and they were perfect. The enhancing frame of the comic book, approximately $2\frac{1}{2}$ by $2\frac{1}{2}$, facilitated a world of inked-in colors, bound by the fineness of a cartoonist's pen, forever non-blurry, and when the artist got to the head, the hair, they could color it in. Black. Crowned with a head of blue-black hair in a world in which darkness was cop, the system of order—my boys had power, black ruled.

No cartoonist could resist having at least one black-haired character. After the Archies, the Iggies with small spikey lines as code for hair, their crewcuts—eventually they'd come along. My father's name was Terrence. He had black hair. There was a clear line from him to my dream world and back. My father insisted from the get go that he was in the same frame as me. He elbowed his way into my consciousness. That's Eileen, That's Eileen. As if the world were a school about me. Relatives participated in the plot. One of them, my father's white-haired brother, Ed, gave us a story book about a little girl with braids, who loved to play with kittens, and as if I were an idiot my father showed the book to me and said That's Eileen. I mean yeah, I had braids and a cat. But was I cute? As a picture in a book. Childhood is wide and impersonal. Something that was not me, but showed me the world on its way, is gazing down at a bowl of milk with rice crispies glistening in the morning sun. Breakfast. So beautiful I didn't want to eat it.

The darkest part of my house was the stairs. You had to come down so the day could begin. My father went to work very early. He was a mailman. Weekends, however, he would hold court in the parlor. Atmosphere would be pumped out on 78s all day. Nelson Eddy & Jeanette MacDonald, Bing. Danny Kaye singing those boisterous, eerie tunes: Oh Thumbaleena don't be dumb—tum, tum, tum. My mother's participation in the weekend music festival was evidence that they loved each other. The occasional dance through the house, my mother's sighs at the appropriate song, as she worked. That this was going on all the time was a fact of life and the weekend, like my Dad. One morning moving down through the darkness from the kid's world, a song came on downstairs and with its opening bars my father yelled out: This is Eileen's song. Gordon MacRae was belting out: Oh what a beautiful morning, Oh what a beautiful day. I've got a wonder-ful fee-ling, everything's going my way. The singer went on to describe how the cows were doing, and the beauty of the fields. He was this big happy farmer. I must have expressed appreciation of the tune at some point. That had to be it. But I never wanted to hear it every weekend when I came down the stairs. Even today it's accompa-nied by reluctant floods of light. You didn't want to be thought about that much, before you even knew "you" were there. I can remember a time when my name was for other people, before I even knew it was mine. The anonymous quality of its vowels—"Ei" being a word you heard a lot. Later I would know it was a pronoun, but before I could write, before anything had established that different contexts for sounds, words, meant different things, the "Ei" I heard a lot when people spoke seemed to mean "you." Sometimes they talked about themselves and said "Ei" but if they looked at me, or said it loudly, it meant "you." Then "Leen," that part. It sounded like meat. Roast beef. It had something to do with that. Usually what was going to happen was contained in the second part of what they called me. The "Ei" got my attention. The "Leen" either went really high which meant I was in trouble or slow and soft, the part when the tongue hit the roof of their mouth meant something nice. I was good. If they hit the first part with the second part really fast I was bad or in danger.

As I was travelling down the stairs from the bright kid world, through the dark soft tunnel with carpets towards the place where my parents would move me around, before I really knew I was anybody at all just that movement, never really awake, but very wide, hearing and feeling everything, I heard my name, that thing that made me know that something was going to happen, that woke me up. Now something my father was playing was also mine and I had to remember what I had done the first time I heard this song in front of him, that was the shock of the first time I heard "This is Eileen's song." After that, everytime I heard the song wherever I was in the house I knew that he was sitting in the parlor thinking about me and I was supposed to do something, probably go look at him. If I pretended I hadn't heard it my mother would get in on the act. She'd move her head in his direction. Go see what he wants. Sometimes I'd scream, "I'm eating." That was always a good excuse. If I was in the middle of something good, drawing, I would carry what I was doing. I'd walk into the doorway of the parlor, with my large pad of drawing paper and my charcoal pencil in my fingers and I would stand there, looking at him to show him I was mad. He'd be sitting there on the couch in his big baggy pants, cross-legged in his white socks with a cigarette momentarily held to his lips. He'd smile up at me like I was a surprise. He was dreaming. He'd forgotten he'd called my name. It was like I was a note he had sung in a moment that had passed.

We went on errands with my father on his days off. My mother would ask him to pick something up. Take the kids, Ted, she'd say and we'd go trudging out with him. Inevitably these errands brought him to Cambridge or Somerville where liquor was sold. He would pull into a parking place at some point in the journey and he would introduce his departure with a very quick—Back in a moment, Back in a Flash, Gotta take a whizz, Gotta get a Bromo. My father always talked in slang and frequently we just didn't understand him. We'd sit in the car for interminable periods of time, thinking of the sound of his last word: Flash, Bromo. We would look at the signs over the stores that weighed ever so heavy in our eyesight. Was that Bromo. Was all this time "Flash." Other time words, ten minutes, a second were often used in these breaks from us my father would make and I would try to remember if the last time we had stopped was a moment or a second. I would pull the button on the car door up and down. Don't do that said my brother. Why I'd ask. Dad wouldn't like that. The roof of the car was covered with all rough fuzzy stuff. A light sat in the middle of it and it looked like a big piece of candy. We weren't allowed to turn it on because it hurt the car. There was a tear on the side of the roof and inside of the tear, Look Terry said, revealing it to me, a St. Christopher medal. We would always be safe in this car. You could look out its windows slightly spotty from rain and dirt and first pretend the world looked like that, then remove it and let it be the window. I liked making the world spotted. The world got the shape of the car windows and that was good for a while. There were little round handles like stirrups on the walls of the car and I would hold on to one and pretend to be a horse, Ker Klop, Ker Klop I would yell and chug in my seat until Terry would yell stop you are driving my crazy. Terry never moved. He climbed behind the steering wheel as soon as Daddy left. He would sit there looking straight ahead like an adult. Once we saw Aunt Nora walking along the sidewalk. Look Terry, Look—Aunt Nora. You shut up. Terry she likes us. It's Aunt Nora. Shut up Eileen. He acted like we were doing something bad. Once Daddy had a day off during the week so when we parked Terry got to put nickels in the meter. He let me come out and watch. What are those lines, I asked pointing at the meter. That's how long Daddy's gone. When it's red I put another nickel in. And then he comes? *No*, he said.

Once we had stayed a really long time in Inman Square. It always reminded me of M&M Square. I would think about that when we sat in the car—looking for something that had to do with M&M's. Back in a Flash, M&Ms. My father always reminded me of comic books. That's why I was always looking for him in them. He came out really happy with a friend that time. Uncle Joe's inside he said. Why don't you kids come in. It's really late, Dad, Terry said. It was getting dark. And we hadn't gone to the A & P which is where we were supposed to go. Party pooper he said which made me laugh. The word poop always made me laugh. Inside was not like a store. It was more like a home where you bought drinks and potato chips. It was kind of stinky and smokey and it was all men. Uncle Joe was sitting in a booth. Hi kids he said. It was sort of like a soda fountain but it was all dark wood like houses in Somerville. The radio was really loud, a woman was singing. And there was a green parrot in a cage. It was all men and it was like a pirate place and I began to understand that my father was like a pirate and that's where he would go and come back different.

Everything was different when we got back home. Hello my father would yell from the foot of the stairs. It was like we were all kids now and we were in trouble. Terry and I were holding a big potted plant, a red chrysanthemum. My father had a finger to his lips, almost laughing. Go ahead he said giving us a light shove up the stairs. Surprise Terry and I yelled when she saw us holding the chrysanthemum. Shit on you Ted my mother said to my father who was standing in back of us and then it got really sickening. She didn't make us not eat but we were sent upstairs really fast. My brother and I both had stuffed rabbits we slept with. It was how we talked late at night. If we didn't want to be alone we had our rabbits talk to each other because they couldn't be heard. I knew Terry was crying. He didn't want to carry the flower when my father told him about it. Do you want to have a bunny talk, Terry. No, he screamed and he got up and slammed his door.

Once he took us to the fireworks and he left us there. By now he had joined the American Legion which was right on the other side of the park. Now you kids stay right here, don't move, I'll be right back. Pretty soon the fireworks were over and everyone left. Kids asked us if we wanted to go home with them. We're okay, we smiled. We told our father we'd meet him here. Maybe you should just come home with us—we can give you a ride. Finally when we were the only people left on the bleachers and even the fire department had left down in the field—then we just knew we had to go home. We were in bed when my father came in that night—there were some other voices down there with him—it sounded like his friends had given him a ride. Fireworks still make me kind of anxious. Once I took some acid and watched them through binoculars on the roof. It was perfect.

My father's work day ended before I came in from school. He had to be the source of the gifts that appeared for me on the table when I got home. A harmonica sitting there, a Hohner, not a toy. It was like he was reading my mind. Slides for my microscope—the most amazing one being egg of silkworm—a hot pink sphere with a small slice removed so it appeared to be biting something. A clear tiny bubble had escaped, was drifting away from its pink insides. Sometimes I'd run to the parlor where he was invariably sleeping on the couch. I'd run in, jump on his stomach and jounce until he woke up. I'm up, I'm up, I'm up.

Dinner was often a scene. There were times when my mother would force him to the table from the bedroom. He couldn't walk. He couldn't sit up. She'd put food on his plate and his face would fall in it.

She would pick his head up by his hair. His face would be covered in cabbage and potato and the juice from the corned beef. Nobody wanted to eat after that. He looked like a baby crying. His expression just sagged. I remember her screaming but I don't remember a word that she said. Because she was always angry and he was always sad it's easy to think of my mother as mean in those days. He finally fell off his chair and implored us all on his hands and his knees: I'm sorry, I'm sorry. There was still food on his face. Then he got mad and turned to the kitchen door, all glass and slammed his fists through it—I'll show you something he blubbered crying like a baby and a man.

I had this game with my sister, called Dirty Kids and Clean Kids. We would make real hobo sloppy boy kids, bums with filthy clothes. Despite my sister's entreaties I would only draw boys for this game. I didn't know how to draw girls. It made me feel funny plus I didn't have the same feelings about wanting to see them go from bad to good. Anyhow the bad kids would go through a factory I had also drawn. Once they came out the other side all beautiful and fresh with new clothes we knew that things were better and it made us feel good. It was our favorite game for a while. Just the fact of my sister's existence makes me think this game was fairly late in my father's alcoholism. I would say Bridget want to play Dirty Kids and Clean Kids? We would rush upstairs. More than once my mother remarked that this game must be pretty great the way we were so excited about it. Maybe we could sell it and make some money.

One Halloween he took us out trick or treating. Not just Terry and me, but Bridgie too and all the kids on the street. My father wore some big black old dress and he put a mop on his head and he had some kind of tall witch hat and he put red stuff on his nose. I think he looked like from the Wizard of Oz, more like the scarecrow, but he was a witch. He just sort of trailed behind us, watching out. I was a cat that year. My father painted whiskers on my face. It's funny to remember being so little that someone taking you places meant you could go. My father wasn't like a parent. He was like an older brother. Kind of, when he was good. Some punks tried to take our candy on Lombard Terrace and my father asked them why they were bothering his friends and the punks ran away. My father let us stay out so late our bags were all breaking and we couldn't carry them. It was great.

At home some nights it was hard to tell if he was good or bad. My father would put on a show. He had a skimpy little muscle man bathing suit. He would slick his hair back and come out in that and lift his arms and flex his muscles. I felt like I didn't get it. My mother seemed to be very happy and was laughing a lot. Then he ran into the bedroom and came out again. He wore his big army coat and he had a toothbrush, a black one under his nose and clicked his heels together. He was Hitler. Hitler always reminded me of the Devil. It was scarey. Oh Ted, my mother would exclaim. Then he would come out as a woman. That was the worst. I remember a big pink coat that may have been my mother's, and a tight little scarf around his head. I don't remember any makeup, maybe some rouge on his cheeks. It was like he was doing Grandma, his mother who was in a mental hospital. The woman part was really the scariest. My mother was really happy I think because she could keep an eye on him when he was acting funny and making us watch. He was her boy. But I wasn't so sure he was being good—the house felt hot, it was manic and scarey.

Late at night my mother would scream Oh Ted you've done it again. He had wet the bed. She could have left him. She could have thrown him out.

He had many car accidents and then he couldn't drive anymore. People always gave him a break. I can tell he's a nice guy said some woman who drove him home—so I'm not going to turn him in. I made him promise me he wouldn't drink and drive again.

On Friday nights my mother would go to the priest. It was dark out after supper. She was going to discuss my father's alcoholism. The priest's name sounded something like corn, like corn chowder on Friday nights. My father and I would sit in the den and watch teevee. It must've been before supper which makes no sense, but that's when war movies were. My father was in the Air Force in World War II. He was in a part of the Air Force called the red ball line. Men drove all over Europe in trucks. Jeeps I guess because the Germans would string these thin pieces of wire across the road and my father would make that clucking sound as his fingers pointed across his throat—the guys in the Jeep would get their heads cut off. My father was always interested in suicide. He told me about the Kamikaze pilots on the Japanese side who died for the Emperor and rode their planes right into the same building and died. My father loved to talk about hari kiri. He always wore a white teeshirt around the house and would demonstrate how these other Japanese guys with swords would stick their swords in one side of their stomach and pull it across. My mother and father were fighting in the kitchen once and my father grabbed the big butcher knife and stuck it in my mother's hand. He pulled his teeshirt up: C'mon, Gen, do it to me. Don't tempt me, Ted, she said.

My father was really sad that he didn't get to be a pilot in the war. He failed an eye exam. He washed out.

We sat on the couch and looked at the black and white movies about the war. My mother was out talking with the priest. The movie was about a club of men who went out on flying missions and some of them never came back. They were British. My father had been in England during the war. He loved the English countryside my mother said. The letters he wrote, *uh*. She groaned at their beauty. Apparently, she had thrown them out.

Each time a man didn't come back from a mission the men in the club turned over his mug on the mantle piece. My father loved it. He started crying. He had been really quiet up to there. He was being good. That's what I hope they'll do when I die. Here's to Ted Myles, never hurt anyone but himself. With that he picked up a green bottle of beer from the side of the couch. It was the most interesting bottle of beer I had ever seen in my life. It was magic. It was like he had invented that bottle. He lifted the beer to his lips. It had a horse on its label. Daddy! Oh I'm sorry he said. He was surprised he was drinking too.

A few minutes later he vanished into the kitchen. He was too quiet. He was standing by the sink holding a glass of whiskey. I'd never seen my father drink before. Before he lost his license I heard he'd pull over at the top of Route 2 before coming home and knock back a pint of Old Thompson. Rye. He was standing in the kitchen with his cup of gold. Did he call me one of those names I hated? Princess. Kiddo. Eileeny-Beanie-my Queenie. I became my mother. I grabbed the glass out of his hand and dumped it down the sink. He fell down on his knees, apologizing, repeating again and again. I'm sorry I'm sorry I'm sorry. The light in the kitchen was neon, incredibly bright.

My mother got her license. I'd go with her after school to pick up my father at the post office. He worked on Mt. Auburn Street in Harvard Square. He delivered mail in Harvard Yard. We sort of felt like Harvard was ours, so many members of my family worked there. Aunt Anne cleaned rooms. Toilets, she insisted. My cousin Brian worked in the cafeteria. So did my brother, briefly. My uncle's uncle owned a drugstore in Harvard Square. Harvard was the best college in America so it was nice that we lived near it. Sometimes my father would talk in his sleep. He'd be calling his route from the couch: Dunster, Adams, Leverett. I was standing outside a building one night with a boy I met at a mixer. What's that I pointed. Leverett House. Wow.

Often my father would take us to see the museums. I liked the dinosaurs and all the rocks. He liked the glass flowers. Everyone does, I guess. They remind me of death. Glass flowers make no sense to a child. Actually Harvard just seemed really old. It reminded me of a big bank. Our hi-fi came from Harvard. It cost 85 bucks. The students at Harvard were rich. They were always leaving and selling things. A whole collection of records came with the stereo—Ornette Coleman,

Gerry Mulligan, John Coltrane. They had a dense musty smell. I listened to this Harvard music in college. A Love Supreme, A Love Supreme. My father's clothes came from Harvard: Burberry coats, London Fog. My father liked to look like F. Scott Fitzgerald, that was the idea, an Irish Ivy Leaguer.

There was a drawing pad, Aqua-bee, he gave me, with charcoal pens. It was half drawn on. They just used it for doodling, this big expensive pad and then they threw it out. There was a little pen and ink drawing: the lines were really shakey and sort of scribbled over, but it looked cool, like modern art, the person wasn't working hard but they were smart. It was a man's face with sort of a hat on: Don't be such a Philistine it said. I didn't get it. Wasn't Goliath a Philistine? It meant something else. I asked my mother. Isn't it from the Bible? My brother laughed. I hated it when he knew something and wouldn't tell me.

There was a drawing that came from Harvard, rolled up, with an elastic around it, I believe. It was drawn in blue and black, soft pencils, with lines and shading. It was a man's face, long and thin and he wore a turban and his nose was pointed and his lips were curled into a sneer. I looked at it and closed it quickly. It was evil. I would hide it and look for it again and again. It was like someone's secret, it was something I didn't want to know. It was insidious.

So we'd park on Mt. Auburn Street and wait for my father. He'd come to a window, the head, he said, and wave and come out in a few minutes. I don't think my father ever came out of work drunk so it was a good time. Then we headed over to Aunt Anne's who still lived in Somerville. Once my father met us there and he had just had all his teeth pulled out. He was forty. I guess my father always had bad teeth. Oh your father was always self-conscious about his teeth. That's why he doesn't smile in pictures. He made friends with Mrs. Matheson who also had false teeth. Be true to your teeth or they'll be false to you, he'd say when he took them out.

And later there was something wrong with his ass, hemorrhoids. I guess Mrs. Matheson also had that. It was a joke. And so did Aunt Anne. They all went to the same doctor. They called him the Rear Admiral. Then my father had to sit on this black balloon—it looked like an innertube. I tried it once. It was like a toilet seat. My mother seemed to like my father getting sick because it kept him home and there were more jokes and we could take care of him. Things were under control. And he had ulcers too. It all seemed normal, all these things in his body going wrong. It was about being an adult, being a man. He was falling apart.

In the summer my family took a trip to New Hampshire. My father drove even though he didn't have a license. It was okay if she was with him. My father seemed very quiet and sad. He wasn't drinking. And that was good. We were going to this place called the Polar Caves in the White Mountains. I thought of bears. There's a black and white photograph of this trip. My sister and my mother and I are standing by an outside bathroom. It's labeled squaws. My sister always looked upset in pictures, my mother looks nervous—I have a tan and am good looking. My father took the picture. We all have kerchiefs on. And sweaters. It was an overcast day.

When we got to the caves my father decided not to go in. You okay, Ted, my mother inquired. I don't know if it's another photograph or a memory of my dad. He's standing outside there with a cigarette to his lips. He's a grown man, an adult but he looks extremely vulnerable out there, smoking, worrying. You really did want to take care of him. He had that. Inside it was all these boulders pushed together by nature, by the Ice Age. There were little tunnels you could push your way through. They were tight. You had alternatives, though, and I had heard about these. There was the lemon peel and the orange squeeze. One was tighter than the other, easier for kids to get through. I was getting older so it was important to get through the smaller kid one. My mother even had a hard time with the lemon peel in which you only had to crouch. The orange squeeze you had to climb and then slip through. There were little lamps on all the walls. *Good* thing your father didn't come said my mother. We all got cokes and went back to the motel. Our motel had postcards free at the front desk. It was called the Mar-Jon and it had a pool. Too bad the sun never came out.

Ted, my mother screamed. He was down on the floor. His legs were kicking a little bit and there was some spit forming around his lips. He was just lying there on the tile floor between the kitchen and the room you sat in. What did we do? I can't remember. He was just there. It was like the biggest thing I ever saw. It was like the world stopped. He had on his plaid cotton shirt, black and white with maybe some red. It looked pink. He had the sleeves rolled up, to mid-forearm. He had his watch on. And then it stopped. He sat up. What happened. Ted, you were out like a light. I think we went home early on our trip.

One Christmas, I don't know when, we went over to Aunt Anne's. She had a tiny house and her sons, my cousins Brian and Gerald had tiny rooms. She was on the first floor of a three-family house. They had even less of a backyard than we did. It was cement. You could rollerskate on it. And everywhere you looked there was another house. The fences between them were more like bars. Rusty metal ballet bars you could put your leg up on. My cousin Brian was an athlete. His room had catcher's mitts. There were pictures of baseball players on the wall. Gerald was a deejay, liked electronics, was mean. He saved things. There was a big jar of pennies on his bureau. There were bottles of booze. There were millions of comic books to read which was lucky. Everytime we ate at Aunt Anne's we had to wait for hours to eat while the adults laughed and drank. Ted had a beer my mother said proudly when she meant he'd been good. Gerald was crazy about Elvis Presley. The sad part was he wanted the adults to think Elvis was good. It was weird. So everytime we listened to a Johnny Mathis or a Bing or a Mario Lanza, then Elvis had to come on and show that he could do that too, whatever it was. My father had brought a Danny Kaye record to the party. It was a Christmas Party. I guess he wanted to entertain. To tell you the truth I bet he wanted to do a Danny Kaye imitation. He knew the record by heart. Everytime they changed the record my father would start, Hey Gerald, I—Okay Uncle Ted Gerald would go like a wiseguy, but just let me play Aunt Genny a song I know she will like. This went on many times and then my father vanished. There weren't many places to go in that tiny house. Where's Ted, Aunt Genny finally said. That was my mother. In the bathroom Gerald said putting down another platter. She got up. She knocked on the door. Ted? He sheepishly slipped out of the bathroom. You okay she said. Fine, Mum, he said. Uh-oh. He tried his record one more time and Gerald ignored him. It was so stupid. He had been gone. It meant something. He got up. Suddenly he was roaring drunk. He was white. He was red. He smashed the hard little 78 on the corner of the hi-fi. Don't play the Goddamn record, see if I care. He was screaming and he was crying. It was like the inside of our house was at Aunt Anne's house. Everybody wanted to throw up. Too huge, too big.

The worst part was after dinner. Gerald vanished and then he put my father's record on. He had glued it. It went Cara mia, up. Cara mia, up. Stop it Gerald said my Aunt Anne. It was making everybody sick.

We found bottles all over the house after my father died. In the toilet tank, in our comic book box. He used to come home from church on Sunday and my mother would make him open his coat. She'd find all these little nips and hide them. She said she started to forget whose bottles she was finding. We always thought it was because we had been born. It was our fault. There's a picture of me and Terry in those Pilgrim stocks—you know, heads and wrists poking through holes. It was some day we went to Plymouth or Salem. My father's standing behind us. We're laughing, he looks worse, a prisoner. All the pictures look like that after a point. Me and Terry goofing around in front of an old car, my father in the square of the driver's seat, looking sad, looking trapped.

I think he was gay, said my brother. Was he? Certainly not says my mother. He liked sex, she insisted. He was oversexed. There was a letter she received after his death from a woman who was on his route. Such a wonderful man, she expressed. Now, why would you do that, asked my mother. I think there was something going on there. Once my father wrote a story. He wanted to write my mother said as if that was the problem. He always read books on the nights he was good. Big fat historical novels. It was part of the writer pose: dark-haired man in a soft chair with pipe in his mouth, reading a book. He wrote this story and she sat him down. Your father wants to read you his story. She stood behind him, wanting us to be serious. His story was terrible. And naturally he was drunk.

excerpt from

One True Thing

(1994)

ANNA QUINDLEN

No one came to see us. No one, except for the UPS man when Jules sent me books from the office, and manuscripts, too, so I wouldn't lose my editing touch. I stacked them in the corner of my bedroom and continued with *Anna Karenina*, even though I knew very well how it ended. I felt as though I had an obligation to go on until the train thundered out of the station.

Sometimes, when I went out to buy groceries or some books or a bouquet of daisies, because such things gave my mother pleasure out of all proportion to the act, I would run into some old friend, one of the Minnies, a faculty wife, and I could almost see the sentence forming in their minds before they said it: "I've been meaning to stop by, but . . ."

Another small spark of anger would flare in my chest, then die through lack of oxygen, except for the afternoon when I went into the bookstore to buy a magnifying glass. Teresa said she thought it was the medication affecting my mother's vision. But I think it was just one more part of her too tired to go on.

When Mrs. Duane began to say she'd been meaning to stop by, I looked into her clear blue eyes, the color of sky, wise and so aware of the duplicity of what she was saying that they darted away from my own, and without thinking I interrupted, "Then do it. Don't tell me about it. Don't regret that you didn't. What she has is not catching."

"Ellen—"

"Don't," I said, my voice getting higher and louder. I realized that people in the store had stopped to listen but I didn't care. "No one has come to see my mother since the week before Christmas. She's lonely and she's sad and she thinks that everyone's forgotten her, and all because it's too uncomfortable for anyone to deal with anything deeper than winter ski plans and shopping for dinner." And I picked up my packages and left without paying.

I came home and put the magnifying glass on the table in the living room next to *Anna Karenina*. But I saw no evidence that it was being used. Still, I would not put her book back on the shelf with the two others. I would not declare the Gulden Girls Book and Cook Club defunct.

The next day Mrs. Duane called and asked if she could come over for lunch. I fixed chicken sandwiches and she and my mother ate at a properly laid table in the dining room—"placemats, Ellen," my mother had said. Mrs. Duane scarcely met my eyes. She gossiped with my mother about whose children were doing what and the January slump on Main Street.

I noticed that she assiduously avoided discussing the shortcomings of men, perhaps the greatest talking point when Jules and I had lunch together. And I wondered whether that was yet another difference between women of my mother's age and women of my own, or whether it was a difference between women who were single and women who were married and therefore had much, much more invested in their men than we did. Or perhaps it was because of how her friends felt about my mother and what they knew about my father. I wondered whether Mrs. Duane and the women like her had always done that around my mother, or whether they did it as a matter of course, not certain that any of their marriages were safe from being served up with the spinach salads and the iced tea.

My mother let me help her from her wheelchair into the dining-room chair in which my father usually sat, the one with arms, and that was where she was when Mrs. Duane arrived. She was wearing a sea-green turtleneck with a crewneck sweater in the same color, but the collar of the one and the bulk of the other could not quite hide her frailty.

The morning after her "lovely lunch," as she called it when she spoke of it to my father, she slept late and I was in the kitchen cleaning when I heard her faint footfalls on the old pine floors above me. There was the sound of the water running, the faint wailing of our pipes like a small and halfhearted banshee, the muffled closing of drawers and doors and then silence.

I sat down at the table with one of my mother's magazines, looking at spring perennials, although where I was going to plant perennials and why, when gardening bored me so, I could not have told you. I read the recipes and the instructions for making a bedskirt for a crib. Perhaps my mother was saving it for Halley, whose daughter must be overdue. From above me I heard a sound that I thought at first must be the pipes again, or a child calling from down the street, or perhaps a sudden bad-tempered fit of winter wind whipping around the dormers. It came again and I lifted my head. Again, and I went to the foot of the stairs.

"Ellen," came the cry.

I ran up those stairs as I had not run up since I was in high school, running to see if my father was in early, to tell him news and make it real—"I got into Princeton!" "I won the essay contest!" "I'm valedictorian!" How many times had I run in, banging doors, breathless, to tell him something and had to settle for her instead? How plain had it been on my face?

"Ellen," came the cry again.

Her bedroom was empty, the covers thrown back. Before my mother was sick I think the only time I had seen my parents' bed un-made was when they were in it, when I came in frightened after a bad dream, when I stuck my head in to tell them I had gotten home safely at one in the morning. A pair of knit pants and a tunic were on the chair, which had been moved closer to the bathroom door so that my mother could walk, stopping for a handhold as she went, from bed to table to chair to bath. The bathroom door was closed, and I knocked softly.

"You have to come in," my mother said with a catch in her voice.

The room was warm and smelled rank, the smell of perspiration and something sweeter, deeper. My mother lay in the tub, her arm across her eyes, perhaps practicing the child's fiction of believing that if she could not see me I could not see her.

"I can't get out," she said.

Silently I picked up the towel that was on the bench just next to the tub—she had made the bench from a kit, I remember, then painted it and sanded some of the paint down so it would look old—and hung it over my arm. I took her by the hands and tried to pull, but her legs scrabbled helplessly in the water, slick with bath oil, finding no purchase on the smooth porcelain of the tub. Then I reached around her chest and, with one great tug, pulled her over the edge and onto the bench. I was panting and the front of my denim shirt was wet with bathwater and, perhaps, perspiration. She weighed nothing, but felt so heavy.

I had never before and have never since set about a task which required me so completely to act without thinking. My mother leaned her elbow on the edge of the tub and her head on her hand and wept as I toweled off her poor ravaged body. I took it piece by piece, bit by bit, because I knew that if I allowed myself to really look at her, at what she had become, I would be done for.

But she knew, and while I couldn't speak, she couldn't keep silent. Suddenly she wiped her face with her hand and said, "I never wanted you to see me like this. I should have just stayed there until your father got home. I couldn't figure out what was worse, having you see me like this, or him."

"I would have come up eventually," I said, drying her shoulders.

"I would have died before I would have let you see me like this. Just . . . rotten. That's what I look like now, like a peach when it's all rotten. Like bad fruit. Why can't I just die and be done with it? It's a crime for a human being to have to live like this. Rotten like this." And she let her head drop down again.

It was an apt description. Her skin was slack on her body in places, like soft fruit when it's past its prime, on the insides of her thighs, her upper arms. But most of her flesh was stretched tight over her bones, a faint shroud for the skeleton: the two long bones running parallel beneath the skin of her arms and legs, the cage of pelvis and ribs. In her face every bit of skull was visible where the flesh had gone, leaving only the clear outlines of the understructure, the yawning Os of the eye sockets, the sharp peaks of the cheekbones, the hinge of the jaw, from which all the padding had disappeared. Her breasts were flat and sagging, like those of old women I'd seen in pictures of primitive tribes, and her pubic hair was nearly gone.

I went behind her, and, hooking my hands under her armpits, pulled her into a standing position. She held my arm tightly and shuffled into the bedroom. I helped her on with her underpants and her pants, her tunic, as she held on to the edge of the dresser. But I never touched her, not really, never patted her, much less held her close. And if I told you today that I've wondered about that a hundred times since then, whether I should have wrapped my arms around her instead of the towel, whether I should have rocked her as she had done so many times for me, I would be lying about the number, because it has been many many more.

I never try to remember how she looked that morning. I remember that I never touched her, and I never looked her in the eye. When I was done she moved slowly to the bed, like a blind person in an unfamiliar room, and she lay down on her back, staring at the ceiling. For the first time I noticed that the scarf Jeffrey had given her for Christmas had been slung over the mirror atop her dresser, so that a spill of glossy purple grapes and green grape leaves and the sinuous twist of vines hung in place of any reflection.

"I'm going back to sleep," she said.

That January, when they delivered the hospital bed, leaving the den in disarray and the living room crowded with furniture, leaving a long scratch in the oak floor of the hallway because they were careless with a metal side rail, she didn't say anything. She just got in and turned on her side so that she was looking out the window, out the window that looked out on our driveway and the side of the house next door. It was as though something was broken, but I think it broke in the bathroom, on that bench.

At the end she was both child and mother, both teacher and student, both strength and supplicant. At the end she lay in the den, in the bed with the high bars on the side, so that she would not roll out at night. Sometimes I would stand in the doorway in the dark, quiet and observant as a Peeping Tom, and watch her thrash and cry and talk, bits of disconnected things, about my father, about her babies, always babies. About people whose names meant nothing to me, who might be ghosts, figments, or regrets and missed opportunities. When she talked to her brother Steven one night, her eyes open even though their glaze made their blindness as clear as a white cane, that was when I stayed until the sky outside began to lighten. Somehow I thought if she talked to her brother, dead so many years ago, it meant she was seeing another country in her mind's eye and that her heart was hammering toward its inevitable full stop.

Often I watched with tears dripping down my face onto the front of my nightgown, but it was as though they were an inert function of my body, like a runny nose. There were no sobs, none of the heaves that you associate with a crying jag. There was no sound but my mother's thick and arduous breathing as I stood across the room, bleeding tears.

Once, when I came downstairs, the side of her bed had been lowered, and my father was wedged uncomfortably next to her. He and I looked at one another in the darkness, but I turned and went upstairs and if he followed afterward I did not hear him.

That room had white pine paneling on the walls and flowered curtains at the windows, a rose-and-green print I can still evoke in memory. The green couch had been carted into the living room, the hospital bed positioned in front of the wall of bookshelves so it faced the television. But all of the light and prettiness evoked by the decor was negated that month by the light, which was dim and gray, the dour grudging clouded sunshine of January and February. Now, today, I feel my heart begin to sink on New Year's Day and lift only— inevitably, ironically—when Easter is on the horizon. My miserable anniversaries.

One night the branches of the Douglas fir at the corner of the house lashed my windows and hers all night long, and by morning the snow was falling thick and fast, so that there was no light in the room at all and I had to turn on the lamps in the middle of the day. The snow began to drift until finally it reached almost to the windows. My mother kept her head turned to the side all day, except when she drank her soup, lifting the spoon to her mouth in a long slow arc, dropping her mouth open when the spoon was only halfway there, as though she could no longer trust herself to coordinate her motions more precisely. "The snow is so beautiful," she said, handing me back the mug, and then she fell asleep.

Beneath the rich yellow light of the lamp I read and, when my eyes became tired, went into the kitchen to judge the progress of the storm by the thickness of the blanket in the back, ripples and hillocks where it covered small bushes, a rise in the yard that marked an azalea I had protected with an upturned peach basket and a burlap bag. The phone in the kitchen rang like a scream in the quiet house, and when I went to answer it I saw that the day had slipped away and it was nearly seven. Only the light told me the time, and the light had been disguised all afternoon.

"Ellen," my father said, "I cannot possibly get home in this. The security people have closed off both the footbridges and no one has been able to get out to plow. I will sleep somewhere here."

"In your office?"

"I don't know. Several of the other people in the department have pullout couches. If I can find someone who's already gone home, I'll use theirs. If you try me here and there's no answer, that's what I've done."

"Uh-huh," I said.

"How is your mother?"

"The same."

"Tell her that I'll see her tomorrow."

"Yes."

"Are you all right?"

"Fine."

I think I remember that when I put down the phone there was a flicker of the thought that if my mother died during the night, with the snow falling thick outside, while my father was marooned on a sofa bed with some erudite honors graduate of a Seven Sisters college with strong opinions of Henry James and a soft spot for narrow handsome married men, that he would suffer with the memory the rest of his life. Or perhaps that was how I remembered it afterward, when memory plays so many tricks.

In the den my mother's eyes were open, looking at nothing. "Who was that?" she said softly.

"Your husband," I said in what I thought was a voice without expression. "He cannot seem to find a way to get home, so he is staying at the college. He says he will see you tomorrow."

"It's a bad storm," my mother said, looking out the window again.

"It's not that bad," I said.

"Ellen," she said, and her voice was stronger than it had been in days, "put down the book." In fact her voice was stronger, sterner, than I had ever remembered it, except the day that I mocked the little girl with Downs's syndrome who once lived at the foot of our hill and my mother turned cold and pitiless in a way I had always thought only my father could. She was like a sprinter now, at rest until those brief necessary moments when she would become herself for just a few minutes.

"What has happened between you and your father?"

"What do you mean?"

"You have been very angry with him since you came home. If you're going to be angry at anyone about all this, you should be angry at me. I'm why you're here, not him."

"Mama, this is not about you. And it's not something we should discuss. I have my own differences with Papa that have nothing to do with you."

"They do have to do with me, especially now. He's all you'll have."

"Stop. Just stop." I raised my hands, palm out, as though to push the words away.

"No, you stop. You and your father will need each other. And you and your brothers. And I hope he can have more of a relationship with the boys, too, if I'm not there to get in the way. But you and he already have such a bond. You're so much alike."

"Please don't say that."

"Why? Because he's not perfect? Because he's not the man you once thought he was?"

"Mama, I can't talk to you about this."

"Ellen," she said, struggling to turn toward me, her hands like pale claws on the railing of the bed, her legs scissoring away the white sheets, "listen to me because I will only say this once and I shouldn't say it at all. There is nothing you know about your father that I don't know, too."

The two of us stared silently into one another's eyes, and I think that after a moment she gave a little nod and then lay back.

"And understand better," she added.

"All right," I said.

"You make concessions when you're married a long time that you don't believe you'll ever make when you're beginning," she said. "You say to yourself when you're young, oh, I wouldn't tolerate this or that or the other thing, you say love is the most important thing in the world and there's only one kind of love and it makes you feel different than you feel the rest of the time, like you're all lit up. But time goes by and you've slept together a thousand nights and smelled like spit-up when babies are sick and seen your body droop and get soft. And some nights you say to yourself, it's not enough, I won't put up with another minute. And then the next morning you wake up and the kitchen smells like coffee and the children have their hair all brushed and the birds are eating out of the feeder and you look at your husband and he's not the person you used to think he was but he's your life. The house and the children and so much of what you do is built around him and your life, too, your history. If you take him out it's like cutting his face out of all the pictures, there's a big hole and it's ugly. It would ruin everything. It's more than love, it's more important than love. Think of Anna."

"Anna?"

"In the book." She gestured toward the end table where my paperback copy of *Anna Karenina* lay.

"But you didn't finish reading it."

"I'd read it before." She looked at the snow falling, tiny floating ghosts tapping against the window, spinning in and out of the blue-black beyond. "I'd read them all before. I just wanted a chance to read them again. I wanted a chance to read them with you."

I leaned over the rail of the bed, its metal cold and hard against my chest, and took her hand in mine, her grip strong, painful almost, and then lax. I slid the railing down and I put my head on the sheets, atop the cage of her pelvis, no fat or flesh to protect it. I cried until the sheets were wet, and she stroked my hair, over and over, the dry flesh making a faint sibilant sound, like the smallest whisper. Then in a softer voice, she began to speak again.

"It's hard. And it's hard to understand unless you're in it. And it's hard for you to understand now because of where you are and what you're feeling. But I wanted to say it, I didn't say it very well, I'm no writer, but I wanted to say it because I won't be able to say it when I need to, when it's one of those nights and you're locking the front door because of foolishness about romance, about how things are supposed to be. You can be hard, and you can be judgmental, and with those two things alone you can make a mess of your life the likes of which you won't believe. I think of a thousand things I could teach you in the next ten years, and I think of how everything important you learned the first twenty-four you learned from your father and not me, and it hurts my heart, to know how little I've gotten done."

"No, Mama," I whispered.

"Yes, yes, yes, yes, somebody let me speak the truth, somebody let me," she cried. "Your father says I'll only upset myself, and you say, please, no, Mama, and only Teresa lets me speak. Saying it is the only thing that makes me feel better, even the drugs aren't as good as that. All the things we don't say, all the words we swallow, and it makes nothing but trouble. I want to talk before I die. I want to be the one who gets to say things, who gets to think the deep thoughts. You'll all talk when I'm gone. Let me talk now without *shushing* me because it hurts you to hear what I want to say. I'm tired of being *shushed*."

"What do you want to say?" I said, lifting my head and pushing my damp hair aside. "Go ahead and say it."

"I just said everything I wanted to say, except that I feel sad. I feel sad that I won't be able to plan your wedding. Don't have a flower girl or a ring bearer—they always misbehave and distract from the bride. And don't have too many people."

"Mama, I don't know that I'll ever get married."

"Don't say things like that, Ellen. Think about what I just told you."

"All right. What else?"

"I feel afraid that when I fall asleep I will never wake up. I miss sleeping with your father."

"Should I tell him that?"

"I already have."

"What else?"

"If I knew you would be happy I could close my eyes now and rest." Her voice was beginning to sink and die, as though it was going down the drain, rush of words to trickle of whisper. "It's so much easier."

"I know it is. I wish you could."

"No, not that. The being happy. It's so much easier, to learn to love what you have instead of yearning always for what you're missing, or what you imagine you're missing. It's so much more peaceful."

"I'll try," I said.

"It doesn't work that way." And suddenly she was asleep. Her mouth hung open and her hair was scraped back from her forehead, lank because we had not washed it for several days, not since the last time Teresa had come. The lines across her forehead were cut deep, as though someone had done them with a ruler and a pencil. The sheet over her midsection was dark with my tears.

Everything you know, I know, she'd said, and it was true. I was the ignorant one. I'd taken a laundry list of all the things she'd done and, more important to me, all the things she'd never done, and turned them into my mother, when they were no more my mother than his lectures on the women of Dickens were my father.

Our parents are never people to us, never, they're always character traits, Achilles' heels, dim nightmares, vocal tics, bad noses, hot tears, all handed down and us stuck with them. Our dilemma is utter: turn and look at this woman, understand and pity her, like and talk with her, recognize that she has taken the cold cleanliness of the spartan rooms in which she grew up and turned them, within her considerable and perhaps wounded heart, into a lifelong burst of cooking and cosseting and making her own little corner of the world pretty and welcoming, and the separation is complete—but when that happens you will have to be an adult. There is only room in the lifeboat of your life for one, and you always choose yourself, and turn your parents into whatever it takes to keep you afloat.

Just before midnight she woke. She licked her lips slowly, twisting and turning her arms on the sheets, then turned her head.

"Is it morning yet?" she said.

"No."

"I need pills," she said.

It was a new vial, nearly full. She gulped one down, her throat working; coughed and then sipped again, her whole body moving with the effort. She sighed and it rattled deep in her throat, half groan.

"Help me, Ellen," she whispered. "I don't want to live like this anymore."

We stared at each other in the half-light of the lamps.

"Please," she said. "You must know what to do. Please. Help me. No more."

"It'll be better in the morning."

"No," she said, and groaned again. "It will not. I will not." She sounded like a tired and irritable child. She wrapped her fingers around my wrist, the wrist of the hand that held the pills. Her grip was surprisingly strong, and for some reason I thought of those people who lift Volkswagens off babies pinned beneath, of people trapped in caves and found alive, saved by a diet of snow, long past the time when they should have died.

"Please," she said. "Help me. I don't want this." But I could tell that the pill was already beginning to take effect, or perhaps that the effort of the words, the request, the hand on my arm, had put her under. She looked at me sadly from beneath lids that began to drop like those of some wise old bird. "Help me," she whispered. "You're so smart. You'll know what to do." Then her eyes closed completely. "Please," she whispered once more.

I slept that night in a chair in the den, fell asleep as the snow continued to fall. It covered everything without any sound except the scratch of the pine branches against the side of the house. I woke to the ugly fluorescent brightness of a world deep in fallen snow, covered with pitiless whiteness. It was a world changed forever, a world in which I found it difficult to meet my mother's eyes.

Versus

(1996)

JENNIFER C CORNELL

This is a story about a fisherman who was so good at his job that he could catch twice the fish in half the time it took his neighbors to catch what they needed to live, so every afternoon he'd haul in his nets and go sit on the rocks which looked out across the sea. Sometimes he'd bring a bit of work with him, a net to mend or a line to untangle, but usually he just liked to watch the waves and think. He did a lot of thinking, about a great many things, and people often came to him for his opinion and advice. No one was ever misled by what he told them.

One afternoon he had just settled into his usual place when he caught sight of a barge drifting unevenly in toward the shore. Thinking its captain must have run into trouble, he leaped down from his post to fetch help. But just as his feet touched the sand he was stopped by the sound of voices singing in a language he could not recognize. The object drew closer, the song more distinct, and the fisherman saw it was not a barge at all but a flotilla of dolphins. He was watching the party approach the shallows when one of the figures stood up on its tail and walked through the water onto the beach. The fisherman, who could scarcely believe he'd seen such a marvel, skirted the cliffs for a closer look. What he saw was a woman with pale blue skin, a long folded garment draped over one arm. She lay this bundle on a mound of dry sand, and then, unaware of the fisherman's presence, turned, and stepped back into the sea. The fisherman's heart was in his mouth; those who had brought her had withdrawn with the tide, and the woman's face hung with such a mournful expression that he feared what she might be planning to do, for already he loved her more than he had felt any emotion, love or hate or anger or pity, in all his life. The woman strode toward the depths at a resolute pace, but just as the water closed round her neck she rolled onto her back like an otter and pointed her chin at the sky. Her knees and shoulders bobbed up like buoys, and she floated.

The fisherman's love for the woman was such that he knew he'd do anything, however ignoble, if the doing of it would win him the chance to speak with her. When he was sure she would not detect him, he bent to examine the garment she'd worn. It was a heavy cloak of an ambiguous fabric, as soft and as solid as mail. His heart pounding, with no clear plan in mind, he gathered it up in his arms and ran off to conceal himself among the stones. He had a vague notion he'd withhold the garment until she had promised to be his wife, but when at length she emerged from the water, her expression now as clear as the droplets that caused her skin to sparkle like jade, he couldn't go through with it. In despair he went to her with his face averted and held her robe open wide. But to his surprise she did not snatch it from him. Instead, she took his face in her hands and read all that was in it; then she slipped her arm through his and walked with him, naked, into his home.

At first the fisherman kept his ears cocked for the sound of that mysterious singing he feared would entice her from him someday. But soon, rather than keep her from things she might love, he made himself miserable by encouraging them. If she found herself suddenly drawn to water he would not try to dissuade the urge. If on the pier where he sold his catch he heard sailors describing some fabulous wonder they'd observed while at sea, he would come home and repeat the tale. And, despite her protests, he took her robe out of its box in the attic and hung it in the closet downstairs, so she'd be in no doubt where to find it should a time come when she chose to look.

Years passed and the couple lived in many houses, each one brighter than the one before, and they had a daughter together who was more precious to them both than any element, yet each time the woman went to the closet to fetch the child's boots or a coat for her man, she'd see her own cloak hanging there. Sometimes when they went out together he would suggest that she put it on, but citing a preference for one of the costumes he'd made or bought for her, she'd always decline. Then one night as they were leaving he slipped the cloak over her shoulders and made her confront the full-length mirror to prove how much she deserved his praise. And indeed the cloak did transform her: against its high collar her complexion shone like burnished turquoise, and blue coral ringlets she'd not noticed previously now trembled at her brow. But when she caught sight of his reflection at the edge of the glass, gazing at hers with forlorn admiration, all at once her own image altered; its contours and colors softened like lamplight diffused under silk, and she saw again the face she always wore when she was with him—different, certainly, than the other, but no less splendid for being familiar.

She shrugged the cloak off, completing the change—too quickly, she hoped, for him to notice that there had been one, in either direction; but she was wrong. From then on, alone in the dinghy checking his nets or sunk up to his armpits in brine, in every slow minute he'd imagine her walking alone on a beach whose waves unrolled toward her like bales of cloth. With anguish he'd note their eager devotion and the great reluctance with which they'd retreat, and he grew certain that given more time they would convince her to rejoin the sea. Though his catch remained bountiful, he ached for the hour when he could quit, yet no matter where he settled, even inland among fields far from water amid the hum of busy insects where sheep and cattle murmured and grazed, he could still hear the spit and crash of breakers, the persistent, unbroken rhythm of waves flung out and reeled back and flung out again, until everything he loved became hard to endure—the livelihood that had been his passion, the daily retreat he'd so enjoyed, the very one whose company had sustained and preserved him until he could not imagine a definition of life that did not use her name as its verb.

As for the woman herself, though she tried to resist it, to have worn the cloak even so briefly crowded her mind with curiosity: was what she had seen a mere illusion, or would her life change for the better if she shed the clothes she had been wearing, however fine they'd seemed until then? In the gloom of the attic to which he'd returned it and where she'd found it, finally, after a desperate search, the cloak emitted a phosphorescence that made her think of quick shoals of fish as agile as jockeys, and she knew that either way it didn't matter.

One night when she could bear it no longer, she rose from the bed she shared with her husband and knelt beside her daughter's cot. She blew three times on the child's brow, and from that moment the girl could open her eyes wide in any water, no matter how deep or fast or bitter with salt, and be able to see what there was in front of her, and know whether to swim toward it or away. The woman stood up then and softly called the fisherman's name. When he turned in his sleep toward her, she ran her fingers through his thinning hair until the gray strands darkened to navy and grew stout as twine, and forever after whenever a storm was conjured at sea he had but to pluck a single blue strand from his scalp, bind it fast to any anchor, and the gale would pass over him like a summer breeze.

These things accomplished, the woman prepared to leave the house as she had entered it. She took her robe from its drawer in her bureau—for the fisherman had since discovered that hidden away or out in the open, the fact of it haunted him just the same. Spread over the banister at the foot of the stairs was the fisherman's workcoat, still damp from his efforts the previous day, and when she saw it the woman paused; she'd quilted that coat for him many years earlier and had patched and restitched so often it had grown very thin, yet still he refused to discard it, and in winter wore it every day. The woman gathered it to her gently, drew the sleeves of her robe into its arms and tucked her cowl within its hood, then hung the two as a single garment on a bright brass hook beside the door. Then she stepped naked across the threshold, into a landscape as white as teeth and sharp as wire, and made her way over ice floes till she reached the sea.

That morning when the fisherman woke to discover her missing and snow all around him in the middle of spring, it was this coat he reached for to keep him warm. He was to wear it for many years before he realized why it fit him more snugly in her absence than it had before. By then their daughter was a young woman soon to leave home, so he gave her the coat and his mind was easy knowing that wherever she traveled it would embrace her shoulders like an arm. Yet still sometimes if he observed of a patch of calm water rising at speed like boiled milk, he would halt his oars and sit very still and strain to hear the same choir whose song he had so dreaded once. Above him gulls would dodge and bicker, the weighted line groaned against the stern, the fish he'd caught gasped on the wet boards beneath him, but to his ears all would be silent, for he could not hear the woman's voice. Then the deafness would pass and he would row on, but in the still moments while he listened a melody would drip from his oars, each note clear and sweet and reassuring to the woman, listening for them from the depths below.

Pork Chops

(1996)

EILEEN FITZGERALD

Gina was standing right beside the boxes she'd piled in the breakfast nook, but neither she nor Phil mentioned them. She knew Phil was worried, but he needn't be. Yes, she was going to move out, but as Gina had said again and again, it was an experiment. It didn't have to be an ending.

She held the Styrofoam meat tray, the six small, premium pork chops, carefully arranged in two rows of three. Affixed to the clear plastic wrap was a bright orange sticker that said "Corn-fed." She pushed a finger into the plastic, then studied the dent in the pinkish grayish flesh. "They're not ours," said Gina. "It's like stealing."

But Phil was already paging through his cookbooks, looking for recipes: pork roast, Chinese pork, pineapple pork. He explained again, patiently: "I went to the store. I picked out my groceries. I waited in line. I paid my money. It's not like I put the pork chops in my pocket or shoved them down the front of my pants, but somehow it happened—they got in my bag. My position"—he laid his hand on his chest for emphasis—"is that if the store screws up, the store should suffer." It was true that he'd noticed the package while he was still in the parking lot at the grocery store, but he was in a hurry then, with barely enough time to get to the dry cleaners before it closed. In any event, he wasn't sorry, and he didn't feel guilty either. He and Gina had come home from the supermarket plenty of times minus some item they'd paid for: dental floss, garlic, laundry soap. Gina was forgetting that, thought Phil. She was forgetting all those other times.

Looking at the pork chops, Gina remembered the foul-smelling petting zoo her parents had taken her to when she was a child, the goats balancing on the fence and bleating, the dank barn and the enormous pig she'd seen there, the ten or twelve snorting, squirming piglets attached to the big sow's nipples. "You like bacon?" her father had said. "That's bacon right there."

It had taken her a long time to decipher Phil's system of morality, and even that understanding was incomplete. If a cashier gave him too much change, he never mentioned the mistake, even if the person seemed very young or very dumb, even if Gina poked him and raised her eyebrows. "How will they learn if I do the math for them?" he reasoned. But at restaurants and stores, he always put spare change into the tins and jars soliciting donations for the Community Kitchen or the Lion's Club or for some kid in Martinsville who needed a kidney. Phil copied computer software but wouldn't tape off CDs, and he offered no convincing reasons as to why one practice was acceptable while the other was not. Was it because software was technology while music was art? Though Gina had spent more than two years with Phil, she still hadn't figured him out.

"We never eat pork chops," said Gina.

"I do," he said. "I eat them at lunch in the cafeteria. I eat them all the time when you're not around."

It was strange to think of, Phil eating pork chops when she wasn't around, one after another, nothing but pork chops. What would he do when she left? "I'm thinking of the people who bought them," she said. "It's not the store that suffers."

The most likely suspects, Phil thought, were the people in front of him in the checkout line, an old couple buying old-people food—saltines and eggs and hard candy, red-and-white peppermints for the grandchildren, yellow-wrapped butterscotches for themselves. The woman wore a tailored coat, the man a suit and tie. They looked like they could get hold of more pork chops if they wanted to. If they really wanted pork chops, Phil decided, they could have them; they could go to a restaurant and order them with mashed potatoes on the side.

"They were old," said Phil, "but they seemed rich or at least comfortable. Anyway"—he held out the unwieldy mass of his keys—"if you feel that strongly, why don't you take them back?" He didn't push the keys in Gina's face or rattle them menacingly; they lay quietly in his opened palm. The relationship might be spiraling downward—it might even be over—but for now they shared a house, a bed, a refrigerator. If he walked on tiptoe and spoke in whispers, she might change her mind. She might decide to stay.

Gina frowned. "You take them back."

"I don't have a problem with them. If it's up to me, I'll keep them."

She stood with her hands on her hips, with the boxes stacked up behind her. "I won't eat them."

"There's tuna," said Phil, flipping through the cookbook. "Turkey, yogurt, eggs. Eat whatever you want."

The pork chops landed on the table with a thud, and Gina left the kitchen. Never the satisfaction of a real fight, she thought. No matter how shrill she got, no matter how nasty, Phil was mild mannered, a compromiser. He was annoying. "Fine, fine, fine," he'd say. And meanwhile, he was making the pork chops; he was doing exactly what he wanted to do.

Of *course* she wouldn't take back the pork chops. They had nothing to do with her. She didn't buy them, she didn't want them, they weren't—were not—her problem. Lying on the couch, she picked up the newspaper, shook out the pages, read.

Phil cut slices of onion and laid the circles flat on a plate. He watched the blade as it sliced through one of the rounds, metal hitting porcelain with a ping. If Gina was in the kitchen now, she'd shake her head and sigh; she'd take the knife from his hand, and he'd have no choice but to stand stupidly by and watch her. She'd have some fast, efficient method—six quick whacks and then sweep the chopped onion into a bowl. Well, she wasn't here now, thought Phil. He could do as he liked.

He imagined the people who'd paid for the pork chops, the old people. Once they got home, they pulled out the heavy black skillet. They melted fat and then reached inside the grocery bag, reached, reached. . . .

Phil wondered if they were the kind of people to turn off the burners and drive back to the store, wave the receipt at the service desk, and demand restitution. Or would they simply resign themselves to the loss and find something else to fry? They'd sit at the table, two old people, eat fried eggs and talk about the pork chops. What could have happened? Had they just plain forgotten to pick them up? No, the receipt said clearly, said without a doubt, that they'd bought them. Oh, well, they thought. Such is life.

Phil wondered what their names might be: Trudy and Oscar or maybe Emily and Warren. No, he decided, they were Millie and Jack, and though they were old, they still enjoyed sex. Sometimes when the weather was mild, they closed all the blinds and went around the house without any clothes on, each at perfect ease with the other's saggy body. Who cared about flab and wrinkles? They loved each other! Sometimes Jack and Millie would stop puttering for an hour or so; they'd lie on the couch or right on the rug and make love. Their children had moved to different states and had good jobs, careers even. They were gynecologists and economics professors. In the summer the whole family convened at a lake in Michigan for canoeing and swimming, sun and trout.

What did they need pork chops for? They had afternoon sex and a lake in Michigan. Phil, meanwhile, had nothing. He had five days a week of junior high math students. He had Gina bringing home more boxes every day. "I hope we'll still be friends," she said. "I hope we'll still do things."

He pushed his fingernail against the clear plastic that was wrapped around the pork chops. The film stretched, then sagged, then finally tore. Phil looked at the punctured plastic, the exposed pork chops. From the living room he heard Gina rattling the newspaper. If she was reading Ann Landers, she'd be in the kitchen in two minutes. "Who does Ann Landers think she is?" she'd say, shaking the paper in Phil's face.

"Don't read it," Phil would advise, and Gina would twist the newspaper into a tube, then slap the table with the mangled pages.

"Everyone reads Ann Landers," she'd say. "How can I not read it?"

Phil would stand quietly and consider his possibilities. If he said, "You're irrational," she'd say, "I'm leaving." And if he said, "There, there," she'd leave him anyway. Every option seemed to have the same outcome: Phil in the kitchen, alone with his pork chops.

Onions, oil, lemon, garlic. Two hours to marinate, then sauté, then bake. There was plenty of time to venture out for bread. Phil put on his jacket and went to the garage for his bike. He thought of the first months after Gina had moved in. On Saturday mornings they used to bicycle to the bakery and buy a loaf of Amish dill. At home they boiled a dozen eggs and made a huge vat of egg salad, which they never came close to finishing. But Phil felt there was an appropriateness to a dozen eggs, the carton full, then empty, the eggs in a single layer at the bottom of the pan.

Gliding silently on his bike, Phil felt like some kind of nocturnal animal. He made out details in the darkness—a cat's yellow eyes and then the brownish orange remains of a pumpkin. Gina had vetoed the idea of Halloween candy when they passed the holiday aisle in the grocery store, and Phil had gone along with her then. But he liked Halloween; he didn't want the holiday to just slip by, just another gray, chilly day. After work on the thirty-first, he stopped at Target and bought an orange plastic pumpkin and a bag of miniature candy bars. He put on the porch light, but as Gina had predicted, no trick-or-treaters came knocking. When the news came on at ten, Gina pointed to the heap of little candy bars. "Now what?"

"We eat them," Phil said, grinning and rubbing his hands together. "We divide them half and half." But Gina didn't want all that candy in the house, and Phil took the plastic pumpkin to school the next day and passed it around in homeroom, to seventh-graders who were already sick from too much candy.

They were going to get married, and now they weren't. They'd been engaged. They'd told people; they'd picked a tentative date, but now she was leaving, and there was nothing Phil could do. He assumed they weren't engaged anymore, but he wasn't sure. Neither of them had issued a statement. When friends asked Phil about the wedding, he said simply, evasively, that they'd hit some snags. He didn't know what Gina said; he wasn't even sure what snags they'd hit. He knew only that she wanted time and space, friends, direction. She'd joined a Masters swim team, and four days a week she went straight from work to the Y. She came home after nine, her hair in wet strings, her skin smelling of chlorine—though she claimed to have taken a shower. "With soap?" asked Phil, and Gina showed him her plastic soap dish, placed his fingers on the wet bar inside. Phil imagined the men she might be swimming with—barrel-chested, hairless men in Speedoes— is that what she liked? He pedalled faster just thinking about it. Big-shouldered, slim-waisted men with hair that looked like metal. At first he had tried to fill the swimming hours with tennis, but now it was too cold to coax anyone to play, and he mostly just watched TV or read the paper or planned for the next day's classes.

"Isn't it boring to swim laps?" asked Phil. "Isn't it like walking back and forth in a little room?"

"I think about things," said Gina. "It's not like I leave my brain in the locker room. On the other hand, it's great sometimes to think of nothing at all, to have water all around and quiet."

Phil would imagine floating on his back in a lagoon in the Caribbean, blue sky and water all around. But no matter how appealing Gina's descriptions and his own mental pictures, Phil didn't like to swim. He flailed, he sank, he got water up his nose, and all the next day he sniffled and sneezed.

At the bakery the racks were almost empty. Instead of French bread, Phil had to settle for a homely, lumpy loaf of German rye. He stood for a time in front of the cookie counter. Maybe he should get dessert. What went with pork chops? The cookies were enormous, almost as big as his outstretched hand. If Gina didn't want hers, it would be more than Phil could manage to eat two. He pictured Gina's cookie sitting in its bag on the kitchen counter, getting stale, grease spots showing through the paper. She wouldn't eat the cookie, and neither would Phil, but they wouldn't throw it away either, until it was beyond hard. Or the more likely scenario: she'd move out and leave the cookie, and Phil would be too depressed to ever throw it away. Did Gina even eat cookies now that she was so serious about swimming? Phil didn't know. He didn't know anything about her anymore.

He'd parked his bike in front of the store, and now as he loaded the bread into his backpack, he prayed he wouldn't see anyone he knew. He still loved Bloomington, but lately the town seemed so small and claustrophobic. He'd lived here since his freshman year in college, and he was thirty now. That was twelve years, long enough. He couldn't go anywhere without seeing someone he knew, friends from undergrad days or men he played softball with or fellow teachers at the junior high or even his students. Stop, chat, move along. When Phil and Gina went to their first appointment for couples' counseling, they saw a college friend of Phil's in the hallway of the medical complex. They had to pretend nothing was happening. "Hello!" they'd said. "And what's new with you?"

For months they had talked of being married; they had decided, had gone so far as to look for rings in the mall, but after no more than five minutes of viewing selections, Gina had fled the store. Phil excused himself and wandered the mall looking for her. He saw twenty or thirty women with straight brown hair and jeans shorts, women who could have been Gina, but weren't. There she is, Phil would think, but then she wasn't. He found her finally on a bench outside Penney's, where she was sitting beside a large, yellow potted plant.

"All those names were driving me crazy," said Gina. "Everlasting. Sweetheart. I hated sitting in those purple chairs, and that man with his hair all puffed out, being so helpful and holding out the rings. He was driving me nuts."

Phil wondered how else such a transaction could be managed—he could pick something out and give it to her, the old traditional way, but he wanted Gina to get a ring she liked. Maybe they could look through a catalogue. Once he'd had a girlfriend who left jewelry catalogues lying around his apartment; she'd open the pages to a spread of diamond rings, with circles drawn around the ones she liked. Once she wrote, "Phil will buy me this ring."

But Phil, who was fast losing interest in the woman, wrote, "No, he won't."

"What do we need rings for, anyway?" asked Gina. "If we know we love each other, shouldn't that be enough?"

"Whatever you want," said Phil. "If you don't want one, we won't get one." But gradually Phil realized: it wasn't just the rings.

A few weeks later—six months ago—Gina joined the swim team. She signed up for a Spanish class once a week. On days she didn't

swim, she jogged, and sometimes Phil would join her. But more frequently, she left without him, and when he got home from work, she'd
be sitting on the floor in the living room, stretching out.

"I would have gone with you," Phil would say, trying to hide his
disappointment.

"Oh," Gina would say. "I just wanted to get it over with."

And now she was starting to go out with her new swimming friends.
On Saturday mornings they all went out for pancakes, for carbo load-
ing. One night after practice a group of people had drinks and dinner,
and Gina didn't come home until eleven. Phil, meanwhile, had waited
anxiously, picturing her car spun out of control and smashed against a
tree, her spine severed and blood pouring out of her nose. "You're
paranoid," she said when he met her on the porch that night.

"I'm not paranoid," said Phil, "but I do worry."

She mentioned names, but she didn't really describe any of her
swimming friends, except the coach, Greg, who was spacey and knew
Mark Spitz. "Greg says, don't come so much out of the water for
butterfly. He says Mark Spitz just did that for pictures, to look cool in
pictures.

"Greg said if I had started swimming when I was nine, I could
have been a good college swimmer. He says I've got a good feel for
the water.

"Should I be disappointed," she asked, "that I didn't swim in college? That I'm twenty-five now and didn't become what I could have
become?"

Phil didn't know what amount of regret was appropriate. The only
similar situation he could think of was when he was in eighth grade in
the all-school spelling bee, and he missed a word on purpose, to avoid
the embarrassment of winning. Then in high school he quit the tennis
team, but that was because he realized he'd never make varsity. Regret
had never seemed like a useful emotion; it just wasted time and made
you miserable. If Gina took her boxes and left tomorrow, he'd miss

her, but he wouldn't necessarily have regrets. If he got to be eighty years old, though, and never married anyone, if he was living in a trailer and eating beans out of the can, maybe then he'd have regrets. Maybe he'd wish he had spelled that word correctly so many years before: c-o-n-f-e-t-t-i.

Back home Phil parked his bike in the garage. Inside the house he could smell onions and garlic, good, strong smells. Gina was gone— out running, apparently—though he'd asked her many times not to go by herself after dark. He reasoned with her, pleaded with her, but to no avail. "You're crowding me," she said.

If she wanted privacy, Phil thought, if she wanted room to breathe, why couldn't she just move into the second bedroom; why couldn't they just be platonic for a while? She could have her own little space. They could buy groceries separately, maybe just share milk and toilet paper. But what would the parameters be then? If she got a new boyfriend, would she bring him home?

In the early days there hadn't been any problems with closeness, with crowding. Gina and Phil did everything together—jogging, shopping, laundry—everything. But now that Gina was so busy with work and exercise, Phil almost always did the shopping by himself. He changed the sheets on the bed; he cleaned the bathroom, hung up the wet towels. On Sundays while Gina was at church, he made cinnamon rolls with icing. He made them for Gina more than for himself, and usually she seemed pleased, though sometimes she didn't want them— she'd eaten doughnuts during the community hour after the service.

Gina almost never thanked him. She asked how much the groceries were and gave him half. Sometimes she asked him to buy tampons or deodorant for her, but that was the extent to which she acknowledged how much of the grunt work he'd taken on in recent months. To be honest, he liked the routine, but he would have appreciated a little gratitude nonetheless.

They almost never fought during the time they'd been together.

Even now that relations had gotten strained, anger came out in brief spurts—a slammed door, a few sharp words. Most often they spoke calmly, reasonably, with Phil making great efforts to understand Gina's point of view. But as careful as he tried to be, he still said things he wished he hadn't: "If you're so unhappy," he'd said one night, "maybe you should move out."

"Maybe that's the answer," said Gina. "Maybe I will."

Phil cracked two eggs into a bowl and beat them with a fork. Why didn't she just get on with it, take her boxes and move in with one of her swimming friends, submerge herself completely in that world of wet hair?

Then he thought of himself bent over the toilet, wiping the porcelain with a sponge, and the question reversed itself: Why would she leave?

He filled another bowl with fine bread crumbs, added spices and parmesan cheese, then sifted the grains with his fingers. Why did it keep coming back to what Gina wanted? Why spend all his energy worrying over that question? Why didn't he wonder what he wanted himself?

He wanted to go to a country where parrots would fly past his window, or to a place that still had glaciers. He wanted to walk along the ocean and pick up sand dollars—with Gina if she'd go, and without her if she wouldn't.

He wanted Gina to stop swimming, to stay home, to get old with him.

Sometimes when they sat on the sofa watching TV, Gina would hold out her arm. "Feel my muscles."

He'd press his fingers against her bicep. "Amazing," he'd say.

During the day, Gina would run through the cemetery near their house, but at night the grounds were too isolated, too scary. Most of the nearby roads were busy, and the sidewalks were unreliable, leading into ditches or ending without warning. When she ran at night, Gina circled the block, around and around, past the same houses until she'd logged four miles. When she moved, she'd live in town, closer to the center of things, and she could run on the high school track. It would be the same thing, running around in circles, but she'd feel less silly somehow.

She'd found a place; she'd signed the lease. He must have guessed about the boxes. It was so strange to think about: they were going to get married—they had interviewed caterers and discussed rice pilaf—and now she was moving out. She hoped they would stay friends, maybe even date, spend Saturday nights watching TV, hanging out.

The air was chilly, but comfortable, and her pace was steady, a bit slower than usual. She felt good, though; she felt strong. She was ready to move on. She had her futon, her answering machine, her dishes, her papasan chair. She'd be paying more for rent than she paid now, but financially she'd be okay. She worked as a secretary at a law firm, and though the job itself was rather grim, the pay was reasonable; the benefits were good.

Of course, Phil was the one who first suggested that she move. And once the idea was out on the table, he certainly hadn't made efforts to convince her to stay. He hadn't done anything except turn into a neat freak overnight, bleaching out the kitchen sink every day and changing the sheets two times a week. She couldn't even use a glass in the kitchen without him washing it as soon as she was finished. And the pork chops—weren't they just another way to annoy her, another way for Phil to prove that he was in the driver's seat?

And yet, how could any of this be Phil's doing? After all, he was the one who wanted them to try counseling. She was the one who couldn't find the time after the first two sessions, after the therapist said, "Some couples decide that they don't have enough common ground for a lasting relationship."

No matter how Gina sliced up the situation, no matter how she arranged the facts, she was the one who wanted to leave. She was the one who panicked in the jewelry store. All that talk of pear cuts and facets, settings and carats and prongs, all the words that conveyed the same terrifying message: forever forever forever.

"We want good value," Phil had said, and that's when her insides seized up, when she ran away, had to run.

She thought of what the swim coach had said—she could have been a college swimmer. She was trying to decide whether she had regret. She wished she'd had the excitement, the camaraderie. But she wondered, can you regret something you never really had a chance at? It wasn't as if she'd been a swimmer and then gave it up because she was lazy or started smoking pot every day. It wasn't as if someone had given her a plane ticket to France, and she'd been afraid to use it, afraid that her French wasn't good enough. Would she regret not marrying Phil? She didn't think so, but it was so hard to know for sure. Maybe they'd still get married. Maybe this was just what they needed, time to think and room to breathe.

Gina turned off Park onto Nancy Lane. Though it was just the first week in November, the house on the corner was blazing with Christmas lights. There was a green plastic sleigh in the yard with an illuminated Santa perched on the seat. The edges of both sleigh and Santa were blurry, as if obscured by a snowstorm, though the night was clear, not even foggy.

She couldn't explain what had happened to the relationship. It wasn't until the moment she said she'd marry Phil that she realized she didn't want to. Now she thought back to the day they'd met, a cold afternoon in February at the counter of Mr. Copy, where she'd gone to get résumés printed, and Phil was copying his tax return.

Over coffee she told him how she'd come to Bloomington to get a master's in English, how she'd dropped out of the program after one miserable semester. And Phil just listened; he let her talk. Unlike the rest of the world, he didn't bombard her with suggestions about careers she should consider: Have you thought of going to library school? What about nursing? That night they went to a movie, and on the weekend they went ice skating. Before a month had gone by, they moved in together, or, rather, Gina moved her things into Phil's house.

It was fun back then: Phil planned picnics to the quarries and long bike rides in the country; he made her a piñata; he bought her a cactus. One weekend they drove up to Chicago on a whim, ate Indian food and visited the aquarium. They'd walked down busy streets in the brisk air, and Gina remembered throwing her hat up, like Mary Tyler Moore, giddy and happy, and then catching it again.

He told her he'd become a teacher in part for the summers off, so he could travel, and Gina had admired his foresight, his adventurousness. He liked to go to travel agencies and bring home booklets about cruises and safaris and wine tours of France, but Gina realized soon enough that he never advanced beyond reading. He never actually went anywhere, except occasionally to Evansville to visit his parents. Once or twice a year he went to the post office and got forms for a passport, but he never finished filling them out.

Of course, thought Gina, these were petty complaints, excuses that would sound foolish if she spoke them aloud. "I'm leaving you because you don't have a passport." "I'm leaving you because you change the sheets too often." She couldn't help it, though. She didn't want her life to be so ordered and so dull: groceries on Thursday, laundry on Friday, egg salad on Saturday.

She thought of the night a few months ago when she'd come home from swimming, still buzzing from the adrenaline of the final sprint, still replaying her flip turn, her push off the wall, her burst of speed. She found Phil slumped in an armchair that had been pulled close to the TV. His legs were stuck out straight in front of him; his hands were folded on his chest. He was watching a car race, absolutely motionless, a television zombie.

"Don't you have anything better to do?" asked Gina.

"I guess not," he said, and he still didn't move.

Back on the porch, Gina cleaned the mud off her shoes on the dirty doormat. Phil was back, and the house smelled wonderful. He didn't say anything when she came in. Gina sat on the floor in the living room and stretched. It had been cool outside, so she wasn't too sweaty. She could get by without a shower.

This is how it would be when she lived alone. No one would call out to her from the kitchen when she came back from running. There wouldn't be this smell of cooking, but there would be quiet and calm. There would be room for her to stretch out; she could take half an hour if she wanted to. She'd go swimming and then eat pancakes. She'd study Spanish. She'd go to work. Every once in a while she'd call Phil and see how he was doing. That would be her life, and she would be happy. She stood and pressed her hands against the wall, stretching her calves, then wandered into the kitchen, where Phil was snapping green beans. She inhaled deeply, with her eyes closed. "Yum," she said.

"I can set you a plate," said Phil.

"Look at this bread." Gina pulled off a chunk, smelled it, then ate it.

Phil decided he wouldn't push; he wouldn't ask her again, but he'd set her plate at the table. He'd say "Dinner" like it was nothing, like he was saying "Phone's for you" or "You got a letter." And she would eat. And she would stay. He should have gotten ice cream—mint chocolate chip or coffee—but he hadn't thought of it until right now. He hadn't realized how important it might be.

"It smells really really good in here," said Gina.

"Just a few more minutes." Phil dropped the beans into the pan and put on the lid.

At the last minute he put candles on the table, turned off the over-head light in the dining room and switched on a smaller lamp. When she sat at the table, Phil passed her the platter of pork chops. He was nice enough not to tease her.

"These are great," said Gina, chewing. "I don't even like pork chops."

Phil described the recipe he'd followed: the marinade and the breading, then sauté and bake. "The green beans are just steamed, and of course, I bought the bread."

"Delicious."

If she was going to make her announcement, he didn't have to make it easy for her. If he made it hard enough for her to say she was leaving, maybe she'd decide to stay. Phil could dream up some elaborate plot, like putting an engagement ring at the bottom of a bowl of chocolate pudding, and they could try again—they could fall in love again.

"You know," said Phil, "all the famous swimmers eat pork chops—Diana Nyad ate pork chops."

"Who's Diana Nyad?"

"You call yourself a swimmer? Didn't you watch that movie in school? She swam to Cuba. She ate a lot of food before she went. The object, I think, is to make yourself look like a dolphin so that you blend in with the rest of the ocean."

Gina laughed. She ripped off another chunk of bread, and watching her chew, Phil could see the future. After they ate they'd settle in on the couch. They'd kiss to try to taste the flavors on each other's lips—garlic, lemon, onion, oil—and from kissing they'd drift seamlessly into sex.

"Did she make it to Cuba?" asked Gina.

"I don't think so. I think she ran into sharks."

"You know," said Gina, "I've been thinking. So what if I wasn't a college swimmer? I'm not a ballerina either. Or a chemist."

"That's true," said Phil. "I wouldn't worry about it."

"It's stupid, I guess, to spend so much time swimming." She stuck her finger to the plate to pick up bread crumbs that had fallen off. "What's it for? I'll still be twenty-five. I can't change that. I can't go back to college."

"It's not stupid if you like it."

"I do like it."

"Then why is it stupid?"

Gina held up her plate and looked sheepish. "Can I have another pork chop?"

After they ate they turned on the TV and sat on the sofa, and one thing followed another, just as Phil had imagined. They kissed first, savoring the taste of meat and garlic, and then they made love with the sounds of CNN in the background: Bosnia, Haiti, unemployment, housing starts. Phil was polite; he was careful. He ran his hand over Gina's back, but he waited for her to unhook her bra herself. He waited for her to move her hand to his pants. But once Phil was inside her, he felt fierce, not gentle. He pushed into her hard, pushed as far as he could go. Maybe he was trying to hurt her, but she wrapped her legs around him and moved with him. When Phil looked down at Gina, her eyes were closed, and she was smiling, and he loved her. He loved her.

Afterward, Gina stood in the shower humming "Sleigh Ride" as hot water ran over her body. She soaped herself once and rinsed off, then soaped herself again just so she could stay longer in the warmth of the water. She felt comfortable, happy, almost free.

Often in the past she'd moved from boyfriend to boyfriend, without leaving any gaps. But now there was no one on the horizon, no cowboy on a white horse. She saw a clear space out in front of her where she could be by herself. She could think about the things that needed to be thought about. She could quit her job and go to Spain, eat paella and sleep in monasteries. She could go to Aspen and work in a ski lodge.

As for Phil, it was just—was it wrong to feel this way?—she didn't need him anymore.

In the living room, Phil sat alone on the sofa. He felt as if his insides had been scraped out, even though she'd kissed him on the nose just before she stood up. He thought of how he'd been afraid that Gina would get shoulders like the East German women swimmers. But Gina, while she certainly got stronger, also got sleeker, sexier. It was steroids that made the East Germans look so misshapen. Swimming alone didn't have such an effect. Swimming made her beautiful.

He knew this was just the moment she was waiting for. Some moment she could call an ending, a special evening to remind her why she'd loved him in the first place. She'd be gone next week, or she'd be gone in the morning. And as time passed she'd forget how they used to ride their bikes to the bakery and to the park; she'd forget her suggestion that they still be friends. She'd forget the head-spinning taste of the pork chops. She'd tell people that Phil had stolen them; she'd say he forced her to eat them, that she hated pork chops.

When Phil heard the bedroom door close, he went into the bathroom. Opening the door he released a cloud of steam. The floral fragrance was from Gina's shampoo, but he couldn't help thinking he was breathing in her essence. She'd hung her wet washcloth on the edge of the tub to dry, and he picked it up. He laid the cloth on his face and breathed in the smell of her soap, her skin. He was smelling soap and crying, sitting on the side of the tub in the steamy intimacy of the bathroom, his body heaving with the force of his sobs. There was nothing to be done. She was going. She was gone.

In bed Gina was asleep already, warm and washed and dreaming. She was moving steadily through the water, over waves and under waves, swimming out to sea.

City Life

(1996)

MARY GORDON

P eter had always been more than thoughtful in not pressing her about her past, and Beatrice was sure it was a reason for her choice of him. Most men, coming of age in a time that extolled openness and disclosure, would have thought themselves remiss in questioning her so little. Perhaps because he was a New Englander—one of four sons in a family that had been stable for generations—perhaps because he was a mathematician, perhaps because both the sight of her and her way of living had pleased him from the first and continued to please him, he had been satisfied with what she was willing to tell. "My parents are dead. We lived in Western New York State, near Rochester. I am an only child. I have no family left."

She preferred saying "I have no family left"—creating with her words an absence, a darkness, rather than to say what had been there, what she had ruthlessly left, with a ruthlessness that would have shocked anyone who knew her later. She had left them so thoroughly that she really didn't know if they were still living. When she tried to locate them, with her marriage and her children and the warm weight of her domestic safety at her back, there was no trace of them. It had shocked and frightened her how completely they had failed to leave a trace. This was the sort of thing most people didn't think of: how possible it was for people like her parents to impress themselves so little on the surface, the many surfaces of the world, that they would leave it or inhabit it with the same lack of a mark.

They were horrors, her parents, the sort people wanted to avert their eyes from, that people felt it was healthful to avert their eyes from. They had let their lives slip very far, further than anyone Beatrice now knew could even begin to imagine. But it had always been like that: a slippage so continuous that there was simultaneously a sense of slippage and of already having slipped.

It was terribly clear to her. She was brought up in filth. Most people, Beatrice knew, believed that filth was temporary, one of those things, unlike disease or insanity or social hatred—that didn't root itself in but was an affair of surfaces, therefore dislodgeable by effort, will, and the meagerest brand of intelligence. That was, Beatrice knew, because people didn't understand filth. They mistook its historical ordinariness for simplicity. They didn't understand the way it could invade and settle, take over, dominate, and for good, until it became, inevitably, the only true thing about a place and the only lives that could be lived there. Dust, grime, the grease of foods, the residues of bodies, the smells that lived in the air, palpable, malign, unidentifiable, impossible to differentiate: an ugly population of refugees from an unknowable location, permanent, stubborn, knife-faced settlers who had right of occupancy—the place was theirs now—and would never leave.

Beatrice's parents had money for food, and the rent must have been paid to someone. They had always lived in the one house: her mother, her father, and herself. Who could have owned it? Who would have put money down for such a place? One-story, nearly windowless, the outside walls made of soft shingle in the semblance of pinkish gray brick. It must have been built from the first entirely without love, with the most cynical understanding, Beatrice had always thought, of the human need for shelter and the dollar value that it could bring. Everything was cheap and thin, done with the minimum of expense and of attention. No thought was given to ornament or amplitude, or even to the long, practical run: what wouldn't age horribly or crumble, splinter, quickly fade.

As she grew older, she believed the house had been built to hide some sort of criminality. It was in the middle of the woods, down a dirt road half a mile down Highway 117, which led nowhere she knew, or maybe south, she somehow thought, to Pennsylvania. Her parents said it had once been a hunting lodge, but she didn't believe it. When she was old enough to have learned about bootlegging, and knew that whiskey had been smuggled in from Canada, she was convinced that the house had had something to do with that. She could always imagine petty gangsters, local thugs in mean felt hats and thin-soled shoes trading liquor for money, throwing their cigarette butts down on the hard, infertile ground, then driving away from the house, not giving it a thought until it was time for their next deal.

Sometimes she thought it was the long periods of uninhabitedness that gave the house its closed, and vengeful, character. But when she began to think like that, it wasn't long before she understood that kind of thought to be fantastical. It wasn't the house, houses had no will or nature. Her parents had natures, and it was their lives and the way they lived that made their dwelling a monstrosity.

She had awakened each day in dread, afraid to open her eyes, knowing the first thing they fell on would be ugly. She didn't even know where she could get something for herself that might be beautiful. The word couldn't have formed itself in her mind in any way that could attach to an object that was familiar to her, or that she could even imagine having access to. She heard, as if from a great distance, people using the word "beautiful" in relation to things like trees or sunsets, but her faculty for understanding things like this had been so crippled that the attempt to comprehend what people were saying when they spoke like this filled her with a kind of panic. She couldn't call up even the first step that would allow her, even in the far future, to come close to what they meant. They were talking about things out of doors when they talked about trees and sunsets. And what was the good of that? You could go out of doors. The blueness of the sky, the brightness of the sun, the freshness of a tree would greet you, but in the end you would only have to go back somewhere to sleep. And that would not be beautiful; it would be where you lived. So beauty seemed a dangerous, foreign, and irrelevant idea. She turned for solace, not to it, but to the nature of enclosure. Everything in her life strained toward the ideal of separations: how to keep the horror of her parents' life from everything that could be called her life.

She learned what it was she wanted from watching her grade school teachers cutting simple shapes—squares, triangles—and writing numbers in straight columns on the blackboard or on paper with crisp, straight blue lines. The whiteness of pages, the unmuddled black of print, struck her as desirable; the dry rasping of the scissors, the click of a stapler, the riffling of a rubber band around a set of children's tests. She understood all these things as prosperity, and knew that her family was not prosperous; they were poor. But she knew as well that their real affliction wasn't poverty but something different— you might, perhaps, say worse—but not connected to money. If she could have pointed to that—a simple lack of money—it would have been more hopeful for her. But she knew it wasn't poverty that was the problem. It was the way her parents were. It was what they did.

They drank. That was what they did. It was, properly speaking, the only thing they did. But no, she always told herself when she began to think that way, it wasn't the only thing. Her father, after all, had gone out to work. He was a gravedigger in a Catholic cemetery. Each morning he woke in the dark house. Massive, nearly toothless, and still in his underwear, he drank black coffee with a shot in it for breakfast, and then put on his dark-olive work pants and shirts, his heavy boots—in winter a fleece-lined coat and cap—and started the reluctant car driving down the dirt road. He came home at night, with a clutch of bottles in a paper bag, to begin drinking. He wasn't violent or abusive; he was interested only in the stupor he could enter and inhabit. This, Beatrice knew early on, was his true home.

Her mother woke late, her hair in pin curls wrapped in a kerchief, which she rarely bothered to undo. She was skeletally thin; her skin was always in a state of dull eruptions; red spidery veins on her legs always seemed to Beatrice to be the tracks of a slow disease. Just out of bed, she poured herself a drink, not bothering to hide it in coffee, and drank it from a glass that had held cheese spread mixed with pimentos, which her parents ate on crackers when they drank, and which was often Beatrice's supper. Beatrice's mother would sit for a while on the plaid couch, watch television, then go back to bed. The house was nearly always silent; there were as few words in the house as there were ornaments. It was another reason Peter liked her. She had a gift, he said, for silence, a gift he respected, that he said too few people had. She wondered if he would have prized this treasure if he'd known its provenance.

Beatrice saw everything her parents did because she slept in the large room. When she was born, her parents had put a crib for her in the corner of the room nearest their bedroom, opposite the wall where the sink, the stove, and the refrigerator were. It didn't occur to them that she might want privacy; when she grew taller, they replaced the crib with a bed, but they never imagined she had any more rights or desires than an infant. The torpor, the disorder of their lives, spread into her quarters. For years, it anguished her to see their slippers, their half-read newspapers, broken bobby pins, half-empty glasses, butt-filled ashtrays traveling like bacilli into the area she thought of as hers. When she was ten, she bought some clothesline and some tacks. She bought an Indian bedspread from a hippie store in town; rose-colored, with a print of tigers; the only vivid thing in the place. She made a barrier between herself and them. Her father said something unkind about it, but she took no notice.

For the six years after that, she came home as little as she could, staying in the school library until it closed, walking home miles in the darkness. She sat on her bed, did what was left of her homework, and, as early as possible, lay down to sleep. At sunrise, she would leave the house, walking the roads till something opened in the town—the library, the five-and-ten, the luncheonette—then walking for more hours till the sun set. She didn't love the woods; she didn't think of them as nature, with all the implications she had read about. But they were someplace she could be until she had no choice but to be *there* again, but not quite *there*, not in the place that was *theirs*, but her place, behind her curtain, where she needn't see the way they lived.

She moved out of her parents' house two days after she graduated from high school. She packed her few things and moved to Buffalo, where she got a job in a tool and die factory, took night courses at the community college. She did this for five years, then took all her savings and enrolled in the elementary education program at the University of Buffalo full time. She'd planned it all out carefully, in her tiny room, living on yogurt she made from powdered milk, allowing it to ferment in a series of thermoses she'd bought at garage sales, eating the good parts of half-rotten fruit and vegetables she'd bought for pennies, the fresh middle parts of loaves of day-old bread. Never, in those years, did she buy a new blouse or skirt or pair of jeans. She got her clothes from the Salvation Army; it was only later, after she married, that she learned to sew.

In her second semester, she met Peter in a very large class: European History 1789–1945. He said he'd fallen in love with several things about her almost at once: the look of her notebooks, the brilliant white of the collar of her shirt as it peeked over the top of her pastel-blue Shetland sweater, the sheer pink curves of her fingernails. He said he'd been particularly taken by her thumb. Most women's thumbs were ugly and betrayed the incompleteness of their femininity, the essential coarseness of it. The fineness of her thumb, the way the nail curved and was placed within the flesh, showed there wasn't a trace of coarseness in her: everything connected with her was, and would always be, fine. He didn't find out until they'd dated a few times that she was older, more than three years older than he was. He accepted that she'd had to work those years because her parents had— tragically—died.

Beatrice knew what Peter saw when he looked at her: clarity and simplicity and thrift, an almost holy sign of order, a plain creature without hidden parts or edges, who would sail through life before him making a path through murky seas, leaving to him plain sailing: nothing in the world to obstruct him or the free play of his mind. She knew that he didn't realize that he had picked her in part for the emptiness of her past, imagining a beautiful blankness, blameless, unpopulated, clear. His pity for her increased her value for him: she was an exile in the ordinary world he was born into, lacking the encumbrances that could make for problems in his life. He believed that life could be simple, that he would leave from a cloudless day and drop into the teeming fog of mathematics, which for him was peopled, creatured, a tumultuous society he had to colonize and civilize and rule.

She knew he felt he could leave all the rest to her, turning to her at night with the anomaly of his ardor, another equation she could elegantly solve. His curiosity about the shape of her desire was as tenderly blunted as his curiosity about her past, and she was as glad of the one as of the other. Making love to him, an occurrence she found surprisingly frequent, she could pretend she was sitting through a violent and fascinating storm that certainly would pass. Having got through it, she could be covered over in grateful tenderness for the life that he made possible: a life of clean linen and bright rooms, of matched dishes and a variety of specialized kitchen items: each unique, for one use only, and not, as everything in her mother's house was, interchangeable.

So the children came, three boys, and then the farmhouse, bought as a wreck, transformed by Beatrice Talbot into a treasure, something acquaintances came to see as much (more, she thought, if they were honest) as they did the family itself. Then Peter's tenure, and additions on the house: a sewing room, a greenhouse, then uncovering the old woodwork, searching out antique stores, auctions, flea markets for the right furniture—all this researched in the university library and in the local library—and the children growing and needing care so that by the time Peter came home with the news that was the first breakup of the smooth plane that had been their life together, the children had become, somehow, twelve, ten, and eight.

He had won a really spectacular fellowship at Columbia, three years being paid twice what he made at Cornell and no teaching, and a chance to work beside the man who was tops in his field. Peter asked Beatrice what she thought, but only formally. They both knew. They would be going to New York.

Nights in the house ten miles above Ithaca—it was summer and in her panic she could hear the crickets and, toward dawn, smell the freshness of the wet grass—she lay awake in terror of the packing job ahead of her. Everything, each thing she owned, would have to be wrapped and collected. She lived in dread of losing something, breaking something, for each carefully selected, carefully tended object that she owned was a proof of faith against the dark clutching power of the past. She typed on an index card a brief but wholly accurate description of the house, and the housing office presented her with a couple from Berlin—particle physicists, the both of them, and without children, she was grateful to hear. They seemed clean and thorough; they wanted to live in the country, they were the type who would know enough to act in time if a problem were occurring, who wouldn't let things get too far.

Peter and Beatrice were assured by everyone they talked to in New York that their apartment was a jewel. Sally Rodier, the wife of Peter's collaborator, who also helped Beatrice place the children in private schools, kept telling her how incredibly lucky they were, to have been given an apartment in one of the buildings on Riverside Drive. The view could be better, but they had a glimpse of the river. Really, they were almost disgustingly lucky, she said, laughing. Did they know what people would do to get what they had?

But Beatrice's heart sank at the grayness of the grout between the small octagonal bathroom floor tiles, the uneven job of polyurethaning on the living room floor, the small hole in the floor by the radiator base, the stiff door on one of the kitchen cabinets, the frosted glass on the window near the shower that she couldn't, whatever she did, make look clean.

For nearly a month she worked, making the small repairs herself, unheard-of-behavior, Sally Rodier said, in a Columbia tenant. She poured a lake of bleach on the bathroom floor, left it for six hours, then, sopping it up, found she had created a field of dazzling whiteness. She made curtains; she scraped the edges of the window frames. Then she began to venture out. She had been so few places, had done so little, that the city streets, although they frightened her, began to seem a place of quite exciting possibilities. Because she did her errands, for the first time in her life, on foot, she could have human contact with no fear of revelation. She could be among her kind without fear every second that they would find out about her: where and what she'd come from, who she really was. Each day the super left mail on her threshold; they would exchange a pleasant word or two. He was a compact and competent man who had left his family in Peru. She could imagine that he and the Bangladeshi doormen, and the people on the streets, all possessed a dark and complicated past, things they'd prefer to have hidden as she did. In Buffalo, in Ithaca, people had seemed to be expressing everything they were. Even their reserves seemed legible and therefore relatively simple. But, riding on the bus and walking out on Broadway, she felt for the first time part of the web of concealment, of lives constructed like a house with rooms that gave access only to each other, rooms far from the initial entrance, with no source of natural light.

By Thanksgiving, she was able to tell Peter, who feared that she would suffer separation from her beloved house, that she was enjoying herself very much. The boys, whose lives, apart from their aspects of animal survival, never seemed to have much to do with her, were absorbed in the thick worlds of their schools—activities till five or six most nights, homework, and supper and more homework. Weekends, she could leave them to Peter, who was happy to take them to the park for football, or to the university pool, or the indoor track. She would often go to the Metropolitan Museum, to look at the collection of American furniture or, accompanied by a guide book, on an architectural tour.

One Thursday night, Peter was working in the library and the boys were playing basketball in the room the two younger ones shared, throwing a ball made of foam through the hoop Peter had nailed against the door. Beatrice was surprised to hear the bell ring; people rarely came without telephoning first. She opened the door to a stranger, but catching a glimpse of her neighbor across the hall, a history professor, opening her door, she didn't feel afraid.

The man at the doorway was unlike anyone she had spoken to in New York, anyone she'd spoken to since she'd left home. But in an instant she recognized him. She thought he was there to tell her the story of her life, and to tell Peter and everyone she knew. She'd never met him, as himself, before. But he could have lived in the house she'd been born in. He had an unrushed look, as if he had all the time in the world. He took a moment to meet her eyes, but when he did, finally, she understood the scope of everything he knew.

She kept the door mostly closed, leaving only enough space for her body. She would allow him to hurt her, if that was what he came for, but she wouldn't let him in the house.

"I'm your downstairs neighbor," he said.

She opened the door wider. He was wearing a greasy-looking ski jacket which had once been royal blue; a shiny layer of black grime covered the surface like soot on old snow. The laces on his black sneakers had no tips. His pants were olive green; his hands were in his pockets. It was impossible to guess how old he was. He was missing several top teeth, which made him look not young, but his hair fell over his eyes in a way that bestowed youth. She stepped back a pace further into the hall.

"What can I do for you?"

"You've got kids?"

For a moment, she thought he meant to take the children. She could hear them in the back of the apartment, running, laughing, innocent of what she was sure would befall them. A sense of heavy torpor took her up. She felt that whatever this man wanted, she would have to let him take. A half-enjoyable lassitude came over her. She knew she couldn't move.

He was waiting for her answer. "I have three boys," she said.

"Well, what you can do for me is to tell them to stop their racket. All day, all night, night and day, bouncing the ball. The plaster is coming down off the ceiling. It's hitting me in my bed. That's not too much to ask, is it? You can see that's not too much to ask."

"No, of course not. No," she said. "I'll see to it right away."

She closed the door very quickly. Walking to the back part of the apartment, she had to dig her nails into the palms of her hands so that she wouldn't scream the words to her children. "They didn't know, they didn't know," she kept saying to herself. It wasn't their fault. They weren't used to living in an apartment. It wasn't anybody's fault. But she was longing to scream at them, for having made this happen. For doing something so she would have to see that man, would have to think about him. An immense distaste for her children came over her. They seemed loud and gross and spoiled and careless. They knew nothing of the world. They were passing the ball back and forth to one another, their blond hair gleaming in the light that shone down from the fixture overhead.

She forced herself to speak calmly. "I'm afraid you can't play basketball here," she said. "The man downstairs complained."

"What'd you say to him?" asked Jeff, the oldest.

"I said I'd make you stop."

"What'd you say that for? We have just as much right as he does."

She looked at her son coldly. "I'm afraid you don't."

The three of them looked back at her, as if they'd never seen her.

"I'll make supper now," she said. "But I have a terrible headache. After I put dinner on the table, I'm going to lie down."

While she was cooking, the phone rang. It was her neighbor across the hall. "Terribly sorry to intrude," she said. "I hope I'm not being a busybody, but I couldn't help overhear the rather unpleasant exchange you had with our neighbor. I just thought you should understand a few things."

I understand everything, Beatrice wanted to say. There's nothing I don't understand.

"He's a pathetic case. Used to be a big shot in the chemistry department. Boy genius. Then he blew it. Just stopped going to classes, stopped showing up in the department. But some bigwigs in the administration were on his side, and he's been on disability and allowed to keep the apartment. We're all stuck with him. If he ever opens the door and you're near, you get a whiff of the place. Unbelievable. It's unbelievable how people live. What I'm trying to tell you is, don't let him get you bent out of shape. Occasionally he crawls out of his cave and growls something, but he's quite harmless."

"Thank you," said Beatrice. "Thank you for calling. Thank you very much."

She put down the phone, walked into her bedroom, turned out all the lights, and lay down on her bed.

Lying in the dark, she knew it was impossible that he was underneath her. If his room was below the children's, it was near the other side of the apartment, far from where she was.

But she imagined she could hear his breathing. It matched her own: in-out-in-out. Just like hers.

She breathed with him. In and out, and in and out. Frightened, afraid to leave the bed, she lay under a quilt she'd made herself. She forced herself to think of the silver scissors, her gold thimble, the spools and spools of pale thread. Tried and tried to call them back, a pastel shimmering cloud, a thickness glowing softly in this darkness. It would come, then fade, swallowed up in darkness. Soon the darkness was all there was. It was everything. It was everything she wanted and her only terror was that she would have to leave it and go back. Outside the closed door, she could hear the voices of her husband and her sons. She put her fingers in her ears so she couldn't hear them. She prayed, she didn't know to whom, to someone who inhabited the same darkness. This was the only thing about the one she prayed to that she knew. She prayed that her family would forget about her, leave her. She dreaded the door's cracking, the intrusion of the light. If she could just be here, in darkness, breathing in and out, with him as he breathed in and out. Then. Then she didn't know. But it would be something that she feared.

"How about you tone it down and let your mother sleep?"

She closed her eyes as tightly as a child in nightmare. Then she knew that she had been, in fact, asleep because when Peter came in, sank his weight onto the bed, she understood she had to start pretending to be sleeping.

After that night, she began staying in bed all day long. She had so rarely been sick, had met the occasional cold or bout of flu with so much stoicism that Peter couldn't help but believe her when she complained of a debilitating headache. And it would have been impossible for him to connect her behavior with the man downstairs. He hadn't even seen him. No one had seen him except her and the woman across the hall who told her what she didn't need to know, what she already knew, what she couldn't help knowing.

She wondered how long it would be before Peter suggested calling a doctor. That was what worried her as she lay in the darkness: what would happen, what would be the thing she wouldn't be able to resist, the thing that would force her to get up.

She cut herself off fully from life of the family. She had no idea what kind of life was going on outside her door. Peter was coping very well, without a question or murmur of complaint. Cynically, she thought it was easier for him not to question: he might learn something he didn't want to know. He had joined up with her so they could create a world free from disturbance, from disturbances. Now the disturbance rumbled beneath them, and it only stood to reason that he wouldn't know of it and wouldn't want to know.

Each morning, she heard the door close as Peter left with the children for school. Then she got up, bathed, fixed herself a breakfast, and, exhausted, fell back into a heavy sleep. She would sleep through the afternoon. In the evening, Peter brought her supper on a tray. The weak light from the lamp on the bed table hurt her eyes; the taste and textures of the food hurt her palate, grown fragile from so much silence, so much sleep.

She didn't ask what the children were doing and they didn't come in to see her. Peter assumed she was in excruciating pain. She said nothing to give him that idea, and nothing to relieve him of it.

After her fourth day in the dark, she heard the doorbell ring. It was early evening, the beginning of December. Night had completely fallen and the radiators hissed and cooed. She tried not to hear what was going on outside, so at first she only heard isolated words that Peter was shouting. "Children." "Natural." "Ordinary." "Play." "Rights." "No right."

Alarm, a spot of electric blue spreading beneath one of her ribs, made her understand that Peter was shouting at the man downstairs. She jumped out of bed and stood at the door of the bedroom. She could see Peter's back, tensed as she had, in fourteen years of marriage, never seen it. His fists were clenched at his side.

"You come here, bothering my wife, disturbing my family. I don't know where the hell . . . what makes you think . . . but you've got the wrong number, mister. My sons are going to play ball occasionally at a reasonable hour. It's five-ten in the afternoon. Don't tell me you're trying to sleep."

"All right, buddy. All right. We'll just see about sleeping. Some night come midnight when everyone in your house is fast asleep, you want to hear about disturbing. Believe me, buddy, I know how to make a disturbance."

Peter shut the door in the man's face. He turned around, pale, his fists not yet unclenched.

"Why didn't you tell me about that guy?" he said, standing so close to her that his voice hurt her ears, which had heard very little in the last four days.

"I wasn't feeling well," she said.

He nodded. She knew he hadn't heard her.

"Better get back into bed."

The doorbell rang again. Peter ran to it, his fists clenched once again. But it wasn't the man downstairs, it was the woman across the hall. Beatrice could hear her telling Peter the same story she'd told her, but with more details. "The house is full of broken machines, he takes them apart for some experiment he says he's doing. He says he's going to be able to create enough energy to power the whole world. He brags that he can live on five dollars a week."

"Low overhead," said Peter, and the two of them laughed.

She was back in the darkness. Her heart was a swollen muscle; she spread her hands over her chest to slow it down. She heard Peter calling Al Rodier.

"Do you believe it . . . university building . . . speak to someone in real estate first thing . . . right to the top if necessary . . . will not put up with it . . . hard to evict, but not impossible. Despoiling the environment . . . polluting the air we breathe."

The word "pollution" spun in her brain like one of those headlines in old movies: one word finally comprehensible after the turning blur: Strike. War.

Pollution. It suggested a defilement so complete, so permanent, that nothing could reverse it. Clear streams turned black, and tarlike, verdant forests transformed to soot-covered stumps, the air full of black flakes that settled on the skin and couldn't be washed off.

Was that what the man downstairs was doing? He was living the way he wanted to, perhaps the only way he could. Before this incident, he hadn't disturbed them. They were the first to disturb him. People had a right not to hear thumping over their heads. Supposing he was trying to read, listening to music, working out a scientific formula.

Suppose, when the children were making that noise, he was on the phone making an important call, the call that could change his life.

It wasn't likely. What was more likely was that he was lying in the dark, as she was. But not as she was. He wasn't lying in an empty bed. He bedded down in garbage. And the sound of thumping over his head was the sound of all his fear: that he would be named the names that he knew fit him, but could bear if they weren't said. "Disreputable." "Illegitimate."

They would send him out into the world. If only he could be left alone. If only he could be left to himself. And her children with their loud feet, the shouts of their unknowingness told him what he most feared, what he was right to fear, but what he only wanted to forget. At any minute they would tell him he was nothing, he was worse than nothing. Everything was theirs and they could take it rightfully, at any moment. Not because they were unjust or cruel. They were not unjust. Justice was entirely on their side. He couldn't possibly, in justice, speak a word in his own defense. Stone-faced, empty-handed, he would have to follow them into the open air.

She heard Peter on the phone calling the people they knew in the building who'd invited them for coffee or for brunch. She kept hearing him say his name—Peter Talbot—and his department—Mathematics, and the number of their apartment—4A. He was urging them to band together in his living room, the next night, to come up with a plan of action before, he kept saying, over and over, "things get more out of hand. And when you think," he kept saying, "of the qualified people who'd give their eyeteeth for what he's got, what he's destroying for everyone who comes after him. I'll bet every one of you knows someone who deserves that apartment more than him."

She saw them filing into her house, their crisp short hair, their well-tended shoes, the smiles cutting across their faces like a rifle shot. They would march in, certain of their right to be there, their duty to keep order. Not questioning the essential rightness of clearing out the swamp, the place where disease bred, and necessarily, of course, removing the breeders and the spreaders who, if left to themselves, would contaminate the world.

And Beatrice knew that they were right, that was the terrible thing about them, their unquestionable rightness. Right to clear out, break in, burn, tear, demolish, so that the health of the world might be preserved.

She sank down deeper. She was there with those who wallowed, burrowed, hoarded, their weak eyes half-closed, their sour voices, not really sour but hopeless at the prospect of trying to raise some objection, of offering some resistance. They knew there could be no negotiation, since they had no rights. So their petition turned into a growl, a growl that only stiffened the righteousness of their purpose. "Leave me alone," is all the ones who hid were saying. They would have liked to beseech but they were afraid to. Also full of hate. "Leave me alone."

Of course they wouldn't be left alone. They couldn't be. Beatrice understood that.

The skin around her eyes felt flayed, her limbs were heavy, her spine too weak to hold her up. "Leave me alone." The sweetness of the warm darkness, like a poultice, was all that could protect her from the brutality of open air on her raw skin.

She and the man downstairs breathed. In and out. She heard their joined breath and, underneath that sound, the opening of doors, the rush of violent armies, of flame, of tidal wave, lightning cleaving a moss-covered tree in two. And then something else below that: "Cannot. Cannot. Leave me alone." Unheeded.

She turned the light on in the bedroom. She put on a pair of light blue sweatpants and a matching sweatshirt. On her feet she wore immaculate white socks and the white sneakers she'd varnished to brilliance with a product called Sneaker White she'd bought especially.

She put on earrings, perfume, but no lipstick and no blush. She walked out of the apartment. She knew that Peter, in the back with the children, wouldn't hear the door close.

She walked down the dank, faintly ill-smelling stairs to the apartment situated exactly as hers was—3A—and rang the bell.

He opened the door a crack. The stench of rotting food and unwashed clothes ought to have made her sick, but she knew she was beyond that sort of thing.

She looked him in the eye. "I need to talk to you," she said.

He shrugged then smiled. Most of his top teeth were gone and the ones that were left were yellowed and streaked. He pushed the lock of his blondish hair that fell into his forehead back, away from his eyes. Then he took a comb out of his pocket and pulled it through his hair.

"Make yourself at home," he said, laughing morosely.

There was hardly a place to stand. The floor space was taken up by broken radios, blenders, ancient portable TVs revealing blown tubes, disconnected wires, a double-size mattress. Beside the mattress were paper plates with hardened sandwiches, glimpses of pink ham, tomatoes turned to felt between stone-colored slices of bread, magazines with wrinkled pages, unopened envelopes (yellow, white, mustard-colored), sloping hills of clean underwear mixed up with balled socks, and opened cans of Coke. There were no sheets on the mattress; sheets, she could tell, had been given up long ago. Loosely spread over the blue ticking was a pinkish blanket, its trim a trap, a bracelet for the foot to catch itself in during the uneasy night.

A few feet from the mattress was a Barcalounger whose upholstery must once have been mustard-colored. The headrest was a darker shade, almost brown; she understood that the discoloration was from the grease of his hair when he leaned back. She moved some copies of *Popular Mechanics* and some Styrofoam containers, hamburger-sized, to make room for herself to sit. She tried to imagine what she looked like, in her turquoise sweatsuit, sitting in this chair.

"I came to warn you," she said. "They're having a meeting. Right now in my apartment. They want to have you evicted."

He laughed, and she could see that his top teeth looked striated, lines of brownish yellow striping the enamel in a way she didn't remember seeing on anyone else.

"Relax," he said. "It'll never happen. They keep trying, but it'll never happen. This is New York. I'm a disabled person. I'm on disability. You understand what that means? Nobody like me gets evicted in New York. Don't worry about it. I'll be here forever."

She looked at her neighbor and gave him a smile so radiant that it seemed to partake of prayer. And then a torpor that was not somnolent, but full of joy, took hold of her. Her eyes were closing themselves with happiness. She needed rest. Why hadn't she ever known before that rest was the one thing she had always needed?

She saw her white bathroom floor, gleaming from the lake of bleach she had poured on it. Just thinking of it hurt her eyes. Here, there was nothing that would hurt her. She wanted to tell him it was beautiful here, it was wonderful, it was just like home. But she was too tired to speak. And that was fine, she knew he understood. Here, where they both were, there was no need to say a word.

But he was saying something. She could hear it through her sleep, and she had to swim up to get it, like a fish surfacing for crumbs. She couldn't seem, quite, to open her eyes and she fell back down to the dark water. Then she felt him shaking her by the shoulders.

"What are you doing? What are you doing? You can't do that here."

She looked at his eyes. They weren't looking at her kindly. She had thought he would be kind. She blinked several times, then closed her eyes again. When she opened them, he was still standing above her, his hands on her shoulders, shaking them, his eyes unkind.

"You can't do that here. You can't just come down here and go to sleep like that. This is my place. Now get out."

He was telling her she had to leave. She supposed she understood that. She couldn't stay here if he didn't want her. She had thought he'd understand that what she needed was a place to rest, just that, she wouldn't be taking anything from him. But he was treating her like a thief. He was making her leave as if she were a criminal. There was no choice now but to leave, shamefully, like a criminal.

He closed the door behind her. Although her back was to the door, she felt he was closing it in her face and she felt the force of it exactly on her face as if his hand had struck it. She stood completely still, her back nearly touching the brown door.

She couldn't move. She couldn't move because she could think of no direction that seemed sensible. But the shame of his having thrown her out propelled her toward the stairs. She wondered if she could simply walk out of the building as she was. With no coat, no money, nothing to identify her. But she knew that wasn't possible. It was winter, and it was New York.

She walked up the stairs. She stood on the straw mat in front of her own door. She'd have to ring the bell; she hadn't brought her keys. Peter would wonder where she had gone. She didn't know what she'd tell him. There was nothing to say.

She didn't know what would happen now. She knew only that she must ring the bell and see her husband's face and then walk into the apartment. It was the place she lived and she had nowhere else to go.

Daily
Affirmations

(1996)

ERIN MCGRAW

A week before flying back to my parents' house for Christmas, my suitcases were already packed. I knew that packing early was an unproductive habit, discouraging me from living in the moment, but by three o'clock one sleepless morning my self-control had ebbed and I hauled out the suitcases for the plain relief of doing something.

It was December 8th, and I had been focusing my support group on families and the holidays since September, talking about strategies, battle. "You're going to be on the front lines. How will you defend yourselves when the choppers start coming in?" I suggested that they take home one another's telephone numbers as well as talismans to carry or wear. Myself, I packed two books of affirmations, the cassettes from the seminars I had led the summer before, and my favorite button—the one I liked to wear to workshops. It showed a stick figure tugging at a huge barbell, and it said LIGHTEN UP.

Thinking about what lay ahead, I pinned the button to my coat. My mother, who insisted on going to daily Mass, had just broken her ankle on a slick spot outside the church, so she would be bedridden— *helpless* was her word—for three months. When I talked to my father on the phone, he said she was making the whole ordeal worse than it had to be: "She won't use the crutches. She talks like nobody's ever been in pain before." I had to fight down my impulse to talk about honoring her pain, which he wouldn't have paid any attention to. Anyway, as long as I was in my own apartment, it was their issue, not mine.

After I finished packing I wandered into the kitchen and flicked open the freezer. I could catalogue every item in it, including the mousse cake left over from dinner with Jon in November. Binge eating in the middle of the night was another behavior I tried to avoid; it channeled into every old complex that had wrecked my twenties. I thought about this, then fished out the cake and went to the cupboard for peanut butter and bread.

In *Returning to the Body* I wrote a chapter called "Eating For Two" about this exact phenomenon. That chapter roped almost as much attention as the ones on sex, and for months after the book came out I fielded phone calls from women who wanted to confess their late-night eating. One woman wept and admitted that she'd eaten a stick of butter like a candy bar. We talked for half an hour, and before she hung up she gave me permission to use her story in my next book. I was already at work on it, a follow-up that my publisher wanted to call *Into the Light*. My suitcases were stuffed with notes, a computer, and the transcripts of fifty workshops. My theory was that by writing while I was home I could distance myself from my past and—a bonus—allow my parents to see the woman I had become.

I tucked a third book of affirmations into my purse. Trips home always courted danger; one step into my mother's kitchen and my whole new life would start to waver and float. I'd found it useful to talk in sessions about the dream I had when I was home—how a warm, dark current pulled me farther and farther from shore. When I described it, every head in the room nodded.

After I finished the cake I crossed my legs, relaxed my shoulders, and closed my eyes. I inhaled to the count of five and began that day's affirmation: *Today I will acknowledge that healing is a lengthy process, and I will give myself permission to take my time.*

I took thirty deep breaths and shifted on the couch, easing my pants at the waist where they bit. This was the fifth night in a row I had dipped into the Skippy. Peanut butter was itself a danger sign—hadn't I counseled clients to purge their cupboards before Thanksgiving?— but my resolve was shrinking the closer in time I got to my parents. A dull recklessness had set in; I was sleeping through the alarm in the mornings, too, skipping exercise classes, and not telling Jon about any of it. He was fond of reminding me that as an adult I had choices. *He* wasn't the one going to visit his parents. "We've learned to avoid the holidays," he said when I asked him. "Damage containment."

After the flight landed in Los Angeles and I shuffled to the terminal behind a grim man carrying an enormous plush kangaroo, the first thing I saw was my father, waving hugely, grinning and hooting like a Texan. Usually it was my mother who stood leaning against the low restraining gate. She was nearsighted but never could find glasses that pleased her, so she would crane over the gate and peer at every passenger until she found me. Dad would be waiting in the car outside, avoiding the parking lot where, my mother had once read, over a hundred muggings occurred every year. But now here was my father, whooping at me, calling my nickname, which only my family used.

"Tracy. Tracybug! Hey, sight for sore eyes," he said, trying to grab me with one arm, my bag with the other.

"Hi, Dad," I said into his shoulder. "Hey, yourself."

"You don't know how glad I am to see you," he said, letting me step back so he could look at me. He was beaming.

"It's funny to see you here without Mom."

"Everything's going to feel different," he said. "We've had McDonald's for dinner the last four nights."

"What, you forgot how to scramble eggs?"

"Your mother won't let me in the kitchen. She thinks I'll ruin her frying pans. But now that you're home, we've got her over a barrel. What say, halibut tonight?"

"Mom doesn't like fish," I said.

"I know," Dad said, wiggling his eyebrows, "but I do." He threw his arm around me again and squeezed. "It's good to have you home, Trace. You look good. Cornfed."

"I've been very busy," I said. I started down the corridor toward Baggage Claim—it was time to get moving, and Dad looked like he was ready to stand there all day. "You can't imagine all the conferences, and then small-group work. And my publisher wants the new book by June."

"Don't count on having much of your own life. This is your mother we're talking about."

I turned back to look at him. He was holding his mouth in a sour smirk, watching me. Usually it took a little longer before he started coaxing me to join in the chorus of his gripes. "You need to be generous with her now," I said. "This sort of challenge can be a good thing—a time of real growth. She's just discovering her own new needs."

"Me too," Dad said. "My need is to get her to quit complaining. When Monsignor called last night she talked to him as if her leg had fallen off. After she hung up she cried and reminded me that faith can move mountains."

I closed my eyes for a second. I'd heard about her faith all my life and hadn't seen it move so much as a note card. Then I told him, "We can fry some potatoes with the halibut—that's always nice. If you have any apples on hand, I'll make a pie."

"Now you're talking," Dad said.

We stopped at the big Thriftimart on the way home and bought seven bags of groceries; whenever I stopped to look at an item he put it in the basket. "I don't know what we have," he shrugged, collecting cornmeal, tortillas, vanilla. By the time we got home it was nearly four, the sun low. I tried to pull my snug jacket tighter against the sharp ocean wind. Dad unlocked the door, then gestured me in with a courtly sweep of his arm, and so I was the first one to see my mother crumpled at the bottom of the stairs.

"I was sure you'd been in an accident," she said. "I told myself you would never take so long to get home unless you were in an accident." She turned and I could see how she had tucked the leg without the cast underneath her to keep warm. I could also see the urine puddled on the back of her robe. "If you understood the pain I'm in you would have been home sooner."

"Mom, I'm sorry," I said, dropping the bag of groceries and squatting, letting her shoulder rest against me.

"Of course you are," she said.

Dad trudged up from the garage with the suitcases, muttering as he always did about how I must have packed bricks. When he saw my mother on the floor he sighed. "For Pete's sake!" he said, setting down the suitcases and bending to lift her up.

"I was trying to get to the bathroom," she said. "You were gone so long." I had never heard this flutter in my mother's voice before; it made her sound dreamy and mild.

"Why do you think the doctor gave you crutches?" Dad said.

"They hurt. You think it's easy, but it's not."

"You're working hard to keep it complicated, I'll give you that," he said, letting her lean on him as she steadied herself on her good foot. "This is quite a homecoming for our daughter."

"Don't worry about me," I said with idiotic brightness. "I'm tough."

My mother glanced at me and twisted her mouth. "I'm not weak. But I could never have believed the pain."

"Now that we've shared that, Mother, let's get you cleaned up,"

Dad said, steadying her hips while she awkwardly hopped ahead of him. "Then you can come down and talk to Tracy. She's going to make dinner for us."

"A blessing," my mother said, breathing hard. Dad turned and winked at me, and I rolled my eyes despite my best intentions. When I finally got Jon on the phone I told him, "It's like trying to skirt quicksand." I'd been home four days. "One foot is always being sucked in."

"This is your opportunity to work on detachment," Jon said.

"I *am* detached, dammit! She talks about God's will, Dad tells her he's sick of her whining, and I try to yell over the fray for timeouts."

"You can only take responsibility for yourself." His voice was hushed and choppy, and I could picture him nodding, waving his hands to hurry me along. His wife was probably in the next room.

"It's such a relief to talk to you," I told him, my voice sticky and wheedling. "Something solid."

"The holidays are a difficult period for everyone," he said. "We're set up to relive the traumas of our youth."

"We've got the mother lode here," I muttered, but he was still talking, reminding me not to let others define my reality for me. I didn't have a chance to tell him about watching Bob Hope on TV the night before. When I had stood up to bring in some cookies, I'd seen my mother's face covered in tears. "It hurts. It's like something gnawing with sharp teeth," she said when I touched her shoulder.

"For God's sake, Mother, why didn't you say something?"

"I didn't want to bother you," she said.

Now Jon was saying something about openness to life's richness. "I'm open, all right," I told him. "I'm taking in every morsel that my rich new life provides me."

Dad came down to the kitchen every night after the news, when I liked to have a snack. "At least you can get some sleep," he would say, breaking off a piece of whatever I was fixing. "She lies there and just moans—in case I forget for one second the torment she's in."

It was so hard to resist. Already I had found myself telling him about washing her hair, when she started screaming because I'd let shampoo seep into the corner of her eye. She pushed me out of the way and hobbled back to bed, soapy water streaming down her neck. "Fastest I've seen her move since I got home," I told Dad.

"Good to know something can make her jump," he said. "She lies in that bed like she wants to make a career of it."

Now that I was home, Mother was making more of an effort to get up, but her lurching progress exhausted her. She collapsed into chairs and sat, pinched and silent, for fifteen minutes before she could gather herself to speak, her suffering face a mask of accusation. I trudged downstairs later every morning and lost whole afternoons to elaborate recipes that called for stacks of phyllo and jasmine rice.

"I really would prefer plain chicken," she kept saying from the armchair we rolled into the kitchen for her. "Rich food doesn't agree with me."

"We're trying some new things," I said, enjoying myself. Every time I suggested a menu, Dad headed to the grocery store—I had never cooked better. With his encouragement I tried chicken stuffed with chestnuts, then chocolate-mint torte. Mom picked at all of it. "Good for the holidays," I said when I served the cashew-rolled tenderloin that, left over, made such good sandwiches. "I never eat this way at home."

In the mornings I stared helplessly at my computer screen. The chapter about coping strategies was only sketched out, so every morning I reviewed my thick stack of notes and case histories, but I couldn't manage to boil them down to the punchy, practical style my publisher liked. After a half hour of twisting on the chair, I would go to call Jon.

I knew my relationship with him was not ideal, but it was a far cry from the terrible entanglements of my twenties. "More affairs than I could count. As long as men were unavailable—emotionally, maritally, fiscally, or physically—I was game," I wrote in the first book. That confession had been crucial to my recovery; it took all the courage I had to publish it. After the book was included in an article about recovery literature in *Newsweek*, my brother Patrick, who used to drive me wild by calling me Saint Tracy when I was a pious ten-year-old, sent a furious letter addressed to Slut Tracy. I brought it to the next session I facilitated, as an example of how families can stand in the way of our growth.

My parents never mentioned the book at all. I waited until two weeks after the *Newsweek* article, then finally asked whether they had seen it. Jon held my hand while I made the call.

"I'm not going to read your book. It doesn't seem like something I'd like," said my mother. "We're both very proud of you."

I didn't bring it up again. When Jon reminded me that issues unaddressed are issues unresolved, I flashed my LIGHTEN UP button and told him to take it one day at a time.

Now I typed: *Health isn't a goal like a high-jump record. Life throws us curves.* I sighed and wiped it out. There was a tap at the door, and then Dad opened it a crack to look in at me. "Just making sure you were off the phone," he said.

"Never was on it. Couldn't get through."

"You've sure been trying."

"You monitoring my calls?"

"Now, now. Your mother frets. She thinks your publisher should be the one paying for long distance."

"I'm not calling my publisher," I said. "I'm calling my collaborator."

"Collaborator. Sounds like World War II." He raised his eyebrows at me; he wanted me to play, but I swiveled back to the keyboard.

"I'll shave my head and you can parade me through the streets,"
I said.

"I'll leave that to your mother. Who wants you to wash her hair
this afternoon. Apparently she's recovered from your last assault."

I quickly typed: *We who seek and strive are heroes. If we really understood the powers we struggle against, we would never even try.* I saved it,
turned off the computer and said, "Tell her majesty I'm on my way." I
pushed back from the computer so hard my chair screed and stuttered
on the wood floor.

After I'd been home a week, I had floated well out to sea. I sat at my
computer from nine to twelve and buried myself in cooking all afternoon. My mother joined me when I came downstairs, so my sautéing
and mincing stopped whenever she needed more pillows, or a sip of
grapefruit juice, or—the most frequent—help in hobbling to the bathroom. Sometimes she sat at the table and phoned one of my brothers,
then handed off the phone to me. "Well," said James, the one closest
to me in age. "Doing your bit for family. Finding stories to tell for
another book?"

"I'm working on it," I said evenly.

"Myself, I thought the first book was plenty."

"That was about opening the door. This one is about starting the
journey."

"Mary's fine, and the twins are great," he said. "They've got
almost all their teeth."

"You should bring them out to visit. Mom tells me all the time how
she wishes you'd let her dote on them." That was the kind of mean-
ness I wouldn't have stooped to a month before, but I was tired now
from treading water. Jon hadn't answered the phone since the first call.
When I took time out to read my affirmations, they felt absurdly child-

ish, chipper as Norman Vincent Peale, and it took an exhausting act of faith to bother opening the book at all.

"It's good to see you and your brothers talking," Mom would say after I hung up. "A close family is one of the graces I pray for every day."

This was an opening volley, but there was no way I could have known. All that time with idle hands and a throbbing ankle had allowed her to conceive a campaign. She launched it on Christmas Day, after we came home from Mass, which had left us undone. She had winced and gasped the whole short ride, then redirected Dad three times inside the church so her wheelchair could be out of the way but she could still see the priest.

After the service she held court outside in the thin December sunshine, and it took a half hour to wheel her away from the people who pressed their cheeks to hers and told her how she never left their prayers for a minute. "And see," my mother kept saying, grabbing my hand, "my daughter is home." I smiled while they nodded coolly at me. Clearly they had read the book. *I have nothing to apologize for,* I wanted to say. But they didn't talk to me, and by the time we came back home I felt as if I'd been flayed.

"I can't tell you the good it does me to go to Mass," my mother uttered faintly, her head resting against the chair back. "I miss it so."

"Until that ankle heals, God's just going to have to understand," Dad said.

"The Mass is a comfort," she said.

"You certainly are popular," I said. "It looked like you knew everybody there."

"We have a community."

"Now that people know what's happened to you, I'm sure they'll call," I said. "You won't feel so cut off."

"It's not the same," she said, twisting fretfully and waving her

hand as if she would reach over the length of her cast and rub it herself. Dad and I watched her for a second, then I went over and rested
her foot on my lap while I got to work. She went on: "The new priest,
Father Jim, he gives such good sermons—even on weekdays. You
wouldn't believe."

"What are you angling for, Mother?" Dad asked.

"Nothing. I'm not *angling for* anything."

"That's good," he said. "Because Trace and I have got our hands
full here."

"I just think," she said, "it would be nice if you two went to Mass
together during the week. It would be a nice sharing time for you. And
you could tell me what Father Jim said."

I kept rubbing and shot a look at my mother's face, which
was serene as the Madonna's. "Mary Grace," Dad said, "you're out
of your mind."

"I don't know why you say that. I think it's a good idea."

"Tracy and I are not going to start getting up at five-thirty to go off
to Mass for you. I can't believe the wild hairs you get."

"I don't see any reason that you should speak for our daughter,"
my mother said, trying to hike herself up in the chair. "She's perfectly
capable of speaking her own mind."

I was bent over her foot, still rubbing away. "I write in the mornings," I said.

"You could manage a half hour for Mass. It would probably help
your writing."

"I don't think so," I said without looking up.

She yanked her foot away from me, swinging the cast out so hard it
jerked off my lap and crashed to the floor. "So you won't even consider it? Both of you just too busy to do this simple thing for me." She
sniffed hard and tried to clamp her mouth. "It's a small enough favor,
God knows."

"Not everyone shares your sense of priorities, Mother," Dad said.

"You've made that perfectly clear," she said. I reached down to hoist her leg back up, but she snapped, "Just leave it alone. I wouldn't dream of putting you out."

"Don't jump all over the girl," Dad said. "You're making a federal case here. It isn't that important."

"I'm glad. I'm certainly glad to know that what I want isn't that important."

"Oh, for Christ's sake, Mary Grace, lighten up."

"I wish you wouldn't swear in front of Tracy."

"She's heard worse," he said.

"I'll go," I said. I was clenching and unclenching my hands, trying to control my breathing. I didn't look at either one of them. "Maybe I'll find something I can use in my book."

"No," my mother said, jerking her chin. "I don't want you to go now."

"Tracy, sweetheart, you can't just give in," Dad said.

I stood up. "I can't stand listening to you two. When did you start going for blood? You never used to fight like this."

Dad shook his head and sighed. "Always. But you didn't notice what you didn't want to see."

"You had your head in the clouds," my mother nodded.

"Things are different now," I said, and went into the kitchen. I had made brownies and icebox bars the day before, from recipes in my mother's oldest cookbook. I put a handful on a plate and then headed for the stairs and my room, but Mother called me back.

"You know," she said, "Doris Dilworth started going to daily Mass when she began her diet last year, and she was finally able to lose the weight and keep it off. Isn't that interesting? You could use a story like that in your book."

"You really don't know when to stop, do you?"

"I don't know what you're talking about," she said, starting to tear up again. "I just made a suggestion."

"Well, I've got a suggestion for you. Next time you're checking in with God and asking for graces, trying asking for the grace to know when to shut the fuck up," I cried as I tore up the stairs.

Jon wasn't home when I called, and he wasn't home half an hour later. Grimly, I settled in for a siege, picking up the phone every twenty minutes. He would have to answer eventually. He and his wife were staying home for the holidays, taking the chance to spend time with their sons. I used his private number, which rang only in his home office. All afternoon and into the evening it rang.

At intervals I went downstairs to snack. Neighbors had been dropping by with cookies and fruitcake; the kitchen counter was crowded with fancy plates, and Mom held court in the living room. Once I ran into my father, who said, "You've been slaving away ever since you got here. What say I go out and pick up some Mexican tonight?" I shrugged, nodded. If he opened the refrigerator he would see enough leftovers piled up to see us into the new year.

I didn't get Jon until after eleven—after one, Chicago time. "I've been trying to reach you all day," I said when he picked up the phone.

"We went ice skating, and then we picked out a tree."

"How nice. Around here it's cruise missiles."

"You're giving in. This is how they win. What good is all your hard work if you don't hold tight under fire?"

"Families aren't supposed to be battlegrounds," I spat.

"Well, they are," he said shortly. "But at least you ought to be getting some good material."

"As a matter of fact, I'm not," I said. "My parents have staged a battle to the death, and my mother has bullied me into daily Mass."

"She can't make you do anything," he said, and I thought that finally he'd said something my mother would agree with. Even as irritated as I was, I was swayed by the heavy, creamy fall of his voice. "You're the only one responsible for your decisions."

"Listen, I got them to stop carping at each other for two minutes."

"Holidays. They should give out operator's licenses," he said. A moment's silence shimmered between us, a rare thing. "Is there anyone there you can talk to?"

"Jon, I'm talking to you."

"When you're in a bottom you need lots of support."

"Good. Support me. Did you tell your wife about the apartment?"

"I told you I don't want to bring it up until after New Year's."

The glittering silence descended again, and I pictured the lines of telephone wire between us shivering. "Look," I said. "I'm having a hard time. Things here are terrible. I need to know that you miss me."

"Of course I do."

"Try sounding like you mean it."

"I do. Of course. But remember," he said, "some needs can't be filled by another person." I could hear the wheels of his desk chair rolling over the floor, and I pictured a woman standing in the doorway of his office. "Some needs it's up to you to find a way to fill."

"Thanks, Jon. Good support. I'll be sure to call again," I said.

"It'll be easier when you come home. You'll remember who you really are. You'll reclaim your new life."

"If my old life lets me," I said.

I groped down the stairs the next morning at quarter to six, stuffing my shirt into my pants. Mom always put on a skirt to go to church, but if God were expecting me this early, He could accustom His all-seeing eyes to pants. Which, too tight, hurt.

Dad was already in the kitchen, dressed and glaring at the front page. "I didn't think you were going," I said.

"Once you gave in I didn't have any choice," he sighed. "What the hell. Let's go out to the Belgian waffle place afterwards. Salvage something out of this."

"What about Mom?" I said.

"I walked her to the bathroom at two, three, four-thirty and five-thirty-seven. If she's not dry as the Sahara, she can hold it." He fished in his pocket and tossed me the car keys. His night vision had gotten dicey, and the sky was still licorice black. "Let's go."

We didn't talk at all on the drive over, and had to grope our way into the tiny chapel where daily Mass was held. A dozen women were already yawning and waiting in sweatsuits and stretch pants, none of them under sixty. They swung their heads up together like deer when we slipped in; Dad and I took the folding chairs by the door. Everyone was close enough to touch.

When the priest walked in without any fanfare, the women rustled to their feet, and he smiled at them, a sweetly generous smile. "Let's begin," he murmured, and crossed himself. The women pitched into prayer with wonderful precision, none of them even bothering to glance at the missalettes. I tried to imagine coming here every morning in the dark, reciting prayers by heart, and then going home to make breakfast. It felt utterly peculiar.

"What do you make of that?" I asked Dad when we were back out in the chilly black air.

"I managed to nod off twice, which is about as much rest as I get sleeping with your mother these days."

"Don't tell her that. She'll count it as a victory."

When we got to the car I turned up both the heat and the radio, and we sang along to "The Lion Sleeps Tonight" all the way to the restaurant. A waitress with eyes that looked like they'd been set in with a wood-burning kit seated us without a word. Dad glanced at the menu, put it aside, and cleared his throat while I was looking at the strawberry waffles. He fiddled with his napkin, folding it into a little pup tent next to his fork until I looked up again. "You know, you're going to have to talk to your mother," he said.

"I'll pay attention to the sermon tomorrow. I'll take notes."

"Not that," he said. "You were pretty hard on her yesterday. She takes these things to heart."

I frowned at him. "She's got to learn to back off."

Dad smiled unhappily and picked up his spoon, trying to catch his reflection in its bowl. "She doesn't realize sometimes. She loses track. But Honey, she cried all night."

"Shit." I closed my eyes. "I lost my temper. I'm not perfect." I looked up; he was nodding, and my anger started to swell again. "We do everything she wants. You say so yourself. Why else are we going to church in the middle of the night?"

"You don't get it, Trace. You'll be gone in a week. When James told her not to come out after his babies were born, she cried every day for a month. She loves you all."

"So who are you trying to help here? You want me to go do a case study on her dieting friend to get her off your back?"

"She thinks you'd be happier if you were thinner. You *are* pretty big, Honey."

I folded the menu closed and shook out my napkin so it had no wrinkles. My stomach growled. I knew I had the words to respond to him; I had a whole speech. But the speech had drifted away, and there was only a table separating me from my father. It wasn't enough.

"Displacement?" I said. That didn't sound right.

"Not funny, Tracy."

"I'm not trying to be funny."

"I don't need your psychoanalysis," he said sharply.

"We're a long way from the couch. I'm just wondering what it means when a father avoids his wife by trying to win over his daughter."

He flattened his hand on the table. "I said *don't* condescend to me."

"Well then, *don't* intrude in my life."

"I'm so far from intruding, I can barely even see you," he snarled. "If I was going to start intruding, I might take your telephone away. I might ask why you're the one doing the calling, and why you don't mention his name to your mother, who would like to know. I could lock up the sugar and butter and feed you lettuce."

"I made the food you told me you liked," I said behind clenched teeth. "I'll be happy to make salads for you in the future. Better yet, I'll hand over the lettuce. You can make dinner to your own exacting standards."

The blank-eyed waitress materialized next to us and stood tapping her order pad. "Just coffee," Dad said, glancing at her. "I can't eat this early."

I opened the menu and pointed to a photo of three waffles mortared by thick layers of whipped cream with blueberries. "That," I said. "And coffee." The air in the restaurant was warm and sweet, full of low laughter and the scrape of cutlery on heavy plates. I was so hungry the images wobbled before me.

"That ought to help things," Dad said after the waitress turned away. "Good choice."

"We came to a waffle restaurant. I ordered waffles."

"Nothing I say makes any difference to you, does it?"

"I'm an adult. I have to make my own decisions."

"You make some piss-poor ones."

"Impressive talk from a man who's spent fifty years arguing with his wife."

Dad leaned across the table. "At least I married the person I sleep with. At least I don't have to plead with her to talk to me."

"No," I said. "You save the pleading for me."

Dad stared at me, then stood up. "You know what your mother says? She says evil takes good and makes it look bad. I *know* you, no matter what you think." He spun around and walked out. When the waitress came back I nodded at his place, as if he were going to be back in a minute, and I went ahead and ate my breakfast. Even though the berries were lost in the gummy syrup and the coffee was faintly burned, I ate every scrap and wiped the plate to get the juice. When I finished my cup of coffee, I drank Dad's.

Tiptoeing into the chapel by myself the next morning I still felt clumsy and shy, but the chair by the door was open and the quiet warmth of the room was comforting. I had joined my parents for TV the night before, apologizing at the first station break. They nodded, and I went up early to bed. When I left, I heard my mother sigh.

I folded my hands now and watched the faces around me—they were uniformly peaceful, as if bread were on the rise in every one of their kitchens. I couldn't imagine my mother wearing such a look. Patrick used to do imitations called "Mom at Mass": preoccupied, muttering, ticking off mysterious lists on his fingers, while James and I roared.

The side door opened and I looked up to see an ancient woman supported by a walker, wearing the shapeless polyester skirt and crepe-soled shoes of a nun. Two women near the door bounced up and guided her to a chair, one on each side, smiling and murmuring. They moved as if they had done this many, many times, waiting until the sister was secure in her chair before they moved her walker to the wall.

I kept staring at the nun, her faint hair coiled into a permanent that exposed rambling pathways of scalp. The way she tottered, she must have gotten up at three to make it to the chapel. Surely, I thought, the priest could have come to her. But when she had entered her face held the same calm, pleasant look as the other women's. If you came every morning, over enough years, did the calm come?

Abruptly tears began to well, and I couldn't stop them, although I knuckled my eyes hard. In fact, I started to cry harder, giving in, and had to bury my face in my hands to muffle the sniffling. After a minute I felt a hand rest on my shoulder. "There, now," a voice said. "There. Is it someone you're crying for?"

"My mother," I whispered, and though I didn't look up, I imagined the woman beside me nodding.

"No prayers are ever wasted," she said. "God hears you. He'll bring your mother to his side. He sends tears as a sign."

I glanced up then, blinking to see her mild face. "It's not that simple."

"I'll pray for her too," she said, smiling and patting my hand. I was saved from having to respond by the priest, who hurried through the door straightening his stole and inviting us to pray. Swiping my hand across my nose, I joined in the communal responses, feeling the tears stop and the sense of warm, liquid collapse drain away. I was back on dry land beached on the shore of my recognizable life, where I stood uncomfortably waiting for Mass to end.

The old nun stayed seated through the opening prayers, but she swayed gently to her feet during the intercessions. After the other women offered their personal supplications—"For my daughter Jenny," "For my cousin's surgery"—she said, her voice dry as a rusk, "God's peace to the believers." The prayer made me uneasy. I couldn't be sure what it meant, but the woman beside me shot up and cried "Amen" with a zeal that made me cringe, and the others echoed her. I craned, trying to see the nun's face—had she intended a call to arms? All I could see was her wavering stance, and then the unceremonious way she tipped over, dropping to her left like a carelessly balanced board.

The women were at her side instantly, straightening her legs, rubbing her hands and feet, and the priest was already moving toward her with the host. I stood watching from the back, caged between folding chairs, as out of place as an ungainly animal. The nun coughed once, tremendously, from the altar. At least she was alive. For the second time tears surged, and I groped to the door and felt my way out.

Ten minutes later I was still sitting in the cold car, listening to my breath shudder and catch. I felt chastised, slapped by some vast hand, and I could stop crying only by focusing on what was directly in front of me: a spindly tree supported on three sides by wires. No leaves. Its branches made shadows like veins in the light from the church.

Going home was out of the question. Mom would ask about Mass, and I'd be helpless to control my ragged crying. Or Dad would shoot me an ironic look. I felt naked, skinned, lacking the barest boundary from the world. When my feet got cold enough to hurt, I started the car, but from the parking lot I turned right, away from East Gables.

Seventeen years had passed since I'd lived in California, but I drove with perfect memory. Jon had some expression about how adolescent knowledge is the hardest to lose. I felt more adolescent now than I had ever felt as a teenager—teary, shaken, driving because movement was soothing.

I turned onto Pacific, the first four-lane street I'd ever known. Windows were starting to light up; coffee-shop parking lots were half full, and a wobbly mechanical Santa on top of a computer store soundlessly waved and laughed. Four stoplights down was the rec center where I'd learned to swim. It had a flashy new sign out in front, listing classes and meetings for the holidays—Weight Watching In Fruitcake Season; Quick-stitch Quilting; Holidays Without Ho-ho-ho: Support Group. Surprisingly, lights were on throughout the building.

If I had been my mother, I would have called that sign the hand of God. I turned into the parking lot from the far lane. Even if the group wasn't a good one, I figured, there would be a coffeepot going in the back. The meeting was practically finished when I crept in—the leader, a shockingly thin woman with hair cut above her ears, was already reading from the closing statements. "We come together without fears or requirements," she read dully. "We allow each other our own needs. If you feel that you belong here, you belong."

The group was fairly large for so early in the morning—I counted twenty-two women listening in the circle. One, near the leader, was so frantic around the eyes and mouth she looked like she'd vibrate if you brushed her arm. "It is our faith that all pain is to be honored," the leader read. I knew all of this; I'd heard it hundreds of times, meeting after meeting, night after night. Sometimes two meetings a day, before I met Jon, when the loneliness was so sheer and bright I burned my fingertips with matches as a distraction. Next came call and response.

"Our experience—" the leader read.

"—is the center of our being," the group chanted back.

"Our responsibility—"

"—is our own healing."

I thought of my mother, her pursed lips and fussy fingers. With some shock, I realized that she would look right at home here.

"Happiness—"

"—is up to us."

"That's wrong, you know," I said to the woman beside me. She looked up with bloodshot eyes and shifted as if she might move, so I put my hand companionably on her arm. "I'm not criticizing. But if it was up to us we'd all be singing."

She stood up then, shaking off my hand like water, and scuttled to another chair in time for the next refrain.

"Honest," I said, standing now and speaking clearly, to be heard over the others. "I've written a book. I know what I'm talking about. Don't you all deserve sweet joy? I do. My mother does."

"Growth comes in knowledge—" the leader began, but the response was stammering and splintered as women turned to look at me and frown.

"Sure," I said, "but what does knowledge lead to? I know every bad habit I have, but I'm still sleeping with a married man. Every day for five years I've told myself I hold my own happiness, but I'm still coming to meetings like this." The group had fallen silent, the tense woman looking at me with a slack mouth. I took off my jacket and moved into the center of the circle, where I liked to stand when I directed groups. "We all want a map because we can't see the road. But there aren't any maps. There isn't a road."

"We all find our own path," said the leader, her voice quivering. "Only by working together can we find our individual paths. We've learned that this is the only answer."

Heads were nodding, but the women looked back to me, waiting for my response. I stood on a chair. "Aren't you listening? Individual paths is the same as no path. Every day is shapeless." As I spoke the welcome tears broke free again, crashing through seawalls and restraints. I couldn't wipe them away fast enough, so that looking at the group I sensed we were all held together by the warm, embracing water. "Listen! There's a new answer every day," I said. "I'm trying to tell you."

Famine Fever

(1996)

HELENA MULKERNS

H e pulls me out of the cabin near the beach and tells me the tide is alive. He says that out in the blue night a million tiny vessels are flowing along the current off to somewhere else, and he wants us to go with them. I say no. I am too scared. The hut near the beach is all we have, where we can rest in relative safety, considering the times.

His eyes are shining, like I haven't seen them in a long while now. And there is more to him that has changed. He seems whole again, not weighed down with the horror, the filth, and the fear of this plague. He is like he was before, when there was never fear on him. *Nuair nach raibh eagla riamh air.* He fought hard through the hunger, but for all his handsome strength, he faded to a shadow like the rest of us in the end.

Yet tonight, here he is now, like a child with his talk of boats—and the sky coming down on us black as a grave, and something in the back of my mind shrieking loud and long like a storm. He is telling me that the moon will soon be out and I will see the boats. It is true he has me laughing—I see no boats yet, but I do see the moon, scattering milky and gentle down the beach like a dancer. I begin to walk with him into its wake, except that I have a terrible pain at the same time, dragging me backwards into the hut, and I am tormented by this shaking in my bones and this fire over my skin, and I am looking at him, but remembering too deep for the sea to wash it from my head. . . .

In Dublin and London, they said it was God's will for the lazy, teeming Irish, stricken for our own good, and they couldn't interfere with God's will. Our own said it was judgment on our sins, but I never could quite work out what they were, to deserve this. The first year, there was fierce talk of the blight, and it coming westwards. Then one morning, I woke up to the fearful screeching of them in Kelleher's, coming across the quiet fields, as they found the crop in the ground stinking black and mushy, like devils' spits, the flowers fouled. Since then it went from bad to worse.

I smell the salt, crisp in the air. It is strange, this sea—the soft sucking swirls of surf curling like cats around the rocks, and the biggest space in the world under the sky. Tonight, a silver mist seeps around him as we walk down the strand, and he says, "Listen: the bay is humming." It occurs to me that it is the fish, the ones out in the deep we could never reach, singing to us. Then I shiver. Maybe it's the dead-already, moaning from the night vapors. My mind keeps pulling back and forth between his light and my deepest horror, I am restless and dithering. But then I concentrate on my bare feet sliding gently into the sands, and it comforts me.

We weren't as bad off as some. We had subtenants, and a decent cottage and animals. But like the rest, we paid the landlord in grains and produce, and kept the potato for living. Oats, butter, barley, eggs, all went to him, even though we'd never seen him in all our days, an absentee. He only sent his bailiffs to do his dirty work. But still, the potatoes did us well enough, and the rents had to be paid.

I was married only a few months then, and Liam was letting on of course that it wasn't a serious thing at all. So just to be sure, we kept the seed potatoes and sowed even more for the next year, and less grains. We thought we might even make some money. We were wrong. But you see, nobody believed it would happen again, let alone a third time with the few seeders we had left for the '47 crop.

"So," he says to me, with that grin on him. "Are you coming?"

I peer out into the dark sea, pearl-speckled under the moon, and sure enough, he is right. You can just about distinguish an odd flurry of activity out beyond the shore's crashing wave line. I glimpse crafts tiny and majestic—some with lone mariners, some with groups, some with masts and riggings for to cross the ocean altogether, some just curraghs. They are heading in what seems like an out-to-sea and westwardly direction. The light is tricky, sometimes they seem not to be boats at all. But it is beautiful, and terrifying at the same time. "Why are there so many?" I ask. "And where are they going?"

I glance back towards the village, empty now. Where once was crowded and bustling, now is dead to the world, and for a moment, the huddle of bothies look like so many ancient burial mounds, for centuries gone. But his shining tempts me. Now he is unmooring a curragh from a stone on the beach with a ring in it, and he begins talking again, the voice low, smiling in that old way of his. I amn't hearing everything he is saying, and I think of just letting him go, and returning to my son, when it strikes me like a blow that of course, the child is gone. They took him away for fear of the fever, and because I had dried out like an old hag—without nourishment for myself, there was nothing to sustain my milk. I sink into a kind of paralysis, and he lifts me into the boat.

After the second year, we had nothing really. We survived awhile on savings and things put by. Then after the second crop failure we killed the sheep, then the smaller animals. Then we ate carcasses of cattle, rabbits, birds, even dogs for food. We made soup from dandelions, nettles, docks, charlock and when we could find them, we ate mushrooms. Through all that, we kept the holding, since to leave the land was death. You could see that in the eyes of the beggars that were coming to my door every day, bands of them. Those who'd been thrown off the land, those drifting souls whose families were dead, children orphaned and widows taken to the roads. The country was haunted by them, and if it wasn't the road fever with its relapsing fits that got them, it was the famine fever, that rotted and roasted a soul alive and emptied the body out like a putrid fruit, a human blight.

Then there were the dreaded corpse men coming round the houses to take away the bodies and throw them into the mass graves in the bogs away up from the roads. Worse: if a family couldn't afford that, or were too weak, they shoved the remains of children or parents into bog holes or ditches nearby, a shame never known before.

In the spring of 1846, the fever hit the West, and I stopped giving to beggars, or even opening my door. The fear was terrible. The authorities had some schemes going, projects to employ people who could hardly stand, or soup kitchens where you had to give up your land for a bite. In the end, it sounds funny, but finally we ate the rent. That was the simple tragedy of it. I would not see us starve while the good grain was being shipped off to a landlord in England. The bailiff gave us an extra month, and then one day they just arrived with an eviction notice, and burned the house to the ground.

We came down from the mountains, then, outcasts ourselves, thinking that maybe the seashore would provide us with some nourishment. You'd only want to have seen the sight of us, staggering along the boreens like bone-brittle ghosts, aching and red with scurvy. My sister's children had their bellies swollen out like pregnant dwarfs, and one was blinded with an eye malady that seemed more to strike the small ones. We found this village deserted and wondered why, probably cleared by the landlord, we couldn't be sure. Then when the tide ran low, we discovered that the sea was no salvation.

The shore had been stripped bare from end to end, not a sliver of seaweed to put into a pot, not a shellfish or a old crab in a pool, nothing. And like the fishermen before us who had pawned their nets to eat after the first year, we had no fishing tools, nor craft to harvest the waters.

My brother-in-law wanted to continue along the coast to the work-house, now only ten miles away. My parents said they would rather die out in the winds than lying screaming under two-day corpses, like the stories went. Nobody got out of there alive anyway. In the filth, the fever raged wild, and there was nothing to eat but the brimstone grain they tried to give us instead of potatoes, ground glass to the stomachs of the starving. We decided to rest a little, but then the fever took Liam, and the rest were afraid to stay in the village.

The water gleams silver and its coldness is a shock. I am shivering. On the buoyancy of the tide, once we get out beyond the rollers, the current is surprisingly strong. I have never left land before, and won-der at the waves, filled with enough life as if they were creatures them-selves. I see faces under the surface, huddled close beneath the water, and am frightened. My shuddering increases, and I toss my head with pain. They are malevolent, and reaching for me. But then I look at Liam and feel renewed. He is facing me, pulling back rhythmically on the curragh's oars, and his silhouette is framed in deepest indigo speckled by a crowd of stars, and a growing glimmer from the west along the horizon. Which is strange, I think to myself, since dawn usu-ally comes from the other way.

It was a desolate dusk, as I stood at the edge of the village, watching them walk away over the hill until they were gone. I gave my child to my sister, since she'd already lost two, and I stayed with Liam. What could I do. He suffered for days, the ghastly bloody flux, the fever, his voice gone and his face withered, until I felt he was almost beyond me. When my weeping wore out, and I so terribly alone, I screamed out loud at the Virgin, asking why I was left here with nothing to give him, only my own ragged arms and the sound of my voice, until I became so weak I lost that, too. Only the shore breaking of the waves answered me.

And now even the waves are far gone, and the humming sea soothes my terror. He is talking low again, that this will be a good journey. Maybe bring us somewhere the pest has not yet taken hold.

Alongside, towering over us or bobbing lowly, a huge fleet is moving now with some speed. It is magnificent, but quite sinister, because I cannot make out who exactly it is sailing with us, their faces are all indistinct and black, but it seems like we are all related, too. The faces on the boats, and the faces in the waves and even under the bogs.

Maybe it is America we were going to, there is always talk of that. On the estate down the road, the landlord paid for all his tenants' passages to Boston, to get them off his hands, like. The land had emptied out entirely, and the cottages were razed, those too weak to travel shunted off to the workhouse. Liam said it was a lonely stretch after that.

I am leaning back in the curragh, with my shawl around my shoulders, although it is warm, warm, almost unbearably so. I am looking at all the boats, when suddenly an old woman leans out towards me from another craft, her face obscured by shadow, and inquires, "What are you doing here so soon, girl? Don't you know where we're all going?"

The dark stink of her comes wafting over to me, and the moment I realize what it is, I am pulled down into the floor of the boat, and I can't see Liam anymore, nor stars nor the milky glow across the heavens from the moon. I am tossed over, gnarled up into a knot of skirts, my shawl flung from me, my body burning again. I am on the floor of the hut, the cramps gnawing my guts, and a lashing pain all around my back and arms and legs, slicing through every bit of me like a fishmonger's knife. My skin is all aflame, but my clothes icy wet. The fire in the grate has almost gone out and as I get up on one elbow, the shaking takes me so badly I fall back again. *Dia eadrainn agus gach olc.*

God between us and all evil. Not long ago Liam was like this, the sweat on his head and body, the tossing and swelling rash. The stench fills me up, and with the new soreness in my fingers and toes, I know it is me. God bless us, but I hadn't meant to fall asleep, only wanting to stay beside him.

I am crying for the sea—the blinding beauty of the open ocean, and all the tiny boats there, sailing steady, and Liam with his hands calmly on the oars, I'll not let that out of my head, I will fight the blackness with this beauty. The pain is battling to take over, it goes from the back of my neck through my eyes, engulfing me. I close them again, I swim back momentarily to the curragh, and he is as I've just seen him, blue-bathed, eyes out over the waters, alight with that old look of anticipation.

But this time, I am under the waves, within the pain-wracked hum of the undercreatures, and there is a terrible fear on me that he will be away off before I can ask him where it is they are all headed, because I know he knows. Pulled down yet again, I fall through black waters into a muddy bed, a muddy shack with a barren hearth, earth under me and an earthen roof to fall on me like a shroud.

I crawl, wretched as an animal, across the few feet of ground to where he lies, tangled in his own old coat, skeletal and still. Even through the wracking fever my heart breaks at the ashen, emaciated face of him, hollow as a holy statue. I start to ask him what place is it out there in the night that we are all off to, but he is already gone.

Achill Ancestors and a Stranger

(1997)

MAUREEN BRADY

Far out along the headlands, Nuala picks up a stone and tries to scratch her name into the boggy ground, but the mossy soil only indents for a second, then bounces back. Clouds streaming rapidly by quicken the beat of her heart and her skin tingles. A wild contentment vibrates in her, as if she's reached a destination she hadn't known she was heading for. She's on Achill Island—one of the farthest reaches of the west coast of Ireland. Soon the mist will come in to fade out the whole land. Soon, too—in one more day—she'll be on her way back home.

A dusky mauve enters the sky to turn the clouds pink. She tries to capture the wildness of the high cliffs in the distance with her camera.

Another half mile and she can see Bertie's, once the lighthouse property, now the perfect B & B where she's staying. Whitewashed, squat and firm. Behind it there's a white picket fence, then the stone wall that takes the lick of the ocean when the tide comes in. Beyond the fence a man now stands on the rocks, arms folded across the chest of his leather jacket, his gaze upon the sea. She saved her last shot for Bertie's, but not sure she wants the man in her picture, she walks on a little closer.

She drove out that day from Sligo, taking several hours to achieve a hundred miles or so. Stopping often for sheep crossing the road, now and again cattle, sometimes simply a lazy dog. But she didn't mind being slowed, for at every peak she imagined she could almost see Mary McGowan and Michael McTigue—her great-grandmother and great-grandfather whose papers are pressed flat back in Pennsylvania in her aunt's Bible. She's only recently woken up to the fact that they left here in 1846. That they were part of the potato famine. *That they left because they had to.*

Her eyes are drawn once more to the drama of the cliffs and the graceful hamlet below her, silently holding the ages. The countryside is rugged, rural, fanciful. So is she. She has the seaworthy carriage of her father, who, indeed, went to sea, became a wanderer but not a searcher, didn't know what to look for.

She gazes down. The man's still there. He's become so much a part of the landscape that when he moves, it jars Nuala. Especially when he turns and looks up at her. She's not sure she wants to be seen while she has that fluttery stir in her chest. And not only that, he no longer has the peace she assigned him when he seemed so at one with the sea. Now that she's closer she sees the ocean has swelled something up in him—a longing in his body that speaks of need. She's dead sure of it, even though she tells herself that she couldn't possibly know this about some total stranger.

As she approaches him, a broad hello comes out of her, not the tentative greeting she might have uttered even the day before when she'd been standing more aloof from the land of her ancestors.

He nods and greets her back. He has a German accent.

"A grand site, isn't it?" she states the obvious, gesturing to the ocean.

"Yes, yes," he agrees. "The wind blows everything out of your head."

"You stay here?" Her English becomes broken though his is not.

"Bertie's? Yes, yes." After a pause, he asks, "You, too?"

"Yes."

"On holiday?"

"A short rest before I return home."

"You have been traveling a long time?"

"No, no," she tells him. "Working hard to finish a novel at an artist's colony over on the other side of the country."

"Ah, a writer," he says. "Successful."

She doesn't deny it, having achieved at least the momentary pleasure of coming to an ending and putting her book down to rest.

"And you?" she asks.

"I am a writer, too, only a failed one."

His statement is blunt, hurtful to him and perhaps even to her by identification, for she has suffered so many years of bewilderment before this book came true for her, yet always stepped around a word like "failure." She wants to say: surely you know a writer is just a writer no matter what happens to the work, but he seemed so firm about calling himself the failed one, she suspects this would deny him. So she falters, leaving a hole in the conversation.

He looks out at the sea again, then returns his gaze to her. "I'll soon be going to the restaurant up the road. There . . ." He gestures in the direction she just walked from.

"Is it a good one?"

"The only one."

"Oh."

"So I assume you may go there, too."

"Yes," she answers. She may be blushing. It's been years since a man asked her to join him.

"If you'd care to come along with me . . ."

"I need to go back to my room first."

"Very well." He stiffens a bit at her hesitation. "I'll be up there if you like . . ." He formally extends his hand, speaking his name, "Dieter."

"Nuala," she answers, offering him a firm handshake, before turning up the footpath that leads to Bertie's.

In the interlude between his invitation and when she goes to meet him, a lusty desire which has grown from mute to a nearly palpable buzz in her, raises up the notion that she might conceivably sleep with him. Despite the fact that she doesn't sleep with men. Hasn't since she came out in her late twenties. *Now why is that?* she wonders as she stands perched on the same rock Dieter claimed for so long, casting to the sea for an answer.

She likes to believe her ideas are freely hers—not bound by the urgings of any collective voices—but now, as she rankles at her leaning toward Dieter, she wonders if she is, in fact, under the influence of the lesbian police? Because surely, if she wants to, she can sleep with a man not as a serious straight thing but as part of her posture as outlaw. What could be more deviant?

The wind whips wildly about her head and the sea crashes in at her feet, leaving foam at the bottom of the rock. *Why not?* she calls out to no one. The moon is full. The clouds conceal it, then waft by, trailing it behind them. She doesn't think clouds move like this in America, or at least she never noticed them. Irish clouds make a wildness in the sky to match the landscape. She imagines the Celts worshiping the moon in those stone circles she saw just the day before on the great plateau of Carrowmore. She has been told all redheads are witches, which makes her wonder at her powers. Does that apply to women only? For Dieter is redheaded also and has a red mustache.

She spots him as soon as she walks in, his eyes cast down on his half-eaten dinner. When the maitre d' approaches her with a menu, her feet don't know which way to go. Why does he not look up and help her out by beckoning? Perhaps she is too late to join him. But when the maitre d' indicates a table on the other side of the room, Nuala points as if she's in a foreign country where she can't speak the language and guides him to Dieter's table. "Would you still like company?" she asks when she's beside him.

He half stands, bows, "Yes, yes, please. I'd be delighted."

His face brightens as she strips off her two jackets and unwinds the scarf from her neck and the sea air wafts off of her. Dieter seems washed by it.

She studies the menu; he studies her. She tells him to go ahead with his dinner, orders hers quickly. They talk of their homes: Berlin, Manhattan. He says Germany is not so good now. Difficult to get published unless you are very conventional. She wonders if he's unconventional. One couldn't tell by his looks, his slate gray woolen sweater, corduroy trousers. "What do you write about?" she asks him.

"A man who goes on holiday and is waiting for something to happen to him."

His statement makes her tingle as if she is standing back at the cliff's edge. She wonders if it's a proposition. It's been so long, she can't remember what men say if they want a woman to sleep with them.

Still, they talk easily together, despite or perhaps because of the excitement of having found a way to join each other. They avoid the sort of personal questions that would reveal a spouse or lover back home. Dieter announces he's celebrating his forty-fifth birthday with his holiday on Achill Island, and Nuala reveals they're the same age. Of course, he tells her she doesn't look it, her Irish complexion may hold her youth forever. He wants to know if she's famous in America. Would he have read her books if he lived there? Not very likely, she tells him.

"Have they been translated into German?"

"Only one piece, in an anthology." She doesn't tell him it's a collection of stories by lesbians.

He sits forward. His face is lean and shapely. His hands are delicate. Thick brows frame his intelligent eyes with an arc of slight puzzlement, which attracts her. He's a university professor, teaches German literature. At the moment he's on sabbatical. Meant to write his own book this year but has no reason to believe he'll accomplish this, since for years he's been saying he'll do it but has not done it. But when she asks him why he can't do it now that he has the time, he grows foxy, and his eyes appear too wide split. Perhaps one is a wandering eye. He acts as if he can't talk about it—claims problems with his English, which is really quite adequate.

"Is this why you call yourself a failed writer?" she asks to draw him out.

He moves about uncomfortably in his seat, which makes her sorry she asked, afraid she's moved herself into a maternal role with him. Maybe she did that to blunt the question that makes her keep feeling like a bad girl: *Is she going to sleep with him?*

"I don't have enough to say," he says about the writing.

"Oh," she says and leaves it at that. Not: *Of course you do, it's a question of daring to reveal it,* which might only reinforce the maternal.

Superimposed upon his man's face suddenly stands his boy's face, full of yearning but also an almost flinching fear. It is this fear that draws her and makes him seem safe to go home with. But what does she really want from him? Does she think she's going to punish Anya, who turned into a tiresome baby as soon as she moved in with her. Or her lover before that, who whirled her high, then dropped her with a smashing blow by going back to her heavy-handed husband. Or will she sleep with him over nothing—no one, no reason.

But as soon as they come into the crispness of the open air, she remembers once again that it is not nothing propelling her but Ireland,

Achill Island, the full moon, her ancestors, her novel. It is finding home so far from home, sheep in her path, sea spray in her nostrils. And it is him, too, with his wistfulness that stops short of a cry just at this moment when hers may be sated.

They are in Dieter's room because he had the presence of mind to invite her in for tea. He puts on the kettle while she's in the bathroom. There are no chairs—only single beds divided by a nightstand. "Please," he indicates stiffly, when she comes out. She takes the bed closest to the sea, which they can hear pounding Bertie's shore. She leans back awkwardly on her elbows. The overhead light is too bright, lighting up her consciousness of how very little she knows him.

Her voice comes out raspy with nerves. "Do you mind if I turn off the big light?"

"As you like," he says, so she turns on the small light and shuts off the overhead.

He brings the tea on a tray and sits it beside her, kicks off his shoes so they land, clunk, and rests back parallel to her. Asks if she knows Günter Grass, a writer who has influenced him.

"Yes," she replies, "*The Tin Drum* mesmerized me. I was a drummer as a child." The other girl drummer in her high-school band pops into her mind—the one who slicked her hair back in a greasy DA. To keep from being associated with her Nuala always stood at the opposite end from her, keeping the boys between them, but secretly noted the girl's agile hands, which beat out such crisp drum rolls.

When the tea is steeped, she pours it the Irish way, which makes it more of a comfort drink. Milk first coating the bottom of the cup, then the tea, then the sugar. She holds the teacup daintily because it's the sort of fine china that commands gesture. Funny that she's been waiting for an Irish woman to invite her to her room for tea because she read in the lesbian and gay guidebook that this is code for: *Will you come to my room and sleep with me?* Maybe it's the same for heterosexuals and Dieter knows that. Maybe once in the room, one is supposed to skip the tea. For certainly the tea service is now in the way and conversation is exhausted.

Finally Dieter relieves her of the cup and saucer, moves the service to the other bed, and returns to take her hands, study them, squeeze them. She squeezes back a little, realizing she is passing up the last possible moment to excuse herself and return to her silent communion with the sea as her solo lover.

She inclines slightly toward Dieter instead and he leans across to kiss her. Gently at first, quietly, almost as she remembers her first cousin kissing her once when they were children playing spin the bottle, his soft lips pressing hers, his tongue restrained but creating heat behind them. It's a tentative exploration, so unobtrusive Nuala relaxes and begins to encourage it to open out into desire. Unlike with her cousin, when her mind kept repeating to her, *oh my God, you shouldn't.*

She lies back and Dieter comes up to hold the full length of her against him. He is warm and gentle. Still, she wishes he were a woman, for she wants to rub her cheek against another soft as hers. Her first time making love with a woman, this meant the most to her, this softness that told her to claim her vulnerability. Dieter rubs his clean-shaven face against hers. There's a prickle and his mustache tickles, but as he kisses her neck and her body begins to yield to him, she knows a vulnerability more profound than she has known in a while. Yet when he crosses her breast, she catches his hand and keeps it pressed into her, and lets herself grow hungry.

He opens his eyes and rolls them in a signal of delirium.

When he lifts up, she strips off her shirt and her V-necked sweater in one stroke, overriding her shyness with a boldness she barely recognizes. She's never done this with a man. Always waited to be undressed, as if she were still a teenager and each item might be the last one permissible, the one that would raise objection.

She's braless and Dieter is apparently a bit shocked.

"You write about a man who goes on a holiday and is waiting for something to happen to him. What happens when something happens?" she teases him.

He smiles, licks his lips, narrows his wide-apart eyes, drops his own clothes beside the bed in a flash, and comes up to lay on top of her.

When he is in her and it feels good, she wonders why she has not thought to do this before. Her low belly draws toward a heavenly fullness, her chest tingles, and the sound of ocean pounding shore grows louder in the silence. They are two alone souls on a faraway night, why should they not come together?

She rides Dieter. She sees horses. She sees a great green valley like so many she saw as she drove westward. She is traveling along with Dieter, then suddenly she discovers that she has gone very far away from him, as if they veered off on different paths at a fork that divided.

She sees a little redheaded girl, her arms stretched wide to embrace a green field as if it can fill her up. But it cannot, for she is starving. The girl is Mary McGowan, her great-grandmother. She's ten years old. Others come in a blur before her eyes. Distended bellies, bumpy bones, hollows that haunt the bewilderment in their eyes. Her forebearers? Some must have withered and died just as the potatoes hollowed out beneath their skins.

She sees the fog that comes in so strong it leaves treetops standing ghostlike without the appearance of earthly communion. Faces form in the fog. Faces like hers. They flicker, then disappear, like the faces of the dead do.

These pictures arrive without invitation while Nuala is still in the middle of her business with Dieter, changing her valence so utterly that what is wet turns cold—the sweat on her belly, the glistening lube between her legs.

Dieter raises up on his arms, heat in his eyes, his mouth soft from kissing, and sees her eyes darting about. "What is it?" he asks, softening and shrinking a little inside her.

She catches a glimpse of his taut, red hair. There is a frizz to it that makes it clearly not Irish hair and she reassured by this distinction between them. "Distraction of the mind," she says. "I'm sorry."

He closes his eyes, opens them again, hesitates, like a man deciding what to write next. He starts to move in her again, but every little collision is felt like a ferry that comes bumping and bouncing into a ferry dock. They are two, not one, their parts distinct and separate. She does not have to tell him to stop. He comes out of her and rolls off onto his side, letting out a deep sigh.

"What is your real story?" he asks after a moment, his eyes narrowing as if to peg her.

"I'm a better lover to women," she says.

"Ah," he says. "Bisexual."

"No," she replies. "Lesbian."

He makes a face and curls into his midsection as if the word is a blunt ax that has struck him. She thinks of those labryses they sell in women's bookstores—harmless, miniature axes on silver chains. Can the word really be this lethal?

"Do you do this often?"

"Never."

"Why with me then?"

She shrugs. "I guess I was a woman on holiday waiting for something to happen. And besides that, I like you."

"What do you like about me?"

"That sadness you try so hard to hide."

"Oh," he says, keeping his face behind his arms.

"Come on," she says, touching the short, springy hair on the top of his head. "My being a lesbian is a choice, or even if I was born with it, we've already established I don't have eyeteeth in my vagina or anything of that sort."

In the silence that follows the air in the room takes on a greater charge than ever it held during their lovemaking.

"It's not you," he says, slowly unfolding from his fetal position. "It's Marlene."

"Who's Marlene?"

"She was my woman for the past twelve years. She went off with another woman three months ago."

Nuala sees the hurt come clean, Dieter's eyes no longer trying to look both ways at once. She tells him she's sorry, keeping hidden the little note of triumph she can't deny feeling for Marlene. It's nothing against Dieter, only an allegiance to her kind.

"Were you married?"

"No. She had one bad marriage and swore she'd never get married again. I would have married her. Now I think maybe it was partly because she knew she might fall in love with a woman."

"Um," Nuala agrees, pulling a blanket up to cover them.

He looks squarely into her eyes. "And you," he says. "Do you have a broken heart, too?"

Does she? Now that he's put it this way she feels her losses echo but not from up close, from far away. Her trials of the last decade often turning her inside out, nurturance more of an enticement than an actual experience.

Dieter is up on his elbow awaiting her answer. The old way she's told her story suddenly no longer seems true. She can tell him anything; he is a stranger. But why should she hide from him or anyone?

Her eyes cast to the ceiling. "I had a major love," she tells him. "I left her a long time ago and have had some other lovers but never let myself all the way in again since the first one."

"Why did you leave the first one?"

Her heart begins to pound again as it did out there on the headlands. She's always told it the most obvious way: how her lover cheated on her, and, when she discovered the betrayal, couldn't bear it. But in this land of many angles of light, she sees an entirely different sight.

"I was always filled with longing," she says. "We kept each other busy, which held that feeling at bay, but whenever we would stop still, I would find myself yearning with a hunger deep down in my gut that made me want to blame her for anything she couldn't provide me. But then if she'd come at me, as if she could fill it up with her, I'd only want to step aside. I stepped aside enough that eventually she snuck off and had an affair with another woman, which blew us up."

"Was that your distraction?" Dieter asks, reminding Nuala of the moment she left him to ride off in a different direction.

She hears the waves crashing in, the undertow sucking the sand out. The sea's constancy steadies her. "No," she answers. "It was not. I was remembering my ancestors. Feeling their hunger and how it must have passed on to me." She closes her eyes, tries to tap the old yearning she knows so well, but it's not there. Dieter is. She looks past him, toward the sea. "Maybe *that hunger* gave me the longing. Because now that I'm here on their island, it's gone."

He nods his understanding, his now calm eyes on hers. "Something is settled for you, no?" He cradles her face with the length of his hand. The gesture is not sexual.

"Yes."

"Now you are ready to go on."

She chuckles. "And you? Will you be able to finish your story?"

"Now we'll see if I have one." He says this lightly, then he adds, "Do you think I'm a man with a special attraction for lesbians?"

"Ah, yes, it would seem that you are. Perhaps you were a lesbian in an earlier life."

"Perhaps on Achill Island," he embellishes the fantasy. "My people are not here but I come here again and again because it's a place where I can hear myself. And when unusual things happen on Achill Island, I do not consider them so unusual."

While Dieter's in the bathroom, Nuala retrieves her clothes from the floor and dresses. He comes out nude but quickly steps into his corduroys.

"Thank you," she says, touching her hand to his bare shoulder.

"Thank you," he says in return, half bowing the way he did at the dinner table.

"Perhaps we will meet again at breakfast," she adds to make the parting less permanent, though she knows that they will not. For she knows that she will skip breakfast to walk out on the headlands again, following the hard ground of the sheep paths until she is high above but next to the ocean. From there she will look back on the land and breathe it in and in, and then she will turn and start for home.

excerpt from

The Map of Ireland

(1997)

STEPHANIE GRANT

When I think back on the last twelve months and try to figure out the exact chain of events that brought me here, try to figure out which mistake led to which other mistake which led to my current fucked-up situation, I realize everything that's happened can be traced to the bathroom fire. And if everything can be traced to the bathroom fire, then everything can be undone by undoing the bathroom fire. What I mean is, if I could go back to that day and just not set the fire in the first place, or maybe somehow set it but keep the fact of it—the smell of it—from my mother, then none of the crazy, evil shit that's happened to me since last November would have happened.

But now I've run into my real problem: I don't want, not honestly, to undo the fire, just change the outcome, which you can't do and everyone knows you can't do, because life isn't like that, doesn't work that way. Life is essentially unfair, like Ma says, and there are rules, even when you're just a kid sitting around trying to imagine your life turning out differently. There are rules even for your imagination.

It's easy to picture my life turning out differently because I never would have pictured myself here, surrounded by nuns and actual lists of rules typed up and stapled to the door frames. I never would have pictured myself anywhere but in our lousy house, an apartment really, but "house" is what people say. The fire I set in the only bathroom of our shitty three-bedroom in the Mary Ellen McCormack Houses was a small fire, a neat fire, but Ma hit the roof anyway. I was a regular fucking pyromaniac when I was a little kid, before I'd seen what fire could do, back when I thought it had some separate, existential value.

In second and third grade, I made money at recess showing the fires I'd built behind the big rocks that bordered the school playground. This was Gate of Heaven, on East Fourth Street. I was surrounded by nuns then, too, but it was different, they wore habits for one, and the most they could do was scare the crap out of you about heaven and hell, they had no real power. At recess we could sit on the rocks, but never go beyond them, into the pathetic clump of trees that passed for woods. The ground just behind the rocks was cool and hard, almost as hard as the blacktop we played on, but natural, not man-made. It was real ground, an oasis brushed clear of dry leaves and covered with a thin layer of dank dirt that reminded me of the silt at the bottom of Ponkapoag Lake, where my family went swimming summers and where the silt felt so gross under my toes that I preferred to lie on the crummy beach and bake. Which drove Ma completely wild. As if I was making her bake, by baking myself.

Anyway, I was burning letters on the brand-new tile of our too small bathroom in the McCormack Houses. Unsent letters. Fourteen letters I wrote but didn't mail that got me thinking about a fire. Thinking about how good it would feel to watch them disintegrate, metamorphose into ash, then silky smoke, then air. Mr. Goldblatt, our chemistry teacher says that nothing in the universe is ever destroyed, just converted into something else, but no way has he ever set fire to anything outside a petri dish and watched it burn—blue, orange, white—into nothing. Into No Thing.

The fourteen letters weren't exactly love letters. But they weren't exactly *not* love letters either. There was no bad poetry or anything. No "my love beats like a bird's wing against my battered breast," for Christ's sakes. But the letters did say certain things. Express certain feelings of mine about a certain person. A female person, if you want to know the truth, which is the purpose of me telling the story in the first place, I suppose. Not that anyone else does. Tell the truth, I mean. For most people, talking is the end as well as the means.

The certain female person was my French teacher, Mademoiselle Eugenie, an African lady on a Fulbright Teaching Fellowship from Senegal, which we learned was on the coast of West Africa, which surprised me because I'd never thought of Africa as having a coast with beaches and all. I'd always thought of it as dark and hot and land-locked with really dark black people working and sweating, their heads unprotected in the sun. A whole dusty continent. Like the Midwest only all black instead of all white and huts instead of houses. But I was wrong. Boy, was I wrong. Mademoiselle Eugenie showed me that, if nothing else.

The fellowship was an exchange program, except with teachers instead of kids. Mademoiselle Eugenie's other half was Mademoiselle Pat, our regular teacher, who'd taught at South Boston High for years, since way back before the busing, when they needed two whole home-room classes for all the kids whose last names started with Mc. Mademoiselle Pat had applied for a Fulbright Teaching Fellowship in Paris, France, and my sophomore year she made her classes do a special unit on the French capital. We each got maps and had to learn the different *arrondissements* by heart, and I kept getting the left and right banks confused, which was stupid I admit, but she took it like a personal insult, my inability to feel the difference between the two banks, like they meant anything at all to me, like they were anything but a bunch of squiggly lines on a page, like they were any place I'd ever get to visit.

Every day in class, we ate Pillsbury Crescent Rolls that Mademoi-selle Pat had baked herself and we pretended that we'd just gotten back from the goddamn Luxembourg Gardens and were on the way to the goddamn Tuileries, which the whole class got in trouble for pronouncing Tooleries. *Où est Didier? Didier est au Centre Georges Pompidou,* wherever the fuck that is.

Then Mademoiselle Pat's acceptance letter arrived saying she'd definitely won a Fulbright, but that Paris was overbooked. It turned out she'd checked a little box saying *YES, I would consider a Fulbright Teaching Fellowship in another French-speaking country.* Mademoiselle Pat had figured that was Belgium, maybe, or Montreal. I don't think she'd ever considered Africans speaking anything but mumbo jumbo. Or maybe it's better to say I don't think she'd ever considered Africans, period.

Which was true of most of us at Southie High, me included, I'm embarrassed to say, before Mademoiselle Eugenie. Blacks sure. I mean we all had to think about blacks whether we wanted to or not because of Judge Garrity and the court order. But not Africans.

Mademoiselle Eugenie was very tall with a pointy nose and matching eyebrows. She was the blackest person I'd ever seen when I met her. The first day of school, the color shone off her skin as she stood in front of the class, and I realized then that black had other colors in it. She was bright, not incandescent like a light bulb, but still, she illuminated the room with her intensity, and I wanted to look away but couldn't. We all watched her move around the class the way French teachers do, darting between the rows of desks, up to the blackboard, then back to us, to her podium, asking questions but moving before you could answer, so you had to crane your neck every which way to follow her complicated trajectory from your seat. I'm sure there's some scientific reason for it, like the part of your brain that learns foreign languages is wired to the part of your brain that cranes your neck, because they all do it. Every goddamn French teacher I've ever met.

But Mademoiselle Eugenie was the best. She was the best because she made you want to learn French. She made you want to be French.

Or at least be another person. Someone not yourself. Someone say, who moved her mouth in a particular way, like she was constantly sucking on a small egg, a robin's egg, maybe, although I don't think there are robins in Senegal. Someone who makes these wicked unusual, wicked un-American expressions with her face because she's always sucking on that imaginary egg, someone who shows surprise, delight even, at sappy French sentences like, "My name is Ann and I want to go to the cinema." Someone who says "cinema" instead of "movies."

It wasn't like there was anything pornographic in the letters I burned in a pile on the bathroom floor. It was just stuff like that, descriptions of the way Mademoiselle Eugenie moved, the way she spoke, the way she always seemed on the verge of bursting out with an explosion of French words not in our vocabulary books.

I was burning the letters on new tile that was supposed to match the old but didn't, was off by a shade, which was worse somehow, more depressing than a tile that didn't try to match, a tile of a totally different color, not because I was ashamed of what the letters said, but because I didn't have the guts to send them. I could picture mailing them—I'd even put on the stupid stamps, fifteen cents times fourteen down the tubes—but I couldn't picture her receiving them. Every time I tried to imagine it, I'd get this panicky feeling in my stomach and throat, this feeling like I didn't have an esophagus at all, like my stomach was sitting right up under my chin.

I could picture her house. She lived in Jamaica Plain, I knew the street, having rode by on my bike once, not that I was fucking following her or anything, I just wanted to see the house, to see whether it looked like her, reflected her in some way. It was a triple-decker, like a lot of houses around here, a narrow gray-green house, but deep, a whole block deep, with three floors stacked like pancakes on top of each other under a flat roof. There was a crummy cement walk, no shrubs, and a yellow front yard that nobody gave two shits about. The cement walk led to a mailbox, a triple-decker in its own right, three separate boxes with three of those stupid little flags attached, two American, and one—black and green—I couldn't say, but figured maybe was Senegalese.

To tell the truth, it was a seedy-looking house, the kind of house people stay in for a while but don't ever live in, and I hated thinking about her being there, which is why I rode by on my bike only once. That and the fact that my mother practically had a conniption fit when I told her I'd ridden all the way over to Jamaica Plain and not on the sidewalks either. That's my mother for you. She still thinks you ride your bike on the sidewalks.

I wanted to burn the letters because every time I got to the point in my mind where Mademoiselle Eugenie hustled down her walk to the mailbox (she made you think of action verbs, Mademoiselle Eugenie did), every time I got to the point where she darted her hand into the box, her face went blank. Not her expression, but her whole face. She didn't have the pointy nose anymore, or that gently puckered mouth, or those upside-down-vee eyebrows that moved whenever she spoke. Nothing, just a blank black face and it scared me. Each time it happened, my stomach would crawl up my windpipe and just sit there, at the back of my throat, and I swore I could touch it, the slimy, acid insides, with my tongue. So I never sent the letters.

I hated not sending them. I felt like a fucking coward not sending them, and the one thing I prided myself on being, the one thing everyone in the eleventh grade at Southie High knew about Ann Ahern was that she wasn't a coward. So I sort of had to burn the letters. To get rid of them, to get rid of the suggestion that I was a coward, when really, truthfully—you can ask anybody who knows me—I wasn't.

Which is where my mother comes in. Literally. The responsible fire had been burning for about three minutes when she came running. She bounded up the stairs two at a time—I could hear her giant steps, her regular hacked-up, smoker's breathing. There are no locks on any of the doors in our house, not the bedrooms, not the bathrooms, my mother insists on twenty-four-hour access, even taking a shit is a quasi-public experience in our house. When she got to the top of the stairs, my mother flung the door open.

I myself had about thirty seconds from the moment I first heard her register the fire until the moment she opened the bathroom door. She must have been sitting at the kitchen table because I heard her chair scrape against the linoleum—it's a very specific sound—I heard the panic of her slight body hurling itself against the vinyl chair. I guess I was paralyzed though. Or resigned maybe. Because I didn't move. I sat there, on the edge of the tub, watching the letters burn efficiently on the mismatched tile. Kind of in a trance, but one where your mind is still working, your thoughts are still flowing. I was pretty much immobilized there on the edge of the tub waiting for my mother to arrive, waiting for whatever was going to happen next to happen. I remember tapping the fire with the corner of my sneaker, to let some air in, I remember wondering why I was the only one in my family who seemed to care that the old bathroom tile was tan and the new bathroom tile was beige—indisputably beige—when suddenly the door flew practically off its hinges and into the room and my mother was there.

Our upstairs bathroom is small: sink, toilet, and half tub, in that order. There was nowhere to go. Ma and I looked at the pile. Half the pages were ash. The rest were stained black and brown by the smoke, their edges curling.

"What are you doing?"

I stood up. What can you say when your mother catches you burning papers and whatnot on the bathroom floor? It's pretty fucking weird, even I knew that.

She put her hands on her hips. "I said, what are you doing?"

I shrugged and gestured to the dwindling pile.

"Are you trying to burn the house down?"

I shook my head.

"Answer me."

"No."

She's skinny my mother. Not thin. Skinny, except for a pouchy stomach, which she blames on us five kids. One of those skeletal Irish ladies with freckles all over and red hair, but not exactly the color you'd want if you could choose. Kind of orange. You see her joints first, before anything, her elbows and knees, her hips sticking out, ahead of the rest of her, like the way soldiers walk, with their shoulders back, behind their hips, and their heads even farther back, behind their shoulders, as if they wanted to be sure their heads were the last things entering a room. She moved like that, my mother, only she wasn't stiff like a soldier. She was hard like one, sharp, yes, but in a flexible way. I know it sounds contradictory, but there she is my mother, a living breathing contradiction in terms.

"Well, don't just stand there like an idiot, put out the fire." She pointed to the faucet.

For a second I didn't move. The sink was right next to her. I had to step toward her to turn on the water. I didn't especially want to get close when she was mad like this. I knew she'd take a swipe at me. It's not like I'm a fucking abused child or anything, but she wasn't above a healthy smack now and again. Which is just what I got when I reached for the sink. Right across the face.

"I could understand this when you were a kid for heaven's sake. A little kid playing with matches. But I thought you were finished with that. I thought it was a phase. That's what Dr. McGragh said. That it was a phase."

Neither of us registered the slap, which hurt, the back of her bony freckled hand. I was pretty good at not crying when she hit me. It drove her wild.

She pointed to the fire. "This is sick."

I ran the faucet and cupped cold water in my two hands and spilled it over the sorry pile. It hissed until it stopped, until a thin stream of smoke rose up and curled under our noses. I wanted to rub my nose but didn't because I couldn't let her think I was touching my face in any way, surreptitiously rubbing the spot where she'd hit me, which was red, I already knew without looking, could tell from the way the pores had opened wide, then closed, then stung.

"Can you tell me what's going on here? I really can't fathom it. I honestly can't."

"It's just. Some writing of mine. I didn't like it anymore."

"So you burned it?"

"Yes."

"Don't you think that's a little extreme? Couldn't you have just thrown it away, like a normal person?"

Shrug from me.

Exasperated sigh from her. "What's so terrible about them that you have to burn them? What's so bad?" She bent down. "What kind of writing is it, anyway? Letters?"

I grabbed her wrist and yanked what remained of my one-sided correspondence with Mademoiselle Eugenie out of her hand. She lost her balance and had to step into the soggy ash pile.

"Shoot," she said, as she caught herself. She didn't use bad language my mother. It was a big deal for her, like the way some people take stands on abortion or gun control. She could be bad in other ways, ways that seemed more important to me, but she hated foul language. Her name was Theresa, and me and my brothers and sisters called her Mother Theresa, whom she in no way ressembled, just to piss her off.

She wiped the edge of her shoe against the tile. The heels were so worn down the leather had started to curl its way up the shaft. Like fringe. She said, "They must be dirty letters."

"They're my letters, that's all."

She put her hands on her knobby hips again and took a step to either side of the wet fire, straddling it. She was wearing a dress, a boring flowered number with a clear plastic belt. Her stomach poked out beneath the belt. The last plumes of smoke went up there, between her legs.

"I know they're dirty letters," she said. My mother and me are the exact same height so she was looking right into my eyes. "You can't kid a kidder, Ann."

She smirked. Her nostrils flared and I could see her thinking I was chip off the old block, which really disgusted me because I wasn't.

"I'm going to count to three," she said. "And when I get to three, those filthy letters better be in my hand." She stopped smirking now and worked her thin lips into a line. She could be really cold when she wanted to.

"One—"

"They're not filthy."

"Two—"

"Just because you're obscene doesn't mean everyone else is."

This time she hit me on the mouth.

I pushed passed her, the burnt letters in hand, and ran down the stairs and out of the house.

The
Other Woman

(1997)

VALERIE SAYERS

It took some people years to see what was going on with the eighties, but I knew right from the beginning. I hated the eighties. I hated New York in the eighties. By the time she came after me, in 1983, I had already zoned into another time, another place.

I was walking down Seventh Avenue—this was Brooklyn, not Manhattan—and I got caught up in the crowd leaving the subway. I had forgotten about subways, about people piling out at rush hour. I'd given birth to my third child in June, and now it was the first week in August. There wasn't anybody left in New York in August, so what were all these people doing getting off the subway?

I was pushed along in the crush and I felt somebody stepping on my heels. That happens in a crowd on a narrow sidewalk. I hadn't been out without the children in so long that you might even say I was glad to have somebody stepping on my heels. I walked faster. After half a block, somebody clipped my left heel again and this time, I heard a woman's merry laugh. I turned around smiling, sure that the laugh was wrapped around an apology.

I didn't stop on the sidewalk—remember, there was a crowd surging along—but I got a good look at her just the same. She was tall, nearly as tall as I am, and she wore her straw-colored hair shoulder length, like mine, with bangs—though hers were cut too short and pressed too flat to her forehead. My name is Feeney, and everyone in my family wears straw-colored hair and pale skin spattered with freckles; she might have been a Feeney. She even had something of a pot belly to match my postpartum swell. Her clothes were just awful—a pink floral shirt and matching stretch pants—but I was trying not to pay attention to clothes. In the eighties, that was all anybody talked about, that and their co-ops and their cheese and their restaurants. They weren't onto gardening yet.

I was right about one thing: she *was* merry. She was just delighted that she'd stepped on me twice. She had a pie face, round and doughy, pocked as if a fork had pricked holes; and, wouldn't you know, that was just about how I was feeling about my face in the eighties. I hadn't gone on an audition since Gracie, the middle child.

I crossed the street, half expecting her to follow me, but she didn't. I told myself I was getting paranoid, but really I was excited to think that she did it on purpose. I had walked out, actually, hoping to catch a young man's eye—another out-of-work actor or a fireman buying groceries—but not a man saw me passing through the streets.

Back home, it took all my energy to climb the stairs. We lived on the top floor of a brownstone in a big sunny apartment with a fireplace and a dumbwaiter leading nowhere. I loved that apartment—it was a seventies place, still rented cheap—but Jean Paul was ashamed of living in a walk-up. We went to look at co-ops every Sunday.

At the apartment door I could hear Helen switching off the television; she must have been the only adult woman still in Brooklyn in August, besides me and my doppelgänger. Inside, it was close to ninety degrees, unless you were standing right beside one of the fans.

All three children were asleep, just as I'd left them, burning with fever. The sun beat down on the flat tar of the roof all day, and they couldn't shake this bug.

Helen stood by the television, glad to be caught. She was a gaunt woman with wattles, maybe forty, maybe fifty. She'd been crying.

"Did you hear about that new disease?" she said.

I thought she had a theory about the kids' viruses. "What disease?"

"AIDS," she said. "You read about that?"

I nodded. It was only a few months old then; rather, it was only a few months since we all knew about it.

"My brother's got AIDS," she said, "but it's not what you think. He's a junkie."

I thought about putting my arms around her, but she stepped back, as if she sensed what was on my mind. "Now you probably don't want me to use the toilet," she said. "Or watch the kids at all."

Not want Helen to watch the kids? How could I reassure her? The whole world was in Martha's Vineyard or the Hamptons, or even, if they were renters like us, in some little North Carolina beach town. We were still in the city because we had a new baby and our children were sick and Jean Paul thought a vacation not taken would count for a lot at bonus time.

Maybe we were still there because of this woman he was seeing. He hadn't said anything about a woman, but I sensed her in every room of the apartment: we lived with her cool slender presence. She was chic and childless. She came from money and she made her own money, too. She was there in his irritation with the apartment, with my clothes, with the babies always sick. He wanted to say something, too, to confess. He came home very late and hung his head down and stared out into dark space. His grandfather wouldn't have thought anything about having affairs, but Jean Paul was second generation, American enough to crave the guilt.

It was so hot. Just don't tell me about it, I used to think. I was too

tired. I couldn't remember loving him, though I must have once, and
not too long before. Three babies. He was very handsome, with thick
black curly hair that he'd cut short for the eighties. He still looked
good, very French movie star, in his little black bikini when we went to
Jones Beach. But he hated going to a public beach and dragging home
sand in the car, so we hadn't gone together in a long time. I drove out
there alone, with the babies, when no one was running a fever.

Helen was hard to get, now that she spent so much time with her
brother in the hospital, and often when she was able to come I had no
plans in mind, just a need to walk the streets alone. One day I found
myself making broad circles of the neighborhood, up to Prospect
Park, down to Seventh Avenue. Finally I went in a daze to the cash
machine, just to look at the balance, to see if finally having enough
money made me feel better or worse.

The air conditioning in the bank lobby steadied me. I put my card
in the slot and punched in Jean Paul's code—the words "red wine"—
but I never saw the figures come up on the screen. From behind me,
she put her hands over my eyes, the way kids do in the schoolyard. Her
fingers were small and cool, though it was ninety-five outside the
bank's inscrutable dark window. My own palms were streaming sweat.
For a millisecond I tried to persuade myself that it was one of the
other neighborhood mothers, back early from the Cape or Maine, but
she pressed her fingers hard against my eyelids, and I knew for sure.
My friend from the crowd.

When I pried her hands loose and swung around to face her, she
grinned, and then she gave me a little slap on the cheek, a gentle slap.
Playful. She had her hair pulled back in a ponytail and so did I. I could
see from her gray eyes, not quite focused, not quite engaged, that she
was on heavy medication. There was a group home up near the park.
I'd gone to the hearing, in fact, to speak in favor of it. Jean Paul

wouldn't talk to me for three days afterward. *You'd put your own children in danger,* he said.

But Jean Paul was not there now to point a finger at her, and suddenly she was not there either. She skipped off the way the schoolgirl who'd covered my eyes might have done, and the bank door swung shut in rhythm with my throat's closing. Now that she was gone, I felt a clutch of fear, and my milk let down in a gush. I walked home with my blouse soaked through, and still the firemen, buying their groceries at the Key Food, looked right over me and around me and through me, as if I weren't there at all.

By the time I let myself in upstairs, the milk had dried sour on my shirt. Helen met me at the door, holding the baby as if he were already a little corpse. "In the space of an hour," she said. "A hundred and four."

"He's two months old. Babies don't run fevers like that. They've been fine all week."

"I was just waiting for the car service," she said. "Your doctor said get him down to emergency, there's meningitis all over the city."

They did a spinal tap—they made me wait outside the door, so I wouldn't run to Gabe when he screamed—but he didn't have meningitis. Jean Paul showed up just as it was all over. He looked so large and capable in his new linen suit that I wanted to burrow my face in his chest. I was still imagining the baby's gasp of betrayal when they dug the needle into his spine.

"My God," Jean Paul said, once he heard Gabe was all right. "What is that on the front of your blouse?"

Everything was feverish in the eighties. Our neighbor was knifed in the ribs, walking home from work at seven o'clock, and everyone on the block talked about moving to Jersey or the Hudson River Valley. But he was released from the hospital after one day, and we all stayed put.

One night I looked down from the living-room window and saw two guys bent over, one almost atop the other. I thought it was another mugging. From the fourth floor, the two figures were shadows, their arms and heads a twilight color that did not define their races. I opened the window to see better, to yell down, and when they heard my *Hey* we all froze. Is that the right word, *froze*, if you're in a fever?

Stretching out the window, I could see that this was no mugging, that they were kids leaning into our car, stealing our battery—we'd already lost one battery and the hubcaps and the rear window—and I had the urge to leap down to the sidewalk. I wanted to grab them by the ears, little boys that they probably were, and make them look me in the eye.

I was glad that I couldn't see what race they were in the evening light. Jean Paul's family was from Marseilles and they were all dark skinned. He liked to speculate what blood might have mixed with the French: African, Portugese, Arab? My family was terrified by his darkness. My oldest, Paul, was also dark. I'd seen people look from him to me and back. The neighborhood was integrated when we moved in, but by the eighties it seemed very white. I began to dislike white people. I had no doubt that they would eye my Paul on the street when he was a teenager, that they would wait for him to stick a knife in their ribs. I began to see all white people as pale freckled Feeneys telling me to move back to their safe enclaves of Long Island. I was sick of their guessing my own fear. You saw these kids on television in the eighties, their eyes not so much vacant as switched off, not so much defiant as mocking. Some reporter in a short skirt, stroking a microphone, asked them what they thought about when they knocked old people down and they snickered.

I'd heard men on our block talk about beating the shit out of the kids who stole their hubcaps and their batteries and their trim. They talked about beating the kids who, when they weren't too stoned, figured out how to take the whole car.

The night after I saw them disconnecting the battery, they got the whole car. Jean Paul was delighted, because now he could get a Saab or a Peugeot, but we had to wait a month for the insurance money. The last month of summer. The children's fevers had dwindled, leaving their faces pinched and pasty, but now I couldn't drive them to Jones Beach. So instead I loaded down the stroller and Paul and Gracie's backpacks and trundled them onto the D train for Brighton Beach.

Jean Paul thought it was madness. There were used condoms on the sand and every once in a while you'd see a hypodermic—the hospital waste washing up—but there were no crack vials yet. This was only '83, remember. And I was so glad to be with my babies, walking on the boardwalk, that there could have been dead bodies on the beach and it wouldn't have fazed me. When we were acting students, Jean Paul bought me a poster of Coney Island, the Weegee photograph. Maybe you know it: a beachful of bodies—I always saw them as immigrants—stretching back for miles. There seem to be as many people as there are grains of sand on that beach and I always imagined there were Feeneys there, straight over from County Kerry, among the darker bodies. They're all happy, happy, mugging for the camera.

As August wore on, I took the children to Brighton Beach or Coney Island every day. After a week, my pale friend learned our route and trailed us up Seventh Avenue to the D train. The children didn't deter her in the least. Paul and Gracie were all over the sidewalk, dragging sticks usually, so she sneaked around them to give me a soft punch in the shoulder or tug my hair or stick her tongue out. It was a scary tongue—short and fat and coated the same yellow as a Brooklyn morning—but only Paul was old enough to be scared. Gracie loved it when our friend made an appearance; she clambered into the back of the double stroller, and I grabbed Paul's hand, and we all took off to catch her. She was quick disappearing into stores, around corners, and Paul's little legs never held out for more than a block or so. Once, though, we followed her all the way home, to a big limestone in a park block, the kind of house bankers and brokers live in, a gracious house with big bowed windows and a sweet old-fashioned front garden of pansies and petunias.

She raced up the stoop and slipped behind the front door. "Go," Gracie whispered from the stroller. "Go."

It was the halfway house for chronic mental patients. We parked on the sidewalk, my children and I, and watched the front windows, roman shades drawn halfway. Roman shades—that's my picture of the eighties—but I had never expected to see them hanging halfway in a halfway house. The children and I giggled, waiting for her to show her face. It gave her so much pleasure to follow me on the street, to make physical contact, that the pleasure had become contagious. I remembered her merry laugh that first day she tripped me. This house looked merry, too, with the yellow and purple flowers crowding the garden. This was the city I wanted, a city crowded with group homes and flowers and immigrants mugging for the camera.

The children got tired of waiting. She never showed herself or peeked out, and finally I walked back home, the beach bags dragging off the stroller. The sun beat down through a Brooklyn haze. Fatigue overtook me; suddenly I could not bear the thought of Brighton Beach, of leaving their dirty diapers balanced on over-flowing garbage cans. I couldn't bear the thought of one more drunken man exposing himself to me. Gracie wept, because we were not going to the beach after all, and Paul, as we trudged up our own front stoop, asked me if I thought we could have imagined that woman who followed us all the time. That was the eighties: even children couldn't tell what was real.

Jean Paul came home at dusk one night and said he had to speak to me, now, before I put Gabe to bed. I held the baby close, a shield against what I knew was coming, but Jean Paul looked ferocious. I lay Gabe down in his cradle and left Paul and Gracie watching *Sleeping Beauty*. They'd developed a special fondness for witches since they'd met my stalker.

Jean Paul and I made our way down the narrow brownstone hall and sat stiffly in the living room. Just don't say it, I thought. Just don't tell me.

"I've been so depressed," he said.

I stared out the window. The sky was darkening fast, and on our leafy block the streetlights were dim.

"I've been seeing someone," he said.

Don't say it. Don't say it.

"She charges ninety-five an hour but I think it's worth it."

I thought he was telling me how much he paid a call girl—really I did—and a funny squirting sound left my mouth.

"She's talking about a prescription, but I think I can stay off medication . . ."

A shrink. When we were all actors, no one could afford a shrink; now I was the only one I knew without one. But I was sure he'd been having an affair. He couldn't bear to brush up against me. In the heat of an August night, when I lay alone in bed crazy with wanting, he sat on the fire escape until he was sure I was asleep. Maybe this was only the first part; maybe I would have to wait for months until he had the courage to tell me the rest of the news. I was so tired. The stoop was so steep. Gabe woke three and four times a night. No one would be home until after Labor Day.

"Oh, Jean Paul. It's all right. Just go ahead and leave."

"Do you think I would leave you," he said, "with three little children?"

His words, his sense of obligation, chilled me. I rose slowly and walked back down the narrow hallway. My shoulder bag hung over the doorknob. I heaved it up and walked out of the apartment, down the three flights of stairs, down the long stoop, out into the gray Brooklyn night. The air was heavy and still.

I was chilled and I was in a fever. I walked to the cash machine, past the barrels of stinking garbage, and I withdrew the maximum. I would have a car service take me to Manhattan; I would spend the night in a hotel. I would call Jean Paul and tell him where I kept the emergency formula. In the morning I would gather my babies up and retreat to the Feeneys on Long Island. They were the only ones who would have me.

But first, I needed to walk by the group house one last time. I needed to see if my stalker spent her nights staring out the windows the way I did. I walked along the avenue, past the new restaurants and the little stores I didn't recognize anymore. The owners turned over every six months in the eighties, because they all thought they could afford the rent and they couldn't. This wasn't their place and it wasn't my place anymore, either.

I turned toward the park. I should have felt light without the stroller, without the babies, but all my muscles strained. I heard footsteps behind me and looked over my shoulder: a couple licking white ice cream off each other's cones. They opened a garden gate and turned in.

I reached the park block alone, but as I started up I heard footsteps again. I crossed the street so that I could get a good look and she crossed, too, behind me. My friend. If it hadn't been darkening so quickly, if the street hadn't been so lonely, maybe we would have been merry. But she was striding along, hell-bent, and I braced myself.

My milk let down again. A punch in the shoulder, a tug of the hair: what was I so worried about? I knew her pretty well by now. I found myself thinking, incongruously, that I should have not have turned away from Jean Paul. Her hair was loose tonight; my own was twisted high on the back of my head. Still I walked uphill, toward the park, the pad of her sneakered feet gaining on me. Go ahead, do your worst.

We walked along in single file, the pair of us. At the top of the block, faces peered around the big apartment building at the corner. Kids.

They saw me see them—maybe they couldn't see her behind me— and they made their move. They came down the block together, five boys, four of them large, their pants slipping down their waists, the bills of their baseball caps bobbing in the night. Goony birds. I moved to walk in the street—even suburban Feeneys know to do that—but as I veered off the sidewalk they split up, three marching to the opposite sidewalk, two staying behind on mine. There was no point to walking in the middle of the road. My breath was short, my thighs trembling. There was a game they played in the eighties, knocking people down with a single blow.

One boy followed the other. I tried to make eye contact with the first, the shortest of them. When I saw him glance sidewise, I knew I would pass him safely. Something flickered in his face—not guilt, just something. The second boy kept his face averted, and I knew he was the one. As we passed he reached his right fist across my body and struck me in the mouth.

My breath came long and easy then. Now that it was real, I wasn't afraid. The five boys crowded me, pummeling, grabbing for the strap of my bag. I was in a barroom brawl. I was facing down Jean Paul's lover. I spat in one face, then another. Later, people on the block told me that I was screaming bloody murder. Actually, they said I screamed: *Look at me. Look at me.* They thought there was a crazy woman loose.

But I didn't know that I was screaming. I could feel my fists flailing, my shoes making contact with shins. A large hand grabbed my foot, and then I was flat on my back. They pulled me to the gutter, between two cars, the smell of shit close to my face. Maybe they would drag me to the park. They leaned over, crowding, pushing each other back, and I memorized each boy's dark face as it hovered. The smallest boy had a high forehead, a nose as long and broad as Jean Paul's, light eyes: startled, startling. His thick lashes might have been my Paul's.

From above I heard windows raised, ineffectual voices calling down:

Hey. Hey!

The jellied mass of them hesitated, wavering. I was on my feet again, fists windmilling. When they turned to run, together, as if on cue, I thought I had defeated them single-handedly. Not bad: one against five. Still drunk on adrenaline, I took off after them. I would follow them into the park as they scattered. I would track one of them down, the one with the startled eyes. I would make him look at me.

I heard the police car behind me grinding up from the bottom of the block. I counted the bodies ahead—how many had escaped?—and saw that where there had been five boys running, there were now six figures in front of me. One of them had long straw-colored hair. The siren came closer. The bodies ahead ran uphill into the night.

She managed to hold one of them at the corner. By now the police lights flashed at my shoulder, but I didn't look their way. It didn't seem real anymore, and I stumbled. Under the streetlight, my crazy friend held the boy by one arm, pulled behind his back, and by one ear. She twisted it, the way the nuns used to do our ears, so that he would have to look at me as I drew near. It was the smallest boy, the boy with the light eyes. Under the street lamp, I could see that they were green. He shifted them back and forth.

I would make him look at me, and maybe I would take his other ear and give it a good twist. I would make him look, and I would get a good long look at him. I should not have turned away from Jean Paul.

She must have been strong to hold a kid, sixteen or seventeen, muscular, sullen. He held his face impassive, the eyes still darting. The two police car doors slammed shut in unison. My stalker grinned and stuck her yellow tongue out at me. We all had so much to answer for in the eighties. I should not have turned away from him like that. I stuck my own tongue out.

I was happy, happy, jostling in a crowd, mugging for the camera, zoning into that other time, that other place.

How Ireland
Lost the World Cup

(1997)

ANNIE CALLAN

You wouldn't think a bottle of beer squirted all over your face would make you fall for someone, let alone change your politics, but then, I suppose I'm not what you'd call normal anyway.

I've been around is how I'd put it, ya know, raised in the inner city, learned street smarts before I learned to read. From the age of five or so (never knew exactly when I was born), I carried a pointy stick 'round with me and almost poked a young fella's eye out with it once when he followed me—"Cissy, Cissy"—down Sean McDermott Street. An iron bar under his arm, and he yelling, "Smelly Emer. Skinny Emer." "Go jump in a a slagheap, why don't you?" I'd scream back.

Grew up, survived the street skirmishes in our neighborhood. Graduated, you might say, a veteran of primitive armed combat, post–Stone Age Dublin-style. I could stick my paw out for spare change outside the Pro-Cathedral with the best of them. I could knock off cheap lacy bras and knickers in Dunnes Stores. Before I was ten, I'd enough underwear stashed behind the twins' bunk beds to start up a lingerie shop.

It didn't bring me luck with the boys though. Maybe I didn't want them anyway. Most fellas I knew were nail tough, crude and all they wanted was a rough and tumble with you in the alley, a scabby finger up your dress, or a tongue the texture of sawdust jammed into your mouth like a bullet. I always thought *a bit of crumpet* was too fancy a word for such a raw act of haste. A crumpet, to my mind, should be consumed with sweet strawberry jam in tiny wedges, delicately, with tatted lace doilies and pale slender fingers, genteely. I never gave any man his fill.

Well, never that is, until Rory. I don't even know so much if he was that different. Maybe it was just timing. At seventeen, I'd given up, left that black bruise of a city, the gray corporation flats, the grime. I got myself a visa for America. No one had to tell me twice. Soon as I got the fare together from double shifts at the Kylemore Bakery, I ate my last eclair, shook hands with my da from the taxi, and flew as far across the sea as the plane'd take me.

Florida. I knew only one person there, Damien Flaherty, a pal of my old man's. "Be sure and look him up," my da had said, slipping a few bob into my hand. I'd made a fist of it, creasing the bills into a ball. I unfolded it, then creased it again, all the way there.

Damien let me a room, more like a long coffin, in the upstairs back of his bar. The odor of liquor and smoke hunched up the drainpipe and in through the open slit of a window, settling under the wallpaper. But the walls were mine. And cheap.

Durty Nelly's they called the pub. I hated how they misspelled "dirty"—it just fed the idea that we Irish were stupid. I worked nights downstairs in the lounge, as it was called. A bare-bones outfit, red vinyl booths, low-hanging lamps with burgundy shades and fringes. A big-screen TV that was always tuned to the sports channel. The clientele was mainly Irish illegals, maids and bricklayers, carpenters and seamstresses. Piece workers. The odd nurse would wander in now and again. I waited on them, poured and measured for them, but hardly passed words. I wasn't keen on keeping company with my kind—after all, if I'd wanted that, I'd have stayed home.

I'd light up when an American would wander in, make a beeline for them, fill their glass a little higher if I was doing bar. They were most often local laborers, huge men with a girth. They'd waddle in, beaming at you, a Cuban cigar clenched between their startling white teeth, sweat dripping through their fingers. And they'd tip you, which is more than any Irish'd ever do. At first I refused their money. But Liam the bartender said I was mad, sure they were only saying thanks for a job well done. "Everyone tips in America, Emer. Get used to it." So I did. I'd stash the dollar bills and loose change in the pocket of my skirt, put it aside.

I loved Florida. Nothing about it was like home—sun every day to greet you. Blacks, Spanish, Haitians, all colors. Big long cars on big wide roads. I'd take the 29 every morning to the beachfront and settle down on a yellow bath towel with the local paper and an iced tea. *This is it*, I thought. Paradise. Never a care that my fair skin went first salmon pink, then puce, then scarlet, before it all peeled off like an onion. I'd rub cool calamine lotion along the raw parts of my skin in the evenings, happy that I was sloughing off my old cover, that grotty, scarred, useless carapace.

This was the new me—I could be anyone here. I studied vocabulary from my pocket dictionary like I was still in primary school, took on three new words a day. "Cachet." "Cadenza." "Canard." Eliza Doolittle, eat your bleedin' heart out! Only Damien had a clue of my past and even he hardly knew me anyway, except as this spindly kid back home who said, "Hello, Mr. Flaherty," in Clancy's Bar when my da'd bring me in after school for his daily special. "Hello to you Dillons," he'd answer.

It was in the *Florida Sun* that I saw the advertisement: *Hotel Hostess wanted. Luna Beach. Afternoons. Good pay.* Seemed a good way to me to earn a bit extra, find my own place, move away from the bar, and still get my mornings in on the beach.

I nearly didn't get the job. Jose, the manager of the Best Key

Western, took one look at my molting skin and said, "Lady, don't you think you a little fair to work in the sun?"

I protested madly. I'd be under the great straw umbrellas mostly, I'd even wear sunscreen. He looked at me slowly from my bony ankles up and said, "So, put on this, and let me see."

I got used to the uniforms in time, tight waist-squelching red blouses with a deep vee down the front, and a short frilly black skirt—more like a tutu, really. Most of the other girls wore silk fishnet stockings but I liked to let my skin breathe and went bare legged. I must have gone through a stick of sunscreen a week, and my feet ached in those pointy red stilettos we had to prance around in. I painted my fingernails *Classy Cherry* and let them grow.

The guests here were as crass as the ones at the pub, only more sly about it. They'd wait till you'd gone to get more limes or something for them till they'd leer at you from behind as you climbed up the steps to the bar. Thought I didn't see them, the drunken sots. They'd leave big tips though, especially for the more devoted hostesses, like Molly with the big boobs, or Tammi whose skirt was more like a scrap of remnant fabric.

Before Rory, I was not what you'd call a political person. One of my uncles—Feargal—used to be a gun runner, I heard, and do the odd bit of propaganda writing for the IRA. But all that *Free Ireland* sloganeering was a lot of bull as far as I could tell. No one within miles of where I lived gave a flying crap about getting back the north. It was England's now was the sentiment, and good riddance. I was more in my da's camp who said, usually after a few rounds, "What's the use of fighting over property? Property doesn't free the man, it enslaves him," and "Better to be a communist when you're poor, right? What's to lose?"

I must have been at Best Key about two months when the beer sizzled out of his bottle like Cupid's arrow and straight into my eyes. It dripped down my face and neck till I smelled rank, like a brewery.

"Christ, I'm sorry, love," the voice was clipped, sharp like a needle, the true mark of an Irish Northerner. "I'm after tripping over this bleedin' hose. I'm terrible sorry, so I am."

My eyes were burning. "Water! Get her some water." I heard Tammi screaming. "Pronto!"

"Hey, lookit! There's a fountain over here. C'mon," and the sharp voice took hold of my hand, gently pulling me along beside him. "You can lead a horse to water . . ." he said, and his laugh was like bubbles rising up in the noon air, a rainbow of colors. "Sorry, lead a gorgeous woman to water, but can you make her drink?"

Even though my face stung, I could feel something twitch inside. No one had ever called me gorgeous before. Nor even a woman. I was used to "mott," "chick," "baby," "piece." I had visions of a soft roundness to my body, my breasts like ripe fruit. Wo-man. I licked the word round my lips. It tasted salty, heady, a mix of hops, barley, and saliva.

The first time I saw Rory, he was dousing me with water from the fountain. His green eyes were big and open like sunflowers. His hair was a tuft of wheaty blond, spiked I suppose. The gold ring in his ear caught the sunlight and gave a honey cast to his face. He looked flushed, concerned, vulnerable.

"You okay, love?" He said so genuinely you'd think he'd poured castor oil on me.

"I'm okay."

"Well, *you* might be, but I don't think your clothes survived," Jose was beside me now, eyeing me and then Rory, seriously. "Better you call it a day, Emer." He always pronounced it Em, as in ahem. Ehmer, no matter how I tried to convince him to lean on the *e*.

"But my tips . . ."

"Please go," Jose was commanding, not suggesting. "You cannot work scenting of . . . alcohol. Tomorrow you can make double tips, okay?"

Rory started apologizing and Jose waved him away. He couldn't afford to be too rude to paying guests. I don't remember much of what happened after that, except a lot of fuming and steaming on my part. And apologies on his.

"You can shower in my room, if you'd like. . . . Anything."

That suggestion drove me into a frenzy. Who did he think he was, barging into my life, ruining my day, and then propositioning me? Asshole. A typical Irish man. Probably a Protestant, too.

"A taxi, then. Let me pay for your taxi." I heard him shout as I marched away, my high heels clicking under me like castanets.

When I got to work the next day, there was a huge bunch of creamy lilies laying on top of my station, and a napkin that read, "Emer, whose lovely eyes I never meant to wound. Forgive me. Big Foot." It sounded like a poem somehow, how it was worded. I couldn't help a smile. Someone's ma raised him proper, I thought, and put the lilies in a jam jar till closing. Next day, I looked for him, not that I had any intent but to say thanks. It was World Cup time again and the place was crawling with soccer fans. Somehow Ireland had made it to the playoffs and half the country was over to watch them, and staying at this hotel.

Jose decided to shift the decor to the gaudy tricolor: he imported green, white, and orange tablecloths and napkins. He even ordered paper lanterns. One day I came to work to find the Irish flag hanging high beside the star-spangled banner.

You couldn't get into Durty Nelly's either for the crowds. Damien hired six extra servers. I hardly slept all night, the ould folk songs going on through the night below my room. But I was earning money, cash in hand, between the two jobs.

Every green-painted face or emerald hair dye made me look twice to see if he was under it. Every day that week a flower would find its way to my station, once a peach rose, once a foxglove. There were no notes, but I knew it was him. I started asking if anyone'd seen a sandy-headed guy from Northern Ireland wandering through. The flowers became a bit of a joke. "Someone has a crush on our Irish Rose," Tammi went on, "I wonder who it is?"

That Friday, I was heading out the revolving door when I saw him, standing erect, like a soldier almost, feet hip-width apart, shoulders back, chest out. Only he was holding a long-stemmed iris in his hand. I spiraled out the door, slightly dizzy.

"For you." He had that soft vulnerable look again that made me want to hug him into my chest. Though maybe he thought I might hit him one. I smiled. "Are you mad or what, wasting your hard-earned cash on me?"

He smiled now, a gap between his two front teeth. It reminded me of Dana, the Belfast singer who won the Eurovision Contest for Ireland in 1970. She had a gap like that, which everyone said was a mark of beauty.

"The only thing I reckon will be hard earned is you, dear Emer."

"I'm not for sale, dear Big Foot," I quipped, surprised at the softness of my tone.

"Your forgiveness, I mean."

"Oh, forget about it, will ya? It was only a bloody beer."

"I almost blinded you."

"But you didn't, so give over now, would you?"

The scent of the iris hung between us.

Well, I'll spare you the blow-by-blow account of how I ended up in Rory's room. In his shower, and later, on his rug. I do want to tell you though how good the rough sweep of his stubble felt against my skin, how his hands moved about me with the slow gestures of a craftsman. I felt like one of those ancient vessels from Tara—something worthy and beautiful—and the ocean sweeping through me.

We drank rum and Cokes and watched the non-Ireland soccer matches on TV. "No way," he said, "I'm going to share you with all them hooligans," when I suggested a sports bar, and I was just as glad.

I'd never in my life just sat around starkers with a guy before. But there was an undemandingness about Rory, a calmness that made me feel okay. Even better than okay. Him looking at me, soft like, made me feel like I was a woman, feminine, like I didn't need the nasty undergear. It sounds *trite*, I suppose, but I felt natural. When the game was slow, we'd run our tongues along all the curves of skin we could find.

"Where'd you get a name like Rory?" I asked him one night. "After the High King of Ireland?"

"To be honest, yeah." He looked away. "Me da's a fierce Republican, ya know. In a long line of patriots. His da was one of the founders of the Irish Republican Brotherhood."

"Who's your brother then? Let me guess . . . He must be named after our mighty folk hero, Cuchulainn?" I was feeling lighthearted, after a large swig of brandy.

"Close," he said. "Diarmaid. Fionn. Lorcan. Our ma was into the Irish myth thing."

Whew! The American phrase "heavy duty" came to mind. "That's some patriotic family you come from. *Distinguished*." I milked my latest vocabulary word like it was a tender cow.

"We use the word 'tribe.' " I couldn't tell if he was joking.

"Well, I suppose that explains why a Northerner'd bother to come all the way to the States to follow the Irish team."

"Yeah, it's nice to get away, a change of scenery . . ."

"Couldn't be more different here, could it? No such thing as a gray cloud in these parts."

"Says you! What if I told you the cloud's still there, bigger than you could ever imagine, that the sun's only distracting you?" He was trying to joke but there was something brittle in his voice, something I didn't recognize.

Rory had tickets to the games that Ireland played in. He wanted to buy me a ticket too but the black-market prices were *exorbitant*.

"Are you a big soccer fan at home?" I asked him one night in bed.

"A little," he said. "I used to play for the Laughlinsland Rovers. My brother Lorcan's a striker for them. They think he might've made the English leagues if only . . ." He stopped so sharply I could feel the hiss of his breath.

"Only what?"

"Oh, he has a gamey leg—knee—all screwed up it was."

"Why didn't he come with you?"

"Couldn't." His voice was emphatic. "He had to stay, help my da. We all work for him. Family business, you know."

I was envious for a minute. The notion of a family all working together like a team was as foreign to me as Timbuktu. My da kept his job at the tire factory to himself. His paycheck too.

"What is it yis do?" My accent was starting to show signs of a northern lisp. I'd always heard how couples who hang 'round a lot together start to sound like each other. The thought pleased me.

"Family crests. Any surname. The Irish annals—you name it— Burke, Brugha, Connolly. We'll find the crest and the motto and do it all up fancy on a plaque for you."

"What's yours mean?" I asked.

"Fierce. Cold hearted. Warrior." Each word came out like a declaration, like a solemn reading of the Constitution or something. The evening breeze drifted in through the window. It was starting to get cool.

"I run the international sales markets. That's why I got to see the games. I had to come anyway. Kill ten birds."

"What about my name?" I was almost afraid to ask.

"Don't know. Don't think Dillon's in my catalogue. Let me do a bit of research on it when I get back."

The thought of his leaving shocked me.

"Give us another swig there, sailor." I reached for the brandy.

Rory leaped up from the floor like an animal, *limber*, his white back disappearing into the bathroom. "Time for this sailor to shower!" I wanted to go after him, scrape my nails along his chest, dig them in so deep he'd have to pry each finger out, *excavate*. But the drink had my stomach all queasy.

His golden earring was dazzling me there under the lamp on the coffee table. I leaned over and slid the thing around in my palm, letting the light catch it this way and that. *Gleamed*, it did. And then I was tossing it up in the air, higher, higher, dancing it from one hand to the other. I could hear myself laughing, but it sounded like something from another planet. Up, further, yeah, further. The sky, girl, reach for the sky. Emer the Immigrant Juggler. I thought I'd explode with the giggling, me leaping round naked in a hotel room, half sozzled, my man in the shower. Emer, chasing a golden circle, and then, whatever possessed me, I leaned to the left and caught the earring coming down in my mouth. Plop. Just like that. It tasted, I don't know, like money maybe. Real money. Next thing, I'd shoved it into my bag.

"Now, love, I'm presentable again," Rory walked dripping into the room. "All fresh and ready for you." And he planted a sopping smack on my cheek. I couldn't catch my breath, though, to kiss him back.

When he walked me to the door later, I yanked the earring out and threaded it in his ear. "Surprise!" I tried to joke, "look what I found." But my throat was all thick and sore.

A few days later, I came across the word "heraldry" in my dictionary. I knew it was a sign.

One evening, we were out on his patio, sipping salted margaritas. A yellow moon was up. Jose was cleaning tables below. "Hey, señor!" Rory yelled down.

Jose smiled, holding up his designer Irish napkin. "Hey, you crazy Irish man. What's these stupid colors of your flag mean anyway?"

"Green," I shouted, "for Ireland."

"Orange," said Rory, "for the bleedin' English."

"And white?"

"White," we said together, as if on cue at a cabaret, "for peace." I raised my two fingers to make a peace sign, feeling like the Pope at his balcony in Rome. *You just never know, do you Emer,* says I to myself, *away you go from Ireland to escape the people, and now look at you, getting soft on one of your own.*

"You know, just before Lynan scored the goal against Italy," Rory turned to me, all dreamy eyed. *Philosophical.* "Oh Emer, you shoulda been there yesterday. Everyone rooting for the team. It'd make you cry to think about it, that fierce unity. And when he scored, they went mad. Everyone hugging and kissing and roaring. Wild animals we were . . ." A tear ran down his face. He pulled me toward him. "I wish you'd've been there beside me," he was whispering now, but I was thinking how I'd just memorized *Ire.* Anger. Bitterness. How I'd never noticed it was part of my own country's name. How close it was to *fire.*

"Well, let's hope Lynan keeps it up tomorrow," I said. The brandy tasted sour on my tongue. *Enough of the booze in my life,* I thought then, and next day, served Damien my notice.

When I walked in with my rucksack to Rory's room, he was watching the telly. "Volume! Where's the fucking volume knob." He was dancing on his feet, jabbing all the buttons at once. John Major was on the screen, looking *somber.* Then it switched to a pub. Delaunty's splashed in red letters over the door. A man in a farmer's cap stood under the sign. The farmer's lips were moving like a puppet's. Suddenly a voice flooded the room. I cupped my ears on instinct. "We was jest sittin there takin in the match and all. Next thing I know, they're firing. I hear these loud cracks in the air and turns me head. There's people slumpin' head down over their Guinnesses . . ." A calm voice: "Did you catch a look at the perpetrators?" There was a long bristle of hair hanging out of the farmer's nose. "I only seen some folk in black, skedalling out the door."

"Fuck! Fuck! Fuck! The bastards! Fuck." Rory was pounding the headboard like it was a punchbag. "Lorcan . . ."

The newscaster went on as if he was discussing the weather. "To sum up, six men, one aged eighty-five, were gunned down in a pub in Laughlinsland yesterday, as they watched the World Cup. A Protestant militant splinter group is suspected."

"The idiots." I sat, stunned, watching Rory pace through the room like a mad panther. "Who! Who's dead? I need names." He went for the phone. Then stopped, turning to me. "I have to go out for a while, Emer." He threw on his trousers. "Later!" And he was gone. A gale force wind blowing out the door.

Before I could consider my next move, he was back. His eyes were burning like black holes. "One thing," he cupped my face in his hands, "Emer, I love you. All right?" And he was gone again.

No one, I mean bleeding *no one* had ever said that to me before. My ma might have if she'd had the chance, but she didn't, did she? It was like hearing a foreign language, vaguely familiar but in the end, you just couldn't translate it.

My heart thumped like a time bomb, as I walked out of the room in his wake.

I never saw Rory alive again. When I checked in for work at the hotel next day, he was gone. Ireland tied Norway, barely making it to the next round. The game was one long tedious exercise in patience. Prolonged. Agonizing. Not knowing. Hoping. Even praying. *If they only make it through this round, he'll come back.* Despairing.

It's the way my thoughts went for months after that, after he checked out, after I found the last red bud, a rose, on my station. I like to imagine there was a note pinned to it, something like, "I'll be back for you, my love. Laughlinsland needs me now. Please wait." What I read instead two weeks later in the international news section of the

Herald, in a square inch of black type was, *Two more casualties in the ongoing Belfast war: Rory O'Bruadair, 35, and his 3-year-old son, of Laughlinsland, died after a petrol bomb ignited their car this morning. O'Bruadair, the eldest son of the Republican O'Bruadair clan, raised considerable sums for the IRA over the years from sympathetic Irish Americans. He was suspected for retaliatory acts following the World Cup murders two weeks ago.*

I packed in the hostess job after that. Too many memories and all that. Thought about heading back to the miserable Ould Sod, but the only image I could summon for that place was an ugly hunting bitch with its head stuffed down its neck, suffocating. Opted for Chicago instead, where I heard there's always a good wind blowing right through you, a wind that'd cut your eyes out. Whip the soft bits out of you. I didn't stay to watch Ireland get whipped 2–0 by Sweden.

I don't know why, but I helped myself to the crystal vase Jose kept specially for wedding banquets. Not worth that much really, but I wanted some kind of souvenir. Once I got to Chicago, I'd find myself sheltering from the snow in the big department stores. Always, I'd end up in fine china, my fingers massaging the lips of all the pretty bowls there. Blown glass, especially, I couldn't keep my hands off them. At night, I'd force myself through the dictionary, *i, j, k,* on and on, stuffing words into my head. It was a way to pass time. Though if you asked me now what was the point of all that, I couldn't tell you.

Maybe three months after, when I'd settled into a second-story walk-up with a Korean woman, who liked her privacy as much as I did, I got a parcel from the Best Key Hotel. Jose had sent on a blouse I'd left after me, and a ten-dollar tip I'd never picked up from the kitty. On a napkin, he'd written, *Say hola! to the Windy City. Tammi's marrying lumber baron. Florida missing you. Ciao, Jose.*

An envelope with an Irish postmark fell out onto the floor. I had to have a drink before I opened it. Inside, a wafer-thin sheet of paper with a sketch of two eagles, talons interlocked, and an arrow jagging through their breastplates. The colors were silvers and blues. Like bruises. Underneath, in fancy black letters snaking my name, it read: DILLON. *Widow. Wanderer. Beloved.*

ABOUT THE AUTHORS

MAUREEN BRADY is the author of the novels *Give Me Your Good Ear* and *Folly* and a short-story collection, *The Question She Put to Herself*, as well as three books of nonfiction. She teaches writing at The Writer's Voice and N.Y.U. and in 1994 enjoyed a stay at the Tyrone Guthrie Center at Annamakerrig, County Monaghan. She lives in New York City.

ANNIE CALLAN was born in Dublin, Ireland, and now lives in Portland, Oregon, where she works as a writing consultant, editor, and creative-writing instructor. Her volume of poetry, *The Back Door*, was published in 1995. A recipient of the Academy of American Poets Award and a 1995 William Stafford Poetry Fellowship, she has recently completed a collection of personal essay-stories about growing up in Dublin.

JENNIFER C CORNELL's collection of short fiction, *Departures*, won the 1994 Drue Heinz Prize of Literature. Her stories have appeared in *TriQuarterly*, the *New England Review*, and the *Chicago Review*, among others, and have been anthologized in *The Best American Short Stories, 1995* and *The Pushcart Prize: Best of the Small Presses, 1996*.

ELIZABETH CULLINAN was born in New York and, after graduating from college, went to work at *The New Yorker*. From 1960 to 1963, she lived in Dublin. She is the author of two collections of short stories, *Yellow Roses* and *The Time of Adam*, many of the stories in which were first published in *The New Yorker*. Her novel, *House of Gold*, received the Houghton-Mifflin Literary Fellowship Award in 1970. She teaches at Fordham University and lives in New York City.

MARY DOYLE CURRAN (1917–1981) was born in Holyoke, Massachusetts. She trained as a maid and ultimately received a masters from Iowa State University. A college teacher, she taught at Wellesley, Queens College, and the University of Massachusetts, Boston. *The Parish and the Hill* is her only novel.

MARY DEASY (1914–1978) gave up her career as a concert pianist to devote herself to writing. She was the author of seven novels, including *Hour of Spring*, an Irish American family saga. Her short fiction was highly praised and included in the 1940s and '50s in the *O. Henry Memorial Award Short Stories* and *The Best American Short Stories*.

EILEEN FITZGERALD received her M.F.A. from Indiana University and has had her fiction published in *The Gettysburg Review* and *Prairie Schooner*, among other publications. Her story "Pork Chops" appears in her first collection of short fiction, *You're So Beautiful*. She lives in Massachusetts.

KATHLEEN FORD is the author of the novel *Jeffrey Country* and has had her short stories published in *The Virginia Quarterly Review*, *Redbook*, and *The Southern Review*, among others. She won the PEN Syndicated Fiction Project and lives in Charlottesville, Virginia.

ALICE FULTON's books of poetry are *Sensual Math, Powers of Congress, Palladium,* and *Dance Script with Electric Ballerina.* A recipient of a MacArthur Fellowship, she teaches at the University of Michigan, Ann Arbor. "Queen Wintergreen" was included by Louise Erdrich in *The Best American Short Stories, 1993.*

TESS GALLAGHER is the author of the recent short-story collection *At the Owl Woman Saloon.* Her most recent books of poetry are *Portable Kisses Expanded* and *Moon Crossing Bridge.*

MARY GORDON is the author of two collections of short fiction and four novels, including *Final Payments* and *The Other Side.* Her most recent book is *Shadow Man,* a memoir of her father. She has received a Guggenheim Fellowship and the Lila Acheson Wallace–Reader's Digest Writers Award. She teaches at Barnard College and lives in New York City.

STEPHANIE GRANT is the author of the novel *The Passion of Alice.* She received an M.A. at New York University and was a Revson Fellow at Columbia Univeristy. Her novel *The Map of Ireland* is set in Boston during the busing crisis of the early 1970s.

MAUREEN HOWARD is the author of six novels, including *Natural History* and *Bridgeport Bus.* In 1978, Howard won the National Book Critics Award for her memoir, *Facts of Life.* She has been nominated twice for the PEN/Faulkner Award and is a professor at Columbia University. Her latest novel, *Almanac: A Winter's Tale* will be published in winter of 1998.

MARY MCCARTHY (1912–1989) is the author of many books, including her memoir, *Memories of a Catholic Girlhood,* and the novel *The Group.* A member of the National Institute of Arts and Letters, she received a national medal for literature as well as two Guggenheim Fellowships. "C.Y.E." first appeared in her collection of short stories, *Cast a Cold Eye*.

ALICE MCDERMOTT is the author of three novels, *The Bigamist's Daughter, That Night*, adapted into a motion picture of the same title, and *At Weddings and Wakes*. She lives in Pittsburgh.

JEAN MCGARRY is the author of four books of short fiction, *Airs of Providence, The Very Rich Hours, The Courage of Girls*, and *Home at Last*, as well as *Gallagher's Travels*, a new novel. She is a professor in the Writing Seminars at Johns Hopkins University.

ERIN MCGRAW is the author of two collections of short stories, *Lies of the Saints* and *Bodies at Sea*. She teaches fiction writing at the University of Cincinnati.

RUTH MCKENNEY (1912–1972) came to New York to write for a newspaper and ended up writing humorous pieces for *The New Yorker* to support her more "serious" writing. In addition to *My Sister Eileen* and her other collections of stories, she wrote *Industrial Valley*, the story of the Goodyear rubber strike in Akron, Ohio. "Noel Coward and Mrs. Griffin" is a chapter from *My Sister Eileen*, which was adapted into a Broadway play and later a motion picture.

MARY MCGARRY MORRIS's novels include *A Dangerous Woman*, made into a motion picture, and *Vanished*, which was nominated for both the National Book Award and the PEN/Faulkner Award. She lives in Massachusetts with her husband and five children.

HELENA MULKERNS, born and raised in Dublin, has lived in the United States for close to ten years. Her fiction has been nominated for the *Sunday Tribune*/Hennessy Literary Award and has appeared in *Irish Edition* and *Ireland in Exile*. She currently freelances for several publications on both sides of the Atlantic. "Famine Fever" was first published in *Wee Girls* by the Spinifex Press in Australia. She lives in New York City.

EILEEN MYLES is a poet and playwright. She directed the St. Mark's Church Poetry Project and writes for *Art in America* and the *Village Voice*. "My Father's Alcoholism" is from her collection of stories, *Chelsea Girls*. She lives in New York City. Her most recent book of poetry is *School of Fish*.

ANNA QUINDLEN won a Pulitzer Prize in 1992 for her column "Public and Private" in the *New York Times*. She has published two collections of essays and two novels, *Object Lessons* and *One True Thing*. She lives in New Jersey.

VALERIE SAYERS is the author of five novels, including *Brain Fever* and *Who Do You Love*, both named "Notable Books of the Year" by the *New York Times*. She has received a National Endowment for the Arts literature fellowship and is a professor of English at the University of Notre Dame.

MAURA STANTON chairs the creative writing program at Indiana State University. Her first book of poetry, *Snow on Snow*, won the Yale Series of Younger Poets Award. She has written two other books of poetry, *Cries of Swimmers* and *Tales of the Supernatural*, and a novel, *Molly Companion*. "Nijinsky" is from her collection of short stories, *The Country I Come From*.

PERMISSIONS ACKNOWLEDGMENTS

Short Stories, *1993*, published by Houghton Mifflin Company. Reprinted by permission of the author.

"The Lover of Horses" by Tess Gallagher. Reprinted by permission of International Creative Management, Inc. Copyright © 1986.

"City Life" by Mary Gordon, copyright 1996, first appeared in *Ploughshares*. Reprinted by permission of the author.

Excerpt from *The Map of Ireland*, a novel in progress, by Stephanie Grant, copyright 1997. Printed by permission of the author.

Excerpt from *Bridgeport Bus* by Maureen Howard, copyright 1965 and renewed 1993. Reprinted by permission of Watkins/Loomis Agency, Inc.

"C.Y.E." from *Cast a Cold Eye*, copyright 1944 and renewed 1972 by Mary McCarthy, reprinted by permission of Harcourt Brace & Company and the Mary McCarthy Literary Trust.

Excerpt from *At Weddings and Wakes* by Alice McDermott, copyright 1992. Reprinted by permission of the author.

"One of Them Gets Married" by Jean McGarry, copyright 1985. Reprinted from *Airs of Providence*, by permission of the author.

"Daily Affirmations" by Erin McGraw, copyright 1996, first appeared in *The Georgia Review*. Reprinted by permission of the author.

"Noel Coward and Mrs. Griffin" from *My Sister Eileen*, copyright 1938 and renewed 1966 by Ruth McKenney, reprinted by permission of Harcourt Brace & Company and Curtis Brown, Ltd.

"My Father's Boat" by Mary McGarry Morris, copyright 1993, first appeared in *Glimmer Train*. Reprinted by permission of the author.

"Famine Fever" by Helena Mulkerns, copyright 1996, first appeared in *Wee Girls: Women Writing from an Irish Perspective*, edited by Lizz Murphy, published by Spinifex Press. Reprinted by permission of the author.

"My Father's Alcoholism" by Eileen Myles, copyright 1994. Reprinted from *Chelsea Girls* by permission of Black Sparrow Press.

Excerpt from *One True Thing* by Anna Quindlen, copyright 1994. Reprinted by permission of the author.

"The Other Woman" by Valerie Sayers, copyright 1997. Printed by permission of the author.

"Nijinsky" was originally published in *The Country I Come From* by Maura Stanton (Milkweed Editions, 1988). Copyright © 1988 by Maura Stanton. Reprinted with permission from Milkweed Editions.

Every effort has been made to contact copyright holders. The publisher would be happy to hear from any copyright holders not acknowledged or acknowledged incorrectly.